The
Soup
Kitchen

A novel

A. K. HILL

First paperback edition August 2025

Cover Design by Jenna Kendle

ISBN 979-8-9927192-0-8 (paperback)

www.akhillauthor.com

For Hayley

1

KATE

Holding her breath, Kate stepped over the homeless man sleeping on the stoop. Judging from the smell emanating from him, Kate thought he must have been baking in the summer sun for more than a few days. She reached for the door handle, trying to ignore the stares and catcalls coming from the group of men loitering on the other side of the street.

The locked door didn't budge.

Peering through the glass, she could see the glow of lights coming from the back hall, but she saw no people.

She tried the door again: no luck, it was still locked.

Becoming increasingly anxious, she tapped on the window using her car fob, when one of the men from the group across the sidewalk—the tall one—extricated himself and joined her on the stoop.

"They don't open till 8:30," he said, pointing at the sign in the window displaying the hours of operation.

"Oh, thank you," Kate's voice cracked. "Is there another door I could use? It's my first day of work."

"Really?" The man took a puff on his cigarette. "What's a girl like you going to do in a place like this?" He stretched his arms out across the stair railings, blocking her in. His friends encircled the stairs, making a quick exit impossible.

"I'm g—going to be the new chef," Kate stammered, as fear crept up her spine. She was alone on a city street in a bad part of town, surrounded by a group of men who appeared to have nothing to do except bother her.

His eyes traveled over her body. "You're too skinny to be a *good* cook," the man crooned, before turning to wink at his friends.

They roared with laughter while Kate tingled with nerves.

The noise awakened the sleeping man. He grumbled and flung a dirty hand over his face.

Across the street, the bells of Holy Family Church pealed. The large wooden doors opened, and people spilled out. Breathing a sigh of relief, Kate recognized her new boss, Nick. She waved, hoping he would hurry over.

At the sound of the bells, the tall man who had cornered her straightened, unblocking her entry. With a flourish of his hands, he bowed. "Welcome to Mary & Martha's Soup Kitchen."

"Thanks," Kate said. Now that she could take a better look at him, she was surprised by his good looks. The man was strikingly handsome, with almond-colored eyes and soft brown skin.

He stepped aside to let Nick onto the stoop. She felt foolish for being so nervous, he was probably just trying to be nice. A "Cool Hand Luke" type of guy.

"Sorry about that, Katie." Nick smiled. "Most of us go to Mass before starting the day. I didn't think about you getting here early."

"Aah, it's alright Nick," the tall, good-looking man said. "Me and my posse were keeping her safe." He tossed his cigarette onto the sidewalk.

"I'm sure you were, James," Nick answered. "Cigarettes go in there," he said, leaning his head towards the ashcan, "*not* the sidewalk. Better yet, why don't you just stop smoking?"

James grinned. "Come on, Nick, a guy's got to have one vice." His posse guffawed as he ambled away from Kate and returned to the group standing on the sidewalk.

The previously sleeping homeless man struggled to stand from the stoop. Nick reached out to help.

With grimy hands and chipped fingernails, the man grabbed Nick's outstretched arm, heaving himself up. Kate stepped away to avoid gagging from the smell, but Nick seemed immune to the pungent breath and body odor radiating from the now standing man. "You good?" Nick asked, steadying the swaying man with a hand on his shoulder. The man mumbled something before turning away.

Pulling a set of keys out of his pocket, Nick smiled. "Katie, welcome to your first day. Are you nervous?"

"A little," Kate said, wincing at his use of the nickname she had stopped using in high school, "Not about the cooking, of course, more about the people. I'm a little out of my element here."

That's an understatement, she thought as she watched the once sleeping homeless man stagger towards the door.

"You'll do fine." Nick stepped aside, allowing Kate to enter the building, but without warning, the homeless man pushed between her and Nick, almost causing Kate to lose her footing.

In a flash, Nick grabbed the man's arm, pinning it behind his back. He pushed the large man outside. "We're not open yet. You can't come in," Nick grunted, slamming the door shut.

"Let me in," the man yelled, his fist hitting the door. "I want a drink of water. I just want a drink."

Nick turned the lock.

"I just want a drink," the man cried softly, his body sliding down to the sidewalk. "I'm thirsty."

"Can't you let him get a drink?" Kate asked, her eyes wide, hands clasping her bag to her chest.

"No, we have to stick to the rules. It's a safety issue. Only our employees can be inside the building until 8:30. This gives us plenty of time to get organized and prepare for the day without interruptions."

Opening the door to his office, Nick pointed to a chair filled with papers. "Take a seat. You can just put those papers on the floor. I'm going to run some bottled water out to that gentleman. I'll be right back."

Kate stared at his office. It was a wreck.

The space looked as though it had been ransacked by a criminal— and a messy one at that. Papers and boxes were everywhere; filing cabinets so full the drawers wouldn't close. Boxes and crates were stacked on top of the cabinets, reaching all the way up to the nine-foot ceiling.

When Kate removed a pile of papers from the chair, a dusty outline remained, framing the cracks on the pleather cushion. With a quick swipe of her hand, Kate brushed off the dirt and gingerly sat on the edge of the seat. Her purse stayed on her lap. There was no way she'd put it on the floor with all the grime potentially lurking there.

Once again, she studied the space. There weren't any personal photographs on the walls, just photos of people eating in the kitchen. A baseball mitt and ball lay in the center of the cluttered but neat desk, which itself appeared organized, with color-coded manila folders arranged in straight lines.

The papers she'd placed on the other chair began sliding down the stack like molten lava striving to reach the ocean, or in this case, the floor. Kate jumped up to stop the flow, dropping her bag onto the floor. After saving the paper mountain, Kate retrieved her bag. Dust bunnies and paper streams clung to the Louis Vuitton strap.

Is there a frickin' dust fairy here? she thought, as she took out a tissue and wiped off her bag and her hand.

"Sorry about that." Nick strode into the office, his presence filling the room. "I hated the thought of that guy being thirsty all morning. His name is Abraham. He's new to M&M and he didn't know the rules."

Nick's chair screeched in protest as he rolled it back from the desk. "Let's talk about your first week. I'd like you to get a real understanding of how M&M works, so I'm going to have you shadow a different person each day. I want you to implement *real* improvements to the kitchen, and to do that, you've got to see how we do things right now. You can't fix what you don't know is broken." His smile was engaging.

God, he's cute. Tall, sandy-brown hair, warm brown eyes, and a smile you couldn't help but return.

"Okay, but I think I can get the gist of the situation in one day. A whole week of shadowing people seems like overkill to me. I've run my own successful gourmet restaurant for over *five* years. I'm pretty sure I can handle a soup kitchen."

"I'm sure you can but managing a soup kitchen is different from cooking in a gourmet restaurant. I'd like you to indulge me." He stretched, opening his arms wide. "It may surprise you what you learn."

Rolling her eyes, Kate wondered what she could learn from a soup kitchen. *For God's sake, I'm a graduate of Le Cordon Bleu.*

"Once you know how we operate, you can better understand the changes needed to make the kitchen better."

There was a knock at the door, and a man's head popped into the opening. "Hey, Nick— oh, I'm sorry."

"Tucker, come in." Nick stood, motioning for the man to enter. "I want you to meet Katie."

A tall black man with a graying mustache wearing an M&M T-shirt and jeans entered. Seeing Kate, he removed his M&M blue ball cap, revealing a balding head. "Ma'am," he bobbed his head.

It's Kate. She held out her hand.

"Tucker Lewis, this is Katie O'Leary, the new cook." Nick made the introductions from behind the desk.

Tucker's eyes widened. His gaze seesawed between Kate and Nick. "The new cook? I didn't know you'd hired a new cook." He shook Kate's hand. "It's real nice to meet you, ma'am. Welcome."

"Tucker coordinates the donations and deliveries for M&M. He'll give you a weekly inventory, so you know what stock there is to create the daily menus. He's also the director of Padre's Pantry, the neighborhood's food pantry." Nick explained.

"Oh, so you'll do all the ordering for me?" Kate asked.

"Well . . ." Tucker raised an eyebrow at Nick.

"Katie's agreed to help us out until her restaurant reopens." Nick leaned against the filing cabinet. "She's going to revamp the menus and work on instituting better kitchen procedures."

"Well, that sounds real good." Tucker rubbed his bald head before placing the backwards baseball cap on. "Nick, what do you want me to do with the personal care kits that were donated by *A2Z?*"

Nick looked out the door. "How many are there?"

"Five hundred."

"Wow that's a lot," Nick gave a low whistle. "Let's see what's in them." Nick and Tucker walked into the hall, and Kate followed.

Boxes filled two grocery carts. Opening one, Tucker pulled out a package the size of a large pencil case. The clear plastic bag with a zip-lock opening contained toothpaste, a toothbrush, dental floss, bottles of body soap, shampoo, conditioner, and moisturizer.

"These are great," Nick said, examining the kit and dropping it back into the cart. "Go ahead and put them in the stockroom. We'll need to speak with Jenny to discuss the best way to distribute them to the clients."

"Hey, Nick," a voice from the foyer called. "Can you come here? We have an emergency."

"Be right there," Nick yelled back. "Tucker, do you think you can give Katie the ten-cent tour? She's going to use Joe's old office." He looked at his watch. "I want to talk to Marika and Dallas." He touched Kate's arm. "I'll see you in the kitchen later."

Tucker smiled at Kate as he adjusted his hat. "Want to come with me?" Tucker started pushing the first and pulling the second cart.

"I've got this one." Kate placed her bag in the cart seat.

"Thanks, Katie," Tucker said.

"I actually go by Kate."

"Oh, didn't Nick call you Katie?" Tucker asked, looking over his shoulder to check her progress.

"Yes," Kate said shrugging her shoulders.

"Well, you might want to get used to Katie, then." Tucker chuckled.

Pushing the carts down the hall, he began the tour. "Behind these doors are different classrooms or offices. They're used for everything from GED classes—that's General Educational Development—and ESL—English as a Second Language – to computer and parenting classes. We also offer career, legal, and financial counseling." He pulled back on his cart, angling the wheels toward the wall. "Stop here a minute. I need to check on the coffee." He jogged into a classroom.

Kate leaned against the cart and looked at her surroundings. Dings and black smudges marked the once-white walls in the hallway. The speckled green linoleum floor was streaked with tire markings, probably from the grocery carts they were currently pushing. She peeked into the room to see Tucker touching the outside of a huge coffee urn. There was a table with mugs, canisters of sugar, powdered cream, and a huge plate of donuts. Ten folding chairs were arranged in a circle.

"I wanted to make sure the coffee was hot." Tucker pushed his cart. "There's an AA meeting each morning at 8:45. I'm in charge of coffee and donuts. Let's get these kits to the stockroom. I'll talk to Jenny about them after my meeting."

"Oh, do you have to attend the meeting too?" Kate quickened her steps to keep up with him.

"I don't have to, but it's part of my ten steps." He turned and looked at Kate. "I've been sober for twenty years. That's how I originally became involved with M&M. After I got out of the army, my civilian job was down the street. The meeting here fit my work schedule."

"Oh...so, when did you start working here?"

"Four years ago. I started out as a volunteer, but then Nick asked me to help start Padre's Pantry." Tucker shoved his cart through the swinging doors into the stockroom. "Leave your cart out there. We'll empty mine and then switch."

The stockroom was dimly lit. Shelving units lined the walls filled with paper products: cups, plates, napkins, toilet paper, paper towels, as well as plastic containers. Tucker rolled the cart to an empty shelf and began unloading the boxes.

"Can you tell me how a normal day works?" Kate handed him a kit.

"Well, most of the employees attend Mass and then head over." He neatly stacked the cartons. "The first person in starts the coffee."

"For the AA meeting?"

"No, for lunch." He took off his cap and wiped his brow. "We go through a ton of coffee here. It takes about two hours to brew enough just for lunch."

"On most days, they prep lunch the day before and they're really just heating the meal and tossing the salad." Tucker pushed the empty cart out of the stockroom and pulled the second one inside. "Since we're closed on the weekends, Mondays are the most hectic days, because all the prep has to be done in the morning."

"Should I get to the kitchen, then?" Kate checked her watch. "What time do we start serving?"

"Not until 10:00, you've got plenty of time." Tucker shook his head.

"Lunch at 10:00, isn't that breakfast? Why so early?

"For lots of people, this meal will be the only food they eat. Serving early helps get them through the day. Today, we're serving brats and metts. I'm sure Marika and Dallas have it under control." He glanced at the clock. "Nick was going to talk to them, anyway. So, we've got a few minutes. Let me show you your office so you can put down your things." Tucker took her elbow. "I wouldn't leave anything of value out in the open, and it's probably best to lock your purse in the desk."

"Oh, I won't be bringing any of my things in here." Kate shifted her bag to the other shoulder. "I own a restaurant, Kate's on Vine. There was a fire, and well— my restaurant burned down. This job is going to help pay my personal expenses until I get the insurance money. I won't be here very long. Make lemonade out of lemons, right?" She laughed, "I can help the poor, get some good publicity about my altruism when I re-open my restaurant, and make some money while I'm waiting."

"Is that right?" Tucker nodded. "Well, okay, then. Your office is right around the corner."

Turning the bend, Kate saw an old woman standing behind a walker. The woman's thin, wispy gray hair was brushed into a bun, a butterfly barrette by her ear. Although it was eighty-five degrees, she wore a red plaid flannel shirtwaist dress and black winter coat, knee highs slouched around her ankles.

"Oh my God, she's peeing," Kate gasped, grabbing Tucker's arm.

"Oh man." Tucker turned the handle on a door and nudged Kate through. "Katie, here's your office. I'm going to take care of that situation." He crooked his head at the woman, "I'll be back in ten minutes."

Closing the door, Kate leaned against it. She rubbed her eyes, trying to erase the image of the peeing old woman.

What have I gotten myself into? I don't belong here. I've got to get my restaurant reopened. I don't want to help the less fortunate, I just want a damn paycheck, so I don't starve waiting for the insurance company to pay up. I've already gone through my savings, and I can't ask my parents for any more help. I don't want them going into their retirement account.

The windowless room was dark and smelled like fresh paint. Feeling along the wall, her hands searched for the light switch. There was no way she was opening that door before Tucker came back. God only knows what she might see.

She flipped the light switch. The fluorescent bulb bathed the dull beige office in a harsh light. The 1960s-era office furniture included a gray metal desk, a five-drawer filing cabinet with cookbooks on top, two green pleather office chairs and a black desk chair.

It was fine.

Nothing like the modern office she had at the restaurant, with its ergonomic chair though.

Placing her bag on the desk, she sat down. The chair wobbled.

What has my life become? I just watched an old lady pee on the floor. I'm about to cook brats and metts for lunch.

She took her phone from her bag and hit speed dial for the fire inspector. Rolling her eyes, she listened to the voicemail message.

Of course, he's not answering.

Hi, this is Kate O'Leary, *again*. I'm just wondering if there's an update on the fire investigation. Could you call me back, please?"

Defeated, she pulled the metal sign from her bag. It had been a spur-of- the-moment decision, tossing the plaque in the bag with the stupid M&M binder. It was a reminder of who she was and who she would be again.

Rubbing her fingers along the metal, she touched the raised letters, remembering the hours she'd spent designing it. The nameplate shape: a scalloped rectangle in antique bronze, the font style: Italic Gastromond, and the name:

Kate's on Vine

The Restaurant

The restaurant sign was her talisman, her touchstone, her reminder.

I am more than just a cook in a soup kitchen.

Moving the cookbooks from the filing cabinet, she leaned the sign against the wall. "I'll see this each time I come into this stupid office." She caressed the sign. "This is who I am. "

"Katie?" Tucker opened the door.

"Oh, you scared me." Kate's hip bumped into the filing cabinet, and with a clack, the sign toppled.

"Ready to go to the kitchen?"

Not really, but I don't have a lot of options right now.

"Sure, lead the way. " Kate repositioned the plaque, dropped her bag into the desk drawer, locked it, and kicked it closed before following Tucker.

The smell of bleach now permeated the hall, and a yellow easel warned *Caution, Wet Floor*—these were the only reminders of the old woman's presence.

They were back in the building's foyer. "Did we just make a big square?" Kate asked.

"Yep." Tucker nodded. "The kitchen and dining room are the center of M&M. All the other activities and services surround them. You can't help anyone if they are hungry."

"Well, I can certainly feed them. I won't be involved in any other way, but I can make sure they eat."

"I need to get to my meeting." Tucker pointed towards the kitchen. "There's Nick with Marika and Dallas. Just go up the ramp and turn left through the door."

"Okay." Kate turned. "Why are all those people in line?" She crooked her head towards the people on the opposite side of the empty dining room.

"Lunch."

"But lunch doesn't start for another hour and a half."

"I know." Tucker smiled. "Some people don't have anything to do but wait."

Walking up the ramp towards the kitchen, Kate watched Nick talking to the two workers. The woman looked angry. She stood ramrod straight, her dark eyes glaring at Nick. Her lips were pursed, and her arms were crossed against her chest. She kept shaking her head. The shorter man, head down, shoulders sagged, didn't look at Nick. He kept nodding his head and wiping the counter with a towel. Nick looked sincere, his arms outstretched, hands down, in a conciliatory manner.

Kate had a funny feeling she was the topic of the conversation. Taking a deep breath, she pushed open the swinging door. "Hello, I'm all finished with the tour."

"Hey, there she is." Nick waved her over. "Katie, I'd like you to meet Marika Johnson and Dallas Huber. Your sous chefs. I'm sure you can count on their help, and I know they're going to learn a lot from working with you." He smiled at each of them. "Marika, Dallas, this is Katie O'Leary, the new cook."

"Nice to meet you, Ms. Katie." Dallas shook Kate's outstretched hand. Marika kept her hands clenched by her side. She didn't speak or smile.

"Dallas." Nick slapped his back. "Why don't you show Katie the kitchen. Marika," he said, touching her elbow, "Can you come with me to my office?" Marika pulled away from Nick's hand. She stomped out the door and down the ramp. "Thanks, Dallas," Nick said, rushing to catch up to Marika.

"So… Katie, welcome. How long did you own your restaurant?" Dallas asked. Grabbing a broom like a lacrosse stick, he waved his arm for Kate to follow him. The short, stocky, black man wore jeans and a Dallas Cowboys T-shirt and cap. He had a towel dangling from his back pocket.

"I actually go by Kate. And it would have been five years next month – I was planning a big anniversary celebration."

"Did Nick call you Katie?" Dallas grinned.

"Yes." Kate rushed to keep up with his quick pace.

Laughing, Dallas shook his head with a smile. "One thing you need to know about Nick: once he gives you a nickname, it sticks." He opened a door. "My name's Darrell, but from the moment I met Nick, he's called me Dallas. Now, that's what everyone calls me. I don't even answer to anything else."

"Are you from Dallas?" Kate asked.

"Nah, never been. I'd written down my name for the job, and Nick thought it said Dallas. It stuck, then he gave me this Dallas Cowboys baseball hat." He tipped the cap. "And soon, everyone was giving me Cowboy stuff. It's all I wear. I guess it's good when the Bengals are having a bad season."

Oh great, not only have I lost my job, my restaurant, but now apparently my name. Katie... who the hell is she?

Placing the broom in the storage closet, Dallas paused before pushing open the double doors with a flourish. "Ta-dah, I give you the Mary and Martha Soup Kitchen." He was practically bursting with pride.

Kate almost cried.

The ancient kitchen was spotless, but the stainless-steel appliances were so old they had lost their luster: the stove and ovens looked early 1950s at least, and the behemoth refrigerator handles were bound in duct tape. The linoleum floor was a faded black and gray.

"Let me show you everything." Dallas guided Kate to the far right of the room to the industrial-sized refrigerator. "Look at all this room." Dallas opened both sides of the refrigerator doors with gusto. "We can put everything in here."

But it's almost empty, Kate thought as she peered inside.

"We have an eight-burner cooktop." Dallas wiped the knobs with the towel from his back pocket. "The automatic igniters don't work, so we just use this lighter." He grabbed a matchlight from the shelf and demonstrated how to light the burner. Admiring the blue-orange flame, he flipped the gas off and returned the lighter to the shelf.

"Ooh." Dallas touched the next appliance. "It's hot. These are the warming ovens. Did you have those in your restaurant?" Kate shook her head no. "Well, both ovens work now, so we can warm six pans at once. Nick just got the second one fixed."

"Listen, we're having a plumbing problem," Dallas said, standing in front of the commercial-sized stainless-steel basin. A white plastic basin filled with sudsy water sat in the basin. "It should be fixed today. We can wash the pots and pans, but nothing can go down the drain." Dallas pointed to the bucket under the open drainpipe leading from the sink. "You don't need to worry about that. I'll take care of filling and emptying the buckets."

"Oh, good." Kate put her hand on her lips to keep from screaming.

"So, do you think you'll be able to cook here?" Dallas, hands on his hips, admired the kitchen, his smile huge.

"I'm sure I can." Kate tried to smile as she leaned against the wobbly prep table.

Her heart was full of dismay. She missed her restaurant's state-of-the-art kitchen. "It looks great. Should we get started on lunch?"

What have I gotten myself into?

"Marika has things under control. She'll let us know what still needs to be done. Here she is now," Dallas said.

Carrying a four-pound bag of lettuce, Marika strode into the kitchen. "I've done everything: vegetables, brats and metts, pasta, bread, and now I'm making the salad." Marika slammed the salad bag onto the prep table. "Lunch needs to be ready in thirty minutes."

"Now, now, I'm going to help. I was showing Miss Katie around," Dallas said, wiping the prep table.

"What can I do?" Kate asked.

Marika reached under the prep table and grabbed a utility pan, ignoring Kate.

"I'm going to get the desserts. You can help me with those." Dallas jogged out the door. "I'll be right back."

Okay, I'll just stand right here then.

Kate put her hands behind her back and watched Marika work. She was tall, voluptuous, about Kate's age, with dark skin, eyes the color of a buckeye, and short, straight hair under a baseball cap.

Marika ripped open a plastic bag of shredded mixed lettuce and dumped it into the silver pan. She walked to the refrigerator and grabbed a gallon container of ranch dressing, unscrewed the top and poured the thin white liquid onto the greens. Marika tossed the salad with gloved hands.

This was salad?

The sound of a cart rolling across the floor made Kate's head turn. Dallas pushed a six-foot-tall cart filled with trays of desserts: cakes, pies, donuts, pastries, brownies, and muffins. "What's your favorite dessert, Miss Katie? I'm sure we've got it here." He transferred the desserts to the buffet station.

"I'm a choc-a-holic, so anything chocolate, I guess." Kate picked up a tray to help.

"Put on an apron and gloves," Marika interjected. "The white aprons are under the table, and you'll need a baseball cap or hairnet to work back here… Health Regulations."

Kate put the strap of the white apron over her head and tied the back strings around the front of her waist. "My hair's in a pony. Isn't that good enough?"

"I was told we need to wear a baseball cap or a hairnet." Marika shrugged. "But I guess you're the boss."

Continuing to plate the desserts, Dallas rolled his eyes and shook his head.

A hairnet. I have to wear a hairnet. Can my life get any worse?

Kate pushed her ponytail under the black hairnet and washed her hands at the sink before donning a pair of disposable gloves. "What should I do?" she asked.

Dallas handed her an apple pie, a knife, and a stack of green melamine dessert plates. "We try to get eight pieces out of each pie."

"So, how does lunch work?" Kate asked as she sliced into the pie.

"Well, if someone wants to eat, they get in line." Dallas pointed to the long line of people waiting against the wall. He looked at the kitchen clock. "Our volunteers will be in soon, and they'll give each client a ticket at the start of the line. When the client gets to the top of the ramp, another volunteer will take that ticket and give them a tray."

"Why pass out tickets? Can't you just give people a tray at the start of the line?" Kate had moved on to slicing a peach pie.

"Quality control. We want to know how many people we're serving, and it stops people from line-jumping. No ticket, no tray." Dallas rolled a second dessert cart over to the table. "Clients can go through the line as many times as they want, but they have to get a ticket."

"How many pies and cakes are we going to cut?" Kate rubbed her arm.

"We have to fill both carts." Dallas laughed. "Keep cutting."

Kate plated the slices of cherry pie. "Does someone bus the tables?"

"Yes ma'am. Volunteers work the dining room, wiping off tables and trays, cleaning up any spills. In fact, here they come now."

A group of people walked into the kitchen. They were wearing blue aprons and M&M baseball caps. Kate gasped when she saw the older gentleman. "That's Dan Hamilton." She pulled off her hairnet.

"Yep, he's one of our regular volunteers," Dallas answered.

"But he owns Hamilton Enterprises." Kate ran her fingers through her hair.

"I know. He's the president of the M&M board." Dallas led her over to the group. "Miss Katie, this here is the finest group of volunteers M&M has."

"Dallas, you tell every group that," said the gray-haired man, shaking Dallas's hand.

"No, no, I don't," Dallas shook his head. "I mean it. You guys are the best. Dan, Rosie, Sylvie, Rick." He pointed to each person he named. "This is Katie, our new cook."

"Mr. Hamilton, it's so good to see you." Kate grasped his hand.

"Hi Kate." He crossed his arms. "I couldn't believe it when Nick told me he'd hired the chef from Kate's on Vine. M&M sure doesn't fit your image. I never thought I'd see you slumming it down here."

"Well, it's just until I reopen my restaurant. Insurance problems, you know?"

"I thought you'd go work with Phillipe." Dan rocked back and forth as if evaluating Kate's character.

"Oh, I could never cook for anyone else after owning my own place." She hoped her huge smile didn't look fake. "Working at M&M is my way of giving back. I'm going to get the kitchen in shape, fix the procedures, improve the meals. I won't be here long."

"We'd better get moving or lunch is going to be late," Dallas interrupted. "Dan, can you finish the desserts, please? Katie, come with me and I'll show you how we prep the buffet line."

"It's good to see you again, Mr. Hamilton." Kate waved, the hairnet dangling from her fingers.

"Call me Dan, and welcome to M&M." Dan rolled the dessert cart to the serving line.

"You need to wear a hairnet." Marika yelled from the sink.

Dallas carried a stack of plates to the front of the buffet line and placed them in the holder. He rolled skids of bread, rolls, and biscuits next to the tray. Touching the warming table, he said, "It's plenty hot. Let's get the food. The potholders are in that drawer." He crooked his head toward the cabinet next to the warming ovens. "We'll put two pans of brats and metts on the line right away." He handed Kate a pan and nodded for her to follow him to the buffet.

"Do we help serve the food, too?" Kate placed her pan on the rack.

"No, no, the volunteers do the serving." He dropped the pasta into the serving slot. "Can you get the carrots?"

Kate opened the warming oven doors.

"Lunch is really an assembly line," Dallas continued, as he moved down the serving cart, explaining each station. "The first volunteer— today that's Dan—will set the pace. He'll put a piece of bread on the plate with a brat or a mett. He'll pass the plate to the next volunteer, who will serve the pasta. The third person scoops out the carrots, and when those are gone, green beans."

Marika elbowed Kate to move aside and dropped the salad pan into the buffet station.

What the hell is your problem? Kate thought giving Marika a dirty look. Moving closer to Dallas she asked, "What's next?"

"The fourth volunteer adds the salad and then hands the plate to the client." Dallas put his hand on the dessert cart. "Once the clients have their meal, they get to choose their dessert. They can pick two. That's why we needed to cut so many pies and cakes." He smiled. "Desserts is where the back-up always happens. People just can't decide."

"After getting their sweets, the client picks up their utensils: a fork and spoon wrapped in a paper towel. We *never* give knives. Finally, they choose their drink: either water or coffee."

"They have to choose between coffee or water?" Kate looked at the array of mugs.

"Yeah, we don't have enough cups for people to have both. A client

can say no to any food item, so the volunteer should always ask if they
want whatever item they're serving. And we always give the same
amount to each person: no extra servings, no matter how much a client
may beg. We have to be fair. If someone wants more food, they can
always get back in line for seconds."

"Dallas, are you ready?" A lady carrying a clipboard walked into the
kitchen. "Hi, you must be Katie." She shook Kate's hand. "I'm Jenny
Littleford. I coordinate the volunteers for the kitchen and dining room.
I'm sure everything is a blur to you right now." Jenny looked at the buffet
line. "If you have questions during lunch, anyone in a blue apron can help
you out. They're our regular volunteers or staff."

Kate looked down at the white apron Marika had told her to wear.

"We're all set," Dallas said.

"It's time to pray!" Jenny yelled, waving her clipboard in the air.
Like a pied-piper, Jenny led the staff and volunteers out the door to the
dining room. With nothing else to do, Kate joined the end of the line and
hoped the day would go fast.

2

NICK

At 9:45, Nick grabbed his well-worn Bible from the corner of his desk and walked to the M&M foyer. Hordes of people clustered together in the air-conditioned lobby trying to avoid the late summer heat. The smell of sweat, body odor, and cooked food filled the air. A line of hungry, hot people snaked from the kitchen door around the dining room tables. He breathed easier when he saw Marika with the staff and volunteers in a circle, waiting to pray.

A voice rose above the din of conversations.

Tucker, standing on a bench, his hands shaped as a megaphone, announced, "Ladies and gentlemen, it's time to pray. We invite all of you to please quiet yourselves and join us in the dining room."

After years of working at M&M, Nick was immune to the noise of the place. There was always some type of ruckus occurring in the building, but the quiet, the silence, still surprised him. When everyone was ready, staff, volunteers, and clients gathered to pray.

Tucker jumped from the pew. "How's it going, man?" He slapped Nick's back.

"Better," Nick grinned. "I'm glad Marika's still here".

"That bad, huh?" Tucker asked.

"After our conversation this morning, I wasn't sure she was going to stay. I know how much Marika wants to be named head cook, but I think she can learn a lot from Katie if she's willing to." Nick tapped the Bible against his leg.

"She's bull-headed, that's for sure." Tucker smiled, shaking his head. They waited for some of the clients from the foyer to join their circle. No one waiting in line stepped out of place. "Nick, we're ready." Tucker's elbow nudged his side.

Nick looked at the small group of people holding hands, all waiting for him to lead them in prayer. He took a deep breath, "Lord God, thank you for the opportunity to be together. Thank you for this food—and for each other—especially our wonderful and dedicated staff, who we appreciate beyond words." He smiled at Marika. She scowled back.

"*Amen,*" the circle responded.

"Everyone," Nick stood behind Kate, placing his hands on her shoulders. "Before we start serving, I want to introduce Katie O'Leary. She's going to be the head cook for the next few months. Please make Katie feel welcome."

Kate's face reddened when the group began clapping. Pushing an errant curl under the ugly hair net, she gave a shy wave.

Marika stomped towards the kitchen and Nick watched her leave.

Well, I guess she's still mad. Why can't she understand? I hired Katie to help her.

Nick returned to his office, reminding himself why hiring Katie was a smart business decision. When the Board of Directors had approached him to become M&M's Executive Director six years ago, he had been hesitant. He wasn't a social worker or a do-gooder. He was a businessman who believed radical change was needed if poverty was ever really going to end. The board agreed to allow Nick to run the non-profit like a corporation.

He asked the questions: why were people poor? How could one affect change? The answers were simple: a lack of education, lack of opportunity, and household composition, and it spurred the creation of an ambitious five-year strategic plan. Refined, The M&M mission became: *Feed the Hungry and Fortify Them for the Future.*

Nick became the change agent for operating the non-profit. He'd upset the apple cart by rejecting all public assistance. The M&M Board had been furious, believing he was passing on "free money," but the red tape and bureaucratic paperwork required to qualify for the government support made the money extremely expensive. Instead, he'd found new revenue streams and developed corporate partners, making M&M entirely privately funded.

These fresh ideas allowed M&M to have a more holistic approach to supporting the community. Sitting in the wobbly office chair, he reviewed all the reasons Katie was the right choice to be head cook: she had incredible credentials, experience, as well as the ability to create new menus. She would revolutionize the kitchen, which was currently in a rut. Katie would implement better and newer procedures and meals, which would ultimately help Marika and Dallas; help everyone.

It was a business decision, nothing more. He was glad a board member had recommended her for the job even if it was just temporary. Slapping the desktop, he turned on the computer. He just wished Marika's hurt-filled eyes would stop haunting him.

Nick looked up from the computer. He'd been working on the same spreadsheet for an hour, but he couldn't get Marika's disappointment out of his mind. Hands on hips, he stood and looked out the window. Muted shouts from outside mingled with laughter and conversations drifting from the dining room. He watched groups of young men loitering on the street.

I'd love to go talk to them. See what's important in their lives. What were their hopes and dreams—did they even have any? How can I help them?

His thoughts returned to Katie. The kitchen needed her to shake it up in the same way he'd turned around the organization. After Joe, their old cook had decided not to return after hip surgery, Katie's availability to work at the kitchen seemed like a golden opportunity. A classically trained chef willing to reorganize a soup kitchen on a cook's salary. It would have been foolish for him not to hire her. He shook his head and looked down at the papers piled on his desk. He needed to get back to work.

"Hi, Nick?" Katie tapped on the door frame before stepping into the office.

"How'd your first lunch service go?" Nick stood, waving her in.

"I think pretty well," Katie said. "Dallas was really helpful in explaining how it all ran." She dragged her fingers through her hair, smoothing back the mussed strands. "Marika didn't say very much."

"Great, I knew Dallas would come through." Nick walked past her and closed the door. "Just put those papers on the floor and take a seat." He pointed at the chair and sat down at his desk. "Marika may take a little longer to warm up to you." He fumbled with some papers. "I should have probably told you this, but I didn't want you to be uncomfortable. Both Marika and Dallas were expecting to be named the new cook." Nick watched her eyes grow wide.

"They actually *wanted* the job?" Kate leaned forward in the chair, her voice going up an octave. "Then why did you hire me?"

"Listen," Nick raised his palms to stop her questions. "Dallas and Marika are both great, but neither of them is quite ready for the position of head cook." He grabbed a baseball from the desk, tossing it up and down. "I was hoping you could act as their mentor."

"Nick, I don't know." Kate's head bobbed with the ball's movement. "They both seem to have a handle on the cooking." She grabbed the ball. "Do they even want a mentor?"

"Katie, c'mon, the meals are terrible. They've got to look and taste better. They could use a complete nutritional upgrade too. That's why we need *you*. Dallas and Marika can execute the work of the kitchen, but neither of them has the skills yet to improve the quality of the food or the menus. I need *you* to bring the kitchen into this century: better procedures and meals. And most importantly, I want you to make certain one of them is ready to replace you when you leave."

"I don't know." Kate laid the ball back on the desk. "I feel a little funny about this. I mean, I'm not here forever, just until I get the insurance money. They know I don't want to be the M&M cook, right?"

"Absolutely. I've told them you're just temporary. I told them you were recommended by a board member. They know you're not here forever." He palmed the ball, leaning back in the chair. "So, what do you think about the place?"

"I'm not sure what I expected. I guess it was surprising how happy everyone seemed?" She shrugged. "I thought people would be sad, and maybe even a little embarrassed about having to eat in a soup kitchen, but they weren't. The dining room looked like a normal cafeteria; a bunch of people meeting to have lunch."

"That's what I like to hear," Nick walked to the window. "I want

M&M to be the neighborhood diner. This place has been around for over twenty years. For a lot of the clients, not coming to lunch would be weird.

He continued, "My wish is for people *not* to eat here because they *have* to—because they're hungry or poor, but because this is where their friends are. More of a community center than a soup kitchen." He stared at the same men from earlier sitting on the stoop. "I want people to find their friends and their purpose here."

He turned and looked back at Katie. "Why don't you work with Dallas and Marika from start to finish tomorrow, and the next day you can follow Jenny?

"Okay," Katie stood. "I'll see you tomorrow.

3

MARIKA

Marika's mind raced as she finished cleaning the kitchen. The new girl wasn't helping.

"I'm supposed to meet with Nick. Do you guys need me to do anything else?" Her highness had asked in a sugary sweet voice.

She didn't wait for an answer, untying her apron and ripping off her hairnet the second the lunch line closed, smoothing down her designer shirt like she was a queen.

"No, no, Miss Katie," Dallas practically bowed. "You go right ahead. Me and Marika got this."

God, he's such an ass kisser.

Marika rolled her eyes, picking up the dirty water bucket to empty it in the washroom sink.

"Okay, then. I'll see you tomorrow," the queen said, putting her hands together and bowing as if she was subservient. "You guys did a great job, thank you."

Thank you? Why in the hell are you thanking me for doing my job? The job I've been doing for the past seven years. Just have your special meeting with Nick.

Fuming, Marika finished putting away the leftover food, sterilized the counter tops, wiped down the appliances, and mopped the floor, all

the while trying to ignore Dallas's idiotic ramblings and off-key singing.
Some days she couldn't take the man.   .

In record time, the kitchen was spotless. "Looks like we're all done
here. I'm going to help at the Quik-mart—I'll see you tomorrow." Dallas
turned off the kitchen lights.

"Bye," Marika grunted, grabbing her bag from the hook in the hall.
She locked the door to the kitchen and headed home, her anger and
thoughts stewing with each step.

*How dare that woman thank me for doing my job. I'm not a
temporary employee. Working at M&M is important to me. Damn Nick, I
am so mad at him. He just didn't want to choose between me and Dallas
for the head cook job.*

How could he hire her? She doesn't even care about the soup
kitchen, she's just here temporarily until she reopens her precious
gourmet restaurant.

"I think you and Dallas will really be able to learn a lot from Katie.
She's an amazing chef." Nick had said in his office.

"I'm a good cook, too," Marika answered, crossing her arms, trying
not to stomp her foot.

"You are," Nick agreed. "But you're just not ready. I'm sorry," he
said shrugging his shoulders.

"Thanks a lot," she'd turned and walked out of his office.

"Marika," Nick had called after her, but she didn't turn back, and he
didn't come after her.

Once Nick had dropped the bombshell about hiring that *cook*, all
Marika had wanted to do was talk to Tucker, but he didn't want to talk
to her anymore. He let her know that when he walked out of her
apartment last week. So, she'd gone to the computer room to research
their new chef.

The first Google hit was about the fire: *The fire at Kate's on Vine was under investigation. The circumstances were suspicious. Kate O'Leary the restaurant's owner and head chef vows to rebuild.*

Marika shook her head and clicked on the article link to the Kate O'Leary bio.

Only Nick would hire a chef whose restaurant burned. She probably burned down the building for the insurance money.

Kate had gone to private schools her whole life. Attended Le Cordon Bleu cooking school, graduating with honors. She'd worked in Europe, Vegas, and New York.

And now she wants to work in a soup kitchen? What's her deal?

Marika's skepticism grew with each paragraph she read. "Are we going to learn how to cook seafood risotto? Is that what Nick wants her to show us because that's her specialty?" Marika talked to the empty room. "Well, I'm going to figure out what her game is. I'm not as gullible as Nick."

"Why do you think she wants to work here?" Marika asked Dallas in the stockroom while they were prepping lunch.

"I think she wants to help," Dallas had said, pulling cans from the shelf. "We can learn a lot. It's only going to be for a short while." Dallas had shown Kate around like he was giving a tour of the Taj Mahal. Charmed by the new chef, Dallas would not be any help. It was up to Marika to get rid of her.

She was pretty. Maybe that's why Nick hired her.

He was a good-looking man, too, probably not immune to her appearance. But why would a woman like that want to work in a soup kitchen? It didn't make sense. No renowned chef would work at M&M without an ulterior motive. Marika would uncover her game, and then the new chef would be gone, and the job would be hers.

After all, she deserved it. She'd been going to M&M almost her whole life; she knew the kitchen and its clients. She had a cooking degree from the community college, and she'd kept the place running since Joe's surgery. How could Nick hire someone who'd never even stepped foot in the place?

Marika walked fast, not even noticing the scenery. She could walk home blindfolded. This was her neighborhood. She knew the different store owners and the latest neighborhood gossip.

She passed the city park, or what the city called a park: asphalt, a swing-set with no swings, and a tall metal slide at least twenty-five years old that wouldn't pass any safety regulation today. She'd been ten when that slide was brand-new and was one of the first kids to soar down its silvery slope. Nowadays, only a fool would let their child play there. She'd lived here her whole life. She was one of them. There was no way a "temporary" cook was going to be better at this job than her.

4

KATE

The sound of Kate's Dansko clogs echoed on the marble floor of Holy Family Church. She genuflected, making the sign of the cross, and tossed her baseball cap into the empty church pew. She'd been backing out of her driveway when she realized she'd forgotten the damn thing, but there was no way she was wearing a hairnet again. So, leaving the car running, she'd run into her house, grabbed the hat and raced to get to Mass on time. She'd arrived fifteen minutes early. Kneeling, she silently offered a quick prayer.

Please God, help me reopen the restaurant... soon.

She didn't want to risk not being able to get into M&M, so she had taken Nick's suggestion to attend morning Mass with everybody. Besides, the way her life was going, she could use all the help she could get.

Pushing her body onto the wooden pew, she folded her hands in her lap and looked around the church. The pews were filling up and the hum of quiet conversations whispered around her. Kate recognized some people from yesterday, including Nick. She watched him walk to the altar, bow his head before the tabernacle, and light the altar candles. The smell of sulphur wafted through the building.

Sincere...he just seems so sincere. Why isn't he married? Kate mused. *When was my last date?*

Her eyes looked upward. *God, it's been so long...I can't even remember. What has my life become?*

She shook her head and looked around the church. Marika was walking down the aisle with a tall, handsome young man. The teenager wore a school uniform: khakis, a white long-sleeved oxford shirt, and a blue and red striped tie. Kate waved and scooted down the pew so they could sit next to her, but Marika walked past without glancing at her.

So, that's how you want to play it. Kate picked up the hymnal to sing the opening song.

"Hi, Marika." Kate waited at the bottom of the church steps. The morning was chilly after the evening's rain, and she held her jacket closed with her hands. "I thought we could walk to the kitchen together. I think Nick wants me to shadow you today." Kate smiled as the frowning Marika walked down the last few steps.

"I usually walk my son to the bus stop. I'll meet you in the kitchen." Marika took the boy's arm and walked towards the corner. His confused eyes looked at his mother.

"Oh, is this your son?" Kate walked beside them. "Hi, I'm Kate."

The boy reached out to shake her hand. "Hi, I'm Jamal."

Marika stopped walking. "Nick hired Ms. O'Leary to be the temporary cook at M&M. Her own restaurant caught fire, so she needed a job."

"Well, that's not exactly how I would have put it." Kate laughed. "So, where do you go to school?"

"I'm a sophomore at St. Katherine Drexel." Jamal switched his backpack to his other arm. "There's my bus. It was nice meeting you." He hugged Marika as she reached up to place a kiss on his cheek.

"Have a good day. I love you." Marika touched his tie.

"Love you too." Jamal called, racing for the bus.

"Bye," Kate waved.

Crossing the street, the sides of Marika's trench coat flailed behind her like a flag. Kate struggled to keep pace. "Jamal seems like a nice young man. You must be proud." Kate fought the urge to ask her to slow down. "I've heard Drexel is really difficult to get into."

Marika stopped to glare at Kate. "Drexel is very difficult to get into." She pointed at the school bus. "Jamal worked his butt off to get into that school. Things weren't just handed to him." She pivoted and walked behind the M&M building, unlocking the door marked *Deliveries*. The hallway was dark, the kitchen to the right of the room and Kate's office down the hall to the left. The smell of bleach lingered.

"I've never come in this way," Kate looked around. "What a great way to avoid the people blocking the front door."

"Yeah, you want to avoid the riffraff." Marika rolled her eyes. "Make sure you lock the door." She tugged off her coat. "You should probably go hang your jacket in your office." Marika placed her coat on a hook lining the wall. "I wouldn't want it to get dirty out here with mine."

"Did you want to hang your coat in my office?" Kate asked.

"No, I know where my coat belongs." Marika tied a blue apron around her waist. "When you're finished, meet me in the kitchen. Nick thinks you need to shadow Dallas and me again today."

"I have to make one quick phone call." Kate turned the knob to her office door. "I'll be there in a minute."

"I was going to show you how to make the coffee." Marika headed towards the kitchen. "But I guess you can learn some other time."

What, you can't wait five minutes to make coffee?

"Oh, okay, just let me put my things away. I'll call the insurance company later." Kate threw her purse in the desk drawer and put her jacket on the coat hook behind the door.

Get real. She thinks I need to learn how to make coffee. I've made chocolate soufflé for fifty people at once. Marika had better learn which side her bread was buttered on if she wants my recommendation to Nick.

The harsh fluorescent lights glaring on the dulled stainless-steel countertops and appliances forced Kate to blink a few times as she entered the kitchen. Marika stood at the sink, filling one of the large coffee urns. The sound of rushing water clanging in the metal pot reverberated.

"The first person in always starts the coffee," Marika nodded to the red coffee container sitting on the counter. "Put the grounds in the brew basket."

"How much?" Kate grabbed a blue apron, tucked her hair under the Cincinnati Red's baseball cap and picked up the container.

"I use three cups of grounds. The clients like the coffee full-strength." Marika carried the urn filled with water to the serving line.

"Really? That seems too strong." Kate pointed to the directions on the canister. "According to this, we should use two cups."

"I'm just telling you what we normally use. I guess you know better." Marika turned on the water to fill the second urn, drowning out further conversation.

"I hate to waste." Kate measured the coffee. "Let's try it with two cups and see if the customers even notice." She closed the lid and hit the start button.

Marika banged the second urn onto the table.

"Good morning, ladies," Dallas pushed a rolling cart filled with pans into the kitchen. "It sounds like you've got the coffee handled." He chuckled, transferring the pans from the cart to the oven.

Marika opened the refrigerator and grabbed bags of lettuce, tomatoes and carrots.

"Hi, Dallas," Kate walked around Marika. "I'm shadowing you and Marika today. It looks like she's going to make the salad again." Kate wiped her hands on her apron. "What would you like me to do?"

"I'm going to warm the chicken and mushrooms." He closed the oven door. "Why don't you make the rice, and once that's cooking, we can both open cans of green beans." He pointed to the case of beans. "Once the line gets moving, we'll start on tomorrow's lunch."

"Sounds like a plan," Kate clapped her hands together.

When the lunch time prayer ended, Jenny and her crew of volunteers walked into the kitchen. "Are you ready?" Jenny asked.

"I think so. Dallas is putting the pans in the server now," Kate answered. Dallas, singing while he worked, hurried between the buffet table and the warming oven. Dropping the stainless-steel pans of chicken and mushrooms, rice, and green beans into the warming bins. Marika arranged the salad pans and desserts.

Jenny stood beside the buffet station, facing the white aproned volunteers in their baseball caps and hairnets. "Give each client a spoon of rice." She heaped a pile of rice onto the plate. She returned that spoon and moved down the line. "A ladle of chicken and... what is this?" A look of disgust crossed her face as she watched the pieces of chicken and mushroom swimming in a brown sauce fall back into the pan.

"It's chicken with mushroom gravy," Dallas said, wiping imaginary spills from the counter.

"Did anyone taste it?" Jenny's eyes moved between Dallas and Marika. "It looks gross."

"It's fine," Dallas laughed, shaking his head.

"I agree, it doesn't look great." Kate stirred the food. "I'm getting the hang of the menus this week. I promise next week things will look and taste better."

"I wouldn't want to eat it." Jenny grimaced, picking up a ladle. She continued with her spiel to the volunteers. "Ask the client if they want the chicken and gravy on the rice or beside it and ask if they want green beans and the salad; about a spoon of each." Jenny stepped away from the line. "Any questions?" The volunteers looked at each other and shook their heads.

"No? Okay, let's get moving." Jenny held the clipboard in front of her. "One last thing, do not give anyone extra food." She looked at each volunteer. "If someone wants more, the answer is *no*. Tell them to finish what they already have and get back in line if they still want more." She circled her finger in the air. "Okay, let's roll."

Leaning back against the refrigerator, Kate remembered the talk from yesterday.

Jenny gives the same volunteer speech each day. I guess nothing ever changes here. The same guy's first in line again.

He was tall, head shaved, and impeccably groomed. He wore pressed jeans, a collared shirt and clean work boots. A black backpack filled with textbooks was slung over his right shoulder. He seemed disappointed with the food, bypassing the chicken and taking just rice and green beans.

"If someone doesn't take the meat, give them two scoops of rice and green beans." Jenny added more rice and beans to the man's plate before handing it to him.

"Thank you." The man smiled.

Oh, my God. He doesn't have any teeth.

Kate stared as the toothless man asked for a piece of apple pie. The food line moved smoothly. The volunteers quickly served the clients and sent them on their way. People filled the dining room eating, talking, and laughing. Kate stood alone, her back against the refrigerator.

She didn't know the last time she had ever felt so lost in a kitchen.

The kitchen was her happy place. Her fondest memories and happiest times inevitably were by the stove. But at that moment, standing in the Mary and Martha Soup Kitchen, she felt sad. Watching the people coil their way through the long line to get a free lunch, Kate wondered, *how had someone with a Master of Culinary Arts Degree ended up here?*

Trays clattering stopped her reverie. Marika slammed two green colored portioned plates onto the counter and was filling each divided section with food: rice, green beans, salad, and chicken.

"What are these for?" Kate asked.

"We don't want the little kids to go through the line." Marika scanned the dessert trays. "I'm taking them their food."

"Can I help?"

"No, I've got it." Marika placed a cookie on a plate. "You can get started on tomorrow's lunch." She picked up the trays and carried them into the dining room.

"But I don't even know what we're having tomorrow," Kate said to Marika's back.

Kate wandered around the kitchen, looking for some sign of what needed to be done. *First thing next week, I'm putting up a chore chart. This is ridiculous. What the hell is Marika doing? I thought she was just dropping off the meals.*

Kate watched Marika in the dining room. She sat at a table next to two little girls. She took the plates off the tray and placed the food on the table in front of each child. She unwrapped the silverware and elaborately put the napkins on the girl's laps. Marika had transformed. Her face softened, and she was actually smiling.

I think that's the first time I've ever seen her smile. She's pretty when she's not being such a witch.

One of the little girls, about three, her hair in braids, grabbed a cookie and took a bite. Marika smiled and shook her head. She gently took the dessert out of the little hand and returned it to the plate. She pointed to the vegetables on the plate. A woman pulled out a chair next to the children. Marika stood, patted each little girl on the head, and strode back to the kitchen. The little cookie-eater grabbed the half-eaten cookie and happily chewed. Kate expected the girl's mom to react the same way Marika had, pointing to the vegetables, but she didn't. She was too busy eating her chocolate cake.

Until Marika or Dallas shared tomorrow's menu with her, Kate had nothing to do. Trying to act busy, she wiped down the already-clean counter and observed the dining room. The clients came in all shapes, sizes, and colors. A black woman dressed entirely in red, from her bedazzled red baseball cap to her red sequined shoes, walked through the line telling all the volunteers, "God bless you on this glorious day."

An older gentleman with gray hair and a mustache kindly asked the volunteer, "Do you have any muffins? I love muffins."

After checking both dessert carts, the volunteer answered. "I'm sorry, they're all gone today, maybe tomorrow."

"I just love muffins. Hey, do you know how to make an egg roll?"

"No…" The confused volunteer looked at Kate.

"Well, you need wonton wrappers—" Kate said.

"Nah, you push it!" the laughing man took his tray. "That's a good one."

Kate had to smile. It was such a corny joke. She turned at the rattle of the cart being pushed through the swinging doors. "Oh, my goodness, Dallas. Why didn't you ask me to help?" Dallas pushed one cart filled with cans of stews and pulled a second filled with cans of vegetables.

"It's not a problem, Miss Katie." He wiped his brow with a towel. "I always get the stock for the next day's menu as soon as lunch service begins."

She placed her hands on the cart and looked down at cans of Dinty Moore Stew. "Okay, what do you need me to do?"

"Get a can-opener and start opening," his smile grew as wide as her eyes. "We should probably open 60 of these cans. Then we'll add some carrots and peas to make the stew thicker." He handed her a can and the opener, "It's easier to serve if the gravy is thick."

"I couldn't find a chore list. What else are we serving tomorrow?" Kate asked.

"Marika's going to make the mashed potatoes. He placed two serving pans on the counter. "As a special treat, we have peaches. They're about to expire."

Kate held the can-opener with disgust. "Maybe I should peel the potatoes."

"We don't have real potatoes, Miss Katie." Dallas laughed as he wiped out the pan. "We use dried ones. Marika knows how to make them taste great."

Kate grabbed the industrial-sized opener and twisted the cans. After opening about twenty, her arm ached, and her hand seemed permanently clenched. She stopped to rub her shoulder. "Boy, this job is making me wish I'd spent more time at the gym than at Cordon Bleu. My arm is killing me."

"Just you wait. By the time your restaurant reopens, you'll have giant biceps." Dallas said, adding peas and carrots to the stew. Marika stood at the stove combining milk, water, and margarine to reconstitute the dehydrated potato flakes into a facsimile of mashed potatoes. Kate picked up another can and continued her "cooking." Dallas sang as he twisted can after can of stew on the opener. Today's song seemed to be a mix of Beyonce and Lady Gaga. A man yelling from the serving line interrupted him. "Hey, Dallas, what's the new girl's name again?"

Kate turned around to see who was asking about her. It was the man who acted like he was the mayor of the kitchen. He spent lunchtime greeting every table.

"Katie?" Dallas tapped her arm. "I think Deacon wants to talk to you."

"Got a minute?" the man beckoned Kate to the serving station.

She put down the can opener and walked over to the counter. "Yes?" Kate wiped her hands on her apron. Marika, stirring the mixture of potatoes, followed Kate's movements.

"Ma'am, my name's Deacon," the man put his hand on his chest. "I eat lunch here every day, and I own the little Quik-mart on the corner. First, I want to welcome you to the kitchen." He tipped an imaginary hat to Kate.

"Thank you," Kate said.

"Ma'am, there's a bit of a problem with the coffee. Marika told me you made it today." He moved the toothpick from the corner of his mouth and raised a coffee mug up in the air.

"Yessss," Kate glanced over her shoulder at Dallas.

"Well, ma'am," his look was stern, "It's too weak. I know you're new here, but we like our coffee to bite us." He slapped the counter. "It needs to be *real* strong. Maybe you can have Marika show you how to make it? That girl makes some good coffee."

"I will definitely do that," Kate nodded, feeling her face grow hot. "Thank you for telling me. Have a good day." Head bowed; she walked back to the prep table to open more cans of stew. She ignored Dallas, biting his lip to keep from laughing, and Marika's smirk.

At 12:30, Jenny shut down the line. As the last client took a seat, Jenny thanked the volunteers for their help and officially closed the kitchen. Dallas emptied the serving station, bringing the leftovers to the counter for Marika to cover with plastic wrap. "Should I put these in the refrigerator?" Kate asked, pointing to the covered containers.

Marika ignored her.

"No, no, leave those out," Dallas said, wiping down the counter. "Some workers will take them home to their families. They always appreciate the free food."

"You can scrub the pots and pans," Marika said, pushing the dessert cart. "Unless you have another meeting with Nick?" She sashayed through the kitchen door ignoring Kate's gaping mouth and eyes wide with shock.

5
KATE

After hitting the snooze button too many times, Kate missed Mass. Parking her car, she walked to the empty M&M front stoop.

At least I won't have to push my way through the crowd of people waiting at the door.

She pulled on the door handle, but the locked door didn't budge. She had no way of getting inside.

Since Mass wouldn't be over for at least another 20 minutes, she had now become the loiterer.

Kate paced back and forth in front of the door. She contemplated taking a seat on the dirty steps, like so many of the clients did.

It'd be nice to have a place to sit down and wait.

There weren't any benches. In her neighborhood, stores and restaurants provided benches or even café chairs with a small table for people to sit and relax. There was nothing like that on the street here.

It's no wonder groups congregate in front of the door. There's nowhere else to go.

She stood, leaning against the side of the building. The neighborhood was quiet, almost peaceful. The occasional honking or the sound of a beeping truck driving in reverse punctuated the muted responses from the church congregation. Lost in her reverie, Kate jumped when a person burst around the corner, almost bumping into her. Jenny jumped too, and they both laughed once they recognized each other.

"I'm locked out," Kate shrugged her shoulders, "I just realized I never got keys."

"I'll let you in," Jenny said, jiggling a heavy key chain in one hand and toting a stack of clean white aprons in the other.

"Can I help?" Kate took the aprons.

"Yeah, the door can be a little tricky," Jenny wrestled with the door. She twisted and turned the key, pulling the door handle at the same time. "Sometimes it sticks," Jenny said, kicking the bottom of the door and tugging on the handle before getting it opened.

"I think you're working with me this morning," Jenny said, re-locking the door and taking the aprons from Kate.

"I am," Kate nodded, "Do I have time to get the coffee started or do you want to go over things now?"

"Let's meet at 8:30," Jenny looked at her watch, "The volunteers will be arriving then, and I can give you an overview at the same time."

"Perfect. I'll meet you in the dining room."

In the kitchen, Kate brewed the coffee, this time following Marika's instructions to the letter. She placed the stew in the oven and started warming the potatoes when Marika walked into the kitchen.

"Oh, you're here." Marika hung her sweater on the hook outside of the kitchen. "When you weren't at Mass, I thought you might have decided the job wasn't for you.

"No, I just hit the snooze too many times." Kate forced a smile.

Shrugging, Marika grabbed the lettuce from the fridge.

"Good morning." Dallas filled a cup with coffee. Taking a swig, he whistled. "Man, you took Deacon's comment to heart. This is one strong cup of joe."

"The customer is always right." Kate laughed, "That coffee could probably walk by itself." Marika dropped heads of lettuce, bags of carrots, and tomatoes on the prep table with a loud thump. She grabbed a knife and began chopping the iceberg lettuce into thin strips. "There isn't a chore chart. What can I help you with?" Kate looked at her watch. "I'm shadowing Jenny this morning, but I have some time before I have to meet with her."

"Those go into the salad," Marika pointed her knife at a bag of carrots.

Without another word, Kate started peeling the carrots. The kitchen was quiet except for Dallas singing the day's tune, 'I Heard it Through the Grapevine' as he prepped the serving station. After washing the carrots, Kate chopped them into bite size pieces.

"What are you doing?" Marika stopped dicing the tomatoes.

"I'm chopping the carrots," Kate said, holding the knife in her hand.

"We don't chop the carrots." Marika's voice oozed condescension. "We *shred* them."

"What? Why?" Kate asked. She tilted her head, confused.

"A lot of our clients can't chew the carrots if they're chopped." Dallas said, reaching under the counter and pulling out an electric grater.

"Oh, I didn't know." Kate dropped the knife onto the prep table.

"That's why you should probably ask someone who *does* know before you just go and do something." Marika scooped a handful of tomatoes and tossed them onto the lettuce.

Dallas plugged the grater into an outlet. "Here you go, Miss Katie, we're all good."

"Thanks, Dallas, I really appreciate your help." Kate said.

How am I supposed to know the carrots don't get chopped? Why is Marika being such a bitch to me? They're carrots, for God's sake.

"When you're finished, sprinkle the carrots on top. I'll add the salad dressing then." Marika dropped the pans of lettuce and tomatoes next to Kate.

Kate hit the "on" button. The whirr of the grater kept her from responding. After scattering the shredded carrots over the pans of lettuce, Kate washed her hands. "I'm going to meet Jenny. Are you guys okay here?"

"Of course we are." Marika poured the ranch dressing over the salad. "We've been doing this job for years."

Mentally, she flipped her off, but Kate pulled her cell phone out of her back pocket, pushing the speed dial for the fire inspector as Jenny walked up. "I have to make a quick call," Kate whispered. "Can I meet you in the dining room?"

"No, we can—"

Kate raised her finger to silence Jenny. "Hi, Captain, it's Kate O'Leary. I'm surprised you answered. I wanted check on the investigation into the fire." Holding the phone away from her face, she mouthed, "Sorry."

"Just come to my office when you're finished." Jenny pointed down the hall.

Nodding, Kate stepped into her office to talk to the inspector. "But I don't understand what's taking so long. It's been almost two months. I've given you all the paperwork information I have. I'm not sure what else you need. I really wanted to be open in time for the holidays. It's taken so long; I've had to take another job. Without the insurance money or re-opening my restaurant I don't have money.

"Ms. O'Leary," the captain sighed. "Like I've said before, the inquiry can't be rushed. By law, I have six months to file my report. I will call you once we completed the investigation. Have a good day."

"Well, I was hoping—"

'*Call ended*' flashed on her phone screen. Kate shoved it into her back pocket and went to Jenny's office.

"Knock, knock," Kate tapped the door frame and walked through the open door.

"Come in, sit down," Jenny glanced over her shoulder from the computer and waved her to a seat. "I just need a minute." Jenny's head moved between her clipboard and the computer screen. "I'm trying to see where I still need to find volunteers."

Kate studied the volunteer coordinator, Jenny. Runner thin, with frizzy gray hair pulled up into a high ponytail. Her eyes moved from the spreadsheets on her desk to the calendar on the wall to the computer screen, her pencil scribbling on the clipboard at a rapid pace. Her attitude was no nonsense.

Taking a seat on one of the two well-worn captain's chairs, Kate pushed aside the accent pillow which told her to *Be Patient, Be Gentle, Be Humble, Be Kind.* The pillow on the opposite chair reminded her to *smile.* Jenny's office was cozy, the walls painted a light powder-blue with an entire wall collage of framed children's artwork: drawings, paintings, and colored pages adorned the back wall. The large plate-glass window, accessorized by yellow curtains tied back with pale blue roping, gave a full view of the dining room. Jenny closed her computer.

"I like the way you've decorated your office," Kate said, tilting her head towards the artwork.

"Thanks. So many of the little kids paint or draw me pictures. I thought hanging them on the wall would be a nice way to thank them. I change the pictures every two or three months, so no one's feelings get hurt."

"That's a great idea."

"Yeah, the kids get a kick out of seeing their pictures framed. Ready?

Can you grab that stack of aprons on the filing cabinet?" Jenny walked out the door. "Basically, I coordinate all the volunteers for the kitchen and its various activities." Jenny talked and walked fast. "Most days, I have four regular volunteers. These are people who come on a steady schedule, usually once a week and aren't associated with a specific church, company, or group." She opened a cabinet door and pulled out some name tags, stickers and pens. "They're my 'Old Faithful's,' completely reliable, dedicated to M&M. They don't need to check in. They go straight to the kitchen."

"They get the blue aprons?" Kate asked, carrying the white aprons.

"Yes," Jenny nodded. "The second type of volunteer is my 'One and Done,' people who are volunteering for the day." She closed and locked the cabinet. It's usually a group from a church or school, sometimes a company. They come here to work for three hours, feel good about what they've done, and then forget about us. Depending on the day, there are usually six to eight volunteers working each lunch. Personally, I don't think there's anything worse than standing around with nothing to do. So, I make sure each volunteer has a specific job.

In the dining room, six people stood around an empty table nervously, trying to avoid staring at the clients already waiting in line. "Hi, I'm Jenny, the volunteer coordinator." She placed name tags, a stack of papers, and pens on the table. "This is Katie, the new cook."

Smiling, Kate placed the aprons on the table.

"Thanks for helping," Jenny spoke to the group. "You'll each need to sign a release form, grab an apron, and put on a name tag. Did everyone bring a hat?" A few of the volunteers nodded yes. "If not, you'll need to wear a hairnet. I can show you where those are."

Damn, I forgot my hat. Kate slapped her thigh. *I can't believe Marika didn't say anything.*

She rubbed her fingers through her hair. *I hate that stupid hairnet.*

She jerked her head up. *Wait a minute, did Jenny say my name was Katie?*

"Okay, let's go into the kitchen." Jenny gathered the pens and extra name tags. "Before I forget, does anyone have a work-release paper to be signed?" A young woman raised her hand.

"Okay, give it to me. You can pick it up in my office when you leave." Jenny added the paper to her clipboard and pointed at her office through the dining-room window.

"Okay, each person gets one plate." Jenny explained the serving procedures to the volunteers. "Questions?"

"So, how much is a scoop?" the 'mashed potato' volunteer asked.

"About this much." Jenny said, ladling a hearty spoonful. She stirred the meat and vegetables. "Katie, did you taste the stew?"

"No," Kate grimaced.

"Well, if the cook doesn't at least taste it, we probably shouldn't serve it." Jenny dropped the spoon into the stew. "I wouldn't want to eat it either."

"Next week, I'll be planning...."

"It's time to pray." Jenny interrupted, walking into the dining room.

"It looks like they have things under control." Jenny said, once the lunch line was moving. "Let's go to my office and discuss how you and I are going to work together."

Jenny sat at her desk. Kate took a seat in the captain's chair, holding the *Smile* pillow.

"So, how are things going? Is the job what you expected?" Jenny asked.

"Everything's good. There's just so much more to this kitchen than just cooking." Kate looked out the window into the dining room. The clients carried their trays of food and searched for places to sit. "I'm used to cooking for people who have an abundance of food and want a foodie experience. Not for people who are starving." She smiled at Jenny. "Le Cordon Bleu didn't prepare me to work here."

"I bet." Jenny walked to the armchair and sat next to Kate. "Between you and me, I think you're exactly what the kitchen needs. The food has gotten terrible." She pointed to a man dumping the stew into a garbage can. "I swear, sometimes the clients throw away more food than they eat. That's sad."

"Why do you think that is?" Kate looked away from the window, crossing her legs. "I'm not trying to be mean, but really beggars can't be choosers."

"I know," Jenny laughed. "But the food is in a rut. It needs to change." Jenny waved at a young girl passing by the window. "I know these people. I see and talk to them every day. They deserve good, nutritious food. People should want to eat here because the food is good, not just because it's free." She looked back at Kate. "If you can make the meals more appetizing on our budget, you'll really be helping these people."

"I'm certainly going to try." Kate watched the clients. They seemed to play with their food. "I guess your window gives you a different perspective on the meals."

"It does. I see everything that goes on out there. The good, the bad and the ugly." Jenny leaned back in her chair. "Nick wanted me to explain my job to you. We really won't interact very much, but our responsibilities will intersect. I recruit all the volunteers for the kitchen and dining room, and any activity the kitchen is involved in daily."

"Where do you get your volunteers?" Kate asked.

"We're really a word-of-mouth organization." She picked up a pen and tapped it. "Different churches or schools send in groups of workers, and the word spreads. The kitchen's a fun volunteer outing." She smiled. "We also work with the court system. Non-violent offenders can work off their community service hours here." She pointed to a paper on the clipboard. "Remember the girl this morning?" Kate nodded. "I'm signing that she's in compliance with her community service court order."

"Wow, I can't imagine trying to find all the volunteers. I had a hard-enough time trying to find good paid employees."

"Recruitment is tough during the summer, but when the holidays come around, people become more altruistic. I'll start getting five or six calls a day. Groups looking for volunteer hours." She tossed the pen. "But December 26th? Radio silence. After that, I'll struggle to find people.

"I think my mom would like to volunteer. She's trying to keep busy since my dad retired. Do you need people now?"

"I'm always looking for people to fill in in an emergency; people who can come at the drop of a hat. Could your mom do that, or maybe help to pick up the donations?" Jenny shuffled some papers.

"Oh, do you get the food donations too?"

"No, I deal with people, not product. Tucker handles all the donations, but I coordinate the volunteers who pick them up. Have you worked with Tucker yet?"

"No, I'm with him tomorrow." Kate rubbed her hands down her jeans. "I've seen the stockroom, but I don't know the procedures. "

"He'll explain all of that to you. It's quite the system." Jenny said.

Deacon tapped on the window, waving at Jenny before performing a soft shoe dance routine.

Smiling, Jenny jumped up and walked to the window. "Wait for me,"

Jenny said to Deacon. "C'mon, Katie. We've got to get to the dining
room. It's Deacon's birthday." Grabbing a box from on top of the filing
cabinet, Jenny walked out the door.

"Birthday? So, what are we doing?" Kate hurried to keep up.
"Singing Happy Birthday to him?"

"No, I've got his cake," Jenny raised the box. "We try to give each
client a cake to celebrate their special day."

"That's nice. Do you just take the donated ones?" Kate asked.

"No, no, I have a group of volunteers, *The Birthday Bunch*. They
bake birthday cakes for the clients."

Jenny stopped. "The first year I worked here, a client mentioned it was
her birthday. When I asked her how she was going to celebrate, she looked
at me like I was crazy and then said, 'I'm eating here." Jenny shrugged her
shoulders. "That made me so sad. I wanted to make the day a little special
for her, so I went to the kitchen to find a piece of cake or a cupcake, so we
could light a candle and sing, but there wasn't anything. I had to put a candle
in a piece of pie." She shook her head and looked down at the box. "I felt
terrible. Everyone should have cake on their birthday. That night, I baked her
a cake. When I gave it to her the next day, you would have thought I had
given her a million dollars. She cried, thanked me, gave me a hug. Her little
girl drew me a picture. It was so sweet. It made her so happy, and it was
such a simple thing to do."

Jenny pulled open the door to the dining room. "It got me thinking…
the kitchen gets hundreds of cake mixes donated each year, but we don't
have the extra eggs or oil to make the cakes. Why couldn't I get volunteers
to bake cakes for the client's birthday? So, *The Birthday Bunch* was born.
Volunteers take the donated cake mixes home to bake and decorate. We
always have four or five decorated cakes in the freezer. So, when we have a
birthday, we have a cake."

"What a great idea," Kate said.

"There's the birthday boy." Jenny put her arm around Deacon. He was holding court in a corner of the dining room. Jenny added seven candles to the top of the chocolate frosted cake. "It would be against fire regulations for me to light all of your candles, so I'm giving you one for each decade." Jenny smiled at the beaming Deacon, "Let's sing!"

The dining room erupted in song, "*Happy Birthday....*" Deacon used his hands to conduct the singers, clapping profusely as the serenade ended. "Thank you, everyone, for sharing my special day." Deacon bowed.

"Deacon, do you want to take this home or should I cut it now?" Jenny asked.

"I don't have anyone at home to share with, so let me celebrate with my friends here." Deacon nodded at his table. "Let's cut it now."

"Katie, can you pass me the plates and napkins, please? Has everyone met Katie, our new cook?" Jenny asked.

It's Kate, not Katie. "Happy Birthday, Deacon," Kate said, placing a piece of cake in front of him.

"Thank you, Katie." Deacon tipped an imaginary hat. "The coffee was much better today. You did a real nice job."

"Thank you," Kate smiled.

"I'm going to close the line. I think we've gone over everything. Do you have any questions for me?"

"No, I think I'm good, thank you." Kate walked with her back to the kitchen.

"No problem," Jenny stopped, taking Kate's hand. "I'm serious about improving the quality of the meals, Katie. People like Deacon deserve to eat something delicious too."

"I understand." Kate nodded. *But I'm not a freakin' miracle worker... There's only so much I can do.*

6

KATE

Horns honked. People shouted. Sirens blared. The quiet of the early morning had erupted into a cacophony of noise as Kate left M&M after lunch. The energy was frenetic. People crowded the block, standing on their front stoops or hanging out on the street corners, yelling, and laughing, but not really doing anything. Gum and trash dotted the sidewalks. The gray government-issued streetlights had broken glass and missing light bulbs. The buildings were in shambles. Boarded-up windows. Graffiti-laden walls. Garbage piled everywhere.

For goodness sakes, you'd think they'd have some pride in where they live.

Kate stepped off the curb to give a pit bull and his owner full access to the sidewalk. The dog pulled against the thick leather leash. His spiked collar strained as the owner waved Kate away. "Stay back. He can be vicious."

That's the first dog I've seen around here, she thought as she looked around the street. There were lots of *Beware of Dogs* signs but no animals. It was unlike her neighborhood, where dogs were common. Store signs proclaimed, *Dogs Welcome*, and pampered pooches strutted on the sidewalks sporting designer leashes and bejeweled collars. Kate's on Vine had even encouraged people to enjoy a glass of wine on the front porch while their dog lazed next to them. A bowl of fresh water and tin of dog biscuits were always available.

Kate missed the peace and quiet of her old life: her street, her restaurant, her people. Her restaurant's neighborhood was leisurely active. Joggers and walkers ambled along the pristine sidewalks at all times of the day. Moms with children in strollers or kids on bikes trekked to school or the local ice-cream shop. The antique gas lamps dotting the streets created a romantic ambience for couples taking an evening stroll.

Almost in a trance, Kate drove to the restaurant, the place she most wanted to be. A little more than a mile separated Kate's on Vine from Mary and Martha's, but the difference between those streets was mind-boggling. The neighborhoods were in the same city, but the lifestyles were worlds apart. The cement, dirt and litter surrounding the soup kitchen blossomed into manicured lawns, English gardens, and overflowing flowerpots. Graffiti-painted cinderblock buildings with peeling paint morphed into gingerbread homes with coordinated trim. Dirty windows protected by steel rods and condemned properties transformed into the land of *House Beautiful* in the space of ten blocks.

Parking her car on the street, Kate stared at her restaurant. Yellow police tape cordoned off the yard. Plywood covered the large porch windows and front door. The few remaining shutters hung crooked and looked ready to fall. The porch swing, a favorite resting spot for the diners, lay crumbled in the corner. The rusting chain dangled over the side railing. The once award-winning landscaping was an eyesore, the yard a complete shamble. Tire ruts from the heavy fire equipment had created long craters in the lawn, which had dried into mounds of brown mud. The rushing water from the fire hoses had turned the flower beds into rivers of debris and mulch. The vegetable and herb gardens in the side yard had lost the battle against the weeds. Wild brambles strangled the tomato plants.

Looking at the burned-out building with fresh eyes, Kate gripped the steering wheel so tight her knuckles turned white. The restaurant looked forgotten... unloved. The grounds neglected. It looked like nobody cared, but *she* did. Fixing the yard wouldn't cost a lot of money, just manual labor... *Hers.*

She shifted the car into drive and started a mental *To-Do List*: fix the ruts, till the garden, reseed the lawn, fertilize the flower beds. Her afternoons were free after serving lunch at M&M. She'd make the restaurant look like it belonged in this neighborhood once more ... just like her.

7

KATE

The next morning, Kate stood at the prep table slicing sheet cakes into perfect two-inch squares. Dallas crumbled bags of donuts, smashed pies, cakes, and cookies into an industrial sized pan singing 'The Wall' by Pink Floyd.

"What are you doing with all of that?" Kate asked. She dipped her knife in a pan of water, wiping it off before making another slice in the iced dessert.

"Making bread pudding." Dallas's gloved hands churned the crumbs into smaller pieces. "We don't waste anything here. These desserts looked so bad nobody would take them." He poured a quart of milk over the concoction. "I break them up and make bread pudding." He stirred the mixture with slow gentle movements. "People love it. In fact; I'm kinda famous for it."

Kate looked at the slurry of chocolate, cream filling, pie crust, and cake tossed together and stirred with milk. "Really?" she wrinkled her nose. "I guess I'll have to taste it."

A buzzer screamed through the kitchen. "Oh my God," Kate jumped. "Is that the fire alarm?" Her head spun around, searching for flames. Marika ignored the noise and continued to toss the salad with her gloved hands.

"It's the back door." Dallas chuckled, "Man, you jumped a foot." He shook his head. "It's a delivery. Tucker will take care of it." Still laughing, he placed the bread pudding in the oven.

Kate wiped crumbs from the prep table with shaking hands.

How was I supposed to know it was a delivery? At the restaurant, we had a doorbell, not a warning siren.

The sound of a cart rumbling through the kitchen door made everyone turn.

"Look what we just got." Tucker said, opening a carton. In a move reminiscent of the presentation of Simba in *The Lion King*. Tucker raised a cantaloupe into the air. "Isn't it beautiful?"

"Where'd they come from?" Dallas walked to the cart and pulled out a melon.

"We never get fresh fruit." Marika cradled a melon, taking a deep breath.

"A case fell off the truck." Tucker put the fruit back in the box. "These little guys were rolling across the parking lot, so we get them. What do you want to do with them?" He put his hand on the cart handle.

Kate waited for someone to answer before realizing the group expected her to speak. She picked up a melon and gently pricked the skin with her fingernail before bringing the fruit to her nose. It smelled delicious. "Why don't we slice them and serve it for today's lunch? We can save the applesauce for tomorrow."

"Cubes would be better." Marika said.

"Slices will be easier to serve." Kate stated.

"Some people can't bite." Marika shot back

"Then they can use their forks to cut the fruit into cubes." Kate slapped the carton lid. "Slices will be faster." She looked at her watch. "Tucker, I'm working with you today. Let me get lunch going and I'll meet you at your office?"

"How about the stockroom? I can show you what we've got," Tucker said.

Nodding, Kate pushed the melon cart over to the prep table. Marika grabbed a melon and using the knife as a machete hacked the fruit in half.

"Cantaloupe?" Jenny smiled surveying the food line before opening it for lunch. "Where'd we get it?"

"It came in this morning," Kate wiped her hands on her apron.

"How much do we have?" Jenny asked.

"I'm not sure," Kate looked at Dallas. "Do you know?" He shook his head.

"We sliced fifty cantaloupes," Marika called from the sink, her hands covered in soapsuds. "About fourteen slices per melon."

"Okay," Jenny said. "Each client can have two slices."

Walking to the stockroom, Kate hated to admit it, but Marika knowing the number and slices of cantaloupe had been impressive.

Too bad she's such a bitch to work with.

She pushed the swinging door open and saw Tucker. His muscular arms lifting cases of vegetables like ten-pound weights. Taking the towel dangling from his back pocket, he removed his backwards baseball cap and wiped sweat from his brow.

"Hi," Kate said. "Is now a good time?"

"It sure is." He turned his baseball cap around and smiled. "I was just rotating stock and checking inventory." He picked up a clipboard laying on a shelf. The large room had four rows of shelving units, each labeled with a different food group: *vegetables, fruits, grains, proteins (meat and beans)*. The products were arranged with military precision. He tapped a can of green beans to align it with the others. "I give you the inventory sheet each Thursday, so you can create next week's menus." He handed her the clipboard.

"So, when does the delivery get here?" Kate looked at the almost empty shelves.

"Delivery?" Tucker gave her a confused look.

"Aren't you getting ready for this week's stock order?" Kate said.

"Katie," Tucker laughed, "M&M isn't like your restaurant. Our budget is miniscule. We can't order whatever we want. We rely on donations from vendors that have stock about to expire and standing orders with a few companies for the basics, but as a whole we're reliant on the charity of others.

"But there's hardly anything here." Kate walked down the rows of shelving, running her hand along the empty shelves. "How am I supposed to prepare a meal for four hundred people every day next week?" She rubbed her neck to release the stress knot she felt forming.

"Let's look at what we have." He tapped the inventory sheets. "M&M lives the Bible story of the fishes and the loaves. No one goes away hungry, and the Lord always provides."

Picking up a large, green five-gallon bucket from the corner, he flipped it upside down. "Take a seat," He nodded at the makeshift chair.

Kate sat, as Tucker upended a blue bucket and sat next to her, taking the clipboard from her hands. "Let me show you how the stockroom actually works. Each shelf is a category on the spreadsheet, the inventory is organized by food group." He pointed to the papers. "See, in the fruit section, we have lots of applesauce and fruit cocktails, but hardly any peaches or pineapples." He pointed to the vegetable heading, "We have one hundred cans of corn, sixty carrots, twenty-five peas, and one hundred and fifty string beans."

"What's this miscellaneous category?" Kate asked.

"Those are the orphan cans. Maybe we have one or two, but not enough to make a meal." Tucker turned to the back page. "We usually get these cans after the schools hold their annual Canned Food Drive competition. They're the vegetables bought by mistake. Rather than throw them away, they give them to us."

Kate read the names. One asparagus, three lima beans, eight red beets, five cans of spinach. "Who buys canned spinach?" her jaw dropped as she looked at Tucker.

"Some of the things we get donated would surprise you. The weirdest has to be a jar of pickled pigs' feet," Tucker laughed. "C'mon, people who eat here are hungry, not stupid." He stood up and held his hand out to Kate. "I can't name one person who wants to eat those."

"This is really helpful." She hugged the clipboard to her chest as she toured the stockroom again with fresh eyes. Tucker walked beside her.

She looked between the shelves and the spreadsheet. Stacked next to boxes of dried potatoes were bags of rice and packages of pasta. "Dehydrated potatoes are considered a grain?"

"In this case, they are. We only serve rice, pasta or potatoes at lunch."

"Do you ever get fresh potatoes?"

"Sometimes."

She stopped next to the rack with cake mixes, brownies and muffins.

"These were donated." Tucker put his hand on the shelf. "Nothing goes to waste here. We give these to Jenny's Birthday Bunch."

Kate nodded and moved to the next row. "What are these?" Kate pointed to six cartons stamped *Express Meals*.

"A local company prepares MRE's for the soldiers."

"What?" Kate tilted her head, confused.

"Meals Ready to Eat. We get the packages that are about to expire."
Tucker tapped the box. "They taste pretty good."

"Can I see them?"

"Sure." he pulled a pocketknife out of his back pocket and sliced
open a carton. Inside were five hundred silver foil packets about six
inches long and one inch thick, labeled with the meal inside.

Kate picked up a foil package, *Southwest Chicken and Rice.* "How
are these served?"

"The kitchen opens the packets, pours the meal into a pan and heats
them up." Tucker slapped his hands together. "Instant lunch."

"Can I take this?" Kate held up the packet. "I want to see what it
tastes like."

"Sure," Tucker rooted through the box. "Let me get you a sample of
each. Here's the chicken rice, pasta marinara, and chili: veggie and meat."
He placed the meals in a plastic grocery bag and handed them to her.
"Questions about the stockroom?"

"I don't think so." Kate swung the clipboard and bag in her hand.

"Okay, let's go check out the freezer, then."

"Oh, thank God, there's more food here," Kate said, stepping into the
cold, crammed room. Tucker frowned as he shuffled past Kate to shut the
door. "So, is this organized by category, too?"

"Yes ma'am," Tucker nodded. He stood in the middle of the freezer
and touched each shelf he named. "Bread, desserts, meat, vegetables."

"There's so many desserts." Kate leaned against the overflowing
dessert racks and stared at the almost empty meat rack. "I wish we could
switch desserts for meat."

"Beggars can't be choosers, and we beg here."

"What's that?" Kate pointed to a mishmash of packages wrapped in
aluminum foil, zip-locked plastic bags, plastic wrap, and butcher paper.

"Those are meatloaves," Tucker grabbed a plastic bag. "The parishioners from some of the local churches donate uncooked meatloaves on Meatloaf Sunday once a month. We usually get about two hundred loaves."

"So, you serve meatloaf?"

"No, we use the meat to make all kinds of different things: sloppy joes, meatballs, casseroles, and once in a while… *meatloaf.*"

Kate looked at the spreadsheet and then the shelves. "There's only twenty-five pounds of chicken?"

"Yeah, chicken is scarce. We don't get it donated very often, and if we do, there usually isn't enough to provide an entire lunch. Kate rubbed her arms to thwart off the goosebumps forming.

"You're getting cold. Do you have any questions?"

"Nope, I'm good."

"Okay, let's head to the walk-in refrigerator." Tucker opened the freezer door and stepped aside to allow Kate to exit. She bumped into a wall of frozen malt cups stacked floor to ceiling by the door.

"Malts?"

"The local dairy donated those. We're down to five hundred from the thousand they gave us."

"Just what every soup kitchen needs." Kate slammed the freezer door. "Ice-cream."

"It's amazing how happy a little bit of ice-cream can make a person." His smile was so sincere.

She knew Tucker was disappointed in her reaction to the stock room, but she couldn't help it. The pantry was dismal. With any luck, the refrigerator would be stocked full of fresh ingredients. But she wasn't getting her hopes up.

Tucker held the heavy door open for Kate to enter. She saw the empty shelves and knew her luck was gone. Like the stockroom and freezer, the refrigerator was meticulous: packages labeled and arranged neatly on the shelves. There just wasn't very much: four bags of lettuce, three packages of shredded cabbage, condiments, a few gallons of milk, several quarts of sour cream, butter, and one lone lemon.

Kate's restaurant's refrigerator had never looked this empty. She only allowed the very best ingredients in her kitchen. She had bought locally and grown her own vegetables and herbs. Organic meat, chicken and sustainable seafood were the staples of her restaurant, and now, she was supposed to make nutritious meals from food she would have never allowed through her doors.

"I don't know how I'm going to do this," Kate slammed the clipboard on an empty shelf, rubbing her face with her hands. "I can't think of one edible meal to make with the food I've seen." She leaned her back against the cold refrigerator door and looked at Tucker. "How have you been able to feed so many people?"

"Follow me. We'll review the menus from the last few months in my office." Tucker sounded every bit like the drill-sergeant he used to be.

Kate obeyed his command. She could almost hear Tucker's thoughts: *Man up, soldier. You've got a job to do.*

Tucker's office was pristine. Two metal chairs placed at ninety-degree angles faced the desk, and a computer and a phone were the only items on there. There were no papers, pens, or even a stapler visible. The only personal item was a picture on the bookshelf behind his chair. In the photo, Tucker had his arm around a young boy holding a basketball. Their broad smiles shined at the camera. The boy looked familiar.

"Take a seat," Tucker ordered. Kate sat. He walked behind the desk and pulled a manila folder from one of the gray matching filing cabinets and handed it to Kate. "These should help you." The folder contained the M&M monthly meal calendar. Each date had the day's menu with the ingredients and supplies needed to prepare the meal. Attached to the calendar were the weekly inventory sheets

Kate breathed a sigh of relief. "Thank you so much." She scanned the papers, and with each flip of the page her smile grew. "These will really help me get organized. I can see a pattern to the meals here." She closed the folder and looked around the room. "Can I make a copy of these?"

"Those are yours," Tucker smiled. "I thought you might need some inspiration."

Kate looked at the folder again and saw her name printed on the label. "Thanks, Tucker. I was feeling overwhelmed."

"It's not a problem." He walked around the desk and sat next to her. "Katie, everyone here wants you to succeed." He tapped her knee. "M&M is a great place. You can make it even better."

"Thanks for showing me everything, Tucker," Kate said, holding the inventory sheets close. "I admire your organization."

"I'm happy to help," he said, wiping his brow before replacing the backwards baseball cap. "We all want the meals to taste better. I hope you can do that."

"I hope so, too." Kate reached out to shake his hand. "I do have one question. If I have a meal in mind, would you be able to get a specific item donated?"

"I can make a few calls for you," Tucker winked. "You just let me know what you need."

Kate smiled and mentally began to prepare her meals.

8

NICK

A wall of hot, humid air hit Nick as he left Mass Friday morning. The never-ending summer heatwave continued to bake the city. The calendar may have said September, but the weather felt like mid-July.

"Nick," Kate waved from the bottom of the church steps.

"Hi," Nick bounced down the stairs. "You did it." He gave her a high-five. "A whole week of working at M&M under your belt. How's it going?"

"Pretty good," Kate said, passing through the crowd waiting to go inside the air-conditioned building. I've made next week's menus." She held up her tote bag. "Can I go over them with you?" She stepped around the man sitting by the kitchen door.

"Sure," Nick said. He stooped down to talk to the man. "Abraham, how are you? I haven't seen you since Monday."

"I'm thirsty. I just want a drink of water." The man said, his red eyes filled with tears.

"Alright, buddy," Nick said, patting his shoulder. He stood and unlocked the door. "Actually, Katie, let's meet after lunch. I've got a few calls to make."

Nick walked past his office, grabbing a case of water from the stockroom, and returned to Abraham. The large man's dreadlocks bounced as he cried, his face buried in his hands. Kneeling beside him, Nick touched the man's shoulder. Abraham jerked away. "I'm sorry," Nick said, "I can't let you in the building yet, but I don't want you to be thirsty." Punching his fist through the carton's plastic wrap, Nick took out a bottle, "Here's some water."

Abraham grabbed the bottle, tossed the lid to the ground and greedily drank. Watching Nick with reddened eyes, he reached into the case and took a second bottle before finishing the first.

"Anyone else thirsty?" Nick yelled over his shoulder to the men watching from the sidewalk. They all raised their hands. "Come and get it."

Back in his office, Nick kept hearing Abraham's words, *I'm thirsty.* Avoiding the stacks of papers and boxes on the floor, Nick sat in the rickety red desk chair, resting his chin on his hand.

God, it would be awful to be so thirsty and not be able to get a drink. Worse, knowing there was water, but other people wouldn't let you have it.

A normal restaurant would never let Abraham enter. The man looked wild, crazy, scary. His clothes were torn and dirty. His dreadlocks resembled snakes coiling around his head, and the smell… a trifecta of bad breath, body odor and excrement exploding in the summer heat.

Nick understood people being afraid of Abraham, but the guy was just thirsty.

The office phone rang. It was time for his conference call. The actual helping people would have to wait.

"Nick?" He looked up from his spreadsheets and documents.

"Katie." Nick glanced at his watch. "Man, I lost track of time. Lunch already started?"

"It's the first time we've said the prayer without you."

Nick watched her shuffle the stack of papers on the chair to another pile before sitting down. She was tiny. The blue M&M apron covering her jeans and T-shirt almost reached the ground when she sat. Wisps of brown hair escaped from under her Cincinnati Red's baseball cap.

"Yeah, my conference call went long, but I think we'll be able to start the renovations next week."

"Renovations?"

"Yep, it's the final phase of the M&M strategic plan. We're going to open The Shepherd's Inn, an overnight shelter. People will be able to come in for a bed and a shower. Get help if they want it."

"That sounds great." She passed him a folder. "Here are next week's menus."

"Let's see what you've got planned," Nick said, taking the papers. His chair squeaked as he leaned back, and his smile grew as he reviewed the pages. Each page had the day's menu, a chore chart, and supplies. She'd highlighted the items not in stock: beef tips, green peppers, eggs. Nick held up the pages, "This sounds delicious, but what are you really going to make?"

"What do you mean?" she tilted her head.

"We don't have half of the ingredients you need to make these meals." Nick's chair squealed as he leaned forward.

"I know," she held up her hand to halt his argument, "I talked to Tucker. He's going to get me the things I need."

"Tucker doesn't have time to do that," Nick tossed the folder on top of the desk. "You've got to work with what we have."

"But you don't have *anything*," Kate stood. "Let's see," she used her fingers to count, "There's meatloaf, brats, metts, packets of MRE's, a few containers of chicken and no fish, except for some cans of tuna." She placed her hands on her hips and tapped her foot, "I'm not a miracle worker. Without better ingredients, the meals will not improve."

Nick stood. *She was cute, all riled up.*

"Katie, Katie, Katie," he walked towards her. "You're not here to create a dining experience. You're here to cook a meal for some very hungry people." He put his hands on her shoulders and stared into her eyes. "You've got to stop thinking like a chef and be a cook. Use what's available. Where are the inventory sheets?"

She slapped the papers into his hands.

"Let's see what we do have and go from there." Moving her chair next to his, he rifled through the pages. "I don't know what you're talking about. There's a bounty of food in stock," he grinned. "You just have to be more creative."

"But Nick, I can't serve the meals the kitchen's used to. I have my reputation to think about."

"Katie, you've got to work with the stock we have." He leaned back in the chair. "I think it's great you want to try new meals, but we can't buy *everything*."

"Well, the meals would be so much better if you could." She studied the inventory sheets.

"I'm sure they would," he laughed. "The clients don't handle change very well, anyway. So, how about one new meal a week? That way, Tucker only has to try to find one special ingredient a week, rather than every day."

"I guess," her voice dejected. "It's just, well, I never saw myself cooking brats and metts."

"I get it." Nick handed her back the menus. "Plan on serving the first new meal on Monday. The volunteers are great that day, very dependable, and they work as a team. Also, the clients are a little more receptive to new things after the weekend."

"Okay," she stood, shifting from one sneakered foot to the other, "I do have one other question."

"Yes," Nick waited.

"I was wondering… Would it be possible for me to get some keys? I know I'm not here forever, but…" She held the clipboard in front of her like a shield. "I mean, I enjoy going to Mass each morning, but if I can't... Well, I'd like to get in without waiting for someone else to arrive."

"Absolutely." Nick pulled open a filing cabinet drawer and took out a key ring. He walked towards her, spinning the ring on his forefinger. "I always make employees ask for a set of keys." He winked, placing the keys in her palm. "It shows more of a commitment."

"Do I need an alarm code or anything?"

"Nope," Nick smiled.

"Well, I guess that's a good thing. I was always setting off my restaurant's alarm." Kate laughed, shrugging her shoulders.

"Just remember to keep the door locked if you're here alone." Nick looked at his watch. "I've got to get going. Anything else?"

"No, I'm good. Thanks." Kate stood. "Big plans this weekend?"

"Yeah, my little league team's playing for the city championship tomorrow. Tonight's our last practice." Nick reached behind the door and grabbed a duffle bag.

"I didn't know you had a son." Kate waited for him to lock the door.

"I don't. The team needed a coach, so I volunteered." He put on a baseball cap. "We've had an amazing season."

Nick stopped outside Tucker's office. "Hey, you ready?"

"I was just coming to get you," Tucker said, turning off the light. "Hi Katie."

"Tucker's the assistant coach for the team," Nick told Kate. "He's the best third base coach there is."

"You got that right," Tucker locked his door.

"Well, you guys have a nice weekend. Good luck tomorrow." Kate said, walking into her office.

"We're bringing home the trophy." Nick pumped his fist in the air.

Grabbing the gear bag from his truck, Nick walked with Tucker the two blocks to the city park. The air was so humid, his T-shirt clung to his body after a few steps. The sun blazed on the black asphalt, reflecting its heat upwards. The only people enjoying the heat seemed to be the trio of kids running through the sprinkler on the street corner.

"So, what'd you think about those menus?" Tucker removed his baseball cap to wipe his brow.

"Well, she had to rework a few things." Nick switched the gear bag to his other arm. "I told her one new meal a week."

"Thank God, there was no way I could get all of the ingredients she wanted on our budget." Tucker wiped his brow again.

Nick said, "I just hope Katie's up to the job."

"Are you kidding?" Tucker's mouth dropped. "Did you read her restaurant reviews online? Everyone says she's an amazing chef."

"She is an amazing chef, but with the budget to order the best ingredients. The real test will be what she can do with the little we have."

Tucker dropped the duffle bag and stretched his back. "This practice is going to be brutal. We don't want to tire the boys out before tomorrow. Maybe take it easy today: slow drills. When we're finished, we can take the boys back to the kitchen. Give them each a malt cup."

"That's a good plan," Nick kept walking. "I know Katie's a great chef, but I need her to be a good mentor to Dallas and Marika too. I want her to show them how a real kitchen operates; how to create delicious meals and new menus with the food we have. I'm just worried I may be asking too much of her. Being a gourmet chef is very different from being a cook in a soup kitchen." He stopped to open the gate to the baseball field. "Is Marika still mad at me?"

"I don't know. She's mad at me too." Tucker dropped the duffle onto the bench.

"Why?" Nick asked, but before Tucker could answer, eleven boys rushed from the field to greet their coaches.

9

KATE

Waving steam from the pan to her nose, Kate took a deep breath. It smelled amazing. Her mom and sister sat on high bar stools at the kitchen island while the men watched football in the family room. For this week's Sunday Supper, Kate had opted to make one of Kate's on Vine's signature dishes: Lobster Risotto. The complicated and time-consuming meal would remind her she *really* was a chef and would keep her occupied while she was bombarded with questions about M&M from her family.

"So, is it completely depressing?" Lynne asked, bouncing her youngest grandchild on her lap.

"Not really," Kate stirred the arborio rice. "I'd say most of the people are happy to be eating there. It's almost like it's the neighborhood gathering spot."

"What's the food like?" Ellen picked up a red crayon to color with three-year-old Lily in her coloring book.

"Pretty bad," Kate slowly added broth to the pan, making rhythmic circles with the spoon. "I had to *beg* Tucker to find some green peppers and chicken so I could make jambalaya on Monday. He got one of my old distributors to donate the items."

"What are the people like?" Lynne squeezed baby Leah in a tight hug. "I worry so much about you being down in that neighborhood. Do you think it's safe?

"Mom, I swear it's safe." Kate tested the consistency of the rice. "Honestly, most of the clients seem normal. They're looking for volunteers if you want to check things out."

"Well, I still worry. Did you know there was a shooting down there last night?" Lynne said. "Do you want me to make the salad? I feel a little guilty just sitting here watching you cook."

"No, no, I've got it. It's nice to be cooking with real ingredients, actually creating a meal, instead of throwing things together from a can."

"How's Nick?" Ellen handed Kate her finished drawing.

"Very nice! Do you want me to hang it on the refrigerator?" Kate asked, tacking the picture to the fridge with a "Kate's Kitchen" magnet. "Nick is so amazing. He walks around the dining room talking to each client like they're the most important person in the world. He even coaches the neighborhood little league team because no parent would volunteer."

"I always liked him when we were in law school." Ellen handed her daughter another crayon. "What about everyone else?"

"Tucker's great. He must have been a drill sergeant in the army with how he keeps that place organized. He's in charge of the stockroom, and I have never seen a better system. He also helps me plan the menus. Dallas, the assistant cook, is super. He's been so helpful answering my questions, and he's never made me feel stupid for not knowing something. He's willing to do anything, and he's funny. He never stops moving, always cleaning something or starting some kitchen project. He's never quiet. He's humming, singing, or talking the whole day."

Kate put the bread in the oven to warm. "The only person I don't like is Marika. She's kind of a bitch."

"What?" Lynne put her hands over the baby's ears.

"She is," Kate laughed. "She hates me. "

"Why would she hate you?" Lynne asked.

"Apparently, she actually wanted the head cook job." Kate tasted the risotto. "Mmm, that's good. Nick wants me to be her mentor, but I don't think that's going to work."

"Why didn't she get it?" Ellen asked.

"Not sure," Kate checked the bread. "I'm guessing she doesn't have a lot of experience with creating menus. She doesn't talk to me, so I can't ask."

"Well, I'm sure you can help her." Lynne placed the baby in the highchair. "Your restaurant menu was wonderful. I know you can show her how it's done, then she can take over. You won't be there long, hopefully."

"Hopefully," Kate placed the risotto, bread, and spinach salad on the table. "It's ready."

"Boy, that looks delicious," Pete said, sitting at the head of the table.

"Thanks, Dad." Kate smiled. "I wish I had plated it just to remember what it's like to be a real chef."

"You *are* a real chef," Lynne grasped her daughter's hands. "Let's pray."

10

MARIKA

Hanging her jacket on the coat hook in the hallway, Marika walked into the M&M kitchen on Monday morning. The heatwave had finally broken, and the air had the clean, crisp smell of autumn. Grabbing an apron from under the stainless-steel counter, she went to fill the coffee urns. The pots were already warm.

"Oh, hi, I skipped Mass this morning. I wanted to make sure everything was ready for my first lunch," Kate said, pushing a cart filled with bags of chicken and sausage into the kitchen.

She looked meticulous in a pressed oxford blouse and jeans, the strings of a blue apron tied into a bow on the front of her waist, her brown ponytail pulled through the back of a Cincinnati Red's baseball cap. Reaching into her back pocket, Kate pulled out an index card and handed it to Marika.

"This is what I need you to do. The entire job chart is hanging on the fridge." She pointed to the prep table. "Start chopping the vegetables right away. The jambalaya needs to simmer for an hour. I want the flavors to blend."

With a flourish, Kate flounced out of the kitchen.

Marika stared at the white piece of paper hanging on the fridge underneath a floral *Kate's Kitchen* magnet.

What the hell? This wasn't Kate's Kitchen.... It was hers.

Marika crumbled the card in her hand.

Daily Chore Chart

Monday's Menu

Jambalaya, cornbread, salad, desserts

Prep Duties

Marika: Dice vegetables

(x50 peppers, x50 onions, x100 celery stalks)

Dallas: Open x20 cans of whole tomatoes, x25 cans of chicken broth.

Wash and prep collard greens

Kate: Cut 25lbs sausage and 15lbs chicken.

Make cornbread

Lunch Duties

Marika: Salad—Tossed with ranch dressing

Dallas: Rice and collard greens

Kate: Jambalaya and cornbread

Marika slammed the index card on the table.

A card. She gave me a card with my duties. She's too good to actually ask me to do a job.

Grabbing a knife, she slew the peppers and onions. The sound of a rolling cart interrupted her angry chopping.

"Good morning," Dallas trilled, placing five cans of tomatoes on the counter. "Did you have a nice weekend?"

"Fine," Marika whacked off the end of the celery stalk. "Can you believe her? A job chart, and she gave me a card telling me to chop these." Her knife pointed to the stack of veggies. "I can't just read the chart. I need a reminder card."

"I know, isn't it great?" Dallas plugged in the can-opener. "It's like we're working in a real kitchen."

"This *is* a real kitchen." Marika threw the diced celery into the colander. "*Kate's* kitchen, according to the magnet on the fridge," she muttered.

Dallas started singing 'Rock the boat' the old hit by the Hues Corporation. Marika was glad when the noise of the electric can-opener drowned out the damn song.

"I helped Deacon at the Quik-mart on Saturday, so I missed the game." Dallas shouted over the whirr of the appliance. "How'd it go?" He picked up another can of tomatoes and hit the lever.

"I wasn't there," Marika rinsed the celery. "Jamal said they lost, 3-1"

"What?" The noise of the can-opener stopped. "You missed the championship game? Were you sick?" Dallas' eyes gaped.

"No, I just didn't feel like going." Marika dropped the bowl of diced vegetables next to the stove. "Tell the chef her vegetables are ready. I'm going to do my next chore."

"Great," Kate said, pushing through the swinging door. "Everything else ready?" She surveyed the kitchen.

"Yes, ma'am," Dallas wiped the counter. "I can't believe Tucker actually got us chicken, peppers and the stuff to make the cornbread."

"I know. It's going to make all the difference in the meal." Kate clapped her hands together. "Marika, work on the salad. Dallas, will you brown the rice?" Kate handed him a large skillet. "I like the nutty flavor the warmed rice adds to the stew."

Marika stomped out of the walk-in refrigerator and bumped into Dan, one of the Monday volunteers.

"Hey, you weren't at the game," Dan held the fridge door open, "Tough loss."

"I couldn't make it." Marika kicked the door closed.

"Well, Tucker seemed a little off. I guess he missed you." Dan adjusted his baseball cap. "I saw Jamal keeping score. He told me he got the job."

"He did," Marika smiled, cutting open the bags of lettuce. "Thank you so much for helping him."

Dan waved his hand brushing aside her thanks. "I didn't do anything. Jamal wowed HR in the interview, and I was happy to get my company involved with Drexel."

Clap, Clap, Clap. The rat-a-tat of Kate's clapping hands reverberated throughout the kitchen. Marika straightened, her eyes narrowing into steel slits.

Now we answer to clapping?

Kate stood on the bottom shelf of the prep table. "Can I have everyone's attention?" She waved her hands for the group to move closer.

So, the queen claps and we're all supposed to listen? Marika shook her head, watching Dallas, Dan, and the rest of the volunteers gather around Kate.

She refused to move.

"I think I met all of you last week, but in case you don't remember, my name is Kate O'Leary. I'll be working as the new chef just until my restaurant reopens. I've been tasked with improving the quality of the food, implementing new menus and meal plans as well as improving the entire kitchen operation. I'm hoping these new procedures will serve to improve the overall experience of the M&M kitchen long after I'm gone."

"It's about damn time." Dan crossed his arms across his chest. "I swear, it was embarrassing to serve some of that crap."

The hairs on the back of Marika's neck bristled. *Really, Dan? The food wasn't that bad.*

"I agree," Kate nodded. "We're trying a new meal today: jambalaya, warm cornbread, collard greens, salad, and, of course, the usual array of desserts."

"What happens when someone asks for regular bread?" Dan asked.

"I don't think anyone will want a slice of stale bread when they can have a slice of warm, freshly made cornbread," Kate smiled.

"I've volunteered here for three years. Somebody is going to want a slice of white bread," Dan stated.

"I'll get a skid of bread from the back counter." Dallas jogged to the pantry.

"Okay, then," Kate looked at the clock. "We've got a half hour before lunch is served." She held up some index cards. "These are the last few chores we need to finish. I'd appreciate your help."

Grabbing a card, Dan turned to Marika, "Five bucks someone asks for a piece of regular bread."

"No way, that's a fool's bet. Of course someone is going to want a slice of bread," grinned Marika as she tossed the salad.

11

KATE

The jambalaya simmered on the stove as Kate pulled the fresh cornbread out of the oven. No authentic creole meal was served without it, and no client would be able to pass it up.

No matter what Dan said.

Taking a deep breath, she inhaled the aroma. For a few moments, she could pretend she was in her own restaurant getting ready for the evening crowd, until the crashing sound of a cafeteria tray hitting the floor shocked her back to reality.

The buffet station looked good. Stepping back, Kate admired the colorful array of food. Wisps of steam rising off the warm yellow corn bread, cut in perfect two-inch squares. The jambalaya, a perfect amber spotted by dots of green pepper and red tomatoes, the deep dark green of the leafy collards.

Properly plated, this meal would be good enough to serve at my restaurant.

Lunch was ready. Kate looked at the hungry clients waiting. Standing on her tiptoes to see over the counter, she announced, "Today, we're trying something new: jambalaya. I hope you like it." Using her arm, she showcased the serving line like Vanna White turning a vowel.

If possible, the clients looked even more bored. Dan handed the first client his meal. "Enjoy," Kate smiled at the man without any teeth. His eyes jerked away as if she was speaking in tongues.

Kate couldn't wait to hear the customers' reactions to the first new lunch dish. Diners at her restaurant would have paid at least twenty dollars for the same meal, and they would want to thank her when they finished eating it.

Surely, the clients of M&M would appreciate the delicious food too. She stood at the dessert station, excited to hear their comments.

"What is *that*?" a client asked.

"Jambalaya," Dan answered.

"What's in it?"

"It has rice, chicken, sausage. It's good." Dan spooned a helping onto the plate.

"Are those collard greens?" a different client asked. "My mama made the best. Can I have extra?"

Sylvie passed a piece of pie to a client, "It really does look delicious."

"Thanks," Kate said. "I guess I thought people would be more excited to try something new. Most of them don't seem to notice anything different."

"I'm sure it tastes much better than what they're used to. Maybe walk into the dining room to hear what they're saying." Sylvie rearranged the dessert plates.

"Oh, I don't want to do that," Kate looked at the crowded tables. "I'll just start working on tomorrow's lunch. I'm sure they'll love it: brats and metts."

Suddenly, a tray was slammed against the top of the buffet station. Kate jumped. "Where's the real bread?" The old man asked, "I don't want any of that cornbread crap."

Winking at Kate, Dan handed the man a slice of stale bread. "Here you go."

Kate finished the next day's lunch prep and looked around the kitchen for something to do. Dallas was helping Tucker in the stock room and Marika was missing again. Kate had noticed Marika habitually disappeared every day for about thirty minutes. Like a ninja, she'd be cooking or cleaning one minute and gone the next. When she returned, she acted as if she'd never left.

She'll need to stop that type of behavior if she wants me to support her becoming head cook. A chef never leaves their kitchen unattended.

The chatter of the kitchen was happy, yet Kate had never felt more alone. She didn't belong here.

She'd made her daily phone call to the fire inspector and the insurance company with the same results: no money until the fire investigation was complete. She wiped imaginary dirt from the counter, missing her shiny nine-burner Viking stove and copper pans even more.

I'd give anything to be at my restaurant instead of here. I'm depressed, I need sugar. She watched the diners choose their desserts. *Some of those pastries don't look half bad.*

Sylvie, the consummate volunteer, served the multitude of desserts, transferring plates of sweets from the holding racks to the serving station. The older woman was attractive, her silver hair cut into a stylish bob that flattered her round face, warm eyes, an amazing shade of cerulean-blue, and a bright smile encouraged the clients to talk. With panache, she wore a blue M&M apron over her T-shirt with a strand of pearls around her neck. Kate saw the woman rub her back after bending down for about the hundredth time.

"Sylvie, would you like me to help organize these dessert trays?" Kate asked.

"That would be nice, dear," Sylvie answered over her shoulder. "Thank you."

Pulling the utility trays out of the rack, Kate organized the desserts by type and flavor. Cake: chocolate, vanilla, white with a variety of frostings. Pies: pecan, pumpkin, cherry, peach. Donuts: glazed, powdered, filled (jelly and cream). Pastries: cinnamon, fruit, cheese, pecan.

"Katie, did you see any cherry pie?" Sylvie craned her head to look through the shelves. "This young lady would like a piece."

"I'm pretty sure I did," Kate shuffled the plates. "Here it is," she handed the plate to Sylvie.

"Thank you. Is there another one?" Sylvie looked back at the rack, "I like to display an assortment."

Kate placed another piece of cherry pie at the buffet station and watched Sylvie interact with the clients.

"Hi there," Sylvie spoke to a man with graying dreadlocks. "I saved you a bear claw." The man took the pastry nodding his thanks. "Where's the baby today?" she asked a young woman.

"He started pre-school. I just dropped him off," the mom answered.

"Already? Gosh, I remember when he was born. They grow up so fast. I feel like I blinked, and my boys were grown." Sylvie put both hands on her face.

"So, you have two boys?" Kate asked.

"Yes, twins: Zach and Xander. They're all grown up now." Sylvie said, her voice sounding sad. She passed a pastry to the next client.

Sylvie had a wonderful knack for keeping the food line moving, all the while seeing each client as a person, an individual, with different needs and dessert preferences.

"Good morning, Miss Sylvie. How are you on this fine day?" A woman in the buffet line pushed her tray down the ledge.

"I'm good, how are you, Bernice?" Sylvie answered.

"Feeling blessed," the woman was dressed entirely in purple from the turban on her head to the gym shoes on her feet. Her big smile was infectious, "Oh my," she held up the lunch plate. "Did you see this jambalaya and cornbread. Doesn't it look delicious?"

'It does," Sylvie pulled Kate forward by her elbow, "Have you met Katie, the new cook?"

"It's nice to know you," Bernice's purple fingernail touched the glass. "Sylvie, I think I'll have that piece of chocolate cake with chocolate icing today."

"Here you go," Kate handed her the plate.

"Well, thank you, and may God bless you on this beautiful day." Bernice beamed a bright smile.

"She seems nice, normal." Kate said watching the older lady take a seat at a table filled with young people.

"Oh, she is," Sylvie nodded. "I just love her outfits. She moved to the neighborhood when her husband passed away. It's been a huge transition, but she's always smiling."

"Do you know everyone?" Kate asked, moving the empty trays from the rack to the prep table.

"Well, I wouldn't say I know them, but I do recognize them and try to remember what they like." Sylvie looked at the people waiting in line, "See the man with the star tattoo on his cheek?"

Kate nodded.

"He's not going to say a word. I have to guess which dessert he wants." Sylvie talked out of the side of her mouth as the man stopped in front of the desserts staring at her.

"Good morning, what looks good today?" Sylvie held up a piece of yellow cake with white icing. He shook his head. She returned the cake to the tray and pointed to a slice of cherry pie. The man rolled his eyes and looked away.

"Okay then," Sylvie scanned the dessert trays. "Aha, I think you'll like this…Boston cream pie." The man reached for the plate, giving Sylvie a slight nod, his star tattoo twinkling at her success.

Sylvie shrugged, wiping her hands on her apron. "I'm not sure if he doesn't know how to speak or if he just doesn't have anything to say."

A man passed the desserts walking directly to the drink station. "Hi, how are you?" Sylvie reached over the counter to catch his attention. "I've saved a piece of peach pie just for you." The man stopped. Sylvie took a plate from under the counter and handed it to him. He took the dish and left.

"He seems a little shaky today. Hmm, I bet he needs protein, maybe some power bars." Sylvie's voice was soft.

"I'm sorry, did you say something?" Kate placed some glazed donuts on the tray.

"Oh no, I'm just talking to myself," Sylvie's eyes followed the man. So, Kate watched him too. To her, he looked like any other client: scruffy beard, dirty hair that needed to be cut or at least brushed, glazed blue eyes, very thin with pock-marked skin. His clothes were filthy fashionable khakis and a T-shirt. He sat by a young girl, who talked with her hands.

"Hi George," Sylvie smiled at the gray-haired man with wire rimmed glasses staring at the desserts. He wore a brown trench coat even though the day had grown hot. She whispered to Kate, "He's going to want a muffin. I secretly call him the Muffin Man."

"Okay," Kate searched the trays. "Does he want blueberry or apple?"

"It doesn't matter as long as it's a muffin. I always try to save a few for him." Sylvie said.

"Do you have any muffins?" George asked.

"Here you go," Sylvie handed the befuddled man two blueberry muffins.

"If April showers bring May flowers, what do May flowers bring?" George put the muffins on his tray.

"I don't know." Sylvie shrugged, "What do May flowers bring?"

"Pilgrims!" George laughed picking up his tray and muffins before walking down the line.

"George likes to tell jokes; the cornier the better," Sylvie giggled.

"How long have you volunteered here?" Kate moved a piece of cherry pie next to a chocolate cupcake towards the front of the display.

"Just about five years," Sylvie watched while Kate rearranged the different treats.

"Are you always on desserts?"

"No, I like desserts the best, but I take tickets or serve on the line too."

Kate sliced a cupcake in half, removed the wrapper and put the two pieces on a plate. Sylvie gave her a questioning look.

"No one takes the cupcakes," Kate said. "I've moved this chocolate cupcake to four different positions, and no one wants it. Lots of people have taken chocolate cake with chocolate frosting, but not this little guy. I'm thinking if we make the cupcake look like a piece of cake. Someone will finally bite."

"Well, I can tell you pies and cookies are definitely the clients' favorites. Someone takes those as soon as I put them out. Anything with cheese is really popular too: cheese crowns, cheese danish, cinnamon danishes go pretty fast too, and bear claws. People *love* bear claws."

Sylvie pointed to a tray of donuts. "Most of the donuts are taken, but not till later in the day. Donuts travel well. They take them home for breakfast or snacks."

"That's good to know. Maybe we shouldn't put the donuts out until later?" Kate asked, rearranging a few more plates. "What else have you noticed about the lunches? As a volunteer, you have a unique perspective. I'd like to hear your opinion."

"Well…the lunches are pretty terrible," Sylvie patted Kate's hand, "No offense."

"None taken," Kate smiled.

"I mean," Sylvie gave a nervous laugh. "I wouldn't want to eat here. Although, the jambalaya looks delicious today."

"Me either," Kate stared into the dining room. "Don't you wonder what happened? How did a person's life get so bad that they have to eat in a soup kitchen?"

"It's drugs, mostly. They're horrible, destroying families and people's lives."

Sylvie stopped to help the next clients. They seemed to be a couple. A young confused-looking black man and transgender woman. "Leon, are you doing okay? Do you need anything? What would you like for dessert?" Sylvie tapped her hands on the top of the counter trying to get the young black man's attention. He ignored Sylvie and looked instead to his companion. The short, balding woman had large, silver hooped earring and bright red lipstick. She wore a flowered sundress, which exposed a red lacy bra.

"He's good, aren't you baby doll?" The woman rubbed the man's arm. "He'll have a piece of lemon meringue pie. I'll take cherry."

"I'm worried about that situation." Sylvie said after giving them their pie.

"Me too," Dallas glared at the couple. "I don't think Leon knows which way is up right now. It looks like Ole Jackie's swooped in to take advantage of him just like she did all those other guys."

Dallas moved the empty jambalaya pan to the counter. "I bet she's moved into Leon's apartment and is taking his assistance. She should be reported." Dallas snapped his towel on the table. "I'm going to talk to Nick."

Lunch was over and Kate stood by the chore chart. "Everyone know what they're doing for clean up?" Kate asked, studying the chore chart.

"Sure do," Dallas answered, using a hose to drain the water from the buffet station. Marika scoured the sink.

"I have an appointment at my restaurant in thirty minutes, but I wanted to go over a few things." Kate motioned for them to join her at the prep table. Dallas trotted over. Marika continued to spray the basin. "Marika, do you think you can join us here?" Kate tapped the table. "It will only take a minute."

Throwing the towel in the sink, Marika joined the group.

Kate silently counted to ten."It looks like the jambalaya was a big hit. According to Jenny, we served four hundred and fifty meals. That's fifty more than usual."

"I guess word got out about how good it was," Dallas grinned.

"It's Monday, some people haven't eaten all weekend," Marika grumbled.

"For whatever reason," Kate shrugged. "The jambalaya can be rotated into the monthly menus. The rest of this week's meals have all been served before. I've tweaked some recipes." She held up index cards, "But they're pretty standard."

"Sounds good," Dallas said.

"We are going to change the dessert station." Kate rested her hand on the dessert racks. "After working with Sylvie, I think we can organize these better. From now on, we'll have a rack for pastries and donuts, and the other for the actual desserts: cakes, pies, cookies. Sylvie says people don't take donuts and pastries until the end of lunch, so we might as well save the counter space until then."

"Some people like donuts," Marika argued, standing rigid, her arms crossed in front of her body.

"Well, if they ask for a donut, we'll get them one. We're just not going to put them out at the very beginning. We need to get a better handle on what people are actually eating." Kate picked up the split cupcake. "I tried all day to get someone to take this cupcake. I tried different placement, different plates, took off the paper wrapper, but no one wanted it." She tossed the dessert into the garbage like a basketball. "Who knew?" She said, "Beggars really can be choosers." She glanced at her phone. "I've got to run. I'll see you tomorrow."

12

MARIKA

"Cupcakes are dry, and they taste old—that's why no one takes them," Marika said as she walked back to the sink.

"You got that right," Dallas flipped off the lights, "Are you ready to leave? I've got to get to the Quik-mart."

"Go ahead, I'll see you tomorrow." Marika leaned against the refrigerator in the darkened kitchen, staring into the empty dining room. Not much had changed since the first time she ate there. The same mishmash of colored plastic chairs with aluminum legs neatly arranged around wooden tables, dull gray walls decorated with colorfully framed posters of the city's events and activities, which her family could never afford to attend: *The Cincinnati Zoo, Summer Fair,* and *The Shakespeare Theater.* A faint smell of disinfectant lingered in the air.

The serving station looked exactly the same, too. Marika could see her five-year-old self peering through the glass at all the pretty desserts while she waited for her food. Her mom never asked what she wanted for dessert, instead ordering three of whatever was available to avoid fights between the siblings.

She'd always hated it when her mom got cupcakes. The icing would be so stale and dry that it would crunch when she'd bite into it. The cake would crumble and stick to her teeth, making it hard to produce enough saliva to swallow the masticated dessert. Back then, the kitchen was only open three days a week, and Marika's family ate there every day they could.

Marika remembered the first time she'd gotten to choose her own dessert. It was also the first time she'd carried her own tray. She'd felt so grown up, sliding her orange tray down the serving line. She'd stared through the glass looking at the sweets: cakes, pies, donuts, chocolate chip cookies and, without hesitation, ordered the cookie. She'd picked up the tray, keeping her eyes on the wriggling plate of chili, spaghetti and carrots. Slowly and carefully, she carried the food through the crowd, maneuvering around tables, chairs, and people to reach her family. She'd made it. She was so proud. But she hadn't noticed the puddle of water by the chair, and in a flash, her body and her lunch were sailing through the air.

With a thud, she'd landed on the floor underneath her tray of food. The memory still made her flush with embarrassment. Marika had been mortified by the fall, and her mom was furious.

"Get up, damn you," her mom had grabbed her arm, pulling her up. The tray clattered to the ground and skittered across the floor. "Now I'll have to get back in line." Her mom slapped her butt, causing chili and milk to roll down Marika's jeans and land on the new pink gym shoes she'd gotten from the second-hand store.

"Just stand there," her mom shoved Marika to the side of the table. "I don't want my food to get cold. You can wait." With tangled spaghetti hanging from her braids, Marika watched her mom eat lunch.

"Honey, are you okay?" The tall skinny woman wearing a blue apron placed her hands on Marika's shoulders.

"She made a mess," Marika's mom pointed at her with a fork full of twirled spaghetti.

"It's okay, accidents happen." The woman stooped down, resting her hands on her knees to look into Marika's tear-filled eyes. "My name's Ginger. What's your name?"

"Marika."

"Why, that is a beautiful name, Marika. How about I help you get cleaned up?"

Marika looked at her mom, who shrugged before taking a bite of spaghetti.

"Finish your lunch, I'll take care of this little munchkin," Ginger said, taking Marika's chili-covered hand. They walked to the bathroom.

Ginger was the kindest person Marika had ever met. She gently placed the little girl on the edge of the sink and picked the strings of pasta from her braids and clothes, keeping a steady stream of silly conversations going the entire time.

"You smell like strawberries," Marika said when Ginger's hair brushed across her face.

"I do?" Ginger pushed the red curl behind her ear. "I guess I ate too many today."

Marika giggled.

"Put your foot up here," Ginger tapped the sink counter. "We've got to get all that chili off your pretty shoes."

"They light up when I jump."

"They do?" Ginger lifted the little girl down, "Let me see."

Marika jumped as high as she could. The lights flashed with each hop.

"That is amazing. I've never seen someone jump so high."

All cleaned and dressed in clothes from the *lost and found* box, Marika walked with Ginger to the front of the food line, where she got a new lunch and got to choose her own dessert: A cookie. With Ginger's guidance, she successfully carried her tray to the table.

"Mrs. Johnson," Ginger said, pushing in Marika's chair. "You have a delightful daughter. You must be so proud."

Her mom didn't answer.

"You are a wonderful little girl," Ginger said kneeling next to Marika's chair and touching her braids. "I would like to be your friend. Will you come visit me when you come to the kitchen?"

Marika nodded.

"Good," Ginger patted Marika's head. "I give all of my friends chocolate chip cookies."

Over time, Ginger had become more than a friend. She was a mentor, a loving mother figure, and the reason Marika wanted the head cook position more than anything in the world. As head cook, Marika would be just like Ginger: the woman she loved so very much.

"Marika?" A girl with strawberry blonde hair called to her from the dining room.

Marika rubbed her forehead to erase the unpleasant memories of her mother. "Oh, hi Rachel. Did you need something?"

"I was wondering, do you think you could help me with this math problem?" The girl hopped from one foot to the other holding up a notebook. "I don't remember what you said when you were helping the GED class, and I have the test tomorrow."

"Sure, let me look at it." Marika walked into the dining room, and they sat down to work.

13

NICK

The conference room at Hamilton Enterprises was impressive. Floor-to-ceiling windows overlooked the rolling hills of the Hamilton Nature Preserve, filled with majestic oaks and a pond perfect for fishing. Muted dusty-blue walls displayed poster-sized photos of Dan Hamilton, the company's founder, enjoying his eccentric life: Dan atop the summit of Mount Everest, Dan scuba-diving at the Great Barrier Reef, Dan wearing a wingsuit gliding between the Swiss Alps. This man, who lived for the thrill of it all, served as the M&M Board President and was a weekly volunteer in the soup kitchen.

Nick sat with the other board members around a huge mahogany table reviewing the kitchen's monthly reports. He leaned back in the soft, tan leather chair and stared at the pond. A fleeting rainbow appeared when the mist of the fountain flirted just right with the sun. A family of ducks floated by on the water.

I wonder if those are the same ducks that were there when we signed the Lazarus deal?

Nick tapped the pen to his lips.

That was six years ago. How long do ducks live?

The Lazarus merger was the last deal he'd made before he left Hamilton Enterprises. The multi-million-dollar agreement had taken him over a year to negotiate and practically guaranteed him being named as the new President of the company. Yet, signing the contract at this very table, he'd felt empty. He remembered looking at the ducks swimming on the pond thinking. *Is this it? Can't I do more?*

His dissatisfaction had prompted him to apply for the M&M position, and now, six years later, the same feeling of restlessness had returned.

Can't I do more?

Dan's voice boomed, bringing Nick back to the present. "So, with the opening of The Shepherd's Inn, the five-year plan is complete a full year early. What's next?" Dan asked. "The new strategic development committee is up and running, but where do we focus, Nick?"

What was next? Not just for M&M, but for me?

Nick gazed at the board members. "The construction for The Shepherd's Inn is on schedule. We'll be fully operational by December." He looked at the ducks still swimming on the pond and turned back to the board. "I think the new strategic plan has to completely change direction. We've got to switch our focus."

"Is that the reason you hired Kate O'Leary? I can't really see her staying around very long. She's way too image-conscious and ambitious to keep working in a soup kitchen." Dan relaxed in the chair, his legs outstretched, hands clasped behind his head.

"Katie's definitely temporary. She's going to get Marika or Dallas ready to be head cook and then move on. We're lucky she was able to help transition between Joe and hiring a new cook." Nick shuffled his papers. "The new plan has to refocus our attention. M&M has been around a long time, and we're still serving the same number of lunches. Why is that? Why do people still need to eat at M&M?"

"Well, after The Shepherd's Inn opens, M&M will have streamlined access to all social services: food, shelter and clothing. I think that's a great accomplishment. We're helping the community." Dan said.

"Yes, but we could be helping them *more*. We've got to inspire people to want *more* for themselves, for their futures... maybe on a spiritual, more personal level." Nick walked to the window.

"I'm not going to be their priest." Dan laughed, swiveling his chair back towards the table.

"No, I'm serious," Nick paced, almost talking to himself. "The people who eat at the kitchen aren't just hungry physically, they're hungry *spiritually*. We need to develop better relationships with the clients; become mentors, get to know them." He paused and turned back to the group. "Why are they eating in a soup kitchen?"

"Bad life choices," laughed one board member.

"Sometimes people are just down on their luck," said another.

"They like eating there. It's the only thing they know," Dan said.

Nick said, "Until we know *why* a person is eating there, we can't really help them. We're just solving one issue: hunger. We're not addressing the underlying problem. We've got to get to know the clients. Let's show them we care; that God cares. There is a poverty of hope in the M&M community."

The board members fidgeted in their seats. Some nodded their heads in agreement, others rolled their eyes. "So, do you want to have a prayer meeting, or what?" Dan tossed his pen onto the table.

"No," Nick leaned forward, "I think more personal involvement with the clients is crucial. Coaching the baseball team, I got to know the boys and their families. I witnessed first-hand the miracles that can happen when people believe in a kid, and someone shows they care." He shook his head and smiled, "A group of rag-tag boys with very little baseball experience, used equipment, and a dusty brown field brought the neighborhood together. The excitement around the game and the kitchen was incredible. Our team was going to the city championship. There was *hope*."

He slapped the table and looked at each board member, "That's what the new strategic plan should focus on. We've got to give people *hope*."

By the time Nick returned from the board meeting, the lunch line snaked through the dining room into the foyer. Several clients watched Dallas transfer loaves of bread, packages of buns, and donuts from the grocery cart to the grab table for anyone to take home.

"Morning, Dallas," Nick slapped the man's shoulder.

"Hey, Nick. Got a minute?" Dallas dropped a loaf of rye bread onto the table.

"Sure," Nick glanced at his watch. "What's up?"

Dallas pulled Nick towards the *Employees Only* door, "I'm worried about Leon."

"Why, what's going on?" Nick looked for Leon.

"I don't think he's taking his medicine anymore, and he's hanging around Jackie. He seems scared."

"Jackie?"

"You know, *Jackie*, she's transgender." Dallas put his fist on the wall, "She won't let Leon talk, and she's bossing him around like he's a dog. There's something wrong. She's taking advantage of Leon."

"It's not against the law to be transgender," Nick grasped his briefcase with both hands.

"No man, it's not that." Dallas crossed his arms back and forth like an ump calling a man safe. "I'm getting a vibe. There's something wrong, and I heard Jackie moved into Leon's apartment."

"Have you talked to Leon about it?"

"That's just it, he's kind of out of it," Dallas shrugged, "Not high, just not with it. Jackie won't let him talk to anyone."

Nick raised his briefcase. "Let me drop this off in my office, and I'll try to sit with him during lunch."

"Okay, thanks, Nick." Dallas went to finish unpacking the free bread. The cart and table were empty.

The tension in the kitchen was palpable. Marika clattered dishes and plates, moving desserts from one tray to another. "What are you doing?" Nick asked, grabbing a cookie from a plate.

"I'm taking all of the donuts off the line," Marika's voice was cold.

"Why?"

"She doesn't think people want donuts." Marika nodded over her shoulder towards Kate. "She thinks they only want desserts." She slammed a tray into the rack. "Apparently, after eleven, they'll want donuts, because that's when we can put them out."

Kate slid a pan of carrots into the buffet station and turned to face Nick. "Since I was hired to improve procedures, I noticed yesterday the donuts weren't being taken until later in the morning. The counter space should be used for desserts people want. If someone asks for a donut, we'll get them one. Is that okay with you, Marika?" Kate clapped her hands together. Marika turned away. "You can go ahead and start serving." Kate told the volunteer.

Nick took another bite of cookie as he watched the two women.

"How you doin', Nick?" The first client in line asked.

"Ted, my man, how are you?" Nick reached across the top of the buffet counter to shake his hand.

"I'm good, Nick" The man smiled a broad toothless smile shifting his book bag.

"How's your grandma?" Nick said.

"No carrots, thank you," Ted told the volunteer. "She's good. Boy, I was sure disappointed the team lost that game."

"Man, I know," Nick shook his head. "Were you there? I didn't see you."

"No, I had to work, but Grandma told me all about it."

"We'll win it next year. Tell her I said hello."

"Thank you, I will," Ted took the plate from the volunteer. "See you later."

"Do you know everyone's name?" Kate stood beside Nick watching the clients move through the line. Each person's head nodding or shaking to answer the volunteer's question, *did they want carrots?*

"Hmm," Nick looked at the ceiling in thought. "Probably not everyone by name, but I do recognize most of them. Ted's a little different. He's an M&M success story."

"Really? He's always one of the first people in line to eat." Kate sounded doubtful.

"Maybe he likes the food," Nick teased.

"Not before I started working here," Kate grinned.

Laughing, Nick leaned against the refrigerator watching the clients. "Ted's the first person in his family to finish high school and now he's in college. His grandma swears the tutors at Kid's Cafe helped keep Ted on the straight and narrow. They encouraged him and gave him hope." He stopped; struck by the clarity he received.

It was the personal connection. That was the key.

Smiling, he grabbed another cookie. "See ya," he said, waving the cookie in the air. "I'm going to work the dining room."

14

KATE

Kate called the fire inspector on the way to her restaurant. "Hello, Chief Randall, it's Kate O'Leary."

"Yessss?" The chief drawled out the word.

"Just wanted to get an update on the investigation – has the fire report been filed?"

"Like I told you yesterday, *and* the day before, I'll let you know when the investigation is over. Calling everyday isn't going to make the process go any faster."

"Well, I was hoping . . ." Sighing, she parked on the street in front of the restaurant. "Do you think I could at least take down the yellow police tape? I want to do some yard work."

"Sure."

"Okay then," Kate sighed. "Thank you. Talk to you tomorrow."

The call had ended.

After putting on work boots and gardening gloves, Kate stepped onto the front yard and ripped the police tape down. Using both hands, she stuffed the streams of yellow plastic into a garbage bag, wishing her memories of the fire could go in there too.

The call had come on an early Sunday morning. She'd answered the phone without looking at the ID. "Hello?" Her voice croaky with sleep.

"May I speak with Ms. Kathryn O'Leary, please?" An authoritative voice requested.

"Yes, this is Kate. Um, Kathryn." Sitting up in bed, she looked at the unknown phone number on the screen.

"This is Officer Pearson with the Cincinnati Police Department. There's been a report of a fire at the restaurant, Kate's on Vine. Is that your business?"

"Yes." Hopping out of bed, Kate began throwing on clothes. "I'll be right there. What happened?"

"I'll let the fire department know you're on your way." The clipped voice disconnected.

She'd called her mom as she finished dressing. "Mom, my restaurant's on fire!" Kate yelled into the phone. "The police just called. I'm heading down there now." She grabbed her keys and slipped on shoes at the same time.

"How did it happen? What's on fire? Who called you?" her mom asked in a rush.

"The police called me, and I don't know what's on fire. I'm driving there now. Just pray it's not too bad."

It was bad.

Fire trucks and police cars had blocked the road to the restaurant that fateful morning. Kate had to park her car at the top of the street and run the last few blocks to the end of the cul-de-sac. She ran under the yellow police tape already encircling the restaurant's perimeter and grabbed the arm of the first fireman she saw.

"I'm Kate," she struggled to catch her breath. "It's my restaurant."

Bending over, she placed her hands on her knees and gasped for air.

She stared, horrified, at the fire. "Is everyone okay? What happened? Who should I talk to?" she choked out.

"Hey, get back here," a cop yelled gripping her shoulder. The fireman clasped her arm and maneuvered her past the burnt rubble, debris, and devastation, which had once been her beautiful restaurant. Kate tried to contort her body in all sorts of different positions, straining to see beyond the two strong, burly men pushing her to the sidewalk. The policeman lifted the tape and shoved her under.

Wiping sweat from his brow, the fireman said, "I'll get the captain." He pointed to the cement, "Stay there. It's not safe for you to be walking in that mess."

Kate's eyes filled with tears. The Georgian front porch was battered. Shattered glass from the floor-to-ceiling windows covered the misty, gray wood floor. Scorch marks and soot graffitied the building's butter-yellow paint. The one remaining hanging planter tilted at a dangerous angle, looking as if the gentlest breeze or softest touch would force it into the mire and mud of her once-manicured front lawn.

The award-winning landscape was destroyed. The lush green grass was matted and worn from the firefighters dragging their heavy hose and haphazardly tossing the rocking chairs, which had welcomed so many diners to the front porch. Hanging baskets and potted plants drowned in the sodden flower beds. Water from the fire hoses rushed down the gentle slope of the lawn, pooling on the soggy ground where Kate stood. The cold water filling her gym shoes was her wake-up call.

It wasn't a nightmare. The destroyed building was her restaurant. Her dream had literally gone up in smoke.

When the fireman gestured for Kate to come forward, she crossed under the tape and immediately tripped on a mud encrusted slab of metal attached to a broken chain. Wiping the grime away, she uncovered the restaurant name plate.

She had spent hours designing the plaque. It was to represent everything the restaurant would be: an eatery with fresh, local, innovative food for the discerning diner.

Kate's on Vine

The Restaurant

Hugging the metal, she spoke to the fireman, "I'm Kate O'Leary. I own this restaurant. What happened?"

"Chief Randall," he took off his glove to shake her hand. "We received a call approximately six-thirty this morning. A jogger heard a popping noise, probably the glass shattering in the windows. She saw flames and called 911." He shrugged, "From the amount of damage, it appears the fire started sometime during the night. We haven't determined the origination point, and there doesn't seem to be a working smoke detector or fire alarm."

The chief straightened a rocking chair lying on the wet grass. It teetered for a second before collapsing back to the ground. Its rocking leg splintered in two. "We've called the state fire inspector to initiate a thorough investigation."

While he was talking, Kate had stared at the smoldering mess. Like a movie, she watched all her hard work and sacrifice to open the restaurant go up in smoke. The fireman's voice was just background noise to Kate until he said, "No working fire alarm."

"Wait a minute," Kate grasped the chief's arm. "Did you say, 'no working fire alarm'?"

He nodded.

"That's not true. I had an entire security system installed when I bought the building four years ago." She shook her head, "You made a mistake."

"Ma'am," the fireman removed his arm from her clutch. "All I can say is this building was on fire for a *very* long time before we were notified." He pushed her back to the caution tape. "And we were called by a passerby—not an alarm company."

The phone vibrating in Kate's back pocket halted her memory. She pulled off her gloves and admired her work. The yard looked better already. With a swipe, she answered her phone, "Hi, mom."

15

MARIKA

One more day and then the weekend, Marika told herself as she walked into the stockroom, before tripping over a case of Power bars. "Damn it! What the hell are these doing in the middle of the floor?" Marika muttered.

"I haven't had time to put them away yet," Tucker answered in a slow drawl. Wiping his hands on a towel, he stepped from behind the shelf.

"Oh, sorry. I didn't know you were in here." Marika was flustered. She spent her days trying to avoid people: Kate, Nick, Tucker. She was irritated with all of them and wanted to be alone. Hiding in the stockroom had become her haven, she could regroup and remember how her life had been before everyone forced their changes on her.

Nick hiring that new cook—he hadn't even given me a chance. I could make new menus like her. He just didn't want to choose between me and Dallas. I'm a much better cook than Dallas. All that fool does is sing. Kate claiming the meals weren't good enough, well, I could have improved them. Those meals had worked great for the past ten years, but now there was a problem. But Tucker—he hurt the most. Why did he want to change everything? Why did he even want to get married? Life was good the way it was. Why couldn't he see that? Why couldn't he just let them keep things the way they were. We were happy, weren't we?

She was so angry at everyone. Her life was in a tailspin and there was nothing she could do to stop it.

"Marika," Tucker touched her shoulder. "Did you need something?"

"Oh, yeah, I need some apple sauce."

Tucker walked to the shelf and grabbed the case.

"Here you go. Anything else?"

"No—no, thanks." Marika turned to leave.

"Hey, I'm stopping by to help Jamal with his algebra tonight. I'm not sure what you'll want to do."

"Oh…okay," Marika said. *I'm not sure what I want to do either.*

"Jamal, I'm going to take a walk," Marika said at home that evening.

"Why? Tucker's on his way over to help with my homework." Jamal asked.

"I know, he told me. But it's such a nice evening, I thought I'd get some exercise while you two work. There's chili on the stove; you guys eat without me. I might stop by and say hi to Grandma." Jamal looked skeptical, but he didn't question her.

It was a nice night, but did she really want to walk for two hours just to avoid seeing Tucker? When was the last time she stopped by to see her mom? Two years ago?

The walk would do her good.

Tying a jacket around her waist, Marika popped in her earbuds and started walking. The neighborhood was alive. She waved at the cluster of people congregating on the stoops and corners, enjoying the last few days of the summer before the chill of autumn sent people indoors. With each step, Marika ignored the catcalls and whistles directed her way and rebuilt the wall Tucker had breached. She needed to discover how, in three short weeks, her life had been turned completely upside down.

When Tucker was hired to be the facilities and logistics manager four years ago, Marika's reputation as a cold-hearted bitch was well-established with the kitchen's male clients. Her Rubenesque figure, smooth brown skin and oval-shaped eyes naturally attracted men's attention, but Marika wasn't interested. She'd sworn off *all* men after Jamal was born: no man would ever again control or influence her life.

She perfected a don't-even-bother glare. If someone did gather the nerve and request a date, Marika's verbal slap inflicted a bruise so deep the mark would last for weeks.

Looking back, Marika could see how Tucker had infiltrated her life. He'd used the skills he learned in the army to break down her barriers. By diverting her attention from his real goal, he'd been able to swoop in and blindside her. She'd believed him when he said, "I had the army telling me what to do for twenty years. I don't need a woman giving me orders now." He was safe. He didn't want anything from her.

Tucker was way too smart to ask Marika out. He found her Achilles heel—*Jamal*—and developed a relationship with him. He made a point of talking to Jamal each day at Kid's Cafe to ask about school, homework, sports. They talked about the Cincinnati Reds, the Bengals, or whatever other sport was in the news. When Jamal mentioned he was trying out for the school's basketball team, Tucker offered to help him practice his jump shot and rebounds. Tucker was the first-person Jamal told after he made the team.

"You have to come and watch me play," Jamal said to Tucker in the M&M kitchen. "The first game is next week."

"I'll be there, buddy," Tucker gave Jamal a high five, ignoring Marika's doubtful look.

On the walk to the gym for the first game, Jamal excitedly chattered, "I can't believe Tucker's coming to my game. I think I'll score ten points!"

"Tucker might not make it. Something might have come up." Marika tried to prepare him for disappointment. In her experience, men weren't very dependable and, as a mom, she wanted to save Jamal from being hurt.

"He'll be there," Jamal pronounced, bouncing the basketball.

At game time, Jamal scanned the bleachers as he walked to center court for the tip-off. He ignored Marika's wave and took his position with sad eyes. Standing up, she pointed towards the gym door. Jamal spun around to see Tucker stroll in, hands in his pockets wearing a red T-shirt—the team's color.

Beaming, Jamal waved to Tucker and pointed to Marika. With a nod and a smile, Tucker climbed the bleachers to shuffle past several parents before plopping onto the bench next to Marika. "Hi," he said, patting her knee. His eyes on the game.

"I'm glad you made it." Marika put her hand over his as she watched Jamal's moves on the court.

The team lost, but after ice-cream and a slow walk home, everyone agreed it was a really great night.

They were a family long before Marika and Tucker became a couple. Tucker slid into the role of father, coach and mentor to Jamal as easily as the last puzzle piece completes the picture. Tucker attended Jamal's sporting events, school programs, and joined them for dinner several nights a week. Marika loved watching Tucker and Jamal devour the dinner she cooked, acting as if they hadn't seen food in five days. Tucker seemed content with the arrangement, too. He had a ready-made family without a long-term commitment or the worries of supporting them.

Jamal was the one to instigate the change in their relationship.

Playing basketball on the court outside of their house, the twelve-year-old asked Tucker, "Why don't you and mom ever go on dates?" Listening by the window, Marika held her breath while she waited for Tucker's response.

"Hmmm, that's a good question." Tucker bounced the ball a few times before taking the shot. "Do you think she'd go out with me?"

"I think so." Jamal rebounded the ball and dribbled down the court. "Don't you think she's pretty?"

"I think she's beautiful," Tucker tried to steal the ball. "Where would I take her?"

Jamal stopped dribbling and looked skyward, pondering the question. "She likes pizza. You could take her to get pizza and go see a movie." He scored a basket. "That's what they do on TV."

Tucker nodded, rubbing his chin as he walked toward the ball. "That's a pretty good idea, but I wouldn't want you to feel left out. Don't you like pizza and a movie too?"

"Sure, I do, but Benji's having a birthday party on Friday. Why don't you take her out then?" Jamal ran down the court with the ball.

Tucker raced after him, stole the ball and made a long shot. "Well, if you're okay with it, maybe I'll see what she's doing Friday." The ball swooped through the net.

With Jamal's blessing, Tucker and Marika became a couple. Life was good. For almost two years, the status quo was maintained. They were happy. She had her own home, a man she loved, a son she adored, and she expected to be named the new head cook at M&M. But three weeks ago, Tucker issued his ultimatum. "Either we get married, or we can't go out anymore."

"What?" Marika asked, dumbstruck by his announcement.

"I want to get married," Tucker stood on the front stoop. "I'm tired of leaving every night to go home to an empty house."

"I don't want to get married. I like things the way they are." Marika stomped her foot. "Why do they have to change?"

"Because I love you and Jamal, and I want us to be a real family," Tucker said.

"We *are* a real family," Marika pouted.

"No, we're not. You won't let us be one. I've asked you to marry me every month for the past year. You're never going to say yes. I think it will just be better if we don't spend time together anymore," Tucker said.

"Tucker," Marika grabbed his hand. "Please...."

"No, Marika. You obviously don't love or trust me enough to make a real commitment, and I'm tired of hoping you'll change." He pulled his arm away. "It'll be better this way."

"What about Jamal?"

"I am not leaving Jamal," Tucker pointed his finger at her. "This is about you." He walked down the steps. "You'll need to explain to him why we aren't together."

Marika couldn't bring herself to tell Jamal about the break-up and was grateful that fifteen-year-old boys were wrapped up in their own lives. Marika had become adept at dodging and evading being with Tucker and Jamal together with all sorts of excuses. It helped that Tucker was so busy with The Shepherd's Inn. She just didn't know how much longer she could keep up the facade. She was tired ... of *everything*: of Tucker's ultimatum, Nick's decision, and that new cook.

The song changed in her ear and Marika looked around at the strange surroundings.

Where am I?

Lost in her thoughts, she hadn't realized how late it was or how far she'd walked. Untying the jacket from her waist, she slipped it on and tried to get her bearings. She peered at the street sign: *Vine Street.*

The quiet neighborhood was beautiful: manicured lawns, fall décor on the houses, glowing streetlights, and clean sidewalks. Marika strolled down the cul-de-sac admiring the houses. It was as if she had walked into another world.

Well, the dilapidated building at the end of the street would fit in her neighborhood, at least.

Doing a double take, Marika recognized the woman working in the mangled yard.

It was Kate.

She'd walked to her restaurant.

Should she go say something to her? Maybe have it out...clear the air. Tell her she didn't belong at M&M? It would feel so good to say how she really felt about her working at her kitchen. For one minute, she thought about confronting her, but instead, she pulled up her hoodie, and jogged home.

16

KATE

Kate placed a pan onto the buffet station as the Monday volunteers walked into the kitchen. "What smells so good?" Dan asked, tying on an apron.

"Beef stroganoff. I'm trying to use the donated meatloaves in more creative ways."

The clatter of dishes caused Kate to turn around. A frowning Marika slammed the salad pan into its slot. "We're having egg noodles too. Marika, have you served egg noodles here before?"

"No," Marika shoved the salad tongs into the lettuce.

"I didn't think so." Kate stirred the noodles. "Tucker had to find them for me. I think it's a nice change."

"I was always told we had to work with what we have," Marika glared at Kate.

"Well, it's nice to be serving something new," Dan laughed.

"Okay, does everyone know where they should be?" Jenny asked, surveying the buffet: beef stroganoff, egg noodles, green beans and a tomato salad. "That actually looks delicious. My stomach is growling."

"It tastes good too. I had a bite," Dallas rolled the plate cart to the front of the line.

"Alright then, Dan, go ahead and start," Jenny waved to the first client. "Ted we're ready."

Standing with Jenny behind the prep table, Kate watched the clients move through the line.

"What is that?" a client asked Dan.

"Beef stroganoff, it's got beef and sour cream in it."

"Yuck," The man grimaced, "I'm hungry, so I guess I'll have to eat it."

Kate rolled her eyes and Jenny laughed, "So, how are things going?"

"Okay, I guess," Kate shrugged. "I'm not getting much feedback from the clients."

"I'm not hearing any complaints. You could always go ask them." Jenny watched a group of women sitting in the dining room.

"Oh, I don't know. Hey, my mom and sister are interested in volunteering. Is there a specific day you need people?"

"I'll check my computer and give you a few dates." Jenny pushed off the prep table. "I'm going to check out that group in the corner. I want to make sure everything is okay. I'll see you later."

"Bye." Kate looked around the kitchen. Dallas had begun the next day's prep and Marika was gone—*again*.

Kate watched Jenny and Nick walk around the dining room talking to clients. They both looked so comfortable. Nick managed the maze of people, chairs, and bags filled with clothes, aluminum cans, or some other client's treasure with aplomb. Watching him hug a man who looked like he hadn't bathed in a month made her want to gag. Seeing an empty chair, Nick sat down and talked while the clients enjoyed their meal. He made it look so easy.

At her restaurant, Kate enjoyed meeting the diners. It was a crucial part of her image to be seen with the CEOs, politicians and local celebrities who frequented the restaurant. She knew how to work a room, but did she want to work this room?

Not really.

She stared into the dining room. The clients looked like zombies in search of a seat, their outstretched arms carrying lunch trays, grocery bags and totes dangling from their wrists and there was Nick, looking so cute, sitting at a table with the "Mayor" and his cronies.

I can pretend to care what the clients think and accidently bump into Nick as I show my deep concern. Why do I want Nick to think I care? I mean he's my boss now, but once I quit, could he be a boyfriend?

Lifting the straps of the apron over her head, she asked, "Do you know what you're doing for tomorrow?"

"We surely do," Dallas stopped chopping vegetables and pointed to the clipboard hanging on the wall. "I've got the vegetables, and Marika will prep the sauce."

"We do know how to read," Marika muttered placing a pan on the stove.

When did she get back?

Kate stared at Marika. "Great, I'm going to go talk to the clients about the new meals."

Kate rubbed her hands together, nervously standing on the threshold of the dining room.

Who looks semi-normal? What should I say?

She wanted to make a beeline straight to Nick. He had changed tables and was sitting with two new people: the confused man and the transgender woman. She was wearing Daisy Duke shorts, a halter top and had a butterfly barrette stuck in her balding hair.

I can't go straight over there. I need to be subtle; have Nick see me talking to the clients.

A volunteer carrying a stack of trays bumped her elbow. Kate stepped aside and knocked into a second volunteer wiping down a table for a waiting client.

It was showtime.

Pushing her hair back under the ball cap, she searched the tables for someone—*anyone*—normal to talk to. The *muffin-man,* the guy who always wanted a muffin and told corny jokes, was sitting with a group of ladies. *Cool Hand Luke,* the handsome guy she'd met on her very first day? He was surrounded by his posse, but he'd probably think she was coming on to him. *Crazy Maizie,* the lady who had entire conversations by herself was sitting alone, but she seemed to be having an argument with herself. There was a seat next to the *Scarecrow,* the guy with tattoos on his face making him look like the scarecrow from the Wizard of Oz, but if he wouldn't talk to Sylvie, would he be willing to speak with her?

Sighing with relief, Kate spied him…Alone at a corner table, his bookbag resting on an empty chair, right in Nick's line of sight. A regular person: Ted. He was normal. She could talk to him.

She strode toward the table, reaching out her hand. "Hi, I'm Kate, the new cook. I'm wondering what you think about the new meals I'm making." Ted looked up from the plate. His eyes were huge, terrified, like a deer caught in headlights. His fork fell to the table. He swiveled his head, looking for someone to save him. Kate dropped her hand.

"Ted, can I join you?" Nick put the bookbag on the floor and swung the empty chair around to straddle the seat. "Have you met Katie? She's the new cook."

Ted nodded showing a toothless smile.

"I thought I'd ask the clients what they thought about the new meals," Kate stammered, rocking back on her heels, hands clasped behind her back. "I've seen Ted here almost every day, so I thought he'd be the perfect person for me to talk to."

"So, how's she doing so far?" Nick's fist knocked on the table.

"What did you think of the jambalaya and today's stroganoff?"

"It tastes pretty good," Ted laughed looking at Nick. "I like foods I don't have to chew too much." He laughed.

"I bet," Nick grinned back.

Not having to chew too much isn't exactly a rave review. Kate forced a smile

"I've got to go," Ted stood grabbing his bookbag. "I don't want to miss my bus. The food is definitely tasting better." He nodded at Kate.

"Thank you," Kate yelled to his back before facing Nick. "He's nice."

"Ted? He's the best." Nick pushed in the chair. "He's studying information systems at Cincy Tech. He has to be first in line to eat so he can catch the bus for work. He works second shift at the factory uptown."

"If he's in school and works, then why does he eat here?"

"Katie, not everyone who eats here is homeless or unemployed." Nick grabbed a tray from an empty table. "I would say the majority of our clients, the ones who aren't using, have a home and some type of job, even if it's only part-time."

Nick placed the tray at the dishwashing station. "A lot of our clients are victims of circumstances. Ted's mom was fifteen when she had him. He was raised by his grandma. She got him into every activity M&M had to offer: Kid's Cafe, the sports program, the mentor program. He's eaten lunch here almost every day. This kitchen is his home."

"What happened to his teeth?" Kate watched Nick wipe down trays.

"He has a genetic disease, cleidocranial dysplasia. You know the kid on *Stranger Things* without any teeth?" Kate nodded. "Ted has the same thing. When you're worried about how you're going to eat, getting to the dentist isn't a priority." He grabbed another tray. "I'm working on finding a dentist willing to help him out at low or no cost. My goal is to see Ted really smile at his college graduation." Nick tossed the towel on the counter and showed his own dazzling white smile.

"That would be wonderful," Kate grinned.

"I think it's great you're trying to meet the clients." Nick propelled her towards the kitchen. "Personal connection is really important, but people are wary of outsiders, even ones as cute as you." He pushed open the door, "So, when you're in the dining room, maybe grab a towel, wipe the tables, or carry some trays. People will be more receptive if they see you doing a job. Oh, and wear your apron. It's important for people to know you work here."

"Okay, thanks," Kate said. *Did he say I was cute?*

That afternoon at her restaurant, Kate finished the fall cleanup. The flowerbeds were cleared of the fire debris and decaying plants, the vegetable garden was turned over and tilled with compost, the bare spots on the lawn created by fire trucks and rushing water were reseeded and covered with straw in hopes grass would take root by spring. Using a broom, Kate brushed the falling leaves off the front porch. She swept around the broken swing still laying in the corner and realized her dad must have rehung the shutters that had been tilting precariously beside the boarded-up windows.

She sighed when she thought about her dad. Pete stopped by the restaurant at least once a week to make certain the building was safe. He had created a to-do list and had a notebook of renovation ideas to get going with once reconstruction could begin. He was almost as anxious as Kate to get started.

Placing the pumpkins she had bought from the market on the steps, Kate sat down on the stoop to enjoy the last few rays of the Indian summer sun. It had been three months since the fire, and she wasn't any closer to reopening. She had stopped calling the fire investigator and insurance company daily and now made weekly touching-base calls.

Reality hit her: the restaurant wasn't going to be open in time for the holidays. It was becoming more and more difficult to remain positive. Mentally, she had changed her thinking from *when* the restaurant reopens to *if.*...Should she start thinking like a cook instead of a chef, now, too?

17

MARIKA

On the walk into work Monday morning, Marika was happy. She had made it through the weekend without having to tell Jamal about the break-up. She'd been wondering how she was going to explain Tucker's absence, but Saturday morning Jamal, still in his boxers, solved the problem.

"Tucker just called," her son said. "He wants me to help him and Nick today at The Shepherd's Inn. We're going to work on the bedrooms, and then I'll just spend the night with him. Is that okay?"

"I guess," Marika said taking a sip of coffee. "What about homework?"

"It's all under control," Jamal gave a thumbs up. "Tucker's going to help me study for algebra after Mass, and then I'll come home."

She breathed a sigh of relief. She wouldn't have to break her son's heart today. She dreaded telling Jamal she and Tucker were through. He was going to be devastated. The longer she could keep the break-up a secret the better.

She'd spent her time alone devising new menus for the kitchen. She was going to show Nick that she was just as capable as that Kate at creating new menus. She had a better idea now of what Nick wanted in a new cook, and her new menus would prove she could do the job.

Sure, Kate's meals were unique, but who couldn't create delicious meals if you could order all the ingredients? I was always told to cook with what the kitchen had. Now, I know better, and my menus are great, and I didn't ask for ridiculous ingredients like snow peas. Why in the world would a soup kitchen need snow peas?

Hanging her jacket on the hook in the hall, Marika walked into the kitchen tying an apron around her waist. Dallas stood at the prep table looking at the day's chore chart; while singing 'Manic Monday' He finished trilling the Bangles' hit before asking, "How was your weekend?"

"Fine."

Marika scanned the page. The chore chart drove her nuts. *Why couldn't that woman just tell us what to do? Is she too good to talk to us peons working in the kitchen?*

Daily Chore Chart
Monday's Menu

Beef Stroganoff, egg noodles, salad, green beans, desserts

Prep Duties

Marika: Boil egg noodles (75 pounds). Open x10 beef broth, Prep salad veggies

Dallas: Open x10 jumbo cans green beans. Open x20 cans mushroom slices

Kate: Brown 30lbs of ground beef and 7lbs chopped onions

Lunch Duties

Marika: Egg noodles in warming tray. Salad-Tossed with Italian Dressing

Dallas: Vegetables and desserts

Kate: Stroganoff

Marika noticed there was also an entry for tomorrow, too.

Daily Chore Chart

Tuesday's Menu

Sausage, mashed potatoes, sauerkraut, carrots, salad

Prep Duties

Marika: 75 pounds mashed potatoes, Prep Salad veggies

Dallas: Open x15 cans sauerkraut, x15 cans carrots

Kate: 30 pounds sausage

Lunch Duties

Marika: Reconstitute mashed potatoes, toss salad with ranch
dressing

Dallas: Warm sauerkraut and carrots

Kate: Brown sausage

Well, that's fine with me. If she doesn't want to talk to me, then I won't have to talk to her. I'd never run my kitchen like this.

Marika's gloved hands churned the Italian dressing through the lettuce, tomatoes and carrots with a ferocity better suited for whipping egg-whites than tossing a salad, when her thoughts were interrupted.

"So, our boy's starting work next week?" Dan adjusted his baseball cap.

"He is," Marika smiled looking up from the salad. "We're doing a practice run to your office tonight. She pulled off the wet gloves and carried the salad pan to the buffet station. "I want to make sure he knows which bus to take and where to get off." She turned to face him leaning against the rack. "I really appreciate your company's internship program.

So many corporations don't want to work with high school students."

Dan arranged the plates and bread for lunch. "Jamal's a nice kid and Drexel is a great school. I was happy to get my company involved. I think Drexel is really going to change kid's lives…starting with Jamal."

"I agree. I just hope he's safe in that neighborhood…" Marika wiped down the counter.

"Are you kidding?" Dan laughed. "My office is practically in Mayberry."

Once lunch was started, and before the next day's prep began, Marika left the kitchen to either tutor at the GED class or mentor the Mother's Group. She loved doing both. The sessions gave her an opportunity to catch up on the neighborhood gossip as well as give back to the community she cared so much about. She had a unique perspective to share with the students and the moms—she'd been one of them.

On her way to tutoring, she stopped at Nick's office and tapped on the open door.

"Hey Marika, what's up?" Nick looked up from the piles of papers on his desk.

She pulled an envelope from her back pocket. "I wanted to give you this."

His face paled and the chair creaked as he attempted to stand. "Marika, I don't want you to quit." He stared at the envelope in her hand.

"What?" She laughed. "Nick, I'm not quitting. These are some menus I put together." She handed him the envelope. "Now that I know we're able to order new ingredients, I wanted to show you some of my menu ideas. I was very creative."

"Whew, thank God," Nick sat back down. "You scared me for a

minute." He opened the envelope and looked at the menus. "These look great, I knew you'd learn a lot from Katie. You should ask her to add a few of these to the calendar."

"That's okay," Marika shrugged. "I just wanted you to know that I can do the job *this* job. We don't need her."

"Marika, I can't—" Nick tried to get out of the chair again.

Sighing, Marika put her hand up to stop him. "I've got to get to the GED class." Walking to the classroom, she tried to give herself a pep talk.

What did you expect? Nick isn't going to fire the new girl just because you showed him some menus. You've got to make him realize he's made a huge mistake in hiring her, find a way to do that.

18

MARIKA

Marika kept a brisk pace on the short walk to meet Jamal at his school.
The bright sun was misleading. The autumn air was crisp, almost chilly,
and she pulled her jacket tighter to keep warm. Arriving on campus, she
waved at Jamal standing on the stoop talking with his friends. *He's so
handsome, and when did he get so tall? Where has the time gone? I can't
believe I have a son old enough to have a job.*

Tossing his backpack over his shoulder, Jamal walked to meet her.

"Hi there, how was your day?" Marika asked resisting the urge to
give her 6'1" son a hug in front of his friends.

"It was good, how was yours?" Jamal patted her head with a smile,
recognizing his mom's wish to give him a hug.

"Good," she nodded. "Are you ready to do this?" She looked up to
see his face. "I checked the bus schedule again, and we'll need to be at
the stop in five minutes."

"Well, since the stop is about twenty feet away, I think we'll make
it," he chuckled nodding towards the street corner. "Mom, are you
nervous?"

"No, no, it's just a practice run, but I don't want us to miss it. I
bought you a monthly bus pass." She handed him the plastic card and
pushed his tall body towards the corner. "There's the bus—see, it's a little

early, you have to be here just in case."

The bus door opened, and Jamal stepped aside allowing his mom to enter.

"Hello," Marika said to the driver, sliding the bus pass through the scanner. She walked to the front row of seats catty-corner to the driver and sat by the window.

Jamal scanned his pass and took the aisle seat next to her. "Try to always sit up front," Marika whispered patting his leg. "That way you'll be sure to see your stop."

"Mom, it's going to be fine. I've ridden the bus before. You can stop worrying," Jamal shook his head.

Oh, to have the confidence of a fifteen-year-old boy.

Marika smiled at her son. Jamal was right, since she didn't own a car, before Tucker, the bus was their only form of transportation.

She looked out the window as they sped down the street past M&M. Tucker was leaving, Jamal was leaving, everyone was leaving her.

She'd met James, Jamal's father at the kitchen. She'd been fifteen, Jamal's age now, and she could still remember how infatuated she'd been with the high school dropout. He was charismatic, and always surrounded by a group of fawning friends.

She'd been attending *Homework Help* at M&M and James had charmed the advisor into believing he was studying for his GED and needed a tutor. His real quest was the warmth of the kitchen in the winter, or the cool in summer, as well as the free snacks.

Marika idolized him. He was the epitome of cool and everything she thought a man should be.

She could still remember the rush of emotion she felt when he had smiled her way one day.

"Hey baby," he said with a wink. "Why don't you sit your sweet self right next to me?" In one fluid motion, James spun a plastic chair away from the table and offered Marika a seat. His friends had laughed, while her friends had gaped at the suaveness of the move.

Marika nervously took the seat, amazed that the handsome boy with his light-brown skin and muscular build was talking to her. She was hooked, and quickly James became her world.

All her energy was spent with him or thinking about him. She ignored Ginger's warnings about James, choosing to believe all the beautiful words he told her. "I love you baby. You're the only one for me. We're forever."

After being sick three mornings in a row, the school nurse had suggested she take a pregnancy test. The positive result was a surprise, but she was ready. She imagined a life with James, their baby, and his big dreams. They would live happily ever after.

With a folder full of pregnancy pamphlets and options, she walked to meet James at M&M, excited about their future.

Reality was as harsh as a baby crying in the middle of the night.

James sat at their table surrounded by his posse. "I've got a surprise for you," she whispered in his ear, wrapping her arms around his shoulders.

"You do?" James tilted his head to look at her. "Marika's got a surprise for me," he leered at his friends. "Maybe you should all give us some privacy." The group whooped and hollered at James's suggestive comment.

Rolling her eyes, Marika stood up. "Hey, baby, don't go nowhere. Tell me, what's the surprise?" James placed his hand on her ass.

"Come outside," she said pulling at his arm. "It's a secret."

He slapped away her hand, "Baby, these are my peeps. We don't have any secrets."

"Please, please come outside with me," Marika begged clasping her hands around his wrist.

"I said no," he smirked. "If you want to tell me something, just say it." He leaned back in the chair, his feet on the table.

"Fine," Marika faced him placing her hands on her hips. "I'm going to have a baby."

James shot up, knocking the chair to the ground, and gaped at Marika. The silence at the table screamed.

"So, James," a posse member said. "You're going to be a daddy. Hope you know how to change a diaper." The table erupted with guffaws and laughs.

"Shut the fuck up," James yelled.

"It's okay, we're going to be fine. We can get a place together." Marika tried to hug him.

"The kid's not mine." He pushed her away. "I don't know why you're even telling me." He kicked the chair under the table and stormed away.

"James, what are you talking about? Of course, the baby's yours," Marika ran after him pulling on his arm.

"Get off me," he shoved her away. "Stay away from me." He slammed the door.

Ginger found her in the bathroom. Taking a seat on the floor next to her, Ginger passed tissues as Marika sobbed through the story of her heartbreak. Wrapped safely in Ginger's arm, Marika laid her head on her mentor's shoulder. "What am I going to do?" Marika whispered.

"Well, you're certainly in a pickle," Ginger said. "But I want you to listen to me, okay?" Ginger handed Marika a tissue and waited for her to wipe her eyes and blow her nose. "Are you really listening?"

Marika nodded.

"Good. I want you to remember a few things. One: every child is a blessing." Ginger smiled, keeping eye contact with Marika. "Now, your blessing could have better timing, but it's still a blessing. Two: you are strong and capable. You can be an amazing mother." Ginger wiped the fresh tears falling on Marika's face with a Kleenex. "Three: it's going to be alright. I'm going to help you."

Marika believed her.

Ginger kept her word. She accompanied Marika to her doctor's appointments and birthing classes. She ran interference with Marika's mom, who had wanted Marika to have an abortion. She helped Marika get a crib, stroller and baby clothes. Ginger also changed the *Homework Help* policy: students were now required to be enrolled in school and under the age of eighteen to receive entrance to the M&M dining room after 3:00 p.m.

"Mom? Mom? Earth to Mom," Jamal tapped her shoulder.

"I'm sorry, I was daydreaming," Marika looked around the bus.

"Can you believe the size of these houses?" Jamal pointed out the window. "And only one family lives in them. Think I'll be able to buy one of those someday?"

"I do," Marika smiled. "You'll need to have a room for your mom."

"No way," Jamal grinned. "I'll buy you and Tucker a house waaaay down the street."

Marika could feel her heart break as she forced a smile.

I'm going to have to tell him we broke up, but I can't today or next week. I'll tell him once he's situated at the internship.

She had to change the topic. "Oh look, see that dome way over there?" she tapped the window. "That's the hospital where you were born. I remember that day like it was yesterday and now you're starting your first job."

The hospital faded from view and the memories floated before her eyes.

She'd been at *Homework Help* studying for the algebra final with her friends. Standing up to get in her backpack, a gush of water exploded from her body. Flabbergasted, two thoughts crossed her mind at the same time: *I'm so glad Ginger made me take that birthing class* and *the baby's coming now.*

Her legs bowed as she looked at the puddle of water pooling at her feet when she felt the first full-fledge contraction envelope her body. Her girlfriends screamed for help as she doubled over with pain.

"Oh, my goodness," Ginger's sweet voice murmured in her ear. "Is that baby ready to be born?" She gently rubbed her back.

"I made a mess," Marika gasped.

"It's going to be alright. I'm going to help you." Ginger said, skirting the water and picking up the bookbag. "Let's get you to the hospital. C'mon we can breathe together."

The pain of labor diminished with the overwhelming love she experienced the first time she held her baby. He was a perfect head of brown curly hair, oval-shaped eyes and the same beautiful light-brown skin as his father. She just knew James would want to meet him.

With shaky hands, she dialed James' number, "Congratulations, it's a boy." There was silence on the other end. "I had the baby. He looks so much like you. I'm going to call him Jamal," she said in a rush. "Do want to come and see him?"

"I told you the kid's not mine," James' voice was stony. "I don't have time for this." He hung up.

She'd been crushed. A small part of her had believed James would change his mind and want to be a father. He would see the baby and remember all the promises he had made to her. She held her son and cried. A tear landed on Jamal's sweet cheek.

Wiping it away, Jamal's tiny hand grasped her finger making her smile. "That's right," she crooned. "It's just you and me, and we're going to be okay. I promise."

She kissed his face. "We don't need a man in our lives."

The jolt of the bus stopped her musing. *Why hadn't she kept that promise to Jamal? Why had she let Tucker into their lives?*

"Mom, this is my stop." Jamal said. He had been talking the entire ride, but Marika couldn't recall a single thing he said.

He stepped aside to allow Marika to exit first. She stopped next to the bus driver. "Excuse me." Marika said. "Do you drive this route every day?"

"Yes," the woman answered.

"Oh good! This is my son, Jamal." Marika pulled him close. "He's going to work at Hamilton Enterprises in that building over there." Marika pointed towards the glass building. "I would be so grateful if you could keep an eye out for him. He starts Monday."

"I'd be happy to," she smiled. "I'm Roberta. It's nice to meet you, Jamal."

"Nice to meet you," a mortified Jamal shook Roberta's hand.

"Thank you, Roberta. I'm Marika. Have a good day." She stepped off the bus.

"I can't believe you did that," Jamal said swinging his bookbag over his shoulder. "I don't need the bus driver to keep an eye on me. I'm not a baby."

"You're right," Marika nodded. "You're not a baby, but you'll always be *my* baby, and I'll feel better knowing Roberta's keeping an eye on you."

Marika admired the building and grounds. "Oh my, isn't it pretty here?"

The short bus ride had carried them to an entirely different world. A park-like setting of landscaped walkways, fountains and statues connected the various office buildings. A large pond to the right of the buildings was surrounded by benches encouraging people to relax, fish or feed the ducks. Oak and elm trees in full autumn splendor dotted the rolling green hills with splashes of yellow, orange and red.

The neighborhood was beautiful, quiet and peaceful. Each street corner flanked with large flowerpots bursting with fall blooms and unstained by graffiti or litter.

"Let's go, Mom," Jamal said as he strode toward the office.

Following her son, Marika prayed: *Please keep him safe here.*

19

NICK

Nick put down the tub of paint and unlocked the door to The Shepherd's Inn. Turning on the lights, he saw progress. The floor still looked like a construction site, with tarps, ladders and pieces of drywall lining the hall, but there were walls, working electricity and actual plumbing. The Shepherd's Inn would open on time and under budget.

Renovating the old rectory connected to M&M had been a monumental task. The building, which had once served as a dormitory for the local priests, had been empty and neglected for nearly three decades. Once the electricity and plumbing had been brought up to code, the upstairs dormitories had been upgraded to include bathrooms with individual shower stalls and lavatories. The main floor was redesigned to serve as a welcome center and community room, and a full-service laundry had been installed in the basement for the clients to use.

The Shepherd's Inn wasn't a homeless shelter and wouldn't house permanent clients. It would serve as a stop-gap for the homeless; a place where they could come, rest, take a shower, do laundry, and sleep for one or two days in a warm safe environment. Its small staff and volunteers would work with the clients who wanted to make the necessary life changes to achieve permanent housing and assistance. The real challenge was how to encourage the clients to *want* to make the change.

Nick had spent Saturday working with Tucker, Jamal, Dallas and Dan, finishing the drywall, sanding and sweeping the rooms to prepare for the paint. When The Shepherd's Inn opened next month, the final phase of the M&M strategic plan would be complete.

Then what?

Nick moved the buckets of paint to the welcome area. He imagined the clients sitting on the couches and chairs, anxious for someone to help them, to notice them.

He wanted to be that person. He wanted to sit next to someone who had been marginalized and lost to society and help them; to connect and encourage them. He wanted to make them believe they were important, that they mattered, were loved and cared for.

Sighing, Nick kicked the paint can. He was on edge. Hiring Katie hadn't gone as planned; the meals were one hundred percent better, but Marika and Katie weren't working together. They were at a stalemate.

"You know the saying, too many cooks in the kitchen?" Dallas said, as they worked. "Well, that's my life right now." Dallas sung the spiritual, 'Nobody knows the trouble I've seen,' in his low baritone.

Nick looked at his watch before switching off the lights. He'd been working long days. After The Shepherd's Inn officially opens, the directives from the Board of Directors will be accomplished. Every service necessary to help the down-on-their-luck will be available on the same city block, but—would anything really change?

After years of working in the community, Nick knew that the real reason a person's life improved wasn't because of another service or program, but rather because someone else believed in them. It was that simple, yet so very difficult to accomplish.

Would The Shepherd's Inn be able to help the desperate find hope? Since the board meeting, he'd been playing in his mind different ways the staff and volunteers at M&M could work with the clients. In his heart, he knew personal connections were the key to making real life changes. At next week's staff meeting, he was going to issue a challenge: invite each employee to develop or create an activity they could share with the clients. He had some great ideas already—out of the box ideas—and he hoped the employees would share his enthusiasm for the project.

In the meantime, he locked the door.

What am I going to do?

He was so restless and edgy. He needed to make a move in his own life, but the direction God was pointing him in wasn't the path he wanted to take.

20
KATE

Leaving church the next morning, Kate mused at the new rhythm of her life. Ending an evening at the restaurant with a cool glass of sauvignon blanc had been replaced with morning Mass, cooking cafeteria-style, finishing with an afternoon of manual labor at the restaurant. Most nights she was happy to crawl into bed by ten o'clock, and she couldn't remember the last time she'd had a glass of wine. Her life had been turned upside down.

Daily Mass had become a peaceful respite in Kate's life. The celebration centered her day and enabled her to better cope with the frustration of the fire and working at the kitchen. Kneeling before the altar she'd pray, "Please God, get me out of here. Help me to open my restaurant soon."

Nick stopped her after Mass, "Katie, can you come see me after lunch gets started?"

"Do you want to meet now?" Kate followed Nick down the church steps.

"No, I don't want to be rushed."

"Okay, I'll come to your office around ten?"

"Good," he nodded jogging back up the stairs. "Father Murray, do you have a minute?"

I wonder what he wants to talk about. He looked so serious.

The food had definitely improved since she started running the kitchen. Not once since Kate took control of the menus had Jenny asked, "What is *this*?"

Tucker and Dallas agreed more food was being eaten, too. People were coming through the line more times and the amount of food waste had drastically declined.

The only problem she could see was Marika; that woman had a huge chip on her shoulder. Her attitude was terrible. She still believed Kate actually wanted to be the M&M cook. The woman was insufferable. She made snide comments about the changes and then ignored the new procedures whenever it suited her, and where did she disappear to each day? Lunch would begin and ten minutes later Marika would vanish.

She just knew the woman was complaining to Nick about her. Is she what Nick wanted to talk about? Had Marika found a way to get rid of her?

By the time ten o'clock rolled around, Kate had convinced herself she was being fired.

It's not like I even wanted this job, but I don't want to be fired either. Granted, it's not a lot of money, but it is covering my expenses. Damn it, I've done a good job. Why is he siding with Marika over me?

Outraged at the injustice of the situation, she rapped on Nick's door and walked in without waiting for a response. "Nick," she said.

"Hey," Nick glanced up from the file he was reading. "Take a seat. I want to review these menus and numbers."

Kate looked around the room. If possible, the boxes had multiplied since the last time she'd been in his office. All the chairs were filled with papers or cartons. Taking a stack from the nearest seat, Kate sat holding the papers on her lap.

"The jambalaya went over really well." Nick read the weekly meal summaries. "The beef stroganoff and taco casserole were popular too. I wasn't sure about the stuffed peppers, but the clients seemed to like them. Overall, I think things are going really well. What do you think?" He looked up from the pages. "Why are you holding those papers?" He looked confused.

"I didn't know where to put them," Kate shrugged.

"Sorry, here give them to me." The chair gave its usual screech as he pushed back from the desk.

"I think things are working well." Kate handed him the stack, breathing a little easier.

I guess he's not firing me.

"I'm getting into the routine and I'm enjoying the challenge of creating menus with the limited stock. I think the clients have noticed the improvement in the meals too."

"I agree. So, I know we talked about a one-month trial and that's over Monday. Are you willing to stay on for a while longer?"

"Yes," Kate nodded. "I'd like to stay until I get my insurance money. I really don't have an answer for how long that will be" She sighed, "It could be next week or in six months?"

"Well, hopefully it will be sooner rather than later. I'd really like you to work on getting Marika or Dallas ready to fill your shoes, but I also have a favor to ask." Nick's smile was contagious, and his eyes practically twinkled with excitement. "I want you to teach a cooking class."

"A cooking class?" Kate's eyes popped with surprise, "For who?"

"The clients, students, really anyone from the neighborhood who's interested." Nick maneuvered around the cluttered office. He picked up a tennis ball from his desk and tossed it between his hands. "We've got to find different ways to connect with the community. M&M offers all kinds of sports programs and tutoring, but we don't have anything that can benefit normal life; teach real life skills that will help them survive on their own. Seeing what you've done with the food here made me think about how we can help people cook their own delicious meals at home. It would be a great opportunity for members of the community to learn from an actual gourmet chef. What do you think?"

"Oh, I don't know," Kate stood and looked out the dirty window. "I have work to do at the restaurant." She hesitated, "I really appreciate being able to work here, but I'm just not certain I want to take on anything more."

"I get that," Nick bounced the ball on the floor. "Just think about it. A cooking class could be a life-changing opportunity for someone. Teaching a person how to prepare a meal for their family and encouraging them to sit down and eat a dinner together." He held the ball and looked at the sky, "Man, what a difference you could make."

"But—" Kate said.

He stopped her argument, "Think about it, and you can let me know at the staff meeting Friday."

"Staff meeting?" Kate said.

"Didn't I tell you? We have a monthly staff meeting the first Friday of the month. It starts at three, and we usually grab a bite to eat afterwards."

"Oh, alright" Kate opened the door. "I'll think about the cooking class, but I'm not making any promises."

Fair enough," Nick's chair screamed in protest as he leaned back to stretch his legs, crossing his feet on top of the desk. "By the way, Katie, you're doing a great job. The change in the food is remarkable. Oh, and

Marika put together some menus. Maybe you could take a look and put a few of the meals into the monthly line-up?" He handed her the papers.

"Sure, I wanted to talk to you about Marika. She disappears once lunch starts…I'm not sure what's going on, but that's no way to run a kitchen."

"Hmmm, have you asked her what she's doing?" Nick asked.

"Well, no." Kate said, "She's a cook. She should be in the kitchen."

"Talk to her... Marika has a lot of knowledge about the kitchen and the neighborhood. It might be good for you to know some of it. You've really influenced Marika, and I think she could do the same for you."

I've had an influence on Marika. How? The woman won't even speak to me.

Kate walked through the dining room holding Marika's menus. The clients seemed to be enjoying the taco casserole. Conversations and laughter filled the room, but no one talked to her.

On the ride home that afternoon, Kate instinctively drove to the restaurant. It was a crisp, sunny autumn day. Walking up the porch steps, Kate watched the lone orange leaf on a tree-branch lose its battle against the breeze and gently float to the porch.

She relished the peace and serenity of the neighborhood. There were no honking horns or people yelling from the street corners. The pumpkin and scarecrow decorations she'd placed on the front porch two weeks ago sat untouched.

There was no chaos here.

She waved to a toddler ferociously pedaling his tricycle down the sidewalk, his mom pushing a stroller behind him. Kate admired the landscaping. The work outside the restaurant was finished; leaves raked, porch swept, shutters hung. The porch swing, which her dad must have hung last week, swayed with the wind. Sitting down, her feet gently pushed the swing back and forth as visions of rebuilding and reopening the restaurant danced through her mind.

When she agreed to the one-month trial period, in her heart of hearts she never imagined she'd be there longer than a month. She knew the fire was an accident, and she'd be getting the insurance money. But until that money was released, she was broke.

Taking the job at M&M was allowing her to save face. She would market the job as a way for her to be altruistic; helping the less-fortunate while she waited to rebuild. The truth was the job at M&M was saving her from asking her family for more help. The small salary was just enough to keep her head above water while she waited for the insurance money. But now, Nick wanted more of a commitment. `Teaching a cooking class? Did she want to get that involved with those people?* True, it would give her something to do, and she would definitely get some good press that way, but would she be giving up on the restaurant? Her feet moved the swing faster and faster.

Teaching the class might be fun. She'd always loved to cook. Closing her eyes, she remembered standing on the kitchen chair helping her mom make chocolate chip cookies, dumping the sugar and cracking the eggs into the Pyrex mixing bowl. As a Girl Scout, the very first badge she earned was the cooking badge. She had made spaghetti and meatballs for her family meal. In high school, the omelet she cooked in the 'Contemporary Living' class at Mount Notre Dame had won first prize. Cooking was second nature to her—should she share her knowledge and passion with other people?

She leapt from the swing. Nick didn't expect an answer right away. She'd think about it. Nick was certain the cooking class would fill up, but he also thought Marika was benefiting from working with her. She was teaching Marika a few things. What a joke! That woman disappeared as soon as lunch started. She wasn't willing to learn a damn thing.

21

NICK

Nick always thought the kitchen had a different energy on the day of the staff meeting. Dallas had an extra bounce in his ever-energetic step, and the whole crew looked forward to kicking back once business was finished, for a night of fun. As soon as lunch closed, Dallas and Tucker rushed the clients out the door to hurriedly clean the dining room. After scrubbing the floors, they arranged three square tables in a row to make one long, boardroom-sized table. Jenny set a veggie tray and some chips on the buffet counter. Surveying the snacks, Nick asked, "Where are Marika's chocolate chip cookies?"

"She didn't make them," Jenny whispered.

He looked over at Marika sitting across from Kate at the table. They weren't speaking.

"Oh, I guess she's still mad at me," Nick grabbed some chips and a Coke. Taking the seat next to Marika at the table, he said, "I was looking forward to one of your chocolate chip cookies."

"Well," Marika said not looking up from the doodle she was drawing on the agenda. "We don't always get what we want."

Touche.

Nick nodded. "Hi, everyone, let's get started. Jenny, can you lock the front door?"

Dallas carried a plate of cheese and crackers in one hand and a soda in the other. He walked to one end of the table. Tucker, holding a cup of coffee, sat at the opposite end. Jenny took the seat next to Kate.

"Dear Lord," Nick said. "We thank you for the gift of your guidance during this past month. We are grateful for the numerous volunteers you have sent our way to help in your mission of feeding the hungry. Please bless our patrons and help us to show your loving care to the people who most need your blessings. In your name we pray. *Our Father...*" The voices of the staff joined his prayer.

"Before we begin, I have a big announcement," Nick had the group's attention. "Katie has agreed to continue as our cook for the near future."

The whole table clapped except for Marika.

"Katie, we thank you. The kitchen is really benefiting from your expertise. Now, let's get down to business." Nick ran the staff meeting as if he was in the boardroom of a multi-million-dollar company. The agenda was strict, allowing only a short time for discussions after each item.

"Looking at the month, our numbers were good. We served 8,400 people." Nick read from the attachment.

"*Really?*" Kate gaped.

"The actual number of meals was probably well over ten thousand, but for accounting purposes, we only count the first time a person goes through the line," Nick answered.

"I can't believe it. During the busiest month at my restaurant, I only served nine hundred," Kate said.

"We're down from last month, aren't we?" Marika tapped her pencil on the edge of the table.

"We are," Nick nodded. "With school starting, we've had fewer kids, but we're up from last year. I'm sure that's because the new cook's food is so good." He winked at Kate, watching her face redden. "Tucker how are the donations going?"

"As expected, donations are down for this month," he rubbed the scruff of his beard. "The holiday canned-food drives will begin in the next few weeks, so I think we'll get back on track." Clearing his throat, he smiled at Kate. "Our new cook has a very long wish list, and I'm working to make certain all her dreams come true. We've been pretty lucky so far, but I'd love to find a corporate chicken donor. Anyone have any ideas?"

Kate gave Tucker a thumbs up. Marika glared at the table.

"I'm sure you've tried the normal avenues?" Nick asked.

"Yep," Tucker nodded, "I think we may have to think bigger."

"Okay," Nick made a note on his page. "Jenny you're up."

"Two hundred people donated over six hundred hours this month. Requests for holiday service hours have already begun, but we really need to increase the pool of permanent volunteers." Jenny put the clipboard down and ran her fingers through her hair. "Any chance we can run some ads or maybe start a marketing campaign to recruit regular helpers?"

A loud bang sounded on the front door. Dallas hopped from his chair and ran to see who it was. "It's Libby," he said unlocking the deadbolt.

"What took you so long?" the woman asked.

Dressed in tight, black-ripped jeans, a "Resist" T-shirt and four-inch platform heels, the woman appeared to be in her late forties. The yellow and white beads in her cornrows clicked against the huge sunglasses hiding her face. She dropped an overflowing tote bag onto the chair next to Kate grabbed an agenda and wobbled over to the snack table.

"What'd I miss?" The woman asked over her shoulder. "You know I don't have keys. Why did you lock the front door?"

"The meeting started at three," Nick checked his watch. "It's three-thirty. We're almost ready for your report." Shrugging, the woman continued to stack cheese, crackers, and vegetables on the dish.

"This is Libby Jackson," Nick told a confused looking Katie. "She's the social worker assigned to M&M. Although she works for the state, she uses an office at M&M to be close to the clients. Libby, this is Katie O'Leary. She's the new cook."

A current of tension filled the room at Libby's arrival. The easy flow of conversation and relaxed camaraderie stopped. Everyone seemed enthralled by the agenda, their eyes stared at the page. Nick tried to hide his frustration with Libby, but her attitude and work ethic infuriated him. Her mere presence changed the tenor of the meeting. Taking a deep breath, Nick continued, "Sorry for the interruption. Jenny, would you please finish your report?"

"Sure," Jenny rested her hands on the table. "The bottom line is we need more permanent volunteers. I need people who can make a weekly or monthly commitment."

"What about putting requests in the church bulletins?" Tucker said.

"I did that," Jenny said. "The local universities and the *Business Courier* too, but our best recruitment tool is still word of mouth…so spread the word." She leaned back in her seat, "I'm done."

"Okay, Libby, you're up." Nick sighed.

Libby licked veggie dip from her finger and reached into her overflowing briefcase, pulling out a stack of manila file folders. "Well," Libby opened the top folder, "I was able to find housing for the Rodriguez family. They can move in next week."

"The Manny Rodriguez family?" Nick interrupted.

"Uh huh," Libby bit into a carrot.

"I helped them move into a new apartment last week," Nick said.

"You did?" Libby slapped the folder onto the table. "I wish you would tell me these things, Nick. I spent days trying to find them a suitable place."

"It's been three weeks since they were evicted from their apartment." Nick threw his pen on the table. "Where did you think they've been living?"

"I can't snap my fingers and get housing." Libby clipped. "I have to follow proper procedures." She opened another folder and shook her head, "That's the problem with these people, everyone wants things right away."

"Having a place to live is important," Nick's laugh was mocking. "Especially when you have four little kids counting on you. I don't think Manny cared about following the proper procedures. Can you give the housing to someone else?"

"That's not how it works, and you know it." Libby stuffed the file in her briefcase. "I've put up a sign for the job training seminars. We'll see if anyone bothers to come to those. Other than that, you're up to date." She bit into a cracker.

"Great," Nick sighed, clearly frustrated by Libby's lack of progress.

"Dallas and Marika, can you give the kitchen update? Katie, you can give the report next month."

"The kitchen equipment is running good," Dallas said. "The warming oven is back in operation and the sink is fixed. We're testing the ventilation system next week to make sure we're ready for winter. The kitchen's been running real smooth since Katie came on board." He smiled at Katie. "Marika, it's your turn."

"The changes in the kitchen haven't gone too bad and some of the clients seem to like the new food." Marika talked to the table.

"Sounds good then." Nick hid a smile watching Kate roll her eyes during Marika's synopsis. "Anything else we need to review?"

He looked around the table. "Okay, let's head to City View, I've got the first round."

22

NICK

Nick walked into City View first. The place was a dive. The entire restaurant-bar consisted of two rooms. The front part had a pool table, a few bar stools grouped in a back corner and a vintage pinball machine against the opposite wall. The pinball machine probably hadn't been vintage when the bar opened, but over the years had become retro. The wooden floors were sticky in some places and creaked in others. Five bar stools lined the bar, their black leather seats worn from years of use. Behind the bar there was an electric griddle used for frying the only item on the menu: burgers. Clients were able to choose their side—potato chips or pretzels.

Off the back room was a screened-in deck. Nick held open the door for the M&M employees to go outside. "You'll see why we come here as soon as you step outside," he told a wary-looking Kate.

The view from the patio was magnificent. The twists and turns of the Ohio river ambled alongside the city's skyline. Boats floated down the river while cars flew up the hills and across the bridge. The last of the autumn leaves burst orange and red.

"What can I get everyone to drink?" Nick asked.

"I'll have a gin and tonic," Jenny said, "I don't know why, but they're the best in the city."

"I'll have a Miller," Dallas said.

"Me too," Marika nodded.

"Coke for me," Tucker added.

"I guess I'll try a gin and tonic with two limes, please," Kate said, "Do you want some help?"

"That'd be great. They don't have waiting staff here." Nick walked back inside with Kate to place the order.

After ordering the drinks, Kate leaned against the bar. "Libby didn't come?"

"Nope," Nick took a swig of beer from the opened bottle.

"Why not?" Kate squeezed two limes into a red solo cup. The bar really was a hole-in-the wall.

"She's not an employee, and she's lousy at her job." Nick said.

"Wow, how do you really feel?" Kate looked stunned by his outburst.

"I think the bureaucracy of the government allows people to remain employed when they should have been fired years ago. Our government rewards incompetence." He grabbed the drinks, and they set off back outside.

Pushing open the deck door, Nick trilled, "Oh, what a beautiful evening, Oh, what a beautiful day," Changing the lyrics to the iconic song from *Oklahoma.*

"Man, that's beautiful," Tucker took his Coke, "Who knew you had such a pretty voice."

"Well, thanks," Nick bowed, "I was a huge star in my high school's performances. In Mass today, it came to me: theater. We should start a theater group. We have to try and reach the kids who aren't interested in sports. We need to think outside of the box. What does everyone think?"

"I think . . . who's going to organize that?" Tucker shook his head.

"Nick, we can only do so much."

"I know." Relaxed in the plastic patio chair, Nick pealed the label from the beer bottle. "We've got to connect with more people; find things they're interested in or maybe something they should know."

"Theater is a good idea," Jenny said. "My daughters love being in the school plays, but we run into the same problem... volunteers. Maybe we could partner with a high school or some other theater program? There's no need to reinvent the wheel if we can partner with an established program."

"Good idea. Would your daughter's school be interested?"

"I can ask," Jenny shrugged.

Nick tapped his bottle to Jenny's plastic cup. "Thanks. Does anyone have other ideas? Maybe something you're already doing that you could get a few people involved in?" Nick looked around the group."I mean really think outside of the box. Not just for kids, but young adults or the senior citizens too."

"I could use some help fixing things around the kitchen," Dallas said. "What if I had some type of handyman class or mentor program. Showing how to do the little things like painting, changing an electrical outlet, minor plumbing? A kinda "shop" class."

"That's a great idea," Nick said, "It wouldn't take a lot of money, and I bet we could get a hardware company to be a sponsor. Maybe have a fix-it day? Tucker and I could help, too. Teach people a skill that they could have learned from their dad or grandpa."

"I think we should do something with the GED kids." Marika leaned forward in her chair. "After seeing the opportunities Jamal has, I think it's important to expand their horizons. They need to see that they can go to college or at least aspire to get a good job."

"I love that!" Nick smiled. "Would you still want to be involved with the mom's club?"

"I can do both." Marika drank her beer.

"I know it's sports related, but I can work with my gym to start a boxing club or maybe taekwondo?" Tucker said.

"You guys are the best," Nick raised his glass in a toast. "Any other ideas?" He stared at Kate, while she looked at the river. "Well, let's keep thinking. Anyone got neighborhood news?"

Nick stood at the bar paying the bill when Marika approached. "Do you think you could give me a ride home?"

"Aren't you going with Tucker?" Nick said.

"Oh, I don't want to bother him." Marika said.

"Sure, my truck's out front." Opening the door, Nick said, "It's a beautiful evening, isn't it?

"It is. Look at all those stars." Marika peered at the sky through the window.

He put the key into the ignition. Music blared over the radio. He hit the off button.

"You listen to rap?" Marika said.

"I like to know what the kids are listening to." He smiled, "Your idea for the GED class was good. You don't think it will be too much with the Mother's Group too?"

"Thanks, It's fine." Marika looked down at her hands. "The Mother's Group practically runs itself. I just pop in during lunch, and with Jamal starting his internship I'll have lots of time after the kitchen closes."

"What about Tucker?" Nick asked, pulling the truck up to her home.

"Tucker...well." Her voice cracked. "He doesn't think we should go out anymore. So, I don't need to worry about him." *Click,* the seatbelt released. "Thanks for the ride."

"Marika, are you alright?" He held her arm to keep her from opening the door.

"I'm fine," she said, but her face looked sad.

"Do you want to talk about it?"

Marika shook her head.

"I hate to see you so unhappy. Look, I know you're upset about Katie, but I really do think you two can work together. I thought the menus you made were great, and Katie is going to put them on the calendar. I'm not sure what's going on between you and Tucker, but I do know you both love each other." He squeezed her hand.

"It's fine," she pulled her hand away and stepped out of the car. "I'll see you Monday."

"Okay, have a good weekend." Nick waved watching her walk up the steps.

Driving off, Nick wondered what happened between Marika and Tucker. He knew neither of them would tell him what was wrong, and he supposed it wasn't really his business anyway.

The brainstorming session at City View had gone great. He was a little surprised Katie didn't commit to the cooking class, but everyone else seemed enthusiastic about finding new activities.

For the first time in a while, he had hope.

The new strategy was taking shape, and the staff were working on making fresh connections with the community.

Nick parked in front of Holy Family Church and went in to pray.

23

MARIKA

Marika unlocked the three deadbolts before entering her house. After hanging up her coat, she walked through the living room and turned on the lamp beside the couch. Running her fingers along the rose-flowered upholstery, she remembered Tucker and Jamal's groans at having to move such a feminine piece of furniture into the house.

"I don't think I'll even be able to sit on it," Tucker had said. "It's way too girly for me."

"We'll probably start wearing perfume if we do." Twelve-year-old Jamal had doubled over with laughter.

"No way," Tucker grunted lifting his end of the couch up the stairs. "We're way too macho for that. We like to smell like men."

"I bet you two won't get off that couch once you set it down." Marika said carrying the cushions behind them.

Positioned in the small living room, all three of them had sat on the couch. "It's comfy," Tucker said reaching behind Jamal to touch Marika's shoulder.

"I love it," Marika snuggled into the soft cushion and squeezed Tucker's hand, "Thanks for helping me get it home."

"If I close my eyes, I can pretend it's a different color, then it's not so bad," Jamal giggled.

How she wished she could go back to that time when it was so easy between the three of them. She'd give almost anything to have Tucker and Jamal sitting here, to be a family.

She walked into the kitchen and opened a can of soup. The night loomed ahead. Jamal was at a school retreat, a boot camp to prepare the students for their new work environments.

And Tucker, where was he?

Usually after a staff meeting, they would sneak off to dinner, try a new restaurant, have a real date just the two of them. They'd make sure Jamal could stay with Benji's family.

He hadn't even asked if she needed a ride home. It was over. He wasn't going to change his mind.

Putting one placemat and napkin on the table, she ladled the soup into a bowl and sat down.

Nick said her menus were good, and that he shared them with Kate.

She was already a good cook; she didn't have anything to learn from that gourmet chef. M&M was in her blood: she knew the community, she lived in the neighborhood, she was one of *them*. As a former client, she had a unique perspective; she knew what it was like to wait in line for food, and she knew the workings of the kitchen and its resources. She was living proof M&M, and its programs were changing the community. The only thing that chef knew was how to make a good lobster risotto.

Placing the rinsed bowl in the dishwasher, Marika turned off the kitchen light and headed towards the bathroom. She'd treat herself to a nice luxurious bath.

She smiled when she passed Jamal's room. The cluttered space was filled with sports equipment, schoolbooks, and a poster of Steph Curry. She'd come a long way since Ginger had forced her to get her act together. She'd become the mom Jamal deserved.

After Jamal was born, Marika still lived with her mother, but Jamal's care was entirely hers. Her days were spent feeding, diapering and pacing the small apartment with her colicky baby. When school started in the fall, Marika was too exhausted to attend. She dropped out.

The life of a high school dropout had an easy rhythm. To avoid arguments with her mom, Marika would spend her days at the kitchen and her evenings on the streets. It had been a cold November day when Ginger had issued her the ultimatum.

In the M&M dining room, Marika sat with the other dropouts. "Okay, everyone, it's time to call it a day," Ginger announced. "Kid's Cafe starts in fifteen minutes. If you're not in school, you need to leave."

A collective groan rose from the table as the occupants looked at the rain pouring outside. "Marika," Ginger put her hand on Jamal's stroller. "Will you come to my office before you leave? I want to talk to you."

"Sure, what about?" Marika asked.

"I want to hold that beautiful baby and just see how things are going. I'll meet you there in a few minutes."

In Ginger's office, Marika grabbed a Hershey Kiss from the candy dish before sitting down swiveling the stroller next to the chair. Shutting the door, Ginger picked up Jamal and began swaying. "You are such a good baby," she spoke in a high, singsong voice to the wide-awake child. "You're such a handsome boy and getting so big."

Turning to Marika she said, "I can't believe how much he's grown. How much does he weigh?"

"I'm not sure," Marika touched his hand. "We go to the clinic next week for his five-month check-up. I bet he's over thirteen pounds."

"Are you reading that book I gave you about child development? Is he meeting his milestones?"

"I guess," Marika unwrapped a second piece of chocolate. "I'm kinda busy."

Ginger watched Marika pop the candy in her mouth. "It was just about this time last year that you found out you were pregnant."

"Yep," Marika sucked on the chocolate.

"Do you remember when I told you I would help you?" Ginger continued rocking Jamal, but her eyes were on Marika.

"Uh-huh," Marika nodded.

"Well, now I have to help this little guy," Ginger hugged the baby against her chest. "This little boy deserves a wonderful life and you're not giving him one."

"I'm a good mom," Marika jumped out of the chair and reached for Jamal.

Ginger stepped back cradling the baby. "I know you love Jamal, but what kind of life is he going to have if all his mom does is hang around a soup kitchen? You've got to give this beautiful baby a future. He's relying on you to get your act together."

Marika's eyes filled with tears. "I can't go back to school. The daycare was awful. The babies were crying, and no one was holding them. I couldn't leave him there." Her voice cracked.

"Then let's find a different way for you to get your degree." Ginger laid the sleeping baby in the stroller and handed Marika a tissue. "I want you to join the Mother's Group. Those women can help you become the mom I know you want to be."

"But they're old," Marika whispered. "I don't have anything in common with them."

"They're not all old, and you're a mom too!"

"None of my friends have their GED."

"Which is why they spend their days here. You're too smart for that, and I love you too much to let it happen." Ginger stood up. "Here's the deal. If you don't at least try the Mother's Group for one month and start working on your GED, you can't hang out here anymore."

"That's not fair," Marika stomped her foot.

"Wait," Ginger held up her hand to stop Marika's complaint. "You can eat here, but once you're finished eating you have to leave. If you take the GED classes, Mother's Group and some of the other courses we offer, you can stay practically all day." Ginger opened the office door. "It's up to you. The Mother's Group meets on Wednesdays. Let me know what you decide."

Spinning the stroller around, Marika marched out the door.

The following week, Marika nervously peaked into the room where the Mother's Group was meeting. The women were sitting on the floor, their children on their laps or sitting next to them. In unison, the women made hand motions as they sang, "The itsy-bitsy spider went up the waterspout."

I don't want to go in there.

Marika remembered thinking as she slowly backed the stroller down the hall before bumping into another stroller.

"I'm sorry, I'm always running late. You're going in, aren't you?" The young woman pushed the stroller with one hand the other holding the hand of a little girl.

"I don't think so," Marika looked back into the room. "I think Jamal is too young."

"Well, we're really here to meet the other moms. C'mon, I'll introduce you to everyone. I'm Briana, this is my little girl Kayla and my baby Benji. He's six months old. How old is your baby?"

"He's five months," Marika was forced to move forward by Briana.

"His name's Jamal. I'm Marika."

"Oh, I bet the boys will go to school together!"

Once in the room, Kayla ran to the toy closet to grab a doll. Briana picked up Benji. "Just leave the stroller there, you and Jamal can sit by me." Scooping Jamal from his seat, Marika joined the women sitting in the circle.

The Mother's Group became Marika's lifeline. The women supported each other in ways she could never imagine. A question about a colicky baby or late-night fever? Marika phoned one of her friends from the group. Need help watching Jamal so she could study for a test? A fellow mom would volunteer. When she passed her GED test, the women threw her a graduation party and encouraged her to attend community college. On Jamal's first day of preschool, a teary-eyed Marika celebrated with Briana at the cafe down the street.

Marika sighed; she had to stop reliving the past. Walking into the bathroom she turned on the faucet and added a bath bomb to the water, a gift from Tucker. She watched the bubbles form. Her mind recalling her past.

It was Ginger who had suggested she study culinary arts. "Wouldn't it be great if we could eventually work together here?" Ginger had asked, paging through the community college catalog.

"It would," Marika agreed. She had registered for the culinary arts program that week.

A few years later, Ginger hired her to be the M&M assistant cook. The moment Ginger handed Marika the keys to M&M Kitchen was so significant. The little girl, who had dropped her plate of chili spaghetti all those years ago, would now cook the food she used to eat. At Ginger's retirement party, Marika hugged her friend and whispered, "Thank you. You changed my life."

Sighing, Marika slid into the warm peony scented water. Nick hiring Kate had been like tossing flour on a fire: he'd doused her dream. Her cooking skills were excellent, and she deserved to be the M&M Head Cook. She was going to make Ginger proud of her, and no gourmet chef was going to get in her way.

24

KATE

A silver lining to the restaurant's fire was that Kate suddenly found her weekends free. For the first time in over a decade, she could actually eat dinner out. Driving to the restaurant to meet her family, Kate hoped she wouldn't run into Phillipe, the chef and owner of the restaurant where they were dining. He and Kate had attended cooking school together and Kate didn't want to have to talk about her current working situation with him. The man was a pretentious ass.

Kate enjoyed telling people she knew *Philippe* as *Phil,* the guy who couldn't get his hollandaise right. Sometime after graduation, Phil had decided it would be more lucrative for him to embrace his family's heritage and become fully French. Hence, the name change.

Phil's family had been in the restaurant business for generations. He'd opened his first venture soon after graduation with the financial backing of their numerous business connections. While Kate was still struggling to pull together financing for Kate's on Vine, Phillipe and his family were on project number two.

In Kate's opinion, Phil's restaurants were mediocre, but his family's notoriety made each establishment a hotspot for a while. After the fire, Phil had offered Kate a job, but there was no way she was going to be indebted to that bombastic oaf.

Walking into the restaurant, Kate tried to temper her envy. The space was spectacular. A mirrored bar on the right wall gave way to a wall of windows which opened onto a patio overlooking the river. She saw her family already seated at a table. "Hi," they greeted her.

"It's really pretty, isn't it?" Kate asked pulling out her chair.

"It is," her mom, Lynne, answered. "We ordered you a sauvignon blanc, and you aren't going to believe who our server is."

"Who?" Kate looked around.

"Oh my God," a voice came from behind her.

Turning, Kate saw the waitress carrying a tray of drinks rushing towards her. "Ella?" she asked.

Placing the tray on the table, the server hugged Kate. "It's so good to see you, how are you?" Ella said.

"I'm good," Kate grasped the back of the chair to support herself. Ella had been one of her best waitresses. "I thought you were working at the cafe?"

"I was," Ella covered her mouth with her hand to speak confidentially, "But between you and me, the restaurant opening here was terrible. Phillipe was desperate to hire more professional staff, so he called everyone who had worked for you."

"He *did*?" Kate collapsed into the chair. The air sucked out of her lungs. "So, the whole gang's back together?"

"Not without you," Ella squeezed Kate's hand. "Abby and Claire stayed at the cafe, but everyone else came here. Don't worry, we're all coming back to Kate's when it reopens. Do you have a date yet?"

"Not yet," Kate lowered her face trying to hide the tears filling her eyes. "I'm hoping the insurance money comes through soon."

"Me too," Ella smiled. "Take a look at the menu, and I'll be back in a few. I really like the Lobster Risotto," she winked at Kate. "It's your recipe."

Kate ripped the utensils out of the napkin ring. "Well, that's just great: my recipe, my employees, why didn't Phil just steal the restaurant name, too?" Her voice dripped with sarcasm.

"They have to work," Lynne patted Kate's hand trying to console her.

"I know, but I found them all jobs. Why are they working for *him*?" Kate's voice cracked.

"Because he called them, and he was willing to pay. Phillipe knows your staff was the best." Her sister tapped the table, "Don't let this get you down. You heard Ella, they'll come back when you reopen."

"I guess." Taking a deep breath, Kate studied the workers, watching their rhythm and remembering how she had synchronized the staff at Kate's on Vine to be a well-tuned symphony. Sighing, she changed the subject. "Did I tell you I went to the M&M staff meeting last night?

"No, how was that?" her dad asked.

"Well, Dallas told me he was a client of the kitchen until a few years ago. I didn't believe him." She took a sip of her wine. "He had to show me his Metropolitan Area ID Card—that's the card people get when they're homeless. It enables them to qualify for services. He said, 'Anyone can have a string of bad luck. You gotta deal with the situation and dig yourself out.' Apparently, he keeps his card to remind himself how far he's come. He's got his own apartment now, money in the bank and a full-time job. 'I've got it made,' he said. 'If you've got your health, two good legs and a pair of good hands, you can climb out of any hole you've gotten yourself into.' He was so proud."

"Wow, that's amazing. Why was he homeless?" Ellen asked.

"I don't know. I didn't want to pry," Kate shrugged. "He has three grown kids who live in the Atlanta area, but he doesn't see them very often."

"That's great he's made such a drastic change in his life." Lynne took a roll from the breadbasket.

"He's so nice. I've gotten used to his singing, which he does all the time. I just wish his cooking skills were as good as his maintenance ones."

"So, Marika's the better cook?" Ellen asked.

"Definitely, it's just a shame she's such a bitch."

"That's not very nice," Lynne pursed her lips.

"I don't care." Kate stared back at her mom. "She's a witch. She doesn't talk to me unless it's absolutely necessary, and if I implement a change, she complains about it or ignores it completely."

"I feel sorry for her," Lynne said.

"What! Why?" Kate couldn't hide her surprise at the comment. "Mom, she's mean to me."

"I don't know. You did say she wanted the cook's job. I'm sure she was disappointed Nick hired you." Lynne patted Kate's arm. "I just wish that insurance money would come through."

"Whatever, she's a pain." Kate broke open a roll. "I did find out she grew up in the neighborhood. She ate at M&M when she was a little girl."

"Really?" Ellen said. "I guess that's two success stories. Any other interesting gossip?"

"Well," Kate leaned into the table. "Jenny told me Tucker and Marika had been dating for over three years, but they recently broke up. No one knows why, but I think it's because Tucker realized Marika was such a crab."

"That's interesting. Did you find out if Nick was dating anyone?" Ellen said.

"No, I didn't want to be obvious," Kate sighed. "He's so dedicated to M&M and the clients. I swear he thinks about the place twenty-four-seven. He asked me to teach a cooking class once a week, but I don't know."

"A cooking class for who?" Pete said.

"The clients," Kate pressed her hands on the table and stared at her family. "The reality is the restaurant is not going to be open by the end of the year. Nick wants each staff member to connect with the community in a new way, and a cooking class would make the most sense for me. I could give back while I wait to reopen."

"I think you'd be a wonderful cooking teacher, and it's just until the insurance money arrives." Lynne said.

"Dad, I think we should probably get the building winterized." Kate sighed.

"Kate?" a man walked up to their table. "I heard you were here?"

"Phil," Kate stood to shake his hand. "How are you?" *Just her luck, Phil would be hobnobbing here tonight.*

"I'm good," he splayed his arms wide. "What do you think about the place?"

"It's beautiful. The menu looks familiar," Kate hoped her smile at least looked sincere.

"What's this I hear about you working at a soup kitchen?" Phil's grin resembled the Cheshire cat.

"I am," Kate nodded. "Just trying to give back to the community. M&M needed help, and I have the time since I'm still waiting on the insurance money."

"That's so nice of you. We send all our leftovers there," Phil patted Kate's shoulder. "Well, I've got to go check the kitchen. Enjoy your dinner. *Adieu.*"

"Bye," Kate plopped back into her seat. "Let's eat and get the hell out of here."

Walking to work on Monday with Nick, she said, "I've decided to teach the cooking class."

"That's great news," Nick smiled opening the door. "I've got a sponsor. It would be great if you could teach not only cooking, but also how to make nutritious, delicious and inexpensive meals. Most of the students are going to be living on food stamps, which averages out to about two dollars per meal per person."

"Wait a minute," Kate stopped mid-stride. "You want me to cook a full meal for *two dollars*?"

"I know," Nick laughed. "It's crazy. I've got a company to underwrite the class for six weeks. So, I think you could probably spend about ten dollars on each meal assuming it will feed a family of four. That's really two-dollars-fifty a person."

"Gee, thanks." Kate grimaced.

"I can put the flyers up this week in Kid's Cafe, Mother's Group and on the kitchen bulletin board. I think we'll be turning away people! Who wouldn't want to learn from a renowned gourmet chef?"

"Hopefully someone will." Kate sounded dejected.

"What?" Nick's gaze was quizzical.

"It's just," Kate hesitated, "Well, I know you wanted me to be a mentor to Dallas and Marika…I'm just not sure how well that's working out."

"Hmm, why not?" Nick leaned against the wall.

"Well, to be completely honest, Marika thinks she knows everything. She likes things the way they were, and she disappears every day once lunch starts. Dallas, he's great at execution and he'll do whatever needs to be done, but I don't think he really has any interest in being the head chef."

"I agree about Dallas. He's much more of a doer than a manager, but I'd really like you to keep trying with Marika. I want her to be the new head cook when you leave. I'm counting on you to get her ready for the job. Did you ask her where she disappears too each day?"

"No, I didn't ask, a good cook shouldn't leave the kitchen. Maybe that's the first thing she needs to learn." Kate said.

"Maybe you should try talking to her and learning from each other. Marika's experience is valuable too." With a smile and a two-finger salute, Nick walked to his office.

25

MARIKA

Marika had spent the weekend preparing Jamal for his new job. She washed and ironed his shirts, giving the pants a crease so sharp she was afraid of getting a cut. She had completed the paperwork necessary for Jamal to participate in the intern program: permission slips, medical forms, tax forms, emergency contact information. She'd also encouraged him to take a shoe-shining lesson from Tucker.

By Monday, Jamal was ready. She just wasn't sure she was.

Her son was growing up and soon he'd be leaving her for college. She would be alone. A feeling of melancholy overwhelmed her as she tossed the salad.

"So, today's the big day?" Dan, the volunteer, stood next to her at the prep table tying his apron.

"It is," Marika smiled. "I was just thinking about how fast the time has gone. I can remember his first day of kindergarten and now he's starting a job. Thanks again for helping him to get the internship."

Dan brushed aside her thanks. "Jamal is going to do great."

"I hope so. I'm going to cook his favorite meal tonight, so he'll sit down and tell me all about it." Marika placed the salad in the buffet station.

"I'm sure he's going to have lots of things to report. I spoke with

Melissa last week. She has plenty of work just waiting for him."

"Marika," Kate yelled looking over her shoulder. "Could you get the mushrooms? I forgot them and I'm in the middle of making the sauce."

Marika rolled her eyes. "Thanks again, Dan, I've got to go. Her majesty has beckoned."

Why couldn't that woman get her own damn mushrooms. She was the chef. Why didn't she make sure she had everything before she started making the sauce?

She didn't want to deal with Kate today, she was too busy worrying about Jamal.

Did he remember his bus pass? Were those forms in his book bag? Would he remember to turn them in? Should I text him a reminder?

Focused on being annoyed with Kate and fretting about Jamal, Marika forgot to avoid Tucker. He was in the pantry.

"Can I help you find something?" Tucker pushed the baseball cap back on his head.

"Uh, oh, hi," she could feel her face growing warm. "The cook needs mushrooms for her sauce. She didn't get the ingredients she needed before starting."

Tucker walked down the middle aisle nodding.

"Thanks for helping Jamal with his shoes," Marika followed him down the rows of canned goods. "They shined up great."

"Was he nervous this morning?" Tucker asked.

"A little bit," she put her hand on the shelf and looked at the floor. "He said you called to wish him luck." She looked at Tucker. "Thank you, I know that made him happy."

"I love Jamal." Tucker put his hands in his pocket, "And his mom... I just wish she loved me back."

"Tucker," Marika groaned. "Of course, I love you."

He rocked back on his feet and shook his head. "I get the distinct feeling you've been avoiding me these last few weeks."

Marika's shoulders slumped, and she leaned against the shelf. "You're the one who said you didn't want to go out anymore. I'm trying to respect your wishes."

Tucker placed his hands on her shoulders and bent his face down to hers, their foreheads touching. "I said I was tired of dating. I wanted to get married. I love you."

Marika stepped closer placing her hands around his waist. He smelled so good, clean, safe, steady. She buried her head in his shoulder, "Why can't we just date?"

"Because I want more," Tucker snapped pushing her away. "Why is marrying me such a bad thing?"

"It's not," Marika said, "I'm just not ready."

"Do you think you'll ever be ready? I've waited three years." Tucker opened his arms as he asked the question.

"I don't know," Her voice was strained. "I know I love you, and I miss you."

"Just not enough to marry me," Tucker grabbed a case off the shelf. "Here are the mushrooms."

"Thanks," Marika took the case.

Almost to the kitchen, she stopped and walked back into the stockroom. "Tucker?"

He stopped sweeping the floor to look at her.

"I'm really sorry," she whispered. "I'm making Jamal's favorite dinner tonight to celebrate his first day of work. Will you please come?"

"Ham, mac and cheese?" Tucker asked.

Marika nodded.

"I'll be there." He returned to sweeping.

Jamal's favorite dinner was the ultimate comfort food, and one a single mom could afford to make almost every week. Traditional macaroni and cheese with pieces of ham and broccoli added to the casserole. For dessert, brownie sundaes with Graeter's toffee chip ice-cream. Marika first looked out the window at five-thirty.

"I thought his bus didn't get here until five-forty-five?" Tucker said, sitting on the floral couch, the television remote in his hand.

"It doesn't. I thought maybe it would be early," Marika said smiling at him over her shoulder.

It's so nice to see him on the sofa again. I wish I could snuggle next to him.

"Well, you're anxious. The bus isn't." Tucker pretended to watch the TV, using the remote to channel surf through the news, history channel and ESPN. "You're making me nervous. Sit down and watch the—"

"There he is," she clapped her hands together and pointed out the window.

Tucker leapt up to move the curtain out of the way and get a better look. "He looks happy," he said, laying a hand on her back.

Relishing the warmth of his touch, Marika stared at her son out the window. "Why is he stopping to talk to Benji and Jayden?" she whined. "Doesn't he know how anxious I am? Jayden is nothing but trouble. I can't believe Briana is letting Benji hang out with him."

"He probably just wants to tell the guys about his day at the office," Tucker laughed. "Let's play it cool. Come on, sit down and act like we're watching TV." He pulled her over to the sofa. "There's no need to make a fuss."

"You're right," Marika took a seat and touched Tucker's knee. "Thanks for being here." She longed to cuddle next to him and pretend to be enthralled with the weather forecast, but she'd lost that luxury. Jamal's key jiggled in the lock. Marika started to stand, but Tucker gently tugged her shirt pulling her back to the settee.

"Hi," Jamal closed the door walking into the living room.

"How was it?" Marika hopped up from her seat to help him take off his backpack. "Did it go okay? How was the bus ride? Are the people nice?"

"How'd it go?" Tucker asked, shaking his hand and pulling him into a hug.

"It was good," Jamal put his keys in the dish by the front door. "I'm starving. Can we eat and I'll tell you all about it?"

"Sure, I've made your favorite." Marika walked into the kitchen. "Will someone turn off the TV?"

"Ham, mac and cheese?" Jamal asked.

"Yes, I thought you'd like that." Marika opened the oven.

"Where in the heck is the remote?" Tucker moved the pillows and cushions around the couch.

"It's probably still by the window." Laughing, Jamal pointed to the remote resting on the windowsill. "You must have left it there while you were stalking me."

"We weren't stalking, we were curious," Tucker said turning off the television.

Marika placed the casserole on the trivet and took the seat between her two boys. *It was nice to see three plates at the table again.* Holding hands, they bowed their heads to pray.

"Thank you, God, for this delicious food, and for allowing us to all eat it together," Tucker said. "Thank you, too, for the wonderful opportunity Jamal's been given. In your Son's name we pray."

"*Amen,*" Marika and Jamal said in unison.

"Okay, tell us everything, don't leave a single thing out," Marika said, placing a heaping scoop of mac and cheese on Jamal's plate.

"Okay, I got out of school and walked to the bus stop. I got on the bus. Roberta said, 'Hello.'" He took a bite of food, "Mmm, this is good…it's hot."

"Who's Roberta?" Tucker blew on the pasta before taking a bite.

"The bus driver, mom introduced me to her last week. She asked Roberta to watch me." Jamal put his fork down and stared at Tucker, "Can you believe that?"

"Oh man, that's funny," Tucker laughed wiping his mouth with his napkin. He gave Marika's knee a gentle squeeze under the table.

"Well, you make sure to tell her I said hello too." Distracted by his touch, Marika took a bite.

"So, I got off the bus and walked to my office," Jamal continued.

"Were you nervous?" Marika asked.

"A little. I was walking along, minding my own business, when I heard this guy yell. 'Hey, kid, where are you going?' You would have been proud mom. I didn't answer, I just started walking faster, but then this guy grabbed my backpack."

Marika gasped and put her hand on her chest.

"I'm telling you it scared me so bad," Jamal shook his head. "I turned around ready to drop my bag and just start running, but it was Mr. Hamilton."

"You're kidding. Dan?" Marika put her fork down, "He asked me this morning if you were starting today."

"Yeah, he told me he wanted to make sure everyone knew we were friends, so he walked with me to the office. He's real nice." Jamal said.

"That was so kind. What's the office like?" Marika said.

"Really cool," Jamal answered, taking a bite of food and talking at the same time. The reception desk has a waterfall behind it and there's a fireplace with chairs and a couch. It's real quiet, except for the jazz music playing in the background. Dan—"

"Mr. Hamilton," Marika interjected.

"He told me to call him Dan; everyone does." Jamal smiled, taking a gulp of milk before continuing the story. "He showed me his office. Man, it is *huge*. It's on the top floor and has windows overlooking the lake. It even has an outdoor patio with tables and chairs. I want to have an office like that. Can I have some more, please?" He held up his plate.

Marika dished up the food. "Would you like some more, Tucker?"

"No, I'm good thanks. It's delicious." He looked at Jamal. "So, what happened next?"

Jamal took a bite of macaroni. "Then we walked down a long hallway on the second floor of where I'm going to work." He put his fork down and slapped the table. "You aren't going to believe this, but I have my own office with a desk, a phone and a computer."

"Your own *office*?" Tucker pushed back from the table. "Man, that's cool. I was almost thirty before I had my own office."

"I know, it's so cool." Jamal fist-bumped Tucker's. "Dan told me I could decorate it however I wanted."

"Do you want a picture of me?" Tucker asked.

"Yeah, get me an eight-by-ten glossy," Jamal cracked up. "I got an ID badge too." He hopped up from the table to pull a lanyard from the front pocket of his bookbag. Showing it to Marika and Tucker, he grinned, "I scan this to get into different parts of the building."

Marika held the card and stared at her son's picture, "You look so grown up."

"Did you do any actual work today?" Tucker asked.

"Yep, it's kind of boring. I'm just inputting numbers onto a spreadsheet right now, but my boss said it would get more interesting soon."

"So, you had a good day?" Marika smiled, handing him back the badge, her fingers caressing the top of his hand.

"It was the best day of my life," Jamal said before taking another bite.

26

KATE

Dropping her raincoat and bag in her office later in the week, Kate noticed that her aloe plant needed water, and that the restaurant sign had fallen again. Straightening the sign, she made a mental note to water the plant. Tying an apron around her waist, she walked into the kitchen.

A grocery cart overflowing with frozen vegetables blocked the entrance, and a puddle of water ran across the linoleum to the drain under the buffet server. Tucker stood with his hands on his hips watching the water flow, while Dallas rolled the mop and bucket over to the cart shaking his head. Marika rested her chin on her hands bending over the prep table.

All three stared at the dripping cart perplexed and irritated.

"What's this?" Kate asked.

"The school down the street called saying their freezer was broken" Tucker answered. "They asked if we wanted their frozen vegetables. I said, yes." He picked up a limp bag and tossed it back into the cart. "This is what we got: a cart full of half-frozen vegetables. What are we supposed to do with these? The board of health won't let me refreeze them."

Kate looked at the melting bags and the rain pouring outside the window. "Why don't I make vegetable soup? It won't take any time, and on such a dreary day people might enjoy a nice warm bowl of soup?"

"I don't think that's a good idea," Marika said.

"Of course you don't," Kate crossed her arms.

"I don't know, Katie." Dallas attempted to stop the flow of water with the mop. "We've never served soup. I'm not sure we're allowed."

"Don't be silly," Kate lifted a soggy bag of peas. "We're a *soup* kitchen. Of course, we can serve soup," She started issuing directions. "Tucker, check to make sure we have bowls and spoons. Marika, slice the ham for sandwiches—there's cheese in the refrigerator, and we have plenty of bread. Once the soup is ready, we'll start an assembly line to make the sandwiches: a piece of bread, some ham, a slice of cheese— three minutes under the broiler, and voila, a ham and cheese melt served with a bowl of homemade vegetable soup. I would charge ten dollars for this meal in my restaurant. Delish!" Kate clapped her hands together.

Rolling her eyes, Marika pulled the meat slicer out from the cabinet. Dallas stepped in front of the cart. "Miss Katie, I've worked here three years, and we've never served soup. I think we should ask Nick about this. Don't you, Tucker? Marika?"

Straightening her spine, Kate coldly eyed the group, "We don't need to ask Nick. I'm the chef and we're going to serve soup and sandwiches today." She pushed the cart to the prep table water trailing its wake.

"Tucker—" Dallas pleaded.

"I don't care what we make," Tucker said shaking his head. "We need to use these vegetables *today*."

"I don't think this is a good idea." Dallas sighed, using the mop to erase the spilled water.

"Don't worry about it." Marika muttered slicing the ham. "She's not going to listen to you anyway. She knows best. Didn't you hear her? She's *the chef*."

Kate stirred the soup and took one last taste. It was delicious. Creating the soup had allowed her to be a chef and not just a cook. She'd surveyed the melting vegetables, found a few additional ingredients and spices from the stockroom and made the watery mess into a satisfying meal. Changing the ham into sandwiches had been simple; the kitchen always had a glut of bread.

Rain continued to pour as the cold and wet clients scurried into the lobby looking for a warm and dry place to shelter. The food line started forming thirty minutes before its normal time. Kate noticed a stranger at the front of the line and realized for once Ted wasn't going to be first.

"Oh my, something smells delicious," Sylvie said walking into the kitchen.

"Thank you, I made soup," Kate said.

After tying an apron over her J. Crew quilted sweatshirt and adjusting her M&M hat, Sylvie checked her pearl earrings and necklace. "What can I do?" She asked.

"Would you mind joining the assembly line?" Kate pointed to the prep table where Dallas and Marika were feverishly working to make the sandwiches. "Marika, Sylvie's going to replace you. Go ahead and make the salad."

"What's for lunch?" Dan's voice boomed as he strolled into the kitchen.

Kate was glad it was Monday. When she'd first started, Nick had said the volunteers on Monday were the best, and since working at the kitchen Kate realized he was right. The Monday group worked as a team and were completely dedicated to the kitchen and its operation. She'd come to count on their help to serve a new meal and correct any glitches that may occur during the lunch.

"Soup with ham and cheese melts," Kate said.

"Soup? I've volunteered here for years, and I've never served soup before. That's kind of funny for a soup kitchen, isn't it?" He laughed.

"I think on such a dreary day, everyone will appreciate a nice bowl of vegetable soup." Kate handed Dan a stack of plastic bowls. "We inherited a cart full of melting frozen vegetables, so I decided to shake things up."

"It's time to pray," Jenny yelled walking into the kitchen.

In the lobby, Tucker stood on a pew and raised his voice, "Ladies and gentlemen, may I have your attention. We invite all of you to join us in the dining room to pray." The clients dispersed: some walked to the dining room to form the prayer circle, some to the food line, while others continued shuffling around the lobby. Looking around the room, Kate saw Dan still in the kitchen watching the crowd. At the end of Tucker's prayer, Kate realized she'd been holding Ted's hand. "You're not first in line today?" she asked.

"I have a test this afternoon, so I stayed home to get some extra studying done. I'm hoping the prayer helps too!" Ted smiled his toothless grin.

"I'm sure it will." Kate squeezed his hand. "I think you'll like today's lunch: soup and sandwiches."

"The soup sounds delicious," Ted said. "It's hard for me to bite into a sandwich, but I might be able to cut it up."

"I should have thought of that," Kate frowned. "I'm sorry."

"It's okay. I'll manage." Picking up his wet bookbag, Ted walked to the end of the line.

"Well, have a good day. Good luck on the test," Kate said.

"Thank you. You have a good day too."

Kate slapped her leg walking back to her kitchen. She should have thought about the clients eating the sandwiches. Marika had mentioned several foods the clients couldn't chew: carrots, celery, apples, but she hadn't mentioned sandwiches. Thinking about Ted, it made sense. If you didn't have front teeth, biting into a sandwich would be almost impossible. Hopefully, people would have enough sense to take the ham off the bread or cut it with a fork.

Leaning against the refrigerator, Kate watched the lunch line. Dan ladled the soup into a bowl and carefully handed the dish to the client. A second volunteer placed the toasted sandwich on a plate with the salad. Sylvie then offered the client their choice of dessert.

"Soup," one of the clients said, "I *love* vegetable soup."

Kate was filled with pride. She had given the clients a great meal.

"I'm going to get started on tomorrow's lunch," Kate said to Dallas. "Where did Marika go?"

"I think she's with the Mother's Group or the GED class." Dallas opened the oven. "I've got to keep watching these sandwiches. Do you think you could get the meatloaves?" He pulled out a tray of sandwiches and carried them to the buffet station. "I can make the meatballs while I'm watching these."

"Sure, where is the Mother's Group? Marika should be helping you."

"Mom's meet in the back classroom. I've got this if you'll get the meatloaves."

Kate washed her hands.

Marika should be helping Dallas. I am so tired of her skipping out of the kitchen all the time. I'm going to get her.

She walked through the dining room on her way to find Marika. The tables were full and clients carrying trays with their meals walked around the room searching for seats.

Tucker jumped onto one of the pews aligning the wall. "Ladies and gentlemen," he shouted, hands cupping his mouth like a megaphone. "We are very busy today. Lots of people want to get out of the cold and the rain. We need everyone to put their personal belongings on the floor so that people with trays can use the chairs. Thank you for your cooperation." Tucker jumped down as Kate walked by him.

"I've never seen it this busy before," Kate said.

"Yeah," Tucker wiped his brow with his handkerchief. "It's the rain and the word on the street that your soup is delicious." Squeezing her shoulder, he rushed to help a man with his tray.

On her way to the classrooms, Kate passed Ted still waiting. "Wow, you're still in line?" Kate said.

"Man, I know. I'm starving." Ted looked at the clock. "I'm going to have to eat and run or I'm going to miss my bus. I can't be late for my exam."

"I guess it pays to get here early."

Kate pushed through the door and bumped into Marika. "Oh, I was looking for you," Kate said. "You're needed in the kitchen. Dallas can't be expected to handle the sandwiches and work on tomorrow's lunch by himself. Whatever you're doing can wait until later."

"No, it can't." Marika's eyes flared. She hip-checked the door before barging through.

"She's such a *bitch*," Kate muttered.

Pushing the cart filled with meatloaves into the kitchen, Kate heard shouting in the dining room and went to see what was happening. She saw Tucker rush towards the yelling from the lobby, and Dallas run from the kitchen to the commotion. All eyes were on the table where two groups glared at each other.

Tucker approached, his palms out trying to calm the situation. "Hey, guys, what's the problem?" Tucker asked.

Pointing to a couple sitting at a table, the standing man said, "These assholes took our seats. We saved them so we could get some food. They just shoved our stuff aside and sat down."

The seated man pointed with his fork, a piece of lettuce dangling from the tines. "Look, man, you can't save seats. People got to be able to sit down when they got their food." His girlfriend nodded, blowing on a spoonful of hot soup.

"Be cool, buddy," Tucker told the man standing. "We're real crowded today. Are these your things? He pointed to the soggy bags strewn across the floor. I'll help you move them." The man holding the tray nodded. Tucker grabbed the bags.

"Over here," Dallas beckoned after wiping a clean table. The man followed Tucker.

The standing woman picked up her soup bowl and dumped it on the sitting woman's head. "Your man should learn some manners," she said. The seated woman, hot broth running down her face, a carrot stuck on the side of her cheek, jumped up, toppling her chair to the floor.

"You fucking bitch," she screamed, grabbing her own soup bowl and tossing it into the woman's face.

The dining room erupted. Trays and chairs were thrown across the room. The women threw punches, pulled hair, and one tried to bite the other. The men tackled each other, shoving everything out of their way.

Soup, sandwiches and salad were tossed everywhere. The diners either ran for the front door or joined the melee.

Dallas and Tucker struggled to separate the men and women. Racing into the ruckus, Nick yelled for everyone to settle down, while Jenny shepherded the volunteers into the safety of the stockroom. Marika rushed to lock the kitchen door.

A paralyzed Kate watched from the kitchen. What should she do? Help in the kitchen or hide with the volunteers?

Within minutes, the police arrived, and the crowd quieted. With the police, Nick and Tucker escorted the four troublemakers out of the building. After a brief discussion, a wet and angry Nick returned to the lobby. "Lunch is over, ladies and gentlemen. Due to the unruly situation, we'll need everyone to exit the building."

The groans of the clients echoed in the abnormal quiet. "This is bullshit, Nick!" a man yelled. "I've been in line for almost thirty minutes."

En masse, they gathered their belongings and headed out into the rain.

"Can we stay in the foyer?" A woman with three children asked, "It's pouring outside."

"I'm sorry, no. It's the policy of M&M to close anytime there is a fight. It's not negotiable," Nick said stoically. He held the door open for everyone to exit, accepting their criticism and anger without a response.

"Nick, Nick," Kate forced her shaky legs to move into the lobby. "Wait. It's raining. We can't send everyone outside without lunch." She saw Ted. He hadn't gotten to eat.

"Kate," Nick glared down at her. "We're closed. Go back to the kitchen while we get everyone out.

"Nick, please." Kate pleaded stomping her foot.

"No, we close when there is a fight," he said. "I'll see you in the kitchen."

"Where is everyone parked?" Jenny asked the volunteers huddled in the stock room.

"I'm in the back lot," Dan said. "But I can stay to help."

"No, it's okay," Jenny said, "I'm sure Nick is going to want to talk to us alone. Can you make sure that everyone gets to their cars?"

"Sure," Dan said, "I'll touch base with Nick later."

"Thank you. I'm sorry." Kate whispered as each volunteer exited the kitchen.

Turning, she looked into the dining room. Furniture was strewn everywhere, and soup splattered every surface, dripping down the wall. Lettuce, ham and cheese clung to the tables and chairs while the still intact sandwiches were trampled and squished into unrecognizable shapes.

Locking the lobby door with a deafening click, Nick strode into the middle of the dining room surveying the damage. Marika, Dallas, Tucker and Jenny congregated next to him. Standing alone in the kitchen, Kate stood frozen in place.

The silence roared.

Stooping to upright a chair, Nick sloshed off the mixture of salad dressing and soup covering the seat. Raising his dirty hands in the air, he asked, "When in the hell did we start serving soup?"

All eyes turned to Kate standing alone in the kitchen. Taking a deep breath, she swallowed. Her hands clenched at her side.

"It was my idea. I'm so sorry." Her words came out in a flurry, "We had all these melting vegetables and the rainy weather. Soup sounded like a perfect solution. I thought the clients would love it."

"Well, that didn't work out very well. Did it?" Nick wiped his hands on the towel Dallas handed him. "Everyone's outside in the rain." He tossed the towel on a messy table. "We don't serve soup—*ever*. It's too easy to spill."

"I didn't know, Nick." Kate walked into the dining room. "Can't we do a quick clean up and reopen for the people who didn't get to eat? Ted has a big test today and he didn't get any lunch."

"We tried to tell her." Marika walked around the room picking trays off the floor. "She wouldn't listen. She knows best. She's the chef." She smacked the trays on a table.

"Let's get this mess cleaned up." Nick pushed a table to the side.

"Nick, please." Kate glared at Marika.

"Katie, we're not reopening. We can't allow any fighting here. If there's a fight, we close. Period. Usually, the threat of closure keeps everyone on their best behavior. The instigators weren't regulars, but I can guarantee they won't make the same mistake again." He didn't look at Kate.

"Were they arrested?" Dallas asked.

"No, I said we wouldn't press charges. I also told them they couldn't come back to the kitchen for a month. Marika and Katie, you two clean up the kitchen. Everyone else grab buckets and rags and let's get the dining room cleaned up." Nick bent to upright a chair.

Walking back into the kitchen, Kate's eyes filled with tears when she saw the trays of ham sandwiches waiting to be popped into the oven. She had to do something. She hurried back to the dining room.

"Nick," Kate touched his arm. "Can't I please put the sandwiches in plastic bags and go pass them out? I could even take one to the bus stop so Ted could eat. No one would even have to come into the kitchen."

"Kate, stop it." Nick dropped the chair. "The answer is *no*. I feel bad people are leaving hungry too, but Mary and Martha's has to be a safe place. Fighting of any kind can't be tolerated. Unfortunately, the good have to suffer with the bad. The consequence of fighting is people go hungry. Hopefully, peer-pressure will stop the next fight before it even starts. Everyone who enters this building needs to know they are safe. It's over, so please just go clean the kitchen."

He turned and walked away.

27

MARIKA

Marika wrapped the trays of sandwiches with plastic wrap watching Kate plead with Nick. "Clients are going hungry because some chef wouldn't listen to the people who actually know better," she muttered.

Disgusted, she dumped two pans of salad into the garbage and ladled the soup into storage containers.

"I feel just awful about this," Kate's voice cracked when she walked into the kitchen, her eyes swimming with tears.

"You should," Marika used the ladle to point at the mess in the dining room. "This *is* your fault. We told you soup wasn't a good idea. You didn't ask why not; you just went ahead and gave us orders. Next time, maybe listen to the people who actually *want* to work here. You're the reason people left hungry, because *you think you know best*."

"How was I supposed to know someone would throw the soup?" Kate sniffed. Wiping her eyes, she began to wipe down the buffet station.

Once the kitchen was clean, the two women grabbed buckets and rags to join the others in washing down the dining room. The work was completed in an uncomfortable silence. The soup had splattered in all directions, finding spaces that had never seen sunlight. Tables and chairs were disinfected, and the dull floor was mopped and scrubbed until it almost sparkled.

"This dining room has never been so clean." Nick said, tossing a rag into a bucket. "Thanks, everyone, I think we're all finished."

Kate was the first to leave, of course. The door had barely closed before Marika erupted, "This was all her fault." Marika shouted glaring at Nick. "Dallas and Tucker told her soup wasn't a good idea, but she knows best. She's *a chef.* She doesn't listen to *anyone.* You should have never hired her. How many people didn't get to eat today because of her?"

"Why didn't you stop her?" Nick's voice was soft. "You know soup is too difficult to serve. It spills too easily which can lead to problems."

"*Me?*" Marika's hand flew to her chest. She gasped, "Why didn't *I* stop her? I can't believe you just asked me that."

"Why?" Nick opened his arms. "You *do* know better. You know we don't serve soup and the reason why. Why weren't you willing to stand up for what you knew was right?"

Marika was stunned into silence.

"Tucker, Dallas, thanks for everything. I'll see you guys tomorrow. Marika, come to my office, I want to talk to you alone."

Dallas shuffled out the door.

"Do you want me to stay?" Tucker placed a hand on Marika's shoulder.

"No," Marika said, shaking her head.

In silence, Marika followed Nick to his office. Turning on the lights, he stooped to pick up the stack of papers on the chair. "Take a seat," he said. She dropped to the chair, crossing her arms over her chest. Nick put the papers on the floor and sat down. Tapping a pen on the desk, he stared at Marika before speaking. "I know you were disappointed when I didn't give you the head cook job."

Marika looked away.

He pointed the pen at her, "Your behavior today confirmed that I made the right decision."

"*What*?!" Marika jumped up from the chair. "Your chef decided to make the soup, not me." Glaring, she pointed her finger at Nick "It was *your* decision to hire that high-and-mighty chef. She caused all of this."

Nick tossed the pen on the desk and raised his hands in a placating gesture. "Just calm down and listen to me."

"You've said enough." Marika was near tears, "You don't think I can do the job."

"That's not what I'm saying," Nick walked around the desk in front of Marika. "I know you can cook the food, but can you manage the kitchen? Today proved you aren't ready, if you had been, you would have explained to Katie why serving soup wasn't a good idea. You would have advocated for the clients and what was best for them."

"She wouldn't have listened," Marika pushed him away and faced the wall.

"Did you try?" Nick spoke softly, sitting on the desk corner. "You didn't even show her the menus you created. *I* gave them to her. She thinks they're good. She had no idea that you worked with the Mother's Group or the GED Classes. She thought you were skipping out of work. You've been so busy being pissed off about not getting the job, you haven't shown her anything you can do. Katie isn't the enemy, and I wish you'd stop treating her like she is."

Marika turned to look at Nick.

"I meant it when I asked you to take this time to learn from Katie. This place was in a rut." Nick spread his arms wide. "Joe hadn't allowed any changes for five years and you seemed willing to go with the flow. Things needed to be shaken up, and Katie could do that. I wanted you to partner with her so that, when she leaves, *you* can be named the head cook, because you'll be ready. You'll have the skills and confidence necessary to be successful."

"You want me to be the head cook?" Marika whispered.

"Yes." Nick took both of her hands into his. "I believe you will be the next head cook at M&M."

"Why didn't you tell me that before?"

"I tried to, but you weren't hearing me. I asked you to learn from Katie. I wanted you to see how a professional chef would organize and manage the kitchen. I wanted you to be a team player and show Katie the heart of the kitchen—that's what M&M is really all about.

Marika's eyes glistened with tears and her smile quivered, "You really want me to be the next head cook?"

"I do," Nick smiled back. "As long as you partner with Katie to gain experience."

"Thank you," Marika hugged him. "I promise I'll be a fantastic one." Marika didn't notice the cold on the walk home. *I wish I could call Tucker. I want him to know that I'm going to be the M&M head cook.* Unlocking the front door, she laughed, "I do have something in common with that chef: we both want her restaurant to open soon."

28
KATE

After Nick proclaimed the dining room clean, Kate couldn't wait to leave. She drove to her restaurant. The pouring rain had stopped, and a soft mist gently atomized the air, reawakening the smell of the fire. The smoky scent permeated the neighborhood. Buttoning her winter coat, Kate walked up the steps and sat on the porch swing. She marveled at the turn her life had taken. In less than three months, she had gone from being a successful restauranteur to causing a riot in a soup kitchen.

Her life was in a downward spiral. It had all started with the fire.

Kate shivered and wrapped her arms around her body. Even in a winter jacket and Ugg boots, she was cold. The air's autumn warmth had morphed into winter's frosty chill. Dampness settled into her bones, causing her to wonder how she would ever get warm.

The growling of her stomach reminded her of all the clients who hadn't gotten to eat because of her decision.

Poor Ted, how did he do on his test? It's my fault if he fails. He had to take his exam on an empty stomach, and I'm sure he was cold and wet.

Kate laid her head on the back of the swing, her feet gently moving the chair back and forth. When was the last time she'd felt this sad; this unsure of herself?

It was after the fire…

Because of the official fire investigation, Kate hadn't been allowed into the restaurant for over a week. On the day they were allowed into the building, she'd walked up the back stairs to enter the kitchen, her dad, toolbox in hand, following close behind. Nervous, she turned the key in the knob and pushed the door open.

The building exhaled, expelling the stink of the trapped smoke into the fresh air. The room was pitch black. The windows were boarded over with plywood. As their pupils adjusted to the darkness, the smell of wet wood blending with smoke enveloped them, filling their pores and hair with its acrid scent.

Pete turned on a Maglite. The small beam radiated around the room, illuminating the damage.

It was total devastation. Nothing was salvageable.

Kate rushed back to the daylight and vomited.

"It's going to be okay," Pete said, patting her back as she expelled the bile that was choking her. "You have insurance." Reaching into the toolbox, he handed her a small bottle of water. "Drink this."

Taking a sip, Kate swished her mouth and spat into the yard. She stared into the fire-ravaged kitchen. "There's nothing left." Her heart raced and panic climbed up her body.

"It doesn't look good." Pete agreed, "But we knew that. Besides, we can't really see what we're dealing with, with the boards on the windows. Let's get those off and go back inside."

Boards removed, the sunlight filtered through the smoky, glazed openings, giving the destruction an almost holy aura. The kitchen was a total loss. The heat of the fire had melted the knobs off the sixteen-burner Viking stove. The stainless-steel refrigerator was streaked with soot marks and burns and reeked from the spoiled and moldy foods rotting inside. The prep tables had collapsed along with all the pots and pans; the flames had been so hot the entire hanging pot-rack had fused into a pile, the alloy giving the appearance of a work of modern art.

The vintage dining room tables and chairs, which Kate had spent months refinishing, had acted as kindling for the fire. They went up without much of a fight. The few remaining pieces were covered with soot and marked with blisters. The entire mahogany bar was gone. The fire had consumed it like a drunken sailor. Broken bottles of liquor and shattered glass covered the still-damp hardwood floors from the water spewed by the firehoses.

Ironically, the one feature still recognizable in the restaurant was the fireplace. The white and gray marble mantel had been a huge factor in Kate's decision to buy the Georgian home. She pictured her clients' sipping drinks by its warm glow as they waited for their dinner reservations. She ran her fingers down the smooth stonework making a swirly design in the blackened soot. She'd spent hours polishing the marble until it glistened, and now it was black.

The smell of smoke overwhelmed her. Instead of evoking memories of childhood campfires and eating s'mores, the stink instilled a visual of sirens, flames and destruction.

The restaurant was a total loss.

She sat on the front stoop and sobbed. Sitting down next to her, Pete put his arm over her shoulder pulling her close. "Whew, it's bad. I'm not sure what I expected, but it's worse than I even imagined."

Sobs racked her body. He let her cry for a few minutes, then, handing her a handkerchief, he said, "Kate, there's no sense in crying. This is where you are, you have to figure out where you're going next."

She stopped pushing the swing and tried to find a tissue. Feeling in her coat pocket, Kate came up empty. She wished her dad was here with his ever-ready handkerchief. Her nose was runny. She was cold, hungry and she didn't know what she was going to do next.

Was this how the clients of the kitchen felt?

She felt so guilty. It was her idea to serve the soup even though Dallas and Marika had said it wasn't a good idea. Her decision to overrule their advice had led to Mary & Martha's having to close for the first time in four years. It was her fault.

Marika had been right. *You should listen to the people who actually want to work here.*

The problem is…I don't want to be working in a soup kitchen. I want to be working in my restaurant.

Kate faced the truth. She had mistakenly believed her culinary degree and restaurant experience was more valuable than Marika and Dallas's real-life work. She had only pretended to listen to their ideas. It was no wonder Marika hated her.

I've been the bitch, the interloper, the snob. I've been acting like I'm doing them a huge favor by working there.

If only they knew the truth, she *needed* this job. She was dead broke. If Nick fired her for today's fiasco, the image and persona she'd worked for years to create would be ruined. Her car would be repossessed. She'd lose her condo. She'd have to move in with her parents. Like her restaurant, her money had gone up in smoke.

"God!" Kate groaned, "My life is a mess. What am I going to do?"

Her thoughts were interrupted by a car pulling into the driveway. Recognizing Nick, she jumped from the swing, wiping her eyes and praying mascara wasn't streaking her face. She stood at the top of the porch and waited for Nick to walk up the sidewalk.

"Nice place you've got here." Nick said, placing a foot on the bottom step. He nodded at the boarded-up windows and charred brick building.

"Well, at least there isn't any soup on the walls." Kate shrugged sitting on the stoop.

"You got me there." Nick sat next to her. "I wanted to make sure you were okay. Katie, the fight wasn't your fault. Those people are adults and are capable of making their own decisions—even bad ones like starting a brawl in a soup kitchen. You didn't cause anything. And, I should have told you about the "No- soup" policy. It's been so long since the kitchen served new meals, the reminder wasn't on my radar."

"No, it's my fault." Kate ran her fingers through her hair. "Dallas and Marika said soup wasn't a good idea, but I overruled them because I thought I knew best. I never thought about the clients spilling it."

Her eyes filled with tears, "I'm really sorry. I know I let everyone down, and poor Ted had that exam. I understand if you want to fire me."

"Katie, I'm not going to fire you. " Nick squeezed her hand. "You're doing a great job, and the food is so much better. You just need to realize working in a soup kitchen is really different than a restaurant."

A rush of relief fell over Kate. She still had a job, and Nick was calling her Katie again. "I swear I've learned my lesson. From now on, my focus is going to be to build a real team where we all benefit from each other's experiences. I'm going to stop being a dictator."

"Sounds like a plan," Nick shook her hand before standing up. "So, why exactly do you come here?" He tapped the porch railing.

"As crazy as it seems." Kate stood and rubbed her hand along the blackened porch column. "Sitting on this burned-out porch brings me comfort. When it was warmer, I'd come here and work on the landscape or gardens, but now…I just sit and dream. I think about reopening the restaurant, the new decor, new menus." She pointed to the swing. "Right there, I get to pretend I'm still a gourmet chef."

"I get it." Nick walked to his car. "It's nice to have a place where you can just be."

29

NICK

This has been the longest day, Nick thought on the drive home. Talking to Katie had been the last step needed to put the day to rest.

He rubbed the back of his neck. The hairs curling up made him realize he could use a haircut.

He opened the door to his house, tossed the keys on the counter, grabbed a beer from the fridge and headed to the couch. After a long cold sip of Miller Lite, he grabbed the remote to watch Sport Center. Checking his fantasy football league scores, he took another sip of beer.

His day had started out great: finalizing plans for The Shepherd's Inn's grand opening, talking to Katie about the cooking class—then the fight. He'd called 911 as soon as he saw Tucker and Dallas in the middle of the melee. If those two couldn't get the situation under control, the police were definitely needed.

Closing M&M hadn't been a difficult decision. It was the only option. If there was a fight, M&M closed for the day—no arguments or discussion. The kitchen had to be a sanctuary of peace and safety for the community and the employees. Maybe Marika and Katie could come to their own truce.

It was good he was finally able to clear the air with Marika. For weeks he'd been walking on eggshells around her. He had tried to make her understand why he hired Katie, and he offered support about the Tucker situation, but Marika hid behind her anger. The woman was so stubborn. He hoped that confronting her bad attitude and telling her he wanted her to be the new cook would change the whole kitchen dynamic. Maybe now, Marika would accept the knowledge Katie had to share.

He went to the kitchen for another beer and peered into the freezer for dinner.

What would he have tonight? Stouffer's lasagna or meatloaf?

He grabbed the lasagna and opened the carton to microwave it. While he waited for the dish to nuke, he thought about Katie.

She really was cute.

When she'd looked up at him with those beautiful brown eyes filled with tears, it took everything he had not to hug her and tell her it was okay. She'd been so worried about Ted and his exam.

The microwave beeped. He turned the dish.

Had he told her Ted was taken care of?

After hearing about Ted's test, he'd asked Dan to help. Dan had picked Ted up at the bus stop, taken him to lunch and then onto school for the exam.

Dallas had told him where to find Katie. He wanted to clear the air so tomorrow would be a new day. Katie seemed determined to become more of a team player and to be the mentor Marika needed her to be. And after seeing the burned-out building, he didn't think the reopening would be any time soon. Katie would have lots of time to share her experience with Marika.

Carrying the lasagna into the living room, he muted the television volume before offering grace and eating his solitary meal.

He tried to lose himself in Monday-night football, but it was no use. He couldn't relax. He was restless and unsettled, not from the day's events, but from something deeper.

His life wasn't making sense anymore.

He turned off the game and headed upstairs to bed. When was the last time he'd really been content?

At Mass this morning.

30
KATE

Going to work at the kitchen the day after the fight, Kate was almost as nervous as her first day. She sat alone in the back of church and left as soon as the priest exited the altar. She'd snuck into the kitchen through the back door, anxious to get settled before she had to talk to anyone.

Heading to her office, she thought she heard a scuffle behind her, but the hall was empty.

Flipping on the light switch, the fluorescent overhead bulb illuminated a jumbo can of vegetable soup with a big pink bow placed on the middle of her desk.

Laughter made her turn around. Dallas and Tucker were outside her door, practically doubled over with glee. "You guys," she said picking up the can. "I am so sorry. Please forgive me. I promise, I am going to listen to you from now on."

"Hey, don't you worry about it." Tucker tipped his hat. "Today's a new day, we're all good."

"Miss Katie, we're just fooling with you." Dallas wiped imaginary dust from the desk with a towel. "This place needed a good cleanin'. The food fight motivated us to get the job done." Dallas snapped the desk with the towel. "I'll see you in the kitchen."

Kate placed the soup can on the filing cabinet next to the Kate's on

Vine sign. They were both reminders; where she was and where she wanted to be.

Putting the blue apron over her head, Kate adjusted her baseball cap and walked into the kitchen. Marika worked at the prep table calmly shredding carrots for the salad.

Placing her hands on the table, Kate took a deep breath, smelling the coffee brewing in the urns. "Marika, I want to apologize for yesterday's incident. I know you didn't think serving soup was a good idea, and I should have listened to you."

Marika didn't answer. She continued to feed the orange vegetables into the grater watching the tiny matchsticks emerge.

"I'm really sorry about everything." Kate's words rushed out. "Yesterday's fight made me realize that I know a lot about cooking, but nothing about the working of this kitchen."

"I appreciate your apology." Marika stared down her nose. "You're right, it was all your fault."

Kate gasped. *What did she expect? Marika to be nice?*

"You came in here with your fancy degree from your fancy cooking school. You didn't bother to learn anything about this kitchen." Marika waved her hands in the air. "But I'll tell you, I *know* this kitchen. I *know* these clients, and I was wrong for not standing up to you." She put her hand on her heart. "I should have stopped you from serving that soup. My cooking degree may not be from a prestigious school, but I know how to feed the hungry, and I intend to do just that."

Tossing the carrots onto the lettuce, Marika stormed out of the kitchen.

Kate stood alone.

31
MARIKA

Man, that felt good. Marika headed towards the Mother's Group room. *What did Kate want her to say? It's okay, you've acted like a queen here for the past few months, but all's forgiven. She deserved a piece of my mind.*

"Why do you look like the cat who just ate the canary?" Tucker carried a crate down the hall.

"I just told that cook off," Marika smiled leaning against the wall. "She tried to apologize for not listening to me and going ahead and serving the soup after I told her it was a bad idea. Can you believe that?"

"I think Katie feels terrible about yesterday and you should accept her apology." Tucker's gaze didn't leave her face.

"What?" Marika put her hands on her hips. "What is she apologizing for? The fact that there was a fight, or the fact that she hasn't bothered to listen to a damn thing I've told her?"

"Well, I know she feels bad about the fight, and I believe she wants to work with you," Tucker said.

"I told her the fight was her fault." Marika's voice softened, and she chewed the side of her thumb nail.

"Now, why did you do that?" Tucker placed the crate on the floor. "You know that's not true."

"I know." She stomped her foot. "She just makes me so crazy. She thinks she's so much better than me because she went to that fancy cooking school. She acts like all I can do is make salads." Marika paced the short hallway.

"Well, I think you're letting your own stubbornness, which I am very familiar with, get in the way of your cooking." Tucker's smile was wry. "I have never heard Katie say she's a better cook than you. Have you even asked to do something different or given a suggestion?" He bent to pick up the crate. "I know Nick wants you to learn from Katie. Have you even tried?"

"Why doesn't she learn from me?" Marika interrupted.

"Baby, she will, but you have to be willing to meet her halfway." Tucker winked and walked away.

Was Tucker, right? Should she have handled Kate differently?

She turned on the stockroom lights. There was a clattering sound followed by an "Oh crap."

Marika walked down the aisle to investigate.

Kate stood next to an upturned pickle bucket amid a pile of donated handwipes. "Sorry, I was looking for some cups." Kate said wiping her tear-streaked face.

"In the dark?" Marika asked.

"Well, I couldn't find the light switch." Kate sniffed and wiped her nose with the back of her hand.

Kate ducked as Marika reached behind her to open a napkin package. "Blow," Marika said handing her the white square.

"I'm sorry for what I said to you in the kitchen," Marika squeezed the napkin package. "The fight wasn't your fault. Sometimes tension in the dining room erupts; your food wasn't the problem; the bad behavior was. The soup just happened to be the weapon of choice. I've been around this kitchen for a very long time. I'd say there's a fight about every two years. We were due." She shrugged her shoulders. "I know it's scary, but I guarantee we won't have another one for a very long time."

Wiping her nose again, Kate reached for a second napkin, "I am so sorry, Marika. I promise I don't think my cooking degree is better than yours. I've watched you in the kitchen, you have wonderful skills. I guess I've been so used to running my own kitchen, I didn't think I needed your advice. My ego got in the way."

"I shouldn't have said that." Marika waved her hand. "I'm sorry too. I've been told I'm too stubborn for my own good."

"I've learned my lesson." Kate stood up and blew her nose one last time. "Please, tell me everything you think I need to know."

"Well... I think we should go finish today's lunch or we'll have another riot on our hands." Marika said.

"What did you come in here for?" Kate asked.

"Oh, I almost forgot. I need to get green beans." Marika stacked the vegetable cans on a cart. "I was thinking," she cleared her throat. "It's a sin to have all that soup go to waste. It really did have a nice flavor. Why don't we make the broth into more of a thick gravy, add some beef tips from the MREs and make a shepherd's pie?

Kate cocked her head. "I think that's a great idea. Are you thinking a cornstarch slurry?"

"Yes, I've already started making the mashed potatoes." Marika said.

"Fantastic! Do you think we have enough beef tips?" Kate walked to the MRE shelf.

"We do. I checked earlier," Marika gave a small smile. "I wasn't sure you'd be back."

"I wasn't sure either," Kate laughed. "Let's get today's lunch going and then make the pie."

Before lunch, Kate asked to speak in the prayer circle.

"Hello everyone," Kate stammered. "I wanted to say how very sorry I am about the mess my meal caused yesterday. I didn't listen to the wise words of my co-workers." She nodded at Dallas and Marika. "And I apologize to anyone who went hungry yesterday. Please forgive me." Rocking back on her heels, she stared at the floor.

"It's okay, Miss Katie," Ted yelled from the front of the line.

32

KATE

Kate's first cooking class was two weeks after the fight. Needing to review some last-minute details, she walked into Nick's office. The disarray no longer surprised her, and she didn't bother to try and sit.

"So, are you ready for tonight?" Nick was leaning back in the chair, his feet on top of the desk.

"I guess. I'm a little worried no one will show up." Kate admitted.

"You're completely full! Here's the class list." He reached across the desk and handed her a folder. "I was a little surprised by the people who registered."

"Why?" Kate glanced at the list.

"I don't know." His chair squeaked as he sat up. "I guess I expected them to be kids, but they're almost all adults." He ran his fingers through his hair. "I recognize some names from Marika's groups. She must have plugged the class."

"Really? I better get going then. Thanks for this." She tapped the folder on her leg.

"Let me know how it goes tonight." Nick rocked back in his chair. "I'm sure you'll do great."

God he's cute.

Kate opened the folder and looked at the names again. She didn't know one person. Well, she didn't know their names. She'd probably recognize a few of them from eating at the kitchen.

Pushing open the kitchen door, she marveled at how different the room felt since the fight. The heaviness and anger that had saturated the space had dissipated, and a spirit of cooperation and respect imbued the workplace.

"Marika, would you be interested in helping me teach the cooking class?" Kate asked.

"Well, hello." Marika stopped chopping the vegetables. Her eyes widened with surprise.

"I just got the class list from Nick." Kate held up the folder. "And I don't know a single person on it. He said most of the people were from the GED or Mother's Group."

Marika wiped her hands on a towel and looked at the names. "Well, I know some of them."

"It's no big deal, but I think the class would run smoother if I had a sous chef. And since you know some of them . . ." Kate stirred the gumbo. "To be honest, I'm a little nervous."

"Why in the world are you nervous?" Marika slapped the folder onto the prep table. "You've won all kinds of awards. You cook all the time."

"It's not the cooking… it's the clients." Kate pushed a strand of hair under her hat. "What if they don't like me, or I can't relate to them?"

"You're being ridiculous, but I can help." Marika laughed.

"Oh, thank you." Kate breathed a sigh of relief. "Tonight's menu is super easy: roasted chicken, steamed broccoli, baked potatoes, and a tossed salad."

"Sounds good. Just tell me what you need me to do."

Following the lunch clean-up, Marika arranged the kitchen into more of a classroom setting. She placed stools around the prep tables, with a notepad and pencil at each seat.

"That's a great idea." Kate pointed to the new table design. "I made recipe cards. Do you think I should pass them out now so they can follow along, or save them until they leave?"

"I'd probably give them out first. That way they can jot down notes." Marika laid the cards on top of the notepads. "I'm going to go get some new aprons, I'll be right back."

Where were the students? It's almost 3:00.

Kate looked at her watch again.

"Knock, knock." A pink turban peaked through the swinging kitchen door.

The peacock.

Today's color was pink: a furry cat appliqued on a long pink sweater, pink leggings and pink furry boots. Kate had never seen her without a smile, and she was notable for thanking each volunteer and telling them to "Have a Blessed Day".

"I'm Kate O'Leary, are you here for the cooking class?" Kate shook her hand.

"Bernice Shaw, am I the first one here?" She looked around the kitchen.

"You are. Why don't you grab a seat, and Marika will give you an apron? The rest of the class should be here soon."

"Tamara was going to get the kids settled and then come. She's my neighbor." Bernice placed the apron over her turban and tied the strings around her waist. "Oh, there she is." Bernice pointed to the door.

"You must be Tamara." Kate smiled at the woman walking through the door.

"No, I'm Sharon her sister." A robust woman with a large afro in a grey sweat suit answered.

I've seen her with Cool Hand Luke. The guy who flirted with me on the very first day.

"I'm Tamara." A shorter version of Sharon stepped into the kitchen. She wore jeans and a T-shirt with a wet spot on the front. "I'm sorry we're late. Aldiez wouldn't let me leave until I fed the baby, and of course he spit up." Self-consciously, she covered the stain with her hand.

"That's okay, go ahead and take a seat. Marika has aprons for you."

As she greeted the students, Kate watched a young man in the lobby surreptitiously glance into the kitchen and then down at the floor. He wore a blue plaid shirt, jeans and a book bag over his shoulder. He wrung his hands together and seemed to be speaking to himself.

"I'll be right back," Kate whispered to Marika.

Walking into the lobby, she approached the young man. "Hi, are you here for the cooking class?"

"I wasn't sure boys were allowed." He spoke with his chin facing into his shirt.

"Of course they are. Some of the most famous chefs in the world are men. What's your name?" Kate asked. The man was in his mid-twenties but acted almost like a teen.

"Leon."

"It's nice to meet you, Leon." Kate shook his hand. "I'm so glad you're here. Let's go meet the others in the kitchen."

He's the guy Dallas is so worried about. He sits with the transgender woman.

"Katie, this is Rachel." Marika introduced a cute young girl with strawberry blond hair and freckles. "She's in the GED class."

"Hello and welcome," Kate said. "I think we're expecting one more person, but let's go ahead and get started since it's 3:15. Marika, can you lock the door?"

"Okay." Kate took a deep breath and smiled at the attentive gazes directed at her. "Let's go around and introduce ourselves and maybe say why you registered for the class. I'll go first. My name is Kate O'Leary. I am the owner and chef of Kate's on Vine, which had a fire and burned down—but I promise you it wasn't my fault!" She gave the girl scout honor sign. "I began working for M&M about three months ago. Nick asked me to teach this class and that's why I'm here." Kate patted Marika's arm, "Your turn."

"My name is Marika Johnson. I have a fifteen-year-old son, Jamal, who goes to Drexel. I've been working as the assistant cook at M&M for five years. Prior to working here, I was very active in the Mother's Group and the GED Program. Katie asked me to be her assistant today, which is why I'm here, but I also know I'm going to learn a lot."

"Thank you," Kate smiled at the students. "Marika is a wonderful cook."

"Hi, I'm Bernice Shaw, I moved to this neighborhood about a year ago after my husband passed. I began to eat at the kitchen to meet new people, and I decided to take this class because the food has gotten so much better." She flashed a bright pink smile. "I thought I could learn a few things from the gourmet chef who was preparing such delicious meals."

"Hi, I'm Tamara Smithers. Bernice is my neighbor," Tamara said. "She talked me into taking this class because I have two little kids, and I should know how to cook."

"How old are your children?" Kate asked.

"Lincoln is two and Emma is three months. They're with their dad, Aldiez," Tamara said.

"How wonderful, I'm so glad you found time to join us," Kate answered.

"My name is Sharon Smithers. Tamara told me about the free dinner, so I signed up. I don't like to cook."

"Hopefully we'll be able to change your mind by the end of class." Kate tapped the table. "Rachel, why don't you tell us a little about yourself."

"I'm Rachel Kern." She put her hands on her chest. "Marika is my GED tutor, and she thought I would like the class so here I am."

"Terrific! Last but not least is our very brave friend, Leon." Kate put her hand towards the man.

"My name is Leon, and I like to cook," he said to the table.

"Wonderful." Kate clapped her hands together. "Now that we know each other, and everyone has an apron, let's get started."

Marika rolled a cart with the lesson's ingredients over to the table. Kate put her hand on the cart. "The most difficult thing about creating any meal is deciding what to make. Once you've made that decision, the rest is easy. You simply create a cooking plan, assemble the ingredients, and get to work. Voila…dinner is on the table." Kate snapped her fingers.

"How do you decide what to cook?" Tamara asked.

"Good question," Kate pointed her finger. "I like to use the freshest ingredients available at the best price. When I was trying to plan today's menu, I looked at the grocery store circular to see what was on sale."

"What's a circular?" Sharon interrupted.

"You know," Kate looked at the students' blank faces. "The grocery store ads. The flyers they put on your mailbox each week or online— usually on Sunday or Monday," her voice trailed off.

"Oh honey," Bernice tapped her pink nails on the table. "This neighborhood doesn't get store ads. That was one of the hardest things for me to get used to when I moved here." She clasped her hands in her lap shrugging her shoulders. "I can't walk to the grocery store anymore. It's over five miles away. I have to take the bus."

"I can't afford to go to the grocery store," Sharon said. "I'd have to change buses twice, and if my kids came too that would cost almost twenty bucks, plus where would I put my grocery bags?"

"They're right," Marika said to the dumbstruck Kate. "Most of the people around here go to the food pantry or the Quick-mart. The grocery store is too far away, unless they have their own transportation."

"But the Quick-mart is so expensive, I think it would be better to pay the bus fare."

Kate rubbed her forehead. *I'm going to have to change my menu planning.*

"Well, okay, then. I looked at what was on sale at the supermarket, which was chicken and broccoli. So, we're going to make a roasted chicken with broccoli and lemon, baked potatoes, and a salad."

"Ooh, that sounds delicious." Bernice clapped her hands together.

"It will be." Kate nodded. "Now that we know what we're having, we need to determine what's going to take the longest to cook. What's going to take the most prep time, and how do we coordinate all the different steps, so the dishes are ready at the same time. What do you think is going to take the longest?"

"The chicken," Tamara said.

"I think the potato," Rachel said.

"Well, you're both—" Kate was interrupted by a loud banging followed by the buzz of the kitchen doorbell. All heads turned towards the back door. A young girl with a riot of curly hair and beautiful brown eyes peaked through the window.

"Hi Kendra," Marika said opening the door. "Did you need something?"

"Am I late?" The young girl asked, pushing her way inside. She dropped her bookbag on the floor and bent over placing her hands on her knees as she worked to catch her breath. "I'm sooo sorry." She slowly stood working to calm her breathing. "I talked to Mr. Nick about taking the class, but I have to drop my brothers off at home before I can get here. I ran as fast as I could." She smoothed down her uniform skirt. "I can still take the class, can't I?"

"Of course, you can." Kate picked up the girl's book bag. "C'mon over, I'm Kate." She walked the girl over to a stool.

"Oh good, I was so excited when I heard about the class. I make dinner for my brothers when my mom works, and boy are they sick of hot dogs and chicken nuggets." She tied the apron Marika handed her around her waist. "They can't wait for me to make a fancy dinner."

Kate laughed, "Well, we're glad you're here. Why don't you tell us a little about yourself?"

"I'm Kendra Phipps." She waved to the group. "Hi, I'm in eighth grade at Holy Family. I have two younger brothers, and we live with our mom. I'm really excited to be here."

"That's great," Kate nodded. "We were just talking about the meal we're going to make today. Tamara and Rachel are both right. The potato will take longer to bake, but the chicken is going to take the longest to prepare. I've given each of you four potatoes. Let's take them to the sink, scrub them with a veggie brush and make sure there aren't any eyes; these little buds here." Kate snapped the blemish off the vegetable. Once they're all washed, you'll want to prick the skin with a fork and then the potatoes are ready to be popped in the oven.

"Don't you wrap them in aluminum foil?" Bernice asked.

"No need," Kate said, "The aluminum foil would make the skin softer, but I like the potato to stand on its own. Just put them on a cookie sheet or straight on the oven rack.

"Interesting," Bernice jotted a note on the recipe card.

"Next, the chicken." Kate held up a vacuumed wrapped whole chicken. "It's certainly easier and more convenient to buy only the breasts, thighs, or wings, but it's much more cost effective to purchase the entire bird and cut it yourself. No part of this bird is going to go to waste. After you've eaten the meat, you can use the bones to make a wonderful broth for soups or gravy."

"I think he wants to dance," Bernice said. Picking the carcass up by its wings, the chicken "danced" as she sang 'The Chicken Dance song' "Da..Da…Da.." The class joined in the singing and clapping, including Leon who had been writing down every word Kate said.

"Okay, so we've washed the potatoes, seasoned the chicken, and now it's time for the vegetable. Broccoli is one of my favorite veggies," Kate held up the green stalks. I like it steamed, but I also think it tastes great in the oven. Since the oven is already hot for the potatoes and chicken, it will be simple enough to roast the broccoli there too. I don't particularly like the stems. So, I tend to cut the pieces relatively close to the florets, but it's really a personal preference. Of course, the larger the pieces the longer they'll take to cook."

"I like the stalks better," Kendra said.

"Then, I would suggest cutting the stems length wise and then in half like this." Marika showed Kendra.

"When you're finished chopping the broccoli, sprinkle it with little salt and pepper toss it with some olive oil, the vegetables shouldn't be swimming in oil, just a nice coating so it gets a crisp texture. Pop it in the oven, and when it's done squeeze a little lemon juice over it. Delish."

Kate clapped her hands together. "Alright, the last thing we're going to make is the salad. Marika, would you mind taking over?"

"Me?" Marika asked.

"If you don't mind." Kate nodded and told the class, "Marika makes the salad every day at M&M. She is a salad professional."

"Well, okay." Marika moved to the top of the prep table. Kate gave each student carrots, tomatoes and a head of lettuce.

"You'll want to make sure your ingredients are all washed and dried, but I've already done that for you." She held up the lettuce. "When you prepare a salad, the goal is to chop all the vegetables into bite size pieces. People shouldn't have to use a knife when they eat their salad."

"Can you show us how to chop really fast like the chefs do on TV?" Kendra asked. "I'd love to be able to do that."

"It's probably more important for you to learn the right technique and the differences between minced, diced, and chopped, rather than to focus on speed right now." Marika laughed, "But I promise. You'll get faster."

She's a natural teacher.

Kate watched the students chop the carrots in all different ways.

The salad finished; Kate gave each student a shopping bag. "Now, when you get home, you'll place the entire roasting pan, still covered with the aluminum foil, in a 350-degree preheated oven. The potatoes can go in at the same time. The chicken will be fully cooked when the juices run clean. That means you'll poke the breast with a fork and the liquid running out will be clear." Kate looked at the clock. "Check it after an hour."

"Wait a minute aren't we going to cook the chicken here? I don't have an oven." Sharon said.

"Me either." Tamara and Rachel said at the same time.

"You don't have an oven?" Kate's voice squeaked. "Well then, we'll bake it here." She caught Marika's eye. "Can you preheat the ovens to 350? And I'll get some snacks for us to eat while we wait."

Sitting around a table in the dining room, Kate asked, "Does anyone have any questions while we wait for the food to bake?"

"Did you always know you were going to be chef?" Kendra asked, biting into a carrot.

"Hmm," Kate said. "I meant about the meal, but okay." She took a sip of iced tea. "I always loved to cook, but I never thought I'd make a living doing it. It was hobby, but when I was a junior in high school, at Mount Notre Dame, my Spanish teacher told me I should become a chef, and from that moment on becoming a chef was my dream."

"Your Spanish teacher?" Bernice laughed, "My goodness, how did that happen?"

"I know," Kate shrugged. "I was bad in Spanish. My teacher, Senorita, told our class about a popular Spanish dish called paella. It has all types of seafood, chorizo and saffron rice. She said it was difficult to make, but *sooo* delicious. It sounded wonderful to me, and I wanted to try to make it. My teacher told me if I did, and I brought her a bowl, she'd give me extra credit."

Kate took a piece of celery from the tray. "I really needed the extra credit, so I spent one whole weekend making the dish. Paella is expensive. My mom made me buy the ingredients myself, but it was worth it. My teacher *loved* it. She told me it was the best paella she'd ever eaten, and she'd eaten paella in four different countries. Then she said, '*you should be a chef*'. It was like a lightbulb went off—that's what I wanted to be. I had loved every minute of making the paella: looking for the right recipe, making tweaks, then shopping for the best ingredients, and finally getting to make the dish. It hadn't seemed like work to me. I was going to be a chef.

My parents thought I was crazy, *a chef*? My school counselor was very supportive and helped me research different cooking schools and programs. Once I was accepted at Cordon Bleu, my parents got on board. They helped me open my restaurant when I was ready." Kate bit the celery.

"Do you know what you want to do after high school, Kendra?" Bernice asked.

"Well, first I have to get into St, Katherine Drexel," Kendra answered. "If I get in there, I'll get to go to college but if I don't..." She laid her head on the table. "I don't know what I'll do."

"Is Drexel hard to get into?" Kate saw Marika nod.

"Oh my gosh, it's so hard." Kendra pressed her hands to her forehead. "You have to take an entrance test and write an essay. My mom's been helping me study for the test all year, and I just finished my essay." She took a deep breath. "I don't know who will cry harder if I don't get in, me or my mom."

Sharon's fist pounded the table. "Look at the stress that poor girl is under. Why does she have to work so hard to get into a private school. Our public ones should be doin' a better job."

"Jamal is really happy at Drexel." Marika wiped an imaginary crumb off the table. "It's worth all the effort."

"Those private schools expect the parents to volunteer all the time. I'm not like you. I got other kids to worry about. I don't have time for that crap." Sharon grumbled. "My boy, Jayden, is supposed to be a sophomore, and I can barely get him to go to school. He's always complaining the teachers are mean and the work is too hard. Our public schools are terrible."

"Oh, my word, that doesn't seem right," Bernice said. "What did the teachers and principal say when you talked to them?"

"I don't talk to them. It's Jayden's problem, I'm just saying the schools should do a better job." Sharon said, crossing her arms over her ample bosom.

"St. Katherine Drexel is difficult to get into and does require parents to be involved in their child's education. The school believes the child must be responsible for their schoolwork, but also recognizes they need a strong support system at home too. The parents are expected to ensure homework is completed and education is a priority." Marika stood to collect napkins and plates. "Jamal and I both signed contracts committing ourselves to Drexel's mission of a quality education and a pathway to college. Jamal is going to be a college graduate." Marika said.

"Well, with only one kid I guess you can dream big." Sharon pushed back her chair.

Wow, what's between those two?

Kate jumped as the ding from the oven timer broke the tension. "Saved by the bell," Kate murmured. "Let's go check those chickens."

Carefully removing the foil from a pan, Kate poked the breast of the chicken with a fork while the students watched. "See how the juice is running clear? This chicken is perfect." Kate squeezed the potato next to the pan. "Can everyone see how the potato is soft enough for me to squeeze yet still hold its shape. It's done too. This chicken looks delicious."

"That's mine," Leon smiled shyly

That's the first thing he's said since the introductions. "It looks great" Kate patted his shoulder, "I know you're going to enjoy it."

The meals packaged for home, Kate locked the door after the last student left and relaxed. "Oh, my gosh, I'm glad that's over. I can't thank you enough for your help, Marika. I almost had a heart attack when they said they didn't have ovens."

"Well, you recovered." Marika laughed.

"I couldn't have done it without you. You seemed to know exactly what I was thinking and what I needed. You're a great teacher."

"Thanks, it was fun."

"Here, take this home." Kate handed her the pan of chicken and vegetables.

"Oh, you don't have to do that." Marika waved her hands to refuse.

"No, I want you to have it. I won't eat it."

"Are you sure?" Marika picked up the pans. "Thank you, Jamal will love it."

"Would you be interested in doing the class with me? We could develop the menus together and maybe team teach? I'd appreciate the help." Kate said as they walked out of the building.

"Really?" Marika asked, "I think I'd like that. To be honest, I'm a little lonely with Jamal working after school."

"Great, we'll teach together then."

33

NICK

"So, tell me about the class," Nick said to Katie, walking from Mass to the kitchen the next day.

"It was good, but I'm going to have to change how the class is organized." Katie grabbed his coat sleeve. "Did you know some of clients don't have ovens? I originally planned for them to cook the meals at home, but that's not going to work."

"Hmm, I hadn't thought about that." Nick unlocked the kitchen door and stepped aside for Katie to enter. "Is it that they don't have an oven, or they do but it's broken?"

"Oh, gosh. I didn't ask." Katie placed her bag on a table in the empty foyer and unbuttoned her coat. Pulling off her hat, she brushed wisps of brown hair from her face, her cheeks pink from the brisk walk.

She's so pretty, why is she still single?

Nick unzipped his jacket. "Can you ask them? If the oven's broken, maybe we can get someone to fix it, but if they don't have an oven…well that's an entirely different problem."

"I'll ask next week." Katie shook her head. "I guess I didn't realize how hard it was to live around here. Did you know there's not a real grocery store? I planned the entire meal using the weekly ads, but they don't get the circulars because there isn't a store nearby." She put her hands up in the air. "The closest store is the Quick-mart. You'd think someone would try to fix that."

"Yes." Nick nodded. "I think someone should fix the grocery store situation."

"Oh good." Katie picked up her bag. "Also, I've asked Marika to team teach with me. She was so helpful yesterday, and she's much more connected to the community and students. So, to bottom line it, I like teaching the class, the people are great, and I'm going to be using the kitchen longer than I thought." Katie headed towards her office. "Oh, and what should we do about the grocery store situation? Do you think Tucker could help with that?"

"Wait a minute," Nick followed her. "I'm glad the class went well, and I think you could help with the grocery situation." He pointed at her with both fingers like a gun slinger.

"Me?" Katie laughed, "How?"

"Education," Nick said smiling at Katie's confused stare. "I mean it." Nick leaned against the dining room wall. "Have you heard the term 'Food Desert?"

"No?" Katie leaned against the opposite wall.

"It's what they call an urban area without access to fresh, healthy and affordable food that's us—this community. We're working with the city planners to entice a grocery store to come here, but until then, the people who live around here are stuck."

He continued, "I think you can help educate the cooking class students about the merits of shopping in an actual grocery store. It's hard for them to see the value of taking the bus to shop at the grocery store when the Quick-mart is right down the street. They don't realize a quart of milk at the corner store is $3.50, but a gallon of milk at the grocery store is $1.99. A few more of those types of savings, and the bus fare is paid. The corner market accepts food stamps so it's easy—but expensive. Use the class to show how to stretch the food stamp dollars. Who knows? In a few months, you could have the whole class clipping coupons!"

"No doubt, but there is still the problem of transportation and babysitting." Katie pushed off the wall. "Let me talk to Marika and see what she thinks."

"Including Marika was a great idea," Nick said. "She definitely knows the community."

He walked to his office. There was a definite change in Katie; she was more invested in the neighborhood, and she'd asked Marika to be her teaching partner. Would wonders ever cease?

34

MARIKA

"There you are," Marika said when Katie walked into the kitchen. "I was just telling Dallas how delicious the meal was last night."

"I'm so glad." Katie took the blue apron Marika handed her.

"Jamal said it was the best chicken he'd ever eaten." Marika opened the refrigerator. "I thought so too, but that may have been because I didn't have to cook it."

"I hope everyone enjoyed it," Katie said, tying her apron. She looked over her shoulder. "I spoke with Nick after Mass. I explained how we needed to rework the class, and that you were going to team teach with me. Was that, okay?"

"Sure." Marika placed a gallon of salad dressing on the prep table. "I thought of some different things we could do last night."

"Let's brainstorm after lunch. Maybe we could get some ideas from Tucker and Dallas too."

"What kind of ideas?" Dallas stopped singing 'This Old Heart of Mine'. "I got a million of 'em."

"Ideas for the cooking class," Marika laughed and pushed him out of her way.

"My whole plan was upturned because some of the students don't have ovens and there's not a grocery store nearby." Katie chopped peppers and onions for the meatball casserole.

"I keep telling Deacon he needs to get with the program." Dallas transferred pasta to the serving pan. "He needs to get rid of all the snacks and start carrying fruits and vegetables. The man's so stubborn."

"Well, keep working on him." Katie stirred the vegetables and peppers into the pasta.

Once lunch was cleaned up, Marika made a fresh pot of coffee and brought it to Katie's office. She looked around the room. "Well, I love what you've done with the place."

The space was devoid of any personal touches.

"Gee, thanks." Taking a sip of coffee, Katie looked around the room. "I probably should hang a picture or two, but as silly as it sounds, I'm too afraid. I don't want to become too comfortable here. I want to reopen my restaurant, and if I decorate… it's like I've given up hope."

"I get it," Marika nodded. "I've never had an office, just a hook on the back of the door. So, an office seems glamorous to me. I'd probably over-decorate with pictures, knickknacks, maybe even a coatrack. I'd definitely paint the walls a nice calm blue."

"A coatrack?" Katie asked.

"Yep, my coat's tired of being on the back of the door."

"Ah," Katie said. "Let's talk about the class. What do you know about the students?"

"For the most part, I think they're a good group. I don't know Bernice very well. She's new to the neighborhood and lives in the same building as Tamara. She's worried about Tamara's living situation and has been encouraging her to take advantage of the M&M programs: Mom's Club, Head Start for Lincoln, and now the cooking class."

"Why is she concerned?" Katie took another sip of coffee.

"Tamara's boyfriend, Aldiez, is not a nice guy. Rumor is he's the big source of drugs around here. If there's trouble in the neighborhood, Aldiez is probably nearby."

"Would I recognize him?"

"Probably not, he's more of a night owl. Tamara usually takes a lunch home to him. Tamara wants to be a good mom, that's why she joined the Mother's Group. She's looking for good role models, something her sister is not."

"Sharon? I've seen her with *Cool Hand Luke*, is that her husband?"

"Cool Hand Luke?" Marika asked.

"You know, the really good-looking guy. He's always at the kitchen surrounded by a group of guys. I met him on my first day.

"Yeah, that fits him," Marika laughed. "She's with him. They're not married."

"You don't like Sharon?" Kate asked.

"No," Marika wrapped her hands around the coffee mug. "Did you notice Sharon never said how many children she had?"

Katie tilted her head thinking. "You're right, she didn't. How many kids does she have?"

"I think six." Marika shrugged. "She's a breeder. The more kids she has, the more money she gets from the government."

"Six kids?" Katie pushed from the desk. "Then she didn't have enough food to feed them last night."

"Did she seem concerned?" Marika walked around the desk and straightened the 'Kate on Vine' sign laying on the credenza. "I've known Sharon for years. Jamal and her son Jayden were in the same class. They stopped being friends years ago when I wouldn't let Jamal hang out on the street. Jamal was expected to do his homework and get good grades. Sharon doesn't care what her kids are doing. I think Jayden is working for his Uncle Aldiez."

Marika continued, "Sharon loves to complain about how bad the public schools are, but I bet you five dollars she's never been to a parent/teacher conference."

"Oh gosh, what do you know about Leon? Isn't he the guy Dallas is so concerned about?"

"Yes" Marika nodded. "Leon's hooked up with Jackie, the transgender woman." Marika sat back down. "Leon didn't grow up in the neighborhood. He has some type of mental health problem. He'll eat at the kitchen for a few months, be gone, and then come back. I don't think he makes good choices when he's off his meds. Jackie is notorious for taking advantage of people. I think Leon may be caught in her clutches. Hopefully, we'll be able to figure out what's really going on there."

"Who else?" Katie looked up at the ceiling. "Rachel, she seems nice."

"She is. I met her through the GED classes. She hasn't been sober very long, and I suggested the class to keep her busy. I think her boyfriend is still using…. So, I guess we'll have to wait and see."

"And Kendra, she's such a sweet girl."

"Oh, she is," Marika answered. "I've known her since she was a baby. Her mom and I were in the Mother's Group together. After Kendra's dad left, her mom had to take a second job to support the family, which is why Kendra has to cook two nights a week. She's a good kid. I hope she gets into Drexel."

"Me too. Now about the class, what did you think?"

"I thought it went really well." Marika leaned back in the chair. "I think everyone seemed really interested in learning to cook. Well, not Sharon, she just wants the free food."

"Them not having an oven is really throwing me over the edge." Katie tapped the desk with her pen. "I wanted to make recipes they could cook at home, but without an oven…Maybe next week we could make spaghetti and meatballs? We could make it on the stove, and ground beef is inexpensive so it's in our budget. Nick wants us to show them how to stretch their SNAP money—any ideas?"

Marika thought for a minute. "What if we comparison shopped?" Leaning forward, she clapped her hands excited, "We could show them what twenty dollars would get them at the Quick-mart versus the grocery store."

"That's a great idea." Katie jotted notes on a legal pad. "What could we make?"

"Hmmm, what about breakfast for dinner? The Quick-mart doesn't have fresh chicken or beef, but they do have eggs and milk."

"I love that," Katie said. "We could make an egg casserole or omelets, even pancakes. How about making that your first class in two weeks?"

"You want me to teach it?" Marika put her hands to her chest.

"Of course," Katie said. "It's your idea. You should run with it. I'll be the sous chef and do whatever you tell me to."

"Okay." Marika nodded. "I'll do it, thanks."

"Now we just have to figure out the rest of the month." Katie said, deep in thought.

Marika bundled up for the walk home. The sun was setting earlier each day, and the walk seemed to take much longer, probably because she was alone. Tucker used to keep her company. They'd hold hands and talk about their day, Jamal's after school activities, even plans for the weekend. On chilly days like this, Tucker would warm up his car and drive her home. He had never wanted her to be cold. Since she told him she didn't want to get married, he didn't seem to care if she froze.

Marika crossed the empty street and forced herself to stop thinking about Tucker. The meeting with Katie had gone great. The community college graduate had impressed the Cordon Bleu chef. But her office – how could she not decorate it?

If I had my own office, I'd hang pictures of all the people I love: Jamal, Tucker and Ginger, right next to my diploma. I'd have a drawer filled with coloring books and crayons for the little kids who needed some extra attention, and a candy dish always filled with chocolates. I might even buy a bean bag chair for the teenagers who wanted to come and talk. Marika opened the front door. *My own office? A girl can only dream.*

35

KATE

At the kitchen on Monday, Kate pulled the donated pot roasts out of the oven. "These smell delicious."

"Oooh, those look good," Dallas whistled. "How long should they rest before I start slicing 'em?"

"Fifteen minutes." Kate looked at the clock. "That should give us enough time before we start serving."

"I tossed the potatoes and carrots with thyme." Marika raised the temperature on the oven. "They'll need about thirty-five minutes.

The kitchen staff was working like a well-oiled machine. Once Kate explained that she needed the chore chart to keep herself organized, Marika had embraced the system and even helped delegate the various responsibilities. The two of them had become a dynamic duo, like peanut butter and jelly or bacon and eggs; each were good on their own but worked much better together. They'd even started a weekly menu meeting to brainstorm on different meals. Those sessions usually led to a request for Tucker to find one ingredient that would make a meal spectacular. Miraculously, Tucker always managed to make the dream ingredient appear, including this week's request for snow pea pods.

"Your wish is granted." Tucker placed a case on the table next to the pot roasts.

"You *got* them?" Kate said opening the box to admire the fresh, firm, green legumes, "You have no idea how much better these are going to make the chicken fried rice. The clients are going to love it." She clapped her hands, "Thank you, you're a magician."

Tucker doffed his cap.

"That's right, I'm a magician." Tucker picked up the crate. "I'm going to make these disappear right into the fridge."

"I think it's amazing what you've done with the food." Sylvie watched Dallas carve the roasts. "I've worked here almost four years, and the meals have never looked so appetizing. The clients are loving it."

"Thank you. That's nice to hear. We don't get a lot of feedback, so it's good to get the perspective of the volunteers who serve and interact with the clients," Kate said.

"Your food looks pretty and taste good. That's a combination the clients haven't been accustomed to."

"Thank you. Today's meal is a super easy pot roast with root vegetables. A local parish donated the roasts, and a volunteer donated the carrots, potatoes and onions from her garden, along with homemade applesauce. Today's lunch is one hundred percent thanks to the generosity of the community. Isn't that wonderful?"

"What's even better is the volunteer who donated those vegetables and made the applesauce is here to help serve them too." Dan adjusted his apron.

"Dan, did you donate the vegetables?" Kate asked.

"Not me, her." He nodded at Sylvie. "She's the resident gardener. Anytime there are flowers on the table or beautiful vegetables donated, I'm betting Sylvie brought them from her garden."

"I'm afraid that's the last of the vegetables," Sylvie blushed. "This is my least favorite time of the year. There is absolutely nothing to do in the garden or the yard—my happy place. I'm thinking about picking up a few more days here just to keep myself occupied."

"It's time to pray!" Jenny yelled. Sylvie walked with Kate into the dining room, while Dan remained in the kitchen.

"The pot roast must be good," Kate said, chopping vegetables with Marika at the prep table.

"Why?" Marika grabbed another bunch of broccoli.

"Ted's gone through the line twice. He never does that."

While Kate didn't know a lot of the clients personally or even their names, she had begun to know their quirks. It was hard not to recognize their habits. While the regulars at her restaurant had been people who dined at Kate's once a week, M&M regulars ate at the kitchen every day: the *Peacock*, aka Bernice; the *Muffin Man*, who always asked for a muffin, the *Scarecrow*, the man with the tattoos on his face to resemble the Scarecrow from the Wizard of Oz but never spoke; *Crazy Maisie*, who spoke only to herself; and *Cool Hand Luke*, the handsome man who Kate had met on her first day. His double entendre comments usually ended with a wink.

"What were we thinking?" Marika put down her knife with a laugh. "Chicken fried rice sounded great when we were planning the menus, but now that I'm chopping all these vegetables, I'm not so sure."

"It's going to be delicious. The chopping is the hard part. The rest will be simple." Kate said.

"Hi Katie, hi Marika." Rachel, from the cooking class waved, "Alex, that's my teacher." She nudged the man next to her, "The one teaching me to cook."

The man with Rachel was older and had the most striking blue eyes.

His clothes were fashionable, but dirty, and he wore gym shoes without any socks. The man nodded at Kate before grabbing the piece of peach pie Sylvie handed him. "Hi Rachel, how are you?" Kate asked.

"I'm good," Rachel said. "I can't wait for the next cooking class again. My boyfriend loved the chicken." Giving the grumbling people behind her a dirty look, she asked Sylvie. "Did you give him the peach pie? It's his favorite. I'll have that chocolate chip cookie, please."

"I know," Sylvie said softly.

"I'll see you Wednesday, Rachel. We're making spaghetti and meatballs." Kate said.

"Rachel, her name's Rachel." Sylvie passed the cookie, "I'll tell Zach socks. He needs socks."

"I'm sorry, Sylvie did you say something? Kate asked.

"Oh, nothing, I'm just talking to myself." Sylvie said.

Back at the prep table, Dallas and Marika were ferociously chopping celery, onions, broccoli, carrots and the snow peas for the next day's meal.

"Man." Dallas wiped his brow with the towel from his back pocket. "I feel like I'm back in the big house. He started singing in a low baritone voice. *"Nobody knows the trouble I've seen."*

"C'mon, it can't be that bad?" Kate laughed.

"You have no idea. There were some days in jail I bet I peeled a hundred pounds of potatoes." Dallas gave an exaggerated shiver. "Sometimes, just the thought of mashed potatoes makes me want to cry."

"Well, look how far you've come!" Marika pointed with her knife. "Now you get to chop snow peas. I believe you've made it."

"You know it." Dallas laughed. "Sometimes I can't believe my luck: good health, a little money in the bank, a good job, and the freedom to enjoy it. Life is—" He stopped talking. Both Marika and Kate looked up from the table, a silent Dallas was a rarity. He stabbed the knife into an onion and glared into the dining room, anger emanating from his body.

"What's wrong?" Marika tried to follow his stare. It was Leon and Jackie.

"Hurry up, you're holding up the line," Jackie said shoving Leon. He struggled to carry two book bags, three shopping totes and his tray of food. Leon was visibly upset. Dropping a bookbag to the floor, he tried to push it with his foot. His eyes were wide and filled with tears as he tried to negotiate the food line, his packages, and the snickers from other people.

Dan tried to calm the situation by stopping food service to allow Leon a chance to regroup. However, Jackie continued to berate him. "You're such a dumbass. Why did you drop that bag? Can't you do more than one thing at a time?" Using her fist, she punched him in the back. "Hurry up."

"Hi, Leon, is everything okay?" Wiping her hands on the apron, Kate stood next to Dan.

"He's fine," Jackie answered. "I know he's holding up the line. The imbecile can't do anything right. All he has to do is carry a few bags and get some food, but that seems too hard for him." She clipped a stray hair back into a butterfly barrette.

"Well, let me help." Kate walked into the line and took the tray from Leon. "I'll carry the tray, and why don't you get the bags?" She told the rattled man. "It's pot roast today, and I know you're going to like it."

Nodding, Leon took a deep breath and picked up the bag.

"Which dessert would you like?" Kate made her voice calm and soothing.

"He doesn't need anything." Jackie said, her tone harsh.

"Well," Kate didn't look at Jackie. "I think we'll let Leon answer for himself. How about a piece of chocolate cake, Leon?"

Leon's head bobbed.

"Sylvie, could you please hand that to me?" Taking the cake and the tray to the table, Kate helped Leon get situated with all the bags before he took a seat.

"I'm Jackie." The transgender woman held out her hand. "Leon's my man. I don't know why he gets so upset. I think he needs more medicine." Placing her food on the table, she handed Kate the empty tray. "By the way, that chicken you made last week was delicious."

"Leon," Kate crouched next to his chair, hoping he would look at her, but he kept his eyes on the table. "If you need anything, come and see me in the kitchen." A tear shimmered on his cheek. Patting his back, Kate stood.

"Hey," Jackie grabbed her arm. "I said, he's fine. He needs more meds. I can take care of my man." Kate jerked her arm away and walked back to the kitchen.

"I feel sick to my stomach." Kate washed her hands at the sink. Speaking over her shoulder to Marika and Dallas, "Leon looks scared and confused. Don't you think we should do something?"

Still chopping vegetables, Dallas watched Leon. "The poor guy's not right, and she is taking advantage of him. It makes me sick. I wish Nick would do something."

"What can Nick do? Leon's an adult," Marika asked. "Does he have any family? Maybe they could help?"

"I don't know." Dallas severed the broccoli florets from the stalks.

"Well, Nick can probably find that out." Marika tossed a handful of carrots into a bowl. "I'm just glad Leon's taking the cooking class. It will give us a chance to get to know him better and then maybe we'll be able to help."

"I guess you're right," Kate said.

"Yoo-hoo! How are you this fine and beautiful day, my wonderful teacher?" Bernice asked.

"I'm good, how are you?" Kate stirred the rice, admiring Bernice's royal blue ensemble, which included a turban and peacock feather.

"I am blessed," Bernice answered. "I finished the chicken last night. It was as delicious as the day we made it. I can't wait to see what we'll be cooking this week."

"Spaghetti and meatballs," Kate said.

"That sounds wonderful. Hello, Miss Sylvie, I believe I'll have that piece of sweet potato pie. Did you know I'm taking a cooking class from Miss Katie?"

"You are?" Sylvie handed her the pie. "That sounds like fun."

"Oh, it is. Who knows? Maybe I'll open a restaurant one day." Bernice laughed, "Now you have a blessed day."

"So, you're teaching a cooking class?" Sylvie asked Kate at the end of lunch.

"I am." Kate wrapped up the leftover pot roast. "Nick thought it would be a good way to engage some of the clients, and to be honest with you, I'm a little bored after leaving M&M. The class gives me something to focus on besides the fire at my restaurant."

"I understand wanting to focus on other things," Sylvie said placing her apron in the laundry bag. "I'll see you next week."

36

KATE

"How did your families like the chicken?" Kate asked the students at the start of their second cooking class.

"My brothers loved it. In fact, my mom and I made it together on Sunday," Kendra said.

"You did?" Kate clapped her hands. "I'm so glad, how did it turn out?"

"Delicious," Kendra took a carrot from the veggie tray Marika had prepared. "I made mashed potatoes this time. It was yummy."

"I had to take some of Tamara's cuz' one chicken don't feed all my kids." Sharon shrugged her shoulders.

"Remind me, how many children do you have?" Kate asked.

"Six."

"That's right," Kate said, ignoring Marika's eye roll. "We'll try to make sure you always get a little extra, so everyone can have plenty to eat."

"Today, we're going to make spaghetti and meatballs. This is always one of my go-to meals because its super easy, inexpensive, and can be made entirely on top of the stove.

Marika is going to give each of you an onion, a clove of garlic, and two large cans of crushed tomatoes. There are lots of variations of tomato sauce, but all sauces have those three ingredients." Kate pointed to the items. "It's up to the chef to add different spices or herbs to make the sauce their own. Let's get started! Go ahead and dice the onions and garlic."

"Dice means they're all the same size, right?" Rachel picked up the knife.

"That's right." Marika nodded.

"Now, that you've got things cooking," Kate watched as the students stirred their sauces. "It's time to add the spices. The standards are basil and oregano, but some people like a little bite to their sauce, so they might add a dash of red pepper. For a sweeter sauce, add a chopped carrot—that will give it a touch of sweetness without any sugar. I like to smell the spices and add the one with the best aroma." Kate rubbed basil between her fingers and sniffed.

She watched Sharon add a whole tablespoon of oregano to her pot. "Remember, you can always add a spice, but you can't take it out, so you'll want to add just a little bit at a time."

"Miss Katie, can you taste this?" Leon held a teaspoon of sauce.

Tasting it, Kate said, "Leon, this is delicious. Which spices did you use?"

"Just like you said, I smelled them and added lots of basil, a little oregano, and a dash of red pepper."

"I could serve this in my restaurant." Patting his arm, she saw him wince. "Are you okay?" Kate asked. "Your arm looks swollen."

"I'm fine." He slowly stirred his sauce

"I need help," Tamara laughed. "There is something seriously wrong here."

"Let me try it," Marika grimaced. "Too much salt. Let's try adding some brown sugar, and if that doesn't work, we'll try lemon juice. Keep stirring and tasting, you'll get it right."

The sauces simmering on the stove, the students sat down to prepare the meatballs. "Now, you can always buy breadcrumbs, but it's just as easy to make them yourself." Kate showed the class a sheet pan covered with broken pieces of bread. "We put these out yesterday to dry."

"Wow, something smells good." Nick walked into the kitchen pushing a dolly with two large boxes. Tucker followed him with two more.

"Wow, it does smell good in here," Tucker agreed.

"Hi." Kate put her hands on her hips. "We're making spaghetti and meatballs. What are you guys doing?"

"This looks wonderful," Nick said opening a pot. "The A2Z Corporation donated a thousand pairs of socks for the clients. We're going to store them in the stockroom. Can I taste this?"

"That's mine, you can try it," Rachel said. "My boyfriend needs socks. Can I have a pair?"

Nick took the spoon Kate handed him. "Sure, Tucker, open a box and give everyone a pair."

"Whew, these are great." Tucker passed the socks around the table. "They're the kind that actually keep your feet warm when it's cold outside. It says they're good to twenty degrees."

"Thank you, Alex will definitely use them. He told me the other day his feet were cold," Rachel said.

"A2Z is great to us. I'd say we get something donated from them about once a month. Is that right?" Nick asked Tucker.

"Yep." Tucker nodded. "We got the personal care kits, the power bars, and now these. They're really good to us."

"This sauce is delicious, maybe we should start popping by every week, Tuck." Nick tasted from a different pot.

"Marika is going to give a shopping lesson next week. You guys should stop by." Kate laughed before waving them off.

37

MARIKA

Marika had spent the week preparing to teach her first cooking class. Rifling through grocery bags, she separated items into two grocery carts. "I thought I'd set up a display with the items from the Quick-mart in one cart and the grocery store purchases in the other. I'm going to do a big reveal—show the difference in buying power." Marika crumpled the bags and tossed them into the recycle bin. "I can't believe how much more you can buy at the grocery store. Honestly, it almost triples the buying power."

"That's a great idea. What do you want me to do?" Kate helped Marika cover the carts with sheets.

"Would you mind placing the ingredients at each person's station? I think it will save time if we have everything out." Marika handed Kate the recipe cards and ingredient sheet.

"Let me just run this by you." Marika ran her fingers through her hair and paced around the kitchen. "So, they'll come." She tapped the table. "You'll have the ingredients organized at their seat, and I'll tell them we're going to make breakfast for dinner." She walked over to the stove. "We'll start frying the sausage." She moved her hand as if stirring the sausage. "As the sausage drains," she walked back to the table. "We'll prep the rest of the casserole. While the casseroles are in the oven, I'll

talk about the different shopping experiences. Does that sound okay?"
She tilted her head.

"I think that sounds great," Kate said. "And you're going to talk
about getting the most out of their SNAP money?"

"Yes, and I'd thought I'd have them brainstorm about
transportation." The doorbell buzzed. "Oh, they're here." Marika rubbed
her hands down the apron. "I'm a little nervous."

"You're going to do great." Kate gave her a thumbs up. "Hi, there,
come on in, Marika's got everything set for you." Bernice, resplendent in
emerald, walked through the door with Tamara and Sharon.

"I can't wait to see what we're cooking today," said Bernice. "I hope
it's as delicious as the spaghetti and meatballs. I shared mine with my
neighbor, and he surely enjoyed it."

"Do you have a boyfriend?" Kate teased.

"Oh, my goodness, no." Bernice waved her hand. "He must be at
least ninety. He isn't very mobile, so I try to visit with him every day. I
believe people should know their neighbors. That's one of the reasons I
eat here and why I'm taking this class." Bernice hopped onto the stool.

Marika listened with one ear as she stood in the back corner
reviewing her notes one last time. Leon walked to his seat at the end of
the prep table pulling a notebook out of his backpack. He didn't speak to
anyone. Rachel and Kendra arrived together.

"You're here early." Kate hung Kendra's backpack on the wall hook.

"I know. We have study sessions all this week for the high school
entrance test. So, I got to leave a little early."

"When's the test?" Kate asked.

"Saturday," Kendra tied her apron. "I'm as ready as I'm going to be.
Now, all I can do is pray!"

"We'll all say some prayers," Bernice touched Kendra's hand and smiled.

"I think it's ridiculous these kids are studying so much." Sharon crossed her arms. "I'm fine with the public schools."

Marika walked to the prep table. She took a deep breath and cleared her throat. "Hi, everyone. Today, we're going to do something a little different. We're going to make breakfast for dinner."

"Oooh, I love breakfast," Bernice said.

"Are we making pancakes?" Kendra asked.

"I *hate* breakfast." Sharon said pushing away from the table.

"Well," Marika frowned. "I think your kids will like this breakfast." She picked up a frying pan. "Let's start with frying the sausage. Everybody ready?"

After placing the casseroles in the oven, Marika and Kate rolled the covered carts with the groceries into the kitchen. "Remember when Katie told us how she decided what to cook by looking at what was on sale?" Marika asked. The class nodded. "Well, since we don't get the ads here, I decided to see where I would get the most bang for my buck: the Quick-mart down the street or the actual grocery store. This was a simple meal—eggs, sausage, bread, milk, cheese, right? All these items could be purchased with SNAP?"

"Miss Marika?" Leon raised his hand.

"Did you have a question, Leon?" Marika couldn't believe he'd asked a question, normally he didn't say a word.

"I don't know how to SNAP." He tried to click his fingers together.

"I'm sure you do." Marika bit her lip to keep from laughing. Kendra and the others giggled softly. "We're not really trying to snap." She held his hand. "SNAP is the card you get from the government to help you buy food. The *Supplemental Nutrition Assistance Program*. I'm sure you have a card. It's blue."

"I gave Jackie my card." Leon murmured.

"Oh, honey," Bernice patted Leon's leg. "You shouldn't give away your SNAP card, that's money to help you buy food. You should ask her to give that back to you."

"She's right," Marika nodded to Bernice. "SNAP assumes a meal for a family of four will cost twenty dollars, so that was my budget when I went to each store. Let's see what that actually buys." With a flourish worthy of a magician, Marika and Kate removed the sheets from the carts to reveal the groceries.

"One cart has the groceries from the Quick-mart. The other is from the grocery store, but I had to use bus fare to get there. Any idea of which cart is which? Marika asked.

Both carts had a pound of sausage, a dozen eggs, eight ounces of cheese, and five pounds of flour and sugar. However, the first cart also had a quart of milk and two loaves of bread. The second cart had a loaf of bread, a gallon of milk, a bottle of syrup, and a pint of blueberries.

"I think this one's from the Quick-mart." Sharon pointed to the basket with the blueberries and syrup. You don't have to pay the bus fare to get there so you'd get more."

"That's a good thought, Sharon. Who agrees with her?" Marika asked.

Everyone's hand went up except for Bernice. Slowly, Leon lowered his hand. "Do you disagree, Leon?" Marika asked.

"Yes," He answered speaking into his chest.

"Why?"

"I've never seen blueberries at the Quick-mart."

"Well, you're right," Marika laughed. "The cart with the blueberries and syrup is from Kroger.. Even with paying the bus fare, I was able to buy more at the grocery store."

"Well, you bought two loaves of bread from the Quick-mart, why did you do that?" Sharon asked.

"The bread was two for three dollars or one for $2.49. I decided to buy two. I can always freeze one or give it to a neighbor.

"Why did you get the smaller milk from the Quick-mart?" Tamara asked.

"The quart size of the milk was $3.49, but a gallon of milk from the grocery store is only $1.99. The eggs were the same price, but the cheese and sausage were cheaper at the grocery store. The Quick-mart charged almost double on those items."

"How did you carry everything on the bus?" Tamara looked at the groceries. "I'd have both of my kids too."

"Going to the grocery store wouldn't be easy." Marika agreed. "You'd have to plan for the trip. Could Aldiez stay with the kids, or maybe you could swap babysitting with Sharon or a mom from Mom's Group? Your SNAP money is going to go much further if you take the extra time to get to the grocery store. Do you have a bus pass?"

Tamara nodded.

"Then the cost of the ride is going to be lower too."

"When your SNAP is gone, you can always go to the pantry," Sharon said.

"I agree," Marika said. "But wouldn't it be better to make smarter food choices, so you don't have to go the pantry every month and hope they have what you want?" Marika picked up the flour. "Just for a comparison, the flour at the Quick-mart cost $3.99 and the sugar $4.99. At the grocery store, the flour and sugar each cost $1.99."

"Yeah, but at the pantry they're free." Sharon slapped the table.

Marika rolled her eyes. "The casseroles will be ready in about thirty minutes. Let's make the pancake batter—you can cook them at your house. I have all types of different toppings for you to take home too: chocolate chips, bananas, sprinkles, and of course, blueberries."

Marika smiled, locking the door after saying goodbye. "Whew, I'm glad that's over. I was so nervous."

"You did a great job." Kate wiped down the counter. "I heard Bernice telling Tamara she'd babysit the kids so she could go to the grocery store."

"That's fantastic! Sharon told me it wasn't worth her time. She'd keep using the pantry." Marika threw a towel in the sink. "That woman drives me crazy."

"I think we're done here." Kate took off her apron. "I've got a few things to do in my office. I'll see you tomorrow."

"Okay, thanks for all of your help." Marika turned off the kitchen light and walked into the hall to grab her coat. She jumped when a figure stepped around the corner. "Oh, my goodness, Rachel, you scared me. I thought you had already left."

"No, I wanted to talk to you." Rachel held the bag with her dinner in one hand.

"Okay…is it about the GED class?" Marika buttoned her coat.

"No… um… I think I'm pregnant." Rachel started to cry.

"Oh my," Marika's eyes popped. "It's okay," she said wrapping her arms around the thin girl.

"I'm so scared." Rachel's body shook with sobs

"It's going to be okay," Marika said. "Have you been to the doctor?" Feeling the girl's head shake *no* against her chest. Marika asked, "Would you like me to go with you?"

Her head nodded, almost hitting Marika's chin.

"Okay, we'll go tomorrow." Marika held Rachel at arm's length. She looked into the girl's red, tear-streaked face. "You're not using, are you?"

"No, no." Rachel was emphatic. "I haven't used anything since I first suspected." She put her hands on her stomach. "Do you think I've hurt my baby?" She started crying again. "I didn't even like the drugs. I only did it to be with Alex."

"Is that your boyfriend?"

"Yes," Rachel said.

"Have you told him?"

"No." She wiped her nose on the back of her sleeve.

"Do you want him to go to the doctor with you?"

"No, I want you to go with me. I'm not sure how he'll be."

"Well, then, we'll go tomorrow, right after the GED class."

Taking a deep breath, Rachel hugged Marika. "Thank you, I feel so much better now that I told someone."

"I'm glad," Marika said. *Now, I get to worry.*   •

38

MARIKA

"It's positive," the nurse said, opening the clinic's examining room door. Rachel flopped back on the examination table, placing her hands on her stomach. Sitting next to her, Marika reached over and touched Rachel's knee. The nurse typed on the room's computer. "At the Elizabeth Center, we support mom and baby, so I'm able to give you a prescription for prenatal vitamins, schedule prenatal appointments and your first sonogram." She handed Rachel a stack of brochures and prescriptions. "If you want to take a different path, you'll need to see another provider."

"I'm having the baby," Rachel bolted up, her voice firm.

"I'm happy to hear that. Legally, I do have to share all the options," the nurse said.

"There has been some drug use," Marika said. "Will she need additional tests?"

"Are you using now?" The nurse's eyes bore into Rachels, her tone harsh.

"No, no." Rachel crossed her hands in front of her and then made the Girl Scout honor sign. "I swear. I haven't used since I first thought I was pregnant."

"How far along do you think you are?" The nurse kept typing on the computer.

"Maybe two months?" Rachel guessed. "As soon as I thought I was pregnant, I stopped everything. My baby is going to have a good life. That's why I'm getting my degree."

"Good for you," The nurse smiled. "Putting your baby first is going to make you a wonderful mother."

"The father is pretty heavily into drugs. Is that important to know?" Marika asked.

"It's hard to say," The nurse typed some more. "I'll make a note, but his part in the baby making is really over. It's all up to Rachel now. She has to live a healthy lifestyle to give her baby a great start." Turning off the computer, the nurse asked, "How's your support system?"

Rachel looked down.

"She has friends who are going to help her." Marika squeezed Rachel's hand.

Leaving the clinic, Marika put her arm around Rachel. "Let's get some ice-cream. We need to celebrate. You're having a baby!" Marika was determined to make this day a happy one for Rachel. She remembered wishing someone would have been excited for her when she found out she was pregnant.

"Really?" Rachel pushed her hands into her fleece jacket.

"I know it's cold, but the sun is shining, and a very wise person once told me '*Every child is a blessing…although sometimes their timing could be a little better*'. We should celebrate."

"Okay," Rachel laughed.

Situated with their black-raspberry chip hot fudge sundaes, Marika clicked her spoon against Rachel's. "Congratulations, mom. Now it's time to make some plans."

"I know." Rachel sighed before taking a big bite.

"Are you going to tell Alex?"

"Mmm, this is so good." Rachel closed her eyes savoring the flavor.

"So…?" Marika took a bite.

"Yes, I'm going to tell him." She put down her spoon and looked at Marika. "Do you think he'll stop using when he hears the news?"

"I don't know, Rachel." Marika wiped her mouth with a napkin. "I don't know Alex. What do you think?"

"I'm not sure. I want him to, but…I've only known him on drugs."

"Do you have any family who could help?"

"No." Rachel looked out the window. "I left my foster family when I turned eighteen. I wouldn't want to go back."

Poor kid. "Where are you living now?" Marika took another bite.

"Alex and I share a room with a group of people." She tapped the spoon on the bowl. "It's fine."

"Would you want a baby to live there?" Marika's voice was soft.

"No."

Oh boy, this girl was going to need help.

Marika rubbed her head, hoping to push away the headache that was gathering behind her eyes. "Okay, then the first thing is to find you better housing. Are you working?"

"No, it's hard to get a good job without a high school diploma. That's why I'm taking the GED classes."

"Alright, before the baby gets here you need to: one," Marika raised her forefinger. "Find a place to live; two," she raised a second finger. "Get a job, and three, get your high school diploma. I think you can do it."

"I do too." Rachel gave Marika a high five. "But first I have to tell Alex. I hope he's as excited as me." She put a heaping spoonful of whipped cream into her mouth.

I hope he is too. Marika took a bite.

Returning to Mary and Martha's that afternoon, Marika knocked on Nick's door. "Hey, do you have a minute?"

"Sure c'mon in. What's up?" Nick stopped writing and leaned back in his chair.

Marika scooped up the papers lying on the chair, keeping the files on her lap. "How would we go about helping a young pregnant woman get housing and a job?"

"Anyone I know?" Nick tapped a pen on his chin.

"It's Rachel from the GED and cooking class. I'm worried about her, and she's going to need help."

"Did you talk to Libby?" Nick shrugged as Marika rolled her eyes. "I know, but she *is* a social worker, so you probably should start with her. Is the young lady on any type of assistance now?"

"I have no idea. She grew up in foster care and she's living with her boyfriend, who's a total druggie. She thinks he's going to get clean once he hears about the baby, but I have my doubts."

"Is she using?" Nick rifled through the files on his desk. "If so, we could probably get her placed in a rehab facility until the baby's born."

"No, she's clean."

"Any sober friends?"

Marika stood and put the papers back on the chair. "I guess I can start feeling out some of the GED students and Mother's Group members. Maybe someone will have a room. The thing is, I'm not sure she's going to be willing to leave her boyfriend right now."

Nick stood putting his hands on his hips. "I have to know who needs the room: a pregnant girl or a couple. And I'll be honest, I'm not even going to *try* to find a place for an active drug user. I can try to get him help, but getting clean has to be the first step."

"I understand." Marika nodded. "She's going to tell her boyfriend about the baby tonight. I guess we'll have to see how that goes."

The next morning, clients trickled through the M&M doors early, trying to avoid the cold. The kitchen preparations were in full swing. Marika reviewed the day's chore chart holding a bag of lettuce, her mind a million miles away.

"Marika, Marika," Rachel's hoarse voice called from kitchen door. She beckoned with both hands as if magically pulling Marika towards her. "Marika, I need to talk to you. Please come here." Her hands moved with a flourish.

"Girl, where are your shoes?" Marika looked at the young girl's outfit: black hoodie, pajama bottoms, and bare feet. "How'd it go?" She noticed the girls panicked look. "What's wrong?"

Rachel's face was white, her eyes huge. She spoke in a strained, hushed tone. "Alex won't wake up. I think he's dead." Her voice cracked into sobs.

"*What*?" Marika dropped the bag of lettuce and rushed through the door. She grabbed Rachel's shoulders. "What happened? Did you call 911?"

Rachel shook her head, tears pouring down her face. "I tried to wake him up, but he's so cold. I just came to get you. Please help me." She grabbed Marika's hand and ran for the door.

"I'll be back," Marika yelled to Dallas.

"Where are you going?" Dallas watched Marika rush out the door. "What in the hell happened here?" He looked at the shredded lettuce scattered across the floor.

"Where is Marika going?" Kate asked, pushing a cart filled with bread into the kitchen.

"I have no idea." Dallas said.

39

KATE

Kate looked at the clock for what seemed like the hundredth time. Marika still hadn't returned, and lunch started in ten minutes.

Pushing through the kitchen door, Nick held a Bible in one hand his phone in the other. "Marika just called. She's going to miss lunch."

"Is everything okay?" Kate placed the taco meat into the serving station.

"No, Rachel's boyfriend OD'd this morning. He's dead." Nick stared into the dining room. "Marika's trying to get her settled. I'm heading over to her apartment as soon as we pray."

"Oh *no*," Kate said.

"That's a damn shame." Dallas pounded the prep table with his fist.

"Can I do anything?" Kate asked.

"No, it's just such a waste." Nick shook his head.

"It's time to pray," Jenny's somber voice called from the dining room.

"Dear God," Nick said at the prayer circle. "Our hearts are heavy this morning, and we turn to you for comfort and strength. We ask you to bless this community, and to help us to end the scourge of drugs destroying so many lives. We ask you to protect our families, our neighborhood, and our friends as we fight the good fight to destroy the evil lurking in our community. To you, dear Father, we pray. *Our Father…*"

Lunch was sad. The news of Alex's death spread almost as fast as the rumors. Each table told its own story.

"He got some really good stuff. Do you know where he got it?" A druggie asked.

"He was a user his whole life. His body just quit," Deacon shrugged.

"They found the needle in his arm," Sharon said.

"It was suicide. His old lady just told him she was pregnant. He couldn't take the pressure," Cool Hand Luke offered.

"Excuse me, Miss Katie," Kate turned from the prep table to see Bernice standing at the kitchen door. Donned in a maroon pantsuit with a striped scarf flowing from her head, she beckoned for Kate to come over.

"Hi Bernice, do you need something?" Kate wiped her hands on her apron.

"That young man who died." Bernice put her hand to her mouth as if she was telling a secret. "Was that our Rachel's beau?"

Kate nodded. "Marika's with her right now."

"That poor, sweet girl." Bernice put her hand on her heart. "We've got to help her. I'm going over there right now." She turned so fast her scarf looked like a kite floating in the air behind her.

After lunch was over, Kate and Dallas were busy with the final clean-up when Marika returned. "How is she?" Kate asked.

"She's a mess." Marika brushed her fingers through her hair. "It was awful. I could tell he was dead the second I walked into that filthy apartment." She picked up a towel and began wiping imaginary crumbs. "He was laying on the couch, a hypodermic needle still in his arm. Rachel kept shaking his shoulders saying. '*Marika's here. Alex, it's going to be alright. You're going to be fine.*'" Marika started to cry. "There was nothing I could do but call 911. He was gone." Marika pressed her fingers into her eyes to stop the tears.

Taking a deep breath, she leaned against the prep table. "The EMTs came, but it was useless. Rachel started screaming. '*Please, help him. Marika, don't let them leave, please, please.*' She was begging me to help her. She got on her knees and grabbed my hands, '*Marika, he can't be dead, please make them help him.*'" Marika covered her mouth trying to stifle a sob. "It was horrible. I knelt beside her and put my arms around her and said, '*Rachel, I'm so sorry honey, but he's gone.*'" Marika wiped a tear from her cheek. "I swear. She melted...She disintegrated to the floor. It was so awful."

"Where is she now?" Kate wiped a tear from her face.

"Bernice took her to her apartment." Walking to the sink, Marika started washing the dishes. "Rachel didn't want to stay in that room, and I can't blame her. The place was a pigsty. Six people were living in a one-bedroom apartment. Bernice told Rachel to get her things. She was coming to live with her. Thank God."

Marika threw the towel into the dirty dishwater. "We packed up all her clothes and went to Bernice's apartment. Everything Rachel owns fit into two plastic grocery bags. The poor kid doesn't have anyone or anything. Did you know she grew up in foster care? She said Alex was the only person who was ever nice to her. They met here."

"The rumor in the dining room is that she's pregnant." Dallas dried the pans.

"She is," Marika said. "I went with her to the clinic yesterday. I guess she's suspected for a while, that's why she started taking the GED classes. She really wants to give the baby a good life."

"Do you think he meant to kill himself because of the baby?" Dallas asked.

"I don't think so. Rachel said he seemed happy when she told him. He was going to go to the Suboxone clinic and get well. He told her they would find their own place, and he would get a real job. I'm not sure what happened."

"You don't think she'll start using again, do you?" Kate asked.

"I hope not," Marika said.

"What about a funeral?" Dallas asked.

Marika tossed her apron in the laundry. "Nick's talking to the police and the coroner. The thing is… Rachel isn't a relative. I'm not even sure they would release the body to her. They probably have to search for his next of kin. In any case, she doesn't have money for a funeral."

"Poor kid sounds like she's in a bad way," Dallas said.

Marika started to cry, "I know, my heart is breaking for her. I didn't have the best family, but I was never completely alone. We've got to help her."

"Do you think I could go visit her at Bernice's?" Kate asked.

"We can go together," Marika said.

"I'm going too," Dallas turned off the lights.

Bernice lived two streets away from the kitchen in a fourth-floor walk-up. Marika, Kate and Dallas were out of breath after climbing the stairs to reach the two-bedroom apartment.

"God bless you for coming," Bernice smiled, and stepped aside for them to enter. The apartment was small and crowded. It appeared she had placed all the furniture from her three-bedroom home into the cramped space. Rachel laid on a plaid maroon and tan early American-style couch covered with a blue fleece blanket. Crumpled tissues surrounded her. An uneaten bagel with cream cheese and a can of coke were placed next to the box of tissues on the walnut coffee table. The muted television was tuned to *Dr. Phil.* Watching the group enter through red-rimmed eyes, Rachel tucked the blanket under her chin.

Giving a slight bow, Dallas took off his baseball cap. "Miss Rachel, I'm sorry for your loss. I didn't speak to Alex much, but he seemed like a good man who was battling his demons."

Nodding, Rachel scrunched her face as the tears flowed.

"Rachel, honey, I'm so sorry. What do you need?" Kate handed her a tissue and squeezed next to her on the edge of the sofa. Marika took the seat on Rachel's other side. Dallas sat in the overstuffed recliner in the corner of the room.

"Who would like a cup of tea?" Bernice asked.

"Don't go to any trouble," Marika said. "We're just here to support Rachel."

"He was my only friend." Rachel sobbed grabbing a tissue. "The first time I ate at M&M some guys were bothering me, and Alex scared them away." She shrugged, "After that, I just started to follow him. He made me feel safe."

"Well, we're going to watch out for you now," Bernice called from the kitchen.

"When I told him about the baby, he was happy." Rachel looked at Marika. "He said we could get married." Her voice choked, "I can't believe he's dead. I can't go back to that apartment. I keep seeing him lying on the couch. What am I going to do?" She sobbed.

"You're going to stay here." Bernice walked into the room holding a tray. "As long as you want. We'll make do." She placed a silver tea service on the coffee table. Pouring the steeped liquid into white and rose-trimmed porcelain teacups, "I'm going to take care of you and that sweet baby you're carrying." Bernice kissed Rachel's forehead.

There was a timid tap on the door. "Who could that be?" Bernice wondered.

"I'll get it." Dallas jumped up to open the door. "It's Leon, c'mon on in."

Standing in front of Rachel, Leon spoke to the floor, "I heard about your boyfriend. I'm sorry. I baked you these cookies." He pushed the plate into her hands.

"Thank you." Rachel put the cookies on the table and wrapped Leon in a hug. "Thank you, thank you for coming, Leon. You have no idea how much this means to me."

"Hello?" Tamara walked into the crowded room along with her two children and Sharon. "Oh, Rachel. I'm so sorry. I don't know what to say. I'll help anyway I can."

'It's sad," Sharon stood next to her sister.

"I feel like we should be doing something." Dallas bounced up and down. "Is there someone we should call? His family?"

"I don't think so." Rachel tightened the blanket around her. "Alex didn't like to talk about them. I know his dad is dead. I'm not sure about his mom. I think he was alone…like me."

"You're not alone," Marika said. "We're all here for you."

There was another knock at the door. "Oh, my goodness, you are very popular, Rachel." Bernice opened the door. "Kendra, how nice of you to come by."

"I brought my mom with me." Kendra pulled her mother's arm.

"It's so nice to meet you." Bernice shook Kendra's mom's hand. "I'm Bernice, we love your daughter. She's a delight."

"Thank you, I'm Tessa."

"Mom, this is my entire cooking class." Kendra stepped into the living room.

"Hi, everyone," Tessa smiled. "I'm sorry we're meeting under such sad circumstances."

"Well, it's nice that we're together," Bernice said. "Would you like a cookie? Leon made them."

"Mmm, they look good. I'm starving." Kendra took a bite. "These are delicious, Leon." She pushed some cookie crumbs into her mouth. "I definitely think you're the best baker in the class." Leon's face reddened.

Dallas patted Leon's shoulder. "See, man, you've got skills. You can stand on your own."

Tessa took a cookie. "Well, I know Kendra's cooking has improved. She loves the class, and the boys and I are enjoying the meals she brings home."

"I love the class, too." Bernice squeezed onto the couch. "For the first time since I moved here, I feel like I belong. Just look at us...." She put her arm around Rachel and glanced around the room. "Our friend is in trouble, and we're by her side. We're more than friends. We're family."

40

KATE

On Monday morning, Kate placed the utility-sized pan of chicken pot pie into the serving station. After substituting the phyllo crust with homemade biscuits, the restaurant dish had become economical enough to serve at the kitchen. Would she ever get to cook in her restaurant again? She'd had a frustrating call with the fire inspector and the insurance company. Neither one of them had the answer of when *or if* she'd be getting the insurance money.

She watched Rachel and Bernice navigate the food line. Rachel was crying. Bernice, adorned in yellow, mimicked a mother hen trying to coax her chick through the maze of people.

"Would you like chicken pot pie?" Dan asked a crying Rachel. Wiping her nose with the back of her hand, she shook her head, no.

"You need to eat." Bernice handed Rachel a tray. "She'll have the pot pie, Dan. It looks delicious, and she'll take everything else, too. I'll have the same. Now, you have a blessed day." Bernice smiled at Dan and gave Rachel a gentle push. "Come on, sweet thing, let's keep moving. You're okay, I've got you."

"Hi, Rachel, how are you?" Kate stood next to Sylvie at the dessert station. "Do you need anything?"

Rachel shook her head, wiping the tear on her cheek with the tissue

Bernice pushed into her hand.

"I'll come by tonight and check on you, okay?" Kate said.

Rachel nodded.

"Would you like a dessert?" Sylvie put her hand on top of the counter to catch Rachel's attention. Like a zombie, the girl kept moving down the line.

"I guess." Bernice eyed the desserts. "Give me those chocolate chip cookies and a piece of cherry pie, please." She sighed, "She's got to start eating, poor thing. Maybe the desserts will tempt her."

"I'll bring some chicken noodle soup by tonight," Kate said.

"That sounds good." Bernice placed the desserts on the tray and smiled at Sylvie. "Thank you, Sylvie. Have a blessed day."

"Why is she so upset?" Sylvie's gaze followed Rachel.

"Oh, gosh, it's terrible." Kate watched Bernice and Rachel join Tamara and her children at a table. "Rachel's boyfriend died. He OD'd last week. The poor thing found him dead on the couch with a needle still in his arm."

A dessert tray clattered to the floor, spilling chocolate cake, pies, and cookies all over the kitchen. Sylvie legs buckled, and she collapsed against the wall.

"Sylvie, oh my gosh." Kate knelt on the floor next to her. "Are you alright, what hurts?" Sylvie's blue eyes were filled with tears. Her entire body was shaking.

"Sylvie, Sylvie, what's wrong?" Dan asked. Marika and Dallas rushed over to help.

"Are they sure he's dead?" Sylvie's voice quivered.

"Who?" Kate held Sylvie's hand.

"I think she had a stroke," Marika said. "I'll call 911."

"No," Sylvie shouted. "I'm okay, just answer my question." Tears rolled down her face, and she struggled to stand.

"Let us help you." Kate grasped Sylvie's elbow. "Marika, take her other arm. Dallas, Dan, I need you guys to get the lunch line moving. We'll take her to my office."

Marika and Kate helped Sylvie stand. Sylvie's eyes were wild darting around the dining room and kitchen. "Are they sure he's dead? Where is he? Maybe he passed out?"

"Who?" Marika and Kate stopped. They were confused and concerned.

"That girl crying," Sylvie's voice rasped as she pointed to Rachel. "How do they know her boyfriend's dead?"

"I really think she's having a stroke." Marika talked over Sylvie's head as she helped her to a chair. "I'm going to ask Nick to call 911."

"No, no, no," Sylvie cried shaking her head, tears pouring down her face. "I haven't had a stroke." She grabbed both of Kate's hands. "You've got to tell me. Why do they think that girl's boyfriend is dead?"

"Sylvie, can I call someone for you?" Kate could feel the woman's hand shaking. "Rachel is going to be fine. The entire cooking class is supporting her."

"TELL ME," Sylvie screamed pumping Kate's arms. "Why does Rachel think her boyfriend is dead? ANSWER ME...." Her voice broke. She covered her face with her hands and sobbed, "He's . . . my son."

41

NICK

Nick burst into Kate's office. "Sylvie?"

Sylvie sat in the chair. Sobs racked her body, her face buried in her hands. A pale Katie kneeled next to her rubbing her back. Marika stood next to the filing cabinets, her hands on her chest.

"Rachel's boyfriend is your son?" Kate asked.

Nodding, Sylvie whispered, "He's dead?"

"Sylvie." Nick kneeled on the other side of the chair putting his arm around her shoulder. "I am so sorry. I—we had no idea Alex was your son."

"I know," Sylvie looked up. Her tear-streaked face searched the room. "I need a tissue." Marika handed her a paper towel. "Thank you," Sylvie said with a sad smile. "I need to call Zach. I have to tell him about Xander."

"Sylvie," Kate said. "Rachel's boyfriend's name was Alex. Are you sure he's the same man?"

Sylvie stifled a sob with the paper towel, nodding, "Alexander... We called the boys Xander and Zach... they're twins."

"Thank you for driving me home, Nick, but you really don't have to stay.

I'll be alright." Her voice caught on her words. Sylvie's modest Cape Cod home was twenty minutes from the kitchen. Nick followed her inside.

"No, I want to stay and keep you company. Can I get you something?" Nick asked, standing in Sylvie's kitchen.

She turned on the light over the sink. "No, no. She looked out the window, the grey winter sky casting a shadow over the backyard. "I can't stand how dark it is. I hate the gloom of winter. Don't you?" Sylvie didn't wait for an answer, but walked from the kitchen to the family room, to the living room turning on all the lights. "I hate not being able work outside. I can spend hours in the garden nurturing a delicate plant, eradicating a persistent weed, planting a vegetable, but in the winter. Well…" She sighed and closed the front drapes, "The days are shorter, but the hours seem so much longer."

Nick guided her to the couch. "Why don't you sit down? How about I make you a cup of tea?"

"Tea does sound nice. I can make it. I need to keep moving. Would you like one?"

"Why don't I help you?" Nick followed her back to the kitchen.

Sylvie filled the kettle with water and pointed to a plaque resting on the counter. "There's my M&M 'Volunteer of the Year' award."

"You certainly deserved it."

"Not really." Sylvie opened the cabinet and pulled out a tea canister. "I'm a fraud." She placed the tea bags in the cups. "I didn't really care about helping people. The only reason I volunteered was to see my son," Crying, she hugged the jar.

"Why don't you sit, and I'll make the tea," Nick said.

Nodding, she grabbed a tissue from the box sitting on the coffee table, knocking over the picture next to it. She showed Nick the family photo. "We look so happy here. It was the boys' high school graduation." She stroked the photo. The twins dressed in their caps and gowns. Their arms were wrapped around their parents. The whole family smiled at the camera.

"When did the boy's graduate?" Nick handed her the steaming cup of mint tea.

"Thank you, gosh…they'll have their fifteen-year reunion next year." She took a sip of tea. "How did it go so wrong?" She put the cup down and held the picture. "I remember the day I found out I was having twins like it was yesterday—how can one of my boys now be dead?" Nick sat next to her on the couch and listened.

"Mac and I had tried for years to get pregnant, so when the doctor saw two babies on the sonogram we were thrilled. We wanted to give them everything from A to Z, so we named them Alexander and Zachary. She pointed to the boy on the right, "That's Xander. Look at that big smile of his." She touched the photo. "The boys were mirror twins and had yin and yang personalities, but they were inseparable. Zach was always more serious, the rule follower, a hard worker, but Xander…" She smiled at Nick. "He was the life of the party, happy-go-lucky, a daredevil always looking for the next thrill."

Sylvie took a sip of the tea and nodded at the family room floor. "I can still picture two rambunctious little boys playing Legos, Hot Wheels, or just lying on the carpet to watch cartoons or football. I loved being a stay-at-home mom. I liked driving carpool, setting up play dates, making dinner. As hard as it is to believe, I miss the sound of the door slamming as they rushed in to ask for a snack, or help with their homework, or just to tell me about their day. It seems like another lifetime."

She continued, wistfully, "The years went so fast. They're a blur of baseball, basketball, and football. I used to joke: I knew the season by the sport, not the weather. Life was good. Some of my happiest memories are of me sitting on the sidelines watching the boys. I loved seeing Mac coach their little league teams and attending every game they played in high school." Sylvie's tear-filled eyes peered up at Nick. She grasped his hand. "I need you to understand." Pumping his arm, she emphasized her words. "We were a happy, loving, close family."

"Sylvie, I'm sure you were." Nick nodded. "The camera doesn't lie. You can see the love in that picture."

"We did love each other." She stared at the photo. "The boys decided to separate for college—not different schools, just different rooms on the same dorm floor." Her eyes twinkled as she gave a little laugh. "Their majors suited their personalities: Zach studied information systems and finance, while Xander chose to focus on marketing and promotions." She sighed, "I had expected to feel lost after the boys left, but the truth was I enjoyed reconnecting with Mac. The boys were nearby. They both went to the University of Cincinnati, and I managed to see them whenever they wanted a home-cooked meal, or their laundry done by their mom. I even went back to teaching."

Sylvie laid the picture face-down on the coffee table and walked to the window, looking out into the gray dusky world. "I guess the problems began when Xander broke his leg." She turned to look at Nick sitting on the couch. "A broken leg destroyed my perfect world."

She took a tissue and started pacing the room. "It was the start of the boys' senior year in college. The fraternity was holding a welcome back party, and someone decided it would be a great idea to race grocery carts down a steep hill on campus." She shrugged her shoulders. "It's two o'clock in the morning, you've been drinking all night, why not push a cart as fast as you can, jump in and race to the bottom of the hill? I guess I should be grateful. They did insist everyone wear a bicycle helmet." She brandished her finger. "That was a good thing, because Xander was thrown from the cart and broke his leg in four places."

Sylvie sat down on the chair by the window. "It's true. There's rarely a happy two a.m. phone call. Zach started the conversation. 'He's going to be alright, but Xander's in the emergency room. They think he might have broken his leg. You may want to come down here'."

She continued, "Mac and I raced to the hospital, praying and wondering how a kid on the Dean's List could do something so stupid. I remember thinking when I walked into that hospital room, *I'm going to try to be grateful it's just a broken leg.* Xander looked terrible. Hooked up to an IV, the monitors beeping and screeching. His leg bandaged and bleeding. The whole right side of his face was scraped and bruised. He looked so young," she stopped as if caught up in the memory.

"Poor Zach looked almost as bad—not injured, but worried, scared and probably a little hungover. He sat on the side of the bed holding his brother's hand. As angry as I was at their foolishness, I was so happy he was going to be okay. It was *just* a broken leg."

Sylvie resumed pacing. "Xander had to move home after the surgery. There was no way he could manage the stairs at the fraternity. I took family leave. To be honest, I was happy to be a full-time mom again. I loved caring for my son. Fulfilling all his requests for food, drink, pain medicines, but after a few weeks of recovery, Xander wanted to return to school and graduate with his friends. Zach and the other boys in the fraternity agreed to be his nursemaids."

Sylvie took a sip of tea and sat down on the sofa.

"I'm sure that's cold." Nick pointed to the cup. "Would you like me to warm it?"

Sylvie shook her head. "This is where I go to the why's— *why* didn't I insist Xander stay home to recover? *Why* didn't I keep a check on his pain meds? *Why* would a doctor keep refilling an opioid prescription without question?"

She rubbed her temples. "Mac became suspicious around Christmas. He questioned him, 'Why are you still taking pain medicine? Your leg looks fine. You don't even have a limp.' But Xander's answers always made sense. 'The cold weather really bothers me. The doc said it may be this way for a while.' We let it go. We wanted to believe Xander was fine."

She sighed heavily, "During his last semester at school, his personality changed. The happy-go-lucky guy became belligerent, impatient, a loner. He stopped socializing with his fraternity brothers, and he became almost a recluse, staying in his room all day. Zach tried to help, but he was rebuffed. The once-inseparable brothers now barely spoke."

"That must have been so hard for all of you." Nick said.

Sylvie nodded, "Mac and I tried to explain away the changes: he was stressed because of graduation and the job search, he'd broken up with his girlfriend, his injury had caused him to get behind, he was focusing on his schoolwork. We grabbed any excuse to explain the differences, except for the real one… Drugs didn't happen to people like us. My son isn't a druggie."

Sylvie put her hand on her heart and gave a sarcastic laugh. "The reality check came in the form of a letter. *Dear Mr. Alexander Mitchell, we regret to inform you that you have failed to meet the necessary requirements to graduate.* The boys hadn't changed their mailing address, so all their correspondences came to our house. I'd opened it by mistake or divine providence, I guess?" Sylvie shrugged. "Mac and I went to the fraternity house and confronted him. He cried and then told us the truth. He was addicted to the painkillers the doctor had prescribed to him. He had not attended a single class during the last semester. On the day he should have graduated from college, we moved Xander into an addiction treatment center. Sylvie looked at Nick, her eyes brimming with tears.

She squeezed his hand, "We tried."

"I'm sure you did," Nick squeezed her hand back.

Taking a deep breath and a sip of tea, Sylvie continued, "We were so hopeful, so naive. He was getting help. Xander was going to be okay. After two months of rehab, he came home. We had a huge welcome home party. Fraternity brothers, cousins, aunts, uncles, grandparents, Zach flew in from Silicon Valley where he'd gotten a job. We wanted Xander to know how much love and support he had. He seemed to take his recovery seriously. He attended NA meetings. He registered for his final semester of classes. He worked out every day. Mac and I began to breathe again. We had our child back. We thanked God every day for his healing."

Sylvie breathed deeply before continuing, "After about six weeks, Xander began to stay out after the NA meetings. Mac and I tried not to worry. We'd tell ourselves, *We're just paranoid. NA was a great support system for him. He was a social guy; of course, he was making new friends and hanging out with them. He was young.* But, when he stayed out all night, our worries turned to accusations. Mac and I were sitting on the couch when he walked in bleary-eyed early in the morning. He took one step through the door, and Mac confronted him, 'Where have you been? What did you take? How could you do this to your mother?'"

"'I'm not using,' Xander had shouted back. 'I swear. I lost track of time, and I crashed on a buddy's couch. I'm clean—test me.'"

Sylvie wrapped her arms around her body and stared at Nick. "I wanted to believe him. I ignored the truth. I hugged him and said, 'Honey, we love you. We want to help you. If you've slipped up, let us know. We'll get you more help.' Xander's sweet, blue eyes had pleaded with me.

'Mom, I'm not using. Please believe me, I promise.' He reminded me of his five-year-old self promising me he *did* brush his teeth. I wanted so badly to believe him." She shrugged, "So, I did."

Giving a wry laugh, Sylvie moved about the room picking up knick-knacks, wiping the tops of furniture with her hand. "Mac wasn't as gullible. He watched Xander like a hawk. Not in a vindictive way, but because he was so concerned and scared. He found the evidence a few days later. Xander had hidden the pills in the spare tire well of his car. Mac was livid. The anger he felt at Xander's lies and deception was a visible extension of his body."

Sylvie picked up the photo and touched Mac's face "My husband was a big man. He ran into this house like a tornado after he found the stash. Xander was napping on the sofa and Mac pulled him off the couch by the nape of his shirt. He shoved the bag of pills in Xander's face screaming, 'Where did you get these?' He was so furious. White foam pooled at the sides of his mouth and spit accented each word he yelled. I stood in the doorway crying, watching an obviously stoned Xander try to focus on the bag of pills. Mac was out of control. 'Do you have any idea how much rehab cost us? How dare you treat your mom like this.' Mac was shaking Xander's shoulders so hard. I was certain Xander's neck would break."

Sylvie stood up and began to pace the room, Nick understood. He could see her reliving the memory as she spoke. His heart broke for her.

Turning, she wrapped her arms around herself and stared at Nick, "I tried to intercede. Putting myself between them, I pulled on Mac's arms, pleading. 'Please, let him go. Honey, calm down.' I tried to push Xander back onto the couch. 'Xander, how could you? Pack your bags, we're taking you back to rehab."

"'Fuck no!' Xander had screamed. 'I'm not going back. Get the hell away from me. I'm leaving.' I know he didn't mean to, but he pushed me and knocked me down. I was so stunned. I just laid on the floor and cried. Mac was enraged. He grabbed Xander's belt and practically threw him out the front door. 'Don't you ever touch your mother again. Get the hell out of here. I never want to see your stoned face again, and don't even think about driving that car.' Xander flipped us off as Mac slammed the door."

Sylvie continued, "I sat on the floor and cried. I was so hurt and disappointed. The *why's* came back. *Why* didn't I make him go back to rehab the first night he didn't come home? *Why* didn't we drug-screen him? *Why* wasn't he trying to stay sober? *Why* was he doing this to us? I was so engrossed in my own despair; I didn't notice Mac grasping his chest and gasping for air. The thud of his body hitting the floor made me look up. My strong, loving, kind husband had collapsed. I crawled over to him. 'Mac, Mac, oh my God, honey, what's wrong?' I'd grabbed the phone to call 911 and rushed to the street screaming for Xander. He had disappeared. I tried to remember how to perform CPR: one, two, three compressions; breathe. One, two, three compressions; breathe. It was too late. Mac was dead."

"Oh, Sylvie, I'm so sorry." Nick wrapped his arms around her shoulders.

She gave a weak smile. "I called Zach first. He took the first flight home. I called Xander, but he didn't answer. I left message after message for him to *please call me*. I sent text messages to his friends from college and NA, but no one had seen or heard from him. By the time Zach landed, I had left over a hundred messages for Xander. He didn't respond to any of them."

Sighing, she continued, "Zach spent hours driving around the city searching for him, but Xander was gone. So…one week after Xander stormed out of the house, we buried Mac. Not really knowing whether Xander knew his dad was dead or not. The day after the funeral, I got a text from an unknown number: *I'm Sorry.* I assumed it was Xander and responded immediately. *I know. It's not your fault. Where are you? I love you. Please come home. We'll get you help.* There was no response."

She continued, "I spent the months after Mac died trying to find Xander. I hired private investigators; I drove everywhere searching for him. I could tell you what street corners sold which drugs and the location of secret drug dens, but I couldn't find my son. Xander had simply vanished. I was crazed, I couldn't eat or sleep. Zach was so worried about me. He quit his job and moved back here. I was desolate. My beautiful family was destroyed."

Sylvie laid the photo face-down on the coffee table and sat back down on the couch before continuing her story. "For two years, I lived in limbo." She pulled apart the tissue and stared at the room. "Not knowing where your child is. Well, it's a type of sadistic torture. Thoughts of Xander—*Where was he? Was he alive? Was he scared, alone, hungry, cold, high?* —were destroying me. Moments of peace and happiness were interrupted by hours of panic. There was always a part of my brain pulsing: *where's Xander, where's Xander.*" She clasped and unclasped her fist emphasizing the question.

"Then, I got the phone call, 'Sylvie, I saw Xander!' A family friend volunteering at M&M had seen him come through the lunch line. 'Are you sure it's him?' I'd asked. I couldn't believe it. After two years, he was less than twenty minutes away. My friend was positive. She had called his name, but he ran away."

For the first time, Sylvie smiled, "My heart *soared.* Xander was alive. I had never heard of M&M, but I knew the area. So, I hopped in my car and drove to the neighborhood. The kitchen was closed, but I was renewed. I showed the people standing on the street Xander's photo, hoping someone would recognize him and tell me where he was. Of course, no one admitted to knowing him, but I was rejuvenated. The next day, I parked in front of M&M thirty minutes before it opened. I watched every person who entered and exited the front door for the next two hours. I began to think my friend was mistaken. But then, I saw him: *Xander*! He was dirty, his hair was long and scraggly. He looked so skinny still carrying his bookbag from college. My heart sang and cried at the same time—*There he is. He's alive. He's sick, he's still using.*"

"'Xander, Xander,' I'd jumped out of the car and ran after him. I don't even think I closed the door. He turned when I called his name. I know he recognized me, and then he ran in the opposite direction. I tried to run after him calling, 'Xander, please stop. Honey, it's okay, I love you. I want to help.' He was too fast and too determined. I lost him again."

She continued, "When I got back to the kitchen, my car was gone—*stolen*. I guess an open car door with the keys still in the ignition was too much temptation for someone. Disheartened, I walked into Mary and Martha's to call the police. While I waited for them, Jenny asked. 'Are you here to volunteer?' and without hesitation, I said, 'Yes, yes, I am.' If Xander wouldn't come to me, I'd go to him." She swiped her hands together. "So that's how my illustrious career as *M&M Volunteer of the Year* actually began."

She looked at her watch. "Oh my, I've had you here all afternoon, Nick. You really don't have to stay." She walked to the window and pulled back the drape. "Zach should have landed by now."

"I'd like to meet Zach." Nick picked up her empty teacup. "Can I get you some more tea?"

"Maybe just a glass of ice water? The glasses are next to the sink."

"So, were you ever able to talk to Xander?" Nick asked, handing her the ice water.

Sylvie took a sip. "On the first day I volunteered, I cleaned tables. I saw Xander walk through the door, and I practically knocked over the chairs trying to reach him. He looked so thin and dirty, but all I wanted to do was to pull him into my arms and never let go. I grasped his hand. It was the first time in over two years I had touched my child. I said, 'Xander, I love you. Please come home, I want to help.' He pulled his arm away and ran out the door without eating. The same thing happened the next week. As soon as he saw me, he left."

She sighed, "After that, I changed my tactics. I stopped approaching him. I'd wait until he was in the food line before I spoke. That's why I love serving desserts so much. It was easy for me to hide behind the trays. He didn't see me until he was trapped and had nowhere to go. I was short and sweet: 'How are you? Call me. My number hasn't changed. I want to help, please come home.' If I tried to engage in any deeper conversation, he'd run away. So, over the past few years, we've come to an awkward truce. He doesn't turn at the sight of me, and I don't expect any answers. The truth is, as long as I've been volunteering at M&M, Xander has never said a word to me."

"Wasn't that frustrating?" Nick groaned. "I can't imagine how hard that must have been."

"It was." Sylvie sat down at the kitchen table. "But seeing him became my own addiction. I craved the weekly contact, no matter how unsatisfying it was, that's why I never missed a day of volunteering." Her finger traced the water mark left by the cold glass. "I'd practically be holding my breath until he walked through the kitchen doors each week. Once I knew he was alive, I could breathe and relax for a few days. I'd watch to see how he was acting. Did he seem more sober? Did he need anything…shoes, socks, toothpaste, soap, a warm jacket, gloves? I could get those things for him.

In the beginning, I would hope and pray that he would look at me and say, 'Mom, I want to come home, please help me.' Like the Prodigal Son." She gave a sad smile. "But in the past year, his addiction seems to have gotten so much worse. He had a blank stare. There was maybe a faint glimmer of recognition. It was almost as if he was thinking, *I think I should know you, but I'm not sure why.*"

Sylvie took a deep breath. "I had noticed him and that girl, Rachel? She seemed nice, kind, sober. I was hoping she would be able to help him, but now he's gone."

Laying her head on the table, she cried.

They both jumped when the back door flew open. "Mom?" The tall, dark-haired man looked furious as he rushed towards the table. "Who the hell are you?"

"You must be Zach." Nick reached out to shake his hand. I'm Nick Decker from Mary and Martha's Soup Kitchen."

Zach ignored him. "Mom, are you okay? What's wrong?"

"Oh, honey." Sylvie wrapped her arms around Zach. "Xander's dead."

"What?" Zach's face turned ashen. "Are you sure?"

"We're sure," Nick said. "I'm sorry. We had no idea Alex was Sylvie's son. We've been trying to find his next of kin, but he had listed his name as Alex Malcom."

"Malcom? That's my dad's first name." Zach looked confused. "Alex?"

"In order to qualify for services, people apply at Jobs and Family Services for an identification card. Alex—*Xander*—did that under the name of Alex Malcom. He didn't list any next of kin."

"Of course he didn't." Zach's hand hit the table. "When did he die?"

"Last week. He's been in the morgue all this time," Sylvie's voice broke. "I'm so glad you're here." She touched Zach's cheek, "but I told you to call me when you landed."

"I did, but you didn't answer your phone. You said there was a problem at the kitchen. I thought it was about the sock donation."

"Where is my phone?" Sylvie rubbed her forehead. "Did I leave it in my coat pocket?" She walked to the closet in search of her phone. "M&M got the socks, didn't they, Nick?" She pulled her phone out of the pocket. "I think they need more blankets, though. It's so cold out."

"Okay." Zach typed into his phone. "You should have those by next week." He looked at Nick.

"Wait a minute." Nick put both hands on the table. "Are you the Zach Mitchell from A2Z Corporation?" Zach nodded. "You're one of the kitchen's biggest donors." Nick sat back in the chair.

"Donating was Zach's way of helping his brother. We'd talk each day after I volunteered. Zach would ask how things were, and I'd say the kitchen could use something—protein bars, socks, personal care kits. Magically, the donation would appear by the following week." She hugged Zach. "We both loved Xander and wanted him to get better."

Sylvie walked Nick to the front door. "Thank you for staying with me, Nick. I'm glad I got to tell you about Xander. I've felt like a fraud all these years." Her blue eyes glistened with tears.

"Sylvie," Nick held both of her hands. "Now that I know the real reason you've been a volunteer, I think you are more amazing than ever. Please let me know if I can do anything for you."

After he left, Nick drove straight to Holy Family to pray.

42

MARIKA

At the following week's cooking class, Rachel sulked into the kitchen. "I don't want to cook," she said hopping onto the stool. "Bernice made me come."

"You haven't been out since the funeral. You can't lay around on the couch all day." Bernice handed her an apron. "That baby needs some exercise and fresh air. Cooking will do you good, and you're going back to the GED class tomorrow."

"I am not." Rachel used the apron as a pillow and laid her head on the table.

"You are too! Isn't she, Marika?" Bernice lifted her body onto the seat.

"Well, we've certainly missed you, and you don't want to get too far behind." Marika passed out the recipe cards.

Huffing, Rachel pushed herself up. She still had dark circles under her eyes, but they were no longer brimming with tears. Bernice, clad in an orange sweat suit and baseball cap winked at Marika.

"How are you doing?" Tamara sat on the stool next to Rachel.

"Okay, I guess. I feel sick in the mornings, but Bernice bought me some oyster crackers, and they help."

"Did you talk to the guy's mom? I bet you could get some money out of her." Sharon leaned across the table.

"Oh my, I don't like the sound of that, but I do think she should tell Sylvie about the baby. What does everyone else think?" Bernice looked at the group.

"Well," Marika tapped two fingers on her chin. "If I were Sylvie, I'd want to know about the baby. What are you thinking, Rachel?"

"I'd tell her." Sharon slapped the table. "But unless she gives you some money, don't let her see the kid."

"I don't want her money," Rachel sighed. "If she wouldn't help Alex, then I don't want her to help me or my baby."

"I can't imagine that's the case." Katie placed a stock pot on the table. "Sylvie is so nice. Nick said she offered to take you out to lunch. Why don't you meet her and then decide?"

"I'll see." Rachel stretched her arms. "What are we making today?"

"Comfort food," Marika laughed. "We all need to feel better."

"Even though I don't have the best record, we're going to make soup."

Katie beckoned Leon and Kendra, who had just walked through the door. "Hi, you two, c'mon in, we're just about to get started."

"Any word on the test?" Marika asked, handing Kendra an apron.

"No, I think it will be next week. I'm so nervous." She pulled Marika to the side and whispered, "I think something's wrong with Leon. When I got here, he was pacing in front of the door. It was like he was afraid to come in."

"Hmm, I'll keep an eye on him." Marika watched Leon. He didn't seem to grasp the need to put down his book bag before trying to put on his apron. Something seemed off.

"Is everyone ready?" Katie tapped a spoon against the pot. "Today, we're going to make soup, which is a great way to use up all of your leftovers." She placed half of a rotisserie chicken in front of each person.

"Let's pretend this is the chicken we made the first week. We're going to peel off the skin and shred the breast using two forks like this." Kate separated the crisp brown skin from the meat, holding up the dangling glob of flesh for everyone to see.

"I don't think I can do this," Rachel said turning a strange shade of green. Pushing back from the table, she ran to the bathroom.

"Oh my," Bernice tried to hop down from the stool.

"I'll go." Marika touched Bernice's shoulder. "You stay here and make the soup."

The toilet flushed, and Rachel walked to the sink where Marika waited. "Better?" Marika asked, handing her a towel.

"A little." Rachel dried her hands. "I can't look at meat without feeling sick."

"It'll get better. I brought you a Coke, sometimes that helps." Marika handed her the cold can.

"Thanks." Rachel sat on the bathroom counter and took a sip. "Do you think I should meet with Alex's mom?"

"I think Sylvie is really nice, and it's not going to hurt for you to talk to her."

"But she didn't try to help Alex." She leaned back against the mirror and looked up at the ceiling.

"How do you know that?" Marika tapped the girl's knee. "Did Alex ever mention his family?"

"No."

"Maybe Alex wouldn't let her help him?"

Rachel pinched the bottom of her lip. "I guess I could go to lunch, but you have to go too."

"I will, and I think that's a good idea." Marika brushed a piece of hair from Rachel's face.

"And I'm not calling her." Rachel hopped down from the counter. "You can do that too."

"Why don't we see if Nick will set it up, then he can come to lunch too," Marika said with a smile.

43

NICK

Waiting outside the local restaurant, Nick enjoyed the winter day with the promise of spring in the sunshine. "How are you?" Nick asked Sylvie when she approached.

"I'm good." Sylvie walked with Nick to the table. "Some days are better than others. As much as I anticipated Xander dying, the reality is so much worse than I ever thought possible. A mother shouldn't have to bury her child." Her voice broke, and she searched in her purse for a tissue.

"I'm so sorry." Nick reached across the table to touch her hand. "Thanks for getting here early. I wanted to tell you a little about Rachel."

"Oh, okay." Sylvie looked around the restaurant. "She's still coming, isn't she?"

"Yes," Nick nodded. "Marika's bringing her, but I think you need to understand where Rachel's coming from. She grew up in foster care. She doesn't have any family, and Alex—I mean, *Xander*, was her best friend. He was her safety net."

"Oh, the poor thing." Sylvie folded her hands on the table. "I'd like to help her. I had seen her with Xander these last few months, and I was hoping she would be a good influence on him. She didn't look like she was using."

"She's clean." Nick nodded. "The thing is, Rachel doesn't understand why you didn't help Xander."

"But we tried—" Sylvie's voice pleaded.

"I know you did." Nick held his hand up in a stop motion. "And anyone who knows of your involvement with M&M would recognize your desire to help your son. But Rachel is eighteen, she's never had caring parents, and to her, you're just another mom who gave up on her child."

"But I'm not." Sylvie shook her head holding the tissue to her mouth.

Nick took a deep breath, "What I'm asking you to do is to take it slow. Let Rachel get to know you and your good heart. Don't try to force anything. Let Rachel feel like she's in control. I really want the two of you to build a friendship."

"Okay, I will." Sylvie looked out the window. "Nick, I know about the baby."

Shocked, he asked, "How?"

"I found out when we picked up Xander's things. She's going to keep it, isn't she?"

"That's the plan." Nick sat erect in the booth. "She's going to need help, but she has to believe she's in control."

"I understand." Sylvie nodded. "I'm going to do whatever I need to do to have a relationship with Rachel and the baby. She's the only connection I have to my son."

"They're here." Nick waved to Marika and Rachel standing at the door. He gave an encouraging smile. "It's going to be fine."

They stood as Marika and Rachel approached.

"Hello, ladies, how are you? You know Sylvie." Nick said.

"I'm so glad you both could make it." Sylvie gave a warm smile and stepped aside for Rachel to slide into the booth." Rachel grabbed Marika's hand and pulled her into the seat next to her.

Placing the napkin on her lap, Marika handed the rolled linen to Rachel and nodded for her to do the same. Marika asked, "How are you? We miss you at the kitchen, Sylvie."

"Oh, I'm doing okay." Sylvie played with her silverware. "Some days I can pretend Xander is alive, and I'll see him on Monday at the kitchen. Other days, I know he's dead, and my heart hurts so bad I can barely breathe." Placing her hands on her chest, she took a deep breath.

"Me too," Rachel whispered. "Sometimes I forget he's dead, I just think he's at the store or something, but then I remember him lying on that couch—and I know he's gone." Her voice broke, and a tear fell to the table.

"I'm so sorry you have that horrible picture in your mind." Sylvie touched Rachel's hand. "I've been trying to replace my sad memories with happy ones. I remember all the funny things Xander and his brother did when they were children. Would you like to hear about those?"

Rachel nodded, and for the first time, she looked at Sylvie's eyes, so much like Alex's blue ones. Taking a sip of water, Sylvie shared the story of Xander's life.

Taking the last bite of hot fudge cake, Rachel finally asked a question. "So, you did try to help him?"

"Oh yes." Sylvie nodded. "We all wanted Xander to get better. He refused all our help."

"So, the only reason you were working at M&M was to see Alex?" Rachel asked.

Sylvie nodded.

"I always wondered how you knew his favorite dessert." Rachel played with her spoon.

"I loved saving him a piece of peach pie. Just for a second, I'd feel like his mom again." Sylvie laughed, "Each summer, he'd beg me to bake a pie as soon as the peaches were ripe. He loved anything peach: pie, cobbler, ice-cream.

"I know," Rachel giggled. "One time somebody gave him a gift certificate to Graeter's Ice Cream Shop, and he ordered a peach sundae with peach ice cream. Who does that?"

"What's wrong with that?" Nick laughed. "It sounds delicious. We sure miss you at the kitchen, Sylvie. Lots of the clients have been asking about you, do you think you'll be able to volunteer again?"

"I don't think I can right now." Tears filled Sylvie's eyes. "I think I would spend the entire lunch watching the door and praying for Xander to come through. Before, there was always hope, but now—I don't have any." Her tears fell, and Sylvie fumbled for a tissue. "I'm sorry."

"I have something to tell you." Rachel reached across the table and took Sylvie's hand. "I'm going to have a baby."

Sylvie squeezed her hand back. "I have something to give you." She reached into her purse and handed a small sack to Rachel. "This was in the box of items we took from Xander's apartment. I think he wanted you to have it."

Opening the package, Rachel discovered a small stuffed sheep with a note on the small heart tag.

Rachel, you're going to be a great mom. I love you, Alex.

Rubbing the soft white fur against her cheek, Rachel murmured, "He never told me he loved me."

"Oh, I know Xander loved you." Sylvie said. "I could tell by the way he looked at you as you went through the food line. Xander thought you were very special."

"I want to leave." Rachel stood up pushing Marika out of the booth.

Sylvie stood too. "I'd like to help you and the baby. Will you please let me know if you need anything?"

"Marika, I want to go," Rachel's voice pleaded as she pulled on Marika's hand.

"Okay," Marika said. "Sylvie, thank you for lunch. Nick, I'll see you later." She rushed after the fleeing girl.

"Bye." Sylvie waved dropping into the seat. "I think I blew it."

"I don't think so." Nick sat down. "Give her a few weeks and try again."

44

KATE

At the kitchen the next day, Marika told Kate and Dallas about the lunch with Sylvie and Rachel. They'd gotten the serving line opened and were busy prepping vegetables for the next day's stir-fry. Peeling a pile of carrots, Kate asked. "So, how do you think Rachel's really feeling?"

"I think she's completely overwhelmed with everything right now." Marika chopped the celery in a quick rhythm. "After Sylvie gave her the stuffed sheep, she couldn't wait to get out of the restaurant. I practically had to run to keep pace with her, but by the time we reached Bernice's place she'd calmed down. I'm going to let her chill for a while, maybe talk to her after the class this week."

"Poor kid." Dallas pulled the last casserole pan out of the warmer for the food line. "She's had a rough time of it—What the hell happened to you?" His voice rose as he dropped the meat rotini onto the buffet station. Marika's head jolted up, and she gasped when she saw the bloody and bruised man in the food line holding his tray.

"Oh my gosh, Leon. What happened? Are you okay?" Kate grabbed a towel and walked through the crowd of people waiting to eat. "Let me see." She touched Leon's arm and gently wiped the blood from the scratch on his cheek and upper lip. His left eye was swollen shut. He seemed confused. His arms were stiff holding the food tray straight.

"He's fine," Jackie bulldozed her way through the line. "I told him he shouldn't be so clumsy." She pushed a barrette back into her thinning hair. "He's always falling over things." She patted Leon's back. "You're okay aren't you, baby doll?"

"Leon, I think you should go to the doctor." Kate dabbed his face with the towel. "Your eye looks really bad."

"He's fine," Jackie grabbed Leon's tray. "C'mon, sugar, let's get our food and we'll eat." Leon's one good eye filled with tears as he followed Jackie to a table.

Kate tossed the bloody towel into the laundry room and walked back into the kitchen. Dallas stood with his hands clenched on his hips. His breathing was fast and angry. His stare drilled knives into Jackie. The anger emanating from him was palpable. "If Leon were a woman we'd be calling the police." He pointed at Leon, "That man is being abused."

"I know." Kate filled a plastic bag with ice. "I'm going to try to talk to him again." She walked towards their table in the dining room.

"Sit up straight. Everyone's looking at us," Jackie snarled at Leon. "You look terrible. I'm embarrassed to be seen with you. I should have made you stay home." Leon picked up a cup of water with shaking hands.

Kate took the chair next to him. "Leon, here's some ice. Why don't you hold this on your eye?" She gave him the bag and guided his hand up to his bruised face.

"Baby, why don't you at least try to eat something?" Jackie's tone turned saccharine. "It will make you feel better."

Kate watched Leon move the food around his plate as he held the ice against his swollen eye. "How did this happen?" Glaring at Jackie, Kate's tone was sharp.

"I told you, he's clumsy." Jackie rose, her eyes challenging Kate. "He *fell*." She turned to Leon, "Baby, I'm ready to go. Your mouth must hurt. You can eat later." She pulled Leon up from his seat. His eyes downcast, he stared at the food on his plate.

"I don't think Leon's ready to leave." Kate stood. "I can sit with him."

"Leon and I are together." Jackie slapped his shoulder. "C'mon, I want to get out of here. I don't like the company." She snapped her fingers in front of his face. "Leon, I said we're leaving."

"I'll see you at the cooking class next week, right?" Kate asked as Leon followed Jackie out. He didn't answer.

"Well?" Dallas said as soon as Kate walked into the kitchen.

"He didn't say a word." Kate frenetically cleaned the prep table. "He seemed almost accepting of Jackie's treatment."

"We've got to do something." Dallas mopped the floor with a vengeance. "Leon's about my son's age. If someone was hurting my kid, I'm not sure what I'd do, but it wouldn't be pretty. Jackie is taking advantage of a sick person."

"I agree." Kate threw down her towel and untied her apron. "I'm going to talk to Nick."

"Nick" Kate rapped on the open door to his cluttered office.

Sitting at his desk, Nick looked up and waved her inside. "Hi, how's it going?"

"I think Leon from my cooking class is being abused by his partner. Well—I'm not exactly sure what their relationship is." Kate didn't bother to find a seat.

"Dallas has talked to me about them." Nick closed his computer. "Do you want to sit down?"

"No, I'm fine." Kate rubbed dust off the edge of the desk.

"I know they're living together" Nick picked up a folder. "I'm trying to find out who's paying the rent. If we can prove Jackie is taking advantage of Leon's government assistance, then we may be able to do something."

"But she's *beating* him." Kate placed her hands on her hips. "We need to do something. You should see his poor face. Jackie said he fell, but there's no way."

Nick walked to the window and looked at the clients streaming from the kitchen onto the littered street. "What did Leon say happened?"

"Nothing, it's like he's too afraid to say anything," Kate said.

Nick turned and leaned his back against the windowsill. "Well, then, there's nothing we can do. Leon has to report the abuse, or the police aren't going to get involved. Our best bet is to get Leon to open up about Jackie's abusive behavior, then we can help get him out of the situation."

"Are you kidding me? Leon's a mess." Kate's fist pounded the mound of papers covering the desk. "His eye is so swollen he can't see through it."

"If we don't see the abuse occur, there's nothing we can do."

"If Leon was a woman, would you be telling me the same thing?" Kate asked.

"That's not fair." Nick threw his pen on the desk. "I'm not burying my head in the sand. I'm trying to help Leon, but we need him to tell us what's happening. Jackie has all kinds of excuses as to why Leon's hurt. If we're not careful, she'll claim we're out to harm her because she's trans. She'll try to make it a trans issue and not an abuse issue."

"Well, if you won't do anything, I guess it's up to the cooking class to get him help."

Kate stomped out the door.

Leon and Jackie didn't eat at the kitchen the rest of the week. Dallas, with his many connections, got the neighborhood gossip about Jackie, and none of it was good. "So, Jackie is kind of famous for preying on people with mental health problems," Dallas told Kate as they walked to the parking lot one evening. "She basically finds someone and invades their life. That person thinks she's helping them, but in reality, she's stealing their food stamps, home, and any disability they get. As soon as the person gets suspicious, she moves on to a new schmuck."

"That's terrible, and no one reports her to the police?" Kate asked.

"Think about it." Dallas shrugged. "Leon doesn't seem to know which way is up right now. How is he going to report her?"

"I hope Leon comes to class next week. Maybe we can talk to him alone." Kate looked at her watch. "I've got to hurry. My dad scheduled a meeting with an architect at my restaurant. I'm not sure why, since I still don't have the insurance money, but—" Shouts and yelling on the street corner drew her attention. "What's going on over there?" She pointed to a large group gathered on the corner near the Quick-mart.

"Hit him," a person yelled.

"Leave him alone," someone else screamed.

"Who knew a girl could fight like that?" a different voice laughed.

Dallas looked across the street and darted towards the mob, yelling over his shoulder. "Call 911, it's Leon. Jackie's beating the crap out of him."

Pulling her phone out of her pocket, Kate rushed to follow Dallas. Leon lay on the ground. Jackie was on top of him punching him with her fist. She stood up, but only to kick him in the stomach with her designer combat boots.

Dallas yanked Jackie off Leon. She turned using Dallas as her punching bag. Dallas responded to the hits with force. He pummeled her until Jackie cowered, crying, "Stop, stop, you're hurting me."

"I hope so, you piece of shit." Dallas kept hitting. "How's it feel to be on the other side?"

"Dallas." Kate pulled his arm back. "Stop, the police are coming. Let's help Leon."

"Stay there," Dallas growled, tossing Jackie to the concrete.

The fight over. Deacon unlocked the door to the Quick-mart. "What do you need?" He asked removing a toothpick from his mouth.

"Can you get Nick?" Kate knelt beside Leon. He was lying in the fetal position on the cold sidewalk. Blood flowed from his nose, his eyes, his head. She touched his leg, and he jerked away. "Leon?" she bent her face next to his. "It's Katie." His right eye was swollen shut. The other squeezed tightly closed. "We're going to get you some help. Can you tell me where it hurts?" Leon didn't move. Dallas handed her a towel to cover the bloody gash on the back of Leon's head. Jackie whimpered on the sidewalk.

"What the hell happened?" Nick ran over.

"Katie and I were walking to her car," Dallas said. "We heard yelling and fighting. I looked over and saw Jackie beating up poor Leon." Dallas hit his chest. "I stopped her." He looked down at his M&M sweatshirt. It was covered in blood splatters from Jackie's gushing nose.

"You're a liar," Jackie shouted. "Officer, arrest that man." Her long red fingernails clawed the side of the building as she struggled to stand. A policeman grasped her elbow to steady her. "I was walking with my man and that cretin attacked." She tried to slap Dallas. "I'm going to sue you. Using the back of her hand, she wiped a mixture of blood and tears from her face. Her nose was broken, and she was going to have a black eye. Straightening her torn sweater and skirt, she revealed a black lacy bra. "I need an ambulance too."

"You should be in jail," Dallas shouted. "Look what you've done to Leon."

Nick stepped between them. "Dallas, get over there." He pointed to the Quick-mart door.

Kate sat on the cold sidewalk next to Leon. The paramedics worked to control the bleeding before loading him onto a gurney. "You're safe now," she whispered. She gently touched his forehead as the paramedics placed him in the ambulance. "Do what the doctors say, okay?" Leon nodded his head. A tear fell from his good eye.

"Hey." Nick squeezed Leon's arm near the IV bag. "I'll meet you at the hospital."

The doors shut and the sirens blared as the ambulance drove away.

Jackie stood on the street telling her point of view to anyone who would listen, "I was minding my own business when that lunatic attacked me." She pointed a red fingernail at Dallas. "I am the victim of a hate crime. That maniac should be in jail." Jackie collapsed against the police car. "I need medical attention too," she sobbed.

"It doesn't matter to me if you're a man, a woman, or a unicorn." Dallas puffed up his chest. "You've been abusing Leon for months. Today, you hit him in public."

"That's not true. Leon fell and I was helping him up. You attacked me from out of the blue." Jackie shouted.

"Right," Dallas scoffed. "You helped him up by kicking the shit out of him." Dallas pointed at the crowd. "Officers, ask any of these people. They'll tell you who put Leon in the ambulance. It wasn't me." He shook his head. "I saved the poor guy from her."

"He's right." Deacon approached the officer. "She started the whole thing." He nodded his head towards Jackie. "I saw it. My store has security cameras, so it's on tape."

"Officer, I'm Nick Decker, Executive Director of the Mary and Martha Soup Kitchen." He shook the cop's hand. "Leon, the man in the ambulance, has some type of mental disability. Workers at the kitchen have noticed a decline in his status over the past few weeks. He's been coming in battered and bruised. It's our belief Jackie has been harming him."

"Well," the officer closed his notebook. "There's a warrant out for her arrest, so I'm taking her to the station." He handed Dallas back his license. "Mr. Johnson, I'm going to believe you were acting in self-defense. I'm not going to arrest you this time." The officer touched Jackie's arm. "Turn around, please, hands behind your back."

"Officer, I can't go to jail. I need to go to the hospital," Jackie cried.

"We have medical staff at the jail. We'll get you help." The officer said as he placed her in the back of the police car.

Jackie wiped her bloody nose and glared at Dallas. "I'm going to sue you," Jackie screamed as the police car drove away.

"Good riddance, Jackie." Dallas gave a salute.

Nick clutched Dallas's shoulder and turned him towards M&M. "My office, *now*."

"That's fine, man." Dallas sauntered next to Nick. "We can talk. Things were finally handled."

Nick stormed into the M&M dining room. One of the children from Kid's Café asked, "Why were the cops out there?"

"Everything's fine, get back to work." Nick's voice was sharp. He pushed open his office door and stood aside for Dallas to enter. "Katie, we can talk later." He slammed the door in her face. "What the *hell* were you thinking?" Nick shouted walking behind his desk.

"Man, I wasn't." Dallas put his hands on his hip and shook his head. "I saw Jackie standing over Leon on the ground kicking the crap out of him, and I ran. I don't even remember touching her." Dallas sat down on top of the stacks of paper laying on the chair, "I just wanted to help him."

"But you didn't just help him." Nick was like a caged animal trapped behind his desk pacing back and forth. "You *hit* her. She probably has a broken nose. You never should have touched her."

"So... you wanted me to stand by and watch her beat Leon to death?" Dallas gaped.

"That's not want I'm saying, and you know it." Nick stared at Dallas. "Stopping the fight was one thing, but continuing it is a different story. You are an employee of Mary and Martha's. For God's sake, you're wearing an M&M sweatshirt. The whole neighborhood knows you work here." Nick sat down, defeated. "A representative of M&M cannot be involved in a fight, especially right outside our door. I'm sorry, Dallas, you're fired."

"Nick, wait." Kate burst through the door.

"Are you *kidding* me?" Dallas jumped up. "Jackie has been abusing Leon for months, and you didn't do anything about it." Dallas pointed at Nick. "She finally pounds on him in public, and I stop her, so you *fire* me?" Dallas flung the pile of papers sitting on the desk to the floor. "I thought you were my friend."

"I am your friend, but I'm also the director of this kitchen. We have a reputation to uphold in this community, and I can't have an employee involved in a fight. Mary and Martha's is here to provide a safe haven for the neighborhood. Employees can't beat up the clients."

"So, did you want me to let Jackie keep pounding on Leon? No one else was going to help him. Would you have been happy if Jackie killed him?"

"No, I wouldn't have been happy. You should have broken up the fight and called the police. You stepped over the line when you hit Jackie."

"She hit me first." Dallas shouted.

"I'll give you two weeks' severance." Nick held out his hand. "Give me your keys. You can't be on the premises any longer."

Dallas reached into his pocket and threw the keys across the desk. "Screw you."

"Dallas, wait—" Kate grabbed his arm trying to keep him from leaving, but he brushed her away and left.

"Nick, how could you?" Kate turned to see Nick resting his forehead on his hands, sitting at the desk. "Dallas was right, you weren't there. Poor Leon was trembling on the sidewalk. Jackie looked like she was kick-boxing a punching bag. People were screaming and yelling. No one helped except for Dallas. Leon will probably be in the hospital for weeks."

"This isn't up for discussion." Nick held up his hand to stop the conversation. He was sad and tired. "I don't want to fire Dallas. He's a hard worker, a good person, and my friend, but I can't have an employee fighting with a client, even if that client deserved it. All employees sign a code of conduct, and fighting is a definite violation. I'm sorry, my hands are tied. Dallas has to go."

"You're wrong. Dallas acted honorably," Kate said.

"I agree. Dallas's intentions were honorable—until he threw the first punch." Nick opened his laptop. "There's nothing else to say. I've got a ton of paperwork now. So, I guess I'll see you tomorrow."

45

KATE

She had missed the appointment with her dad and the architect, but Kate still drove to the restaurant. She didn't have anything else to do, and it had been a while since she'd been there. She hadn't thought about reopening in the past months. She couldn't remember the last time she'd called the fire inspector or the insurance company. It wasn't that she'd given up on the restaurant, but her work at the kitchen seemed so much more important.

The afternoon sky was turning to dusk when Kate pulled into the driveway. There was a man sitting on the front porch. Parking, Kate walked up the paved path, sat down, and without saying a word, she put her arm around the man's shoulder.

"I shouldn't have punched her." Dallas took a deep breath. "I was so mad. I knew she had been hurting him for weeks, and to see her kicking him like that in public." He shrugged, "I lost it."

"You had to stop her," Kate said. "Jackie was going to kill him. I can't believe Nick fired you. Maybe he'll change his mind."

"No." Dallas stood. "He's right. The clients have got to feel safe when they come to the kitchen. I wouldn't want anyone to be afraid because of me."

"How is the kitchen going to work without you? What are you

going to do?"

"Now, Miss Katie," Dallas smiled. "No one is irreplaceable, not even me. I don't know what I'll do." Laughing, he shrugged his shoulders. "Oh heck, maybe I'll finally go to Dallas."

The next morning, Nick asked the entire staff to meet in the dining room. "I have an announcement, and I want everyone to hear it at the same time." He read from a piece of notebook paper. "The conduct of Mary and Martha's employees must be above reproach, especially in the neighborhood in which they serve. Dallas Huber's involvement in a physical altercation with a client of the kitchen *cannot* be tolerated. As such, Mr. Huber is no longer an employee of the Mary and Martha Soup Kitchen. He will not be permitted on the premises in any capacity."

Nick folded the paper and placed it in his back pocket. He ignored the stunned faces.

"What happened?" Jenny asked.

"He beat up Jackie," Marika said in a hushed voice.

"For hurting Leon? Well, she deserved it," Jenny spoke out the side of her mouth.

Nick frowned. "I'll start a search for Dallas's replacement, but in the meantime, I hope you can work as a team to serve lunch to the people who need it most. Thank you."

In the kitchen, Tucker tied an apron around his waist. "Nick told me what happened last night. It's not right." He shook his head. "But in any case, I get to be Dallas today. What should I do?"

Kate read from the chore chart. "Dallas prepped the mushroom sauce yesterday. So, all you really need to do is the potatoes. Since it's Friday, Dallas spends most of the day cleaning and closing for the weekend."

They all set to work. Kate sautéed the chicken while Marika tossed the salad and steamed the green beans.

"I can't stand it." Marika slammed the refrigerator closed. "This place is too quiet. We need some music. I can't believe I'm saying this, but I miss Dallas's singing."

"Man, that boy could talk," Tucker said, shaking his head. "I didn't know what he was talking about half the time, but his mouth was always moving. He kept a running commentary on everything he did."

"Oh my gosh, that's so true." Kate poured the mushroom gravy over the chicken. "When I first started working here, I tried to listen to everything he said, but after about a week, I realized he was just talking to himself. He didn't expect a response."

"We're sure going to miss him," Tucker said, placing the potatoes on the serving line.

Nick's prayer before lunch was bittersweet. "Dear Lord, thank you for this day. Please bless the people who helped prepare this food and especially watch over those who can no longer be with us. In your son's loving name, we pray. *Our Father….*"

Leaving the prayer circle, a somber Nick touched Kate's arm. "Katie, once you get lunch moving, I need you to come to my office."

"Sure, five minutes?" Kate said.

"What's that about?" Marika asked.

"I have no idea," Kate said.

Is he mad at me too? Am I in trouble? I didn't do anything wrong, but neither did Dallas.

Kate's thoughts rambled as she brushed a piece of hair under her baseball cap and knocked on Nick's office door.

"Hey, take a seat." Nick pointed to the chair he'd already cleared, before shutting the office door. "I spoke to the hospital," Nick said, sitting on the edge of his desk. "Leon has several broken ribs, a broken nose, and a broken leg, as well as a concussion. The police are filing charges against Jackie."

"Oh my gosh," Kate gasped.

"Apparently, the fight started inside the apartment building. The building has security cameras. Jackie knocked Leon down the stairs and then proceeded to chase him as he tried to get away. Leon's going to be in the hospital for at least a week." Nick shuffled some papers. "Would you like to go visit him with me?"

"Of course," Kate said. "Which hospital is he in?"

"He's at University, in the psych ward."

"The psych ward?"

Nick nodded, "After evaluating his injuries, the hospital staff determined he wasn't really cognizant."

"Poor guy," Kate stood brushing dust off her apron. "When did you want to go?"

Nick opened the door. "Why don't you come and get me when you're finished for the day?"

"Okay," There was a skip in Kate's step as she left the office. *Was it wrong to consider a trip to the hospital a date?*

She smiled at her reflection in the kitchen window. *Why did I wear this shirt today? Do these jeans look dated? Oh, well, a quick spritz in the bathroom. A touch of lipstick, and I'll be ready for Nick . . . I mean Leon.*

Nick opened the door to his truck for Kate. She buckled her seat belt and admired the tan interior of the white Ford F150. "So, you're not a complete slob."

"What?" Nick looked confused as he started the engine.

"Your truck's spotless," Kate smiled. "By the looks of your office, I thought you might be a hoarder."

"My office?" Nick laughed. "It does take on a life of its own." He shifted gears. "I do know where everything is. I just don't have a specific spot for all of it. I'm really a very organized person. You should see my house."

"Really?" Kate looked out the window. *I'd love to see your house.* "I'm really glad you're going with me to see Leon." Nick tapped his fingers on the steering wheel as he drove. "I've run into a brick wall with him."

"Why?" Kate turned in her seat to watch him.

"Leon won't tell us his real last name. I'm hoping you can get through to him; get him to talk about where he's from and any family we can contact. We need to have a safety plan in place before he's released from the hospital."

"Won't Jackie still be in jail?"

"I don't know." Nick shrugged. "She might be able to post bail, but in any case, we've got to stop Leon from returning to a bad or even worse situation."

"Won't the social worker, Libby, be able to help?"

"You're joking, right?" Nick parked the car. "Although Libby's been *helping* Leon for the past two years" He used his hands to make air quotes around the word helping. "She has no idea who he is."

At the hospital, Nick and Kate talked to several people before getting approval to visit Leon in the psych ward. He looked worse than Kate thought possible. His right eye was swollen shut, his nose crooked to the left with a bandage across the bridge, and his left leg was in traction, his torso wrapped to protect his ribs.

"How are you feeling?" Kate's voice cracked. He looked pitiful lying in the hospital bed. She placed the box she was carrying on the side table and took his hand.

"Okay, I guess." Leon sounded like a little boy.

"I'm sorry," Nick stood at the end of the bed. "I should have helped you get away from Jackie a long time ago."

"I didn't think she would hurt me this bad." Leon turned his head away, "I tried to do everything she told me, but I couldn't always remember."

"I know you did," Kate squeezed his hand. "It's not your fault. Jackie is not a nice person. She's in jail, so you don't have to worry about her anymore."

"Leon, we want to help you," Nick said. "Can we call your mom or dad and tell them you're here?"

"I'm not sure," Leon struggled to sit up straight.

"I'm certain your family would want to know you're hurt." Kate straightened the blanket. "Tell Nick their names, and he'll call them."

Leon looked out the window. "Sometimes, they get mad at me because I don't take my medicine."

"But you're in the hospital Leon," Kate rubbed his leg. "You're taking your medicine now, right?" Leon nodded. "Then, they won't be mad."

"Okay," Leon agreed.

Nick left the room to speak with the nurse. "I forgot to give you these." Kate handed Leon the box. Inside was a plate of chocolate chip cookies with a note: *I know these cookies aren't as good as the ones you make, but they're made with lots of love! Feel better soon.*

"Bernice asked everyone in the kitchen to sign the card," Kate said. Leon started to cry. "It's okay." Kate put an arm around his shoulder, trying not to bump any of his bandages. He cried harder. "You're going to be alright," she soothed. "Everyone at M&M is praying for you."

Kate felt helpless. *Should I call the nurse?*

"Does something hurt Leon? Do you need more pain medicine? Can I get you anything?" Leon didn't answer. He laid his head on Kate's chest and cried. "You're going to be okay." Kate kept rubbing his back. "You're safe," she whispered over and over again.

Leon was calmer by the time Nick returned. "Leon, I've talked to the nurse and the social worker. I think we have a good handle on the situation. Katie and I are going to leave, but someone from the kitchen will stop by tomorrow. In the meantime," Nick wrote his cell number on the hospital whiteboard by Leon's bed. "If you need anything, I want you to call me. Do you understand?"

"Thank you," Leon said laying back on the bed.

"I'll see you soon," Kate said. Leon's small wave reminded Kate of her nieces when she told them goodbye on Sunday.

46

NICK

After dropping Kate off at her car, Nick went to M&M. The eerie quiet of the kitchen was comforting. There were no pots clanging, no doors slamming, no clients yelling. He was able to walk the dark hallways without being stopped to solve a problem every few steps.

Unlocking his office door, he turned on the overhead light. The bright bulb illuminated the work that still needed to be finished. Boxes and cartons lined the room's walls. Using both hands, he pushed back the red leather chair.

I need to oil these wheels. It's getting harder to move, and the screeching sounds like fingernails on a blackboard.

He adjusted the seat pad and leaned back into the chair, crossing his ankles on top of the desk. He looked at the top folder: 'Mary and Martha's Next Step: Strategic Plan II.'

What is M&M's next chapter? What is his? The Grand-Opening of The Shepherds Inn had been last week, the First Strategic Plan was officially complete.

He put his hands behind his head and thought about his day. Leon—could he have stopped him from getting hurt? He hadn't seen Jackie hit Leon so he couldn't have stopped the abuse, but he could help him now. He sat up and reached into his pocket for his wallet. The nurse had slipped him Leon's next of kin information. He tapped the business card on the desk. He could call Leon's dad; he could intercede on Leon's behalf and explain how sick and hurt Leon was. Maybe, just maybe, he could help mend that family relationship—there was hope.

After leaving a message, Nick picked up a second folder containing the classified ad he needed to post to find Dallas' replacement. Katie had surprised him when she told him she wasn't sure when the restaurant would reopen, and she didn't seem too concerned about it either. Six months ago, he would have bet a hundred dollars she wouldn't last three weeks.

They'd gone out for drinks after visiting Leon, and it had been fun. Katie was beautiful, smart, easy to talk to.

Why didn't I ask her out? He tapped the pen to his temple. *He was certain she'd be willing to go on a date.* Granted, it had been a while since his last date, but he wasn't so rusty he couldn't tell when a girl was flirting with him. However, asking Katie out didn't feel right. Nothing felt right in his life. M&M seemed stale. The excitement of opening The Shepherd's Inn was over. The strategic plan was executed, and the path the board wanted to take no longer interested him. The neighborhood didn't need more buildings or programs, it needed a more human touch; more of a community where the people were neighbors and friends looking out for each other. How could he help build "hope"?

He looked at his watch. It was still light. He'd take a walk around the neighborhood and talk to people—maybe there was someone who could use a friend. In any case, he would stop by church to pray. Lately, that was the one place he knew he could find peace.

47

KATE

Kate locked her office and headed towards the kitchen to meet the cooking class. After spending two weeks in the hospital, Leon was completing his rehab at his parent's home, thanks to Nick's intervention. Not wanting to miss another cooking class, Leon was going to participate through the magic of Zoom.

Kate's phone buzzed. It wasn't Leon. About to hit decline, she recognized the fire inspector's number.

"Hello, this is Kate O'Leary," she said.

"Ms. O'Leary, Chief Randall from the Cincinnati Fire Department."

"Hello, how are you?" Nervous, she wiped her sweaty palms down the front of her apron.

"Good, good. I wanted to let you know. The fire investigation has been completed, and we've sent the report to the insurance company. They'll have it by the end of the week."

"That's great. Thank you," Taking a deep breath her heart raced. "Can you tell me what the report says?"

"Well, the fire started in the basement at the water heater. The unit was old and should have been replaced years ago—"

"I know it was old, but it still worked. That's why I wasn't in a rush to replace it. Restaurants run on a very tight profit margin." Kate interrupted.

"I understand. We knew the water heater was the ignition source from the very beginning. What we didn't know was why the alarm system didn't work."

Thousands of nervous prickles raced up her spine.

Do they think I did something to the alarm system?

Her breathing was fast and shallow.

Chief Randall continued talking. "Do you remember having work done on your satellite and internet connection?"

"Not really, well…I changed satellite carriers, I guess, about a year ago. Is that what you mean?

"Yes, that's exactly right. The new company never reconnected your alarm system to the phone line, and that means no police or fire notification."

"But I was religious about arming and disarming my alarm," Kate said.

"You probably were, but in reality, you were just pushing buttons. The light pad wasn't doing anything but making noise. We discovered there hadn't been an alarm call to the police in nine months—the exact time you changed satellite service. Your restaurant was listed as a nuisance alarm prior to that.

"A nuisance alarm?" Kate pushed a strand of hair behind her ear.

"That's what the police and fire departments call businesses that have a tendency to set off alarms by accident."

"Well, sometimes my hands were full, and I just couldn't get the alarm turned off fast enough." Kate rubbed her face. "I always tried to cancel it."

"That was noted," Chief Randall said. "No matter, my report was delayed because getting all the various companies to respond to the subpoenas was time-consuming. Once the information was received, we were able to establish a timeline. I'm happy to report the fire has been determined to be an accident."

"Oh my God, thank you." Kate put her hand on her chest.

"You're very welcome. I hope you hear from the insurance company soon. Let me know if I can be of further assistance. Goodbye."

"Bye," Kate slid to the floor, tears blurring her eyes. With a trembling hand, she placed a call. "Mom," her voice cracked. "I'm getting the insurance money."

The cooking class was in full swing by the time Kate entered the kitchen. Marika had the students chopping carrots, celery, onions, mushrooms, and potatoes for the chicken pot pie.

"What's wrong?" Marika asked, seeing Kate's red eyes and flushed cheeks.

"No, nothing." Kate scrunched her face to keep from crying. She shook her head and waved her hands making an X in the air. She finally managed to croak out, "I actually have great news."

"What?" Marika said. The class stopped chopping.

"The fire inspector called, and they've ruled the restaurant's fire an accident. So, I'll be getting the insurance money, and I'm going to be able to completely rebuild." Kate pressed her hands together as if praying.

"Oh my gosh." Marika hugged her. "I'm so happy for you."

"Praise be, Jesus," Bernice proclaimed.

"That's great," Rachel smiled.

"Congratulations," Tamara and Sharon said together.

"So, is this our last cooking class?" Kendra asked.

"No, why?" Kate said.

"Well, if you're not going to work here, will you still teach the class?" Kendra shrugged.

"I haven't thought through the details." Kate looked around the worn kitchen filled with the people she liked so much. *What would happen to the cooking class?* "We'll have to figure some things out, but in the meantime let's finish this dinner."

Sighing, Kate wiped down the dented stainless steel prep table. The students had left with their warm chicken pot pies and lemon squares desserts, so she was alone in the kitchen with Marika.

"What was that for?" Marika stored the leftovers in the refrigerator.

"What?" Kate held the towel up.

"Your sigh."

"I don't know." Kate rinsed the towel at the sink. "I'm feeling a little sad."

"What? Are you crazy?" Marika slammed the refrigerator door closed. "You just got the news you've been waiting months to hear. You're getting the money."

"I know," Kate's smile was wry. "I guess…I'm going to miss working here and being with all of you." She shrugged, "I mean, I want to open my restaurant, but…" Her voice broke, "Ever since the food fight, I've felt like I was part of a team, and like my cooking was really important. The food we made was making a difference." She tossed the towel in the sink. "I'm not sure opening the restaurant will have the same meaning."

"Katie, there are thousands of ways for you to stay involved at M&M. You don't have to give up your dream of reopening the restaurant to make a difference."

"I know, I know." Kate wiped the tears from her cheek. "You're right. It's just so sudden."

"Sudden?" Marika laughed, "When was that fire?"

To celebrate the good news, Kate's family surprised her with a pizza party. "I called the insurance company on my way here," Kate said. "I think they missed hearing from me these past few months." She grabbed a piece of barbecue chicken pizza. "They're cutting the check tomorrow, so I should have it by next week."

"I've been praying so hard. I'm so glad you can quit," Lynne said.

"Well, the kitchen is really short-handed," Kate said. "I've got the cooking class, and Nick still hasn't replaced Dallas, so I can't leave M&M in the lurch. It will be a while before the construction starts, right, Dad?"

"Give them two weeks, then." Lynne grabbed an empty pizza box. "That job was a stop-gap. You've been wasting your skills working there. The restaurant is your dream. How can you not be in a rush to reopen?"

"I don't know." Kate walked to the back door and looked out the window. The yard was showing the first signs of spring. "I haven't had time to get my thoughts together." She turned and looked at her family. "I want to reopen the restaurant, I do." She furrowed her brow. "But I've liked helping the people at M&M. I'm going to miss it."

"You could volunteer. I bet you could still teach the cooking class." Her dad said.

"I know," Kate nodded. "It's just not going to be the same." She sat back down. "As unbelievable as this sounds, I like working there."

After lunch the next day, Kate tapped on Nick's door. "Got a minute?" she asked.

"For you, I've got two," he said, standing to transfer a pile of papers and folders from one chair to another, freeing up a seat. "Sit here." He wiped the chair with his palm and then brushed his hands together to remove the dust. "I just talked to Leon and his dad. He's doing great. He told me he Zoomed the cooking class. That's hilarious."

"It was fun. I'd emailed his dad the recipe card ahead of time, so he was able to cook his own dinner." Kate said.

"That's terrific! So, what can I help you with?" He pushed back the chair, the squeak now gone.

"Well, I got some good news. The fire inspector called, and the restaurant fire was ruled an accident. I'm getting all the insurance money." She smiled.

"Katie, that's great news!" Nick jumped up from his chair and pulled her up into a hug. "I'm so happy for you."

"Thanks." Kate squeezed her arms around him."

He smells so good.

She breathed deeply, "I'm super excited, but I must admit, I'm going to be sad to leave here."

"Hey," Nick put his hands on her shoulders, foreheads touching as he looked into her eyes. "We always knew this was a temporary assignment. I'm happy we had you this long. What's your time frame? Do you think you could give me two weeks?" He walked behind his desk to look at the calendar.

"Of course. I can give you a month if you're willing to be flexible with me leaving early a few times to meet with the architects and builders?"

"That would be fantastic," Nick said. "Any ideas about your replacement?"

"Yes, Marika deserves to be the kitchen's chef. She's completely capable and is a wonderful cook." Kate said.

48

KATE

Kate couldn't believe how fast the month went. Her life had become split between two worlds: the fantasy world of restaurant design—finalizing blueprints, choosing decor, furnishing, and menus—competed with the real world of the soup kitchen—concocting meals with limited ingredients and serving the neediest of the community. Friday would be her last day as an employee of M&M, and the idea was bittersweet. She was going to miss the kitchen and everyone in it.

Carrying a box into her office, Kate smiled seeing Marika sitting behind the desk.

"What's that for?" Marika stared at the box.

"I thought I'd start packing." Kate wrapped the Kate's on Vine sign in paper. "I'm going to leave this here." She held up the aloe plant, which was a gift from her mom. "You may need it. I'll get another one for the restaurant."

"Okay, thanks. Why are you taking that?" Marika pointed to the huge can of soup with the giant pink bow.

Kate dropped the soup into a box. "Because it reminds me that I don't know everything." She brushed her hands together. "I'm all packed."

Shaking her head, Marika returned to the spreadsheets laid out on the

desk. Her phone buzzed. "It's Jamal. Hey babe, how was your day?...
How'd that happen?...Okay, just come to the kitchen. I'll leave the back
door unlocked. We can walk home together. Love you."

"Everything okay?" Kate placed the box by the door.

"It's all good." Marika put the phone on the desk. "He was trying to
finish a big project he's been working on, so he missed the bus." She
leaned back in the chair. "He sounded so happy. He said his head was
spinning with numbers. His boss told him he was the first person to finish
the report early." Marika smiled, "I'm so proud of him."

"You should be." Kate said. "He's an amazing kid. I thought so from
the very first time I met him."

"Thanks." Marika picked up a stack of papers stapled together. "Do
you have time to go over the pantry inventory?"

"Absolutely." Kate pulled a chair around the desk.
Their heads bent together, they spent the next hour reviewing the
spreadsheets and finalizing the menus Marika would prepare in the next
few weeks. Their concentration was interrupted by the sounds of sirens
screaming outside.

"I wonder what happened." Kate moved towards the dining room.

"I wonder where Jamal is?" Marika followed looking at her watch.
"He should have been here by now."

"Wow, they're moving fast." Kate saw three police cars speed past
the kitchen window. "It looks like it's by the Quick-mart. There are tons
of people standing around. Think we should go down?" Kate asked
Marika.

Suddenly, the side door flew open. Dallas ran through, his Quick-
Mart apron covered in blood.

"Oh my gosh, Dallas, are you okay? What happened?" Kate
rushed over.

His breathing was heavy, and his eyes were panicked as he focused on Marika. "It's Jamal. He's been shot. You better come quick."

Screaming, Marika raced out the door.

The crowd seemed to part as they pushed their way through the melee. Kate gasped at the horror of the scene: police and ambulance lights pulsed red and white, giving the buildings an eerie glow; shards of glass and debris coated the sidewalk, and three bodies lay in the street. Paramedics worked on two of them, their hands like conductors directing a symphony, attaching oxygen, IV bags, and bandages to the injured. The third body lay alone, a circle of blood surrounding his head like a halo.

Marika rushed to one of the two bodies being worked on by the paramedics. It was Jamal. She laid down on the pavement, her head next to his. "Jamal, I love you." She caressed his forehead. "He's my son." She told the EMT.

"Ma'am," the female paramedic said. "You need to move."

"He's my *son*," Marika's teary eyes pleaded.

"We're trying to help him. Please step back," The EMT's blood-stained gloves pressed more gauze into the gaping wound on Jamal's chest.

"Marika," Kate touched her shoulder. "Let them work."

Jamal's eyes were closed. An oxygen mask covered his mouth. Marika, kneeling, twisted her body to be above Jamal. She placed both of her hands on his head as if giving a blessing. "Jamal, I'm here. You're going to be okay. You're going to be okay. I love you," she whispered into his ear. "You've got to be strong. You've got to fight. I love you." The paramedic continued working. "Please, please, God, help him." Her shaking hands smoothed his hair and face. "I love you. Please get better. I love you. Please be strong. I love you. God, please help him."

Marika's eyes were closed. She seemed to be willing Jamal to heal, transferring all her strength to him. Kate stood behind them crying, Dallas's arm around her shoulder.

The paramedic stood. "Ma'am, we're transporting him to the hospital. He'll go straight into surgery. They're expecting him. Would you like to ride up front?"

She kissed Jamal's head as they transferred him into the ambulance. "Jamal, I love you. I am so proud of you, be strong, please don't leave me." She ran to the ambulance's passenger seat.

"I'll get your things and meet you at the hospital. Do you need me to do anything else?" Kate asked through the window.

"Would you call Tucker and tell him what happened?" Marika squeezed Kate's hand. "I need you to pray. Please pray."

"I will." Kate nodded as the ambulance drove away.

"Tucker, Tucker?" Kate yelled, running through the Padre Pantry door, Dallas by her side.

"Hey, what's the matter?" Tucker walked down the aisle.

"Jamal's been shot. Marika's with him in the ambulance." Kate tried to catch her breath. Tucker's face paled. He raced out the door.

"Tucker, do you want me to drive you?" Kate yelled as he jumped into his car and sped away.

"Dallas, can you help me lock up?" With shaking hands, Kate turned the dead bolt. "I really want to get to the hospital."

"Sure," Dallas said, locking the doors.

"Do you know who the other boys were?" Kate grabbed Marika's jacket from the coat hook.

"The dead one was Benji. The other hurt kid was Jayden. His mom, Sharon, is in your cooking class."

"Sharon?" Kate's hands flew to her chest.

"Yeah." Dallas flicked off the pantry lights.

"I didn't see her at the scene. Did someone call her?" Kate grabbed her purse from the office.

"I'm sure the police called her." Dallas checked the coffee urns to make sure they were off.

"Are you okay here?" Kate had one hand on the door handle.

"You go; I've got this handled." Dallas waved.

The buzz of the back door made Kate stop. "Katie, what are you still doing here?" Nick called. "You're supposed to slack off your last week of work." He stopped laughing when he saw Dallas. "What are you doing here?"

"He's helping me." Kate stepped in front of Dallas. "Jamal was shot. Marika's at the hospital. I'm taking her things to her."

"I'll drive you. My truck's out back." Nick led Kate to his car. Sitting in the passenger seat, Kate started to shiver. She was so cold her hands were trembling. "Let's turn on your seat warmer." Nick pushed the seat button and directed the warm air vent towards her. He handed her a jacket, which she wrapped around her body like a blanket. He squeezed her hand. "Can you tell me what happened?"

Shaking her head, Kate let the tears slip from her eyes, "I don't know what happened. Jamal called to say he was taking the later bus. He'd had a good day." She wiped her face with her hand and searched for a Kleenex. Reaching over Nick opened the glove compartment to hand her a napkin.

"Thanks," her voice broke. "Marika wants us to pray. Do you think we could start a prayer chain with M&M volunteers? You know, ask them to pray for Jamal and the other kids?"

"There were other people?" Nick sped through the yellow light. "What the hell happened?"

"I don't know." Kate blew her nose. "But one of them died."

49

NICK

The emergency room was organized chaos. Crowds had gathered hoping to find out information about the shooting, reporters were asked to vacate the premises, while police were looking for witnesses. Searching the room, Nick saw Marika and Tucker sitting alone in a corner, sharing a rosary, knees touching, eyes closed.

"Marika," Nick knelt on the floor. He placed his hands over Marika's and Tucker's. "I'm so sorry. How is he? Have you heard anything?"

Marika clasped his hands. "Thank you for coming." A sob fell from her mouth, and she shook her head crinkling a tissue against her lips.

"We really don't know anything." Tucker wrapped an arm around Marika's shoulder pulling her to his side. They've rushed him into surgery." His voice broke. "It's bad. The doctors think he'll be in surgery for at least five hours." Marika buried her face in Tucker's neck.

"What about the other boys?" Kate sat next to Tucker's chair.

"Benji's dead," Tucker took a deep breath. "Jayden's in bad shape too. Sharon is with him."

Tucker nodded. Marika quietly cried.

"Do they know who did this?" Nervous energy made Nick's leg bounce.

"No one saw anything." Tucker waved his hand with disgust. "The police are questioning everyone, but it's not going anywhere."

"That's ridiculous." Nick paced the room. "How can three teenagers get shot and no one sees a thing? I can't believe it." He looked at the crowd of people milling around the waiting room and outside. "Maybe I can get them to talk. I'm going back to M&M." He took a breath and sat next to Marika taking her hand. "Can I do anything for you?" he asked.

"Just pray," her voice was soft.

"I will. I'm going to go check on Sharon and then Benji's family. Katie, do you want to stay here or go with me?"

"I'll stay here." Kate asked Marika, "Is that okay?"

"Yes," Marika nodded taking Kate's hand.

"Okay, can we pray together before I leave?" Nick asked.

"I'd like that," Marika said.

The tiny group joined hands. Nick prayed, "Dear Father in heaven. We ask that you please surround Jamal and Jayden with your loving protection. Please heal them. We ask you to send your Spirit to guide the doctors and nurses caring for the boys. Please, God, give the families of Jamal, Benji, and Jayden strength and peace during this most difficult time. In your son's loving name, we pray. *Our Father....*"

"*Amen.*" The group sniffled.

50

MARIKA

The lamp's glow did nothing to warm the sterile space of the hospital waiting room. Cups of weak, cold coffee sat on the table next to piles of crumpled Kleenex. The emergency room had quieted to its normal tempo of heart attacks, broken bones, and drug overdoses. Worried families congregated in their own areas, the grief and fear too much to share with strangers.

Marika had sent Katie back to the kitchen. "Prayers...Jamal needed prayers. Please contact the members of the Mother's Group and GED classes and ask them to pray."

In their corner, Marika and Tucker were quiet, hands clasped. They waited and prayed. Marika stared at the muted television without seeing, until the local news report. Leaning forward, she used the remote to turn up the volume.

"Senseless tragedy struck the neighborhood surrounding the Mary and Martha Soup Kitchen this evening," The news anchor read, "Leaving one young man dead and two others fighting for their lives—"

Marika stared transfixed. "Baby, let's turn it off, you don't need to hear this." Tucker said, reaching for the remote.

"No, I want to know what they're saying." Marika brushed his arm away.

"According to eyewitnesses," the anchor continued. "The victims were targeted by a black SUV, which started shooting at the boys standing on the street corner. It's believed the teens were caught up in a turf war between two neighborhood gangs. Let's go to Hayley Fitz on location."

"Thanks Emma." The reporter stood on the corner where Jamal had been shot. "I'm here with Deacon Hunter, the owner of the Deacon's Quick-mart. Sir, what can you tell me about the incident?"

"It's a damn shame," Deacon practically grabbed the microphone from the reporter's hand. "A boy can't walk home from school without getting shot. I talked to Jamal right after he got off the bus. He was going to meet his mom. He stopped to talk to Benji and Jayden, and the next thing I know there's people screamin' and yellin', glass is shattered, and the boys are all lyin' on the ground—blood everywhere."

"Sir, do you think this violence is gang-related?" The reporter was back in control of the microphone.

"Well…I don't know about that." Deacon shook his head. "Jamal sure isn't involved with any drugs. He's a good kid, smart, goes to Drexel. The other two, I'm not sure what they were doin'."

"There you have it." The reporter grimaced at the camera. "We'll keep following this story, but as it stands: one teenager dead, and two others fighting for their lives. Hayley Fitz reporting."

Jumping up, Marika's voice was strident. "Are they saying Jamal is in a gang? That's not true, how can they say that?" She paced their six-by-six waiting room space. "Tucker, call that station and tell them Jamal is not in a gang." She pointed at the television. "They should get their facts straight. My son is *not* in a gang."

"Baby," Tucker pulled her into his arms. "Deacon said, 'Jamal isn't in a gang.' You raised him right. Sit back down, the doctor or nurse will be out soon."

"Okay." She let him guide her to the chair. "I think it's a good thing surgery is taking so long. Don't you?"

"I think he's going to be fine." Tucker squeezed her hand.

It was after midnight when the surgeon finished operating. He walked into the now-empty waiting room and stood looming over Marika and Tucker.

"Ms. Johnson, Jamal is alive." The surgeon said.

"Oh, thank *God*," Marika smiled, tears rolling down her face.

"The next few days are critical." The surgeon's face was somber. "The bullet exploded inside Jamal's chest and the damage is quite extensive. Jamal's body was too stressed for me to continue surgery. He's in a medically induced coma, and we've placed a temporary suture over his wound. This will give his body a chance to rest before we finish the repairs.

"Can I see him?" Marika stood.

"Ms. Johnson," The surgeon said, "Jamal is in extremely critical condition. You should prepare yourself."

"He's alive. That's all that matters." Marika said. "Thank you, thank you. Can I see him?

"They're moving him to ICU. Once he's settled, the nurse will come and get you."

"Thank you, is there anything we should be doing?" Tucker shook the surgeon's hand.

"I always suggest praying." The doctor took off his surgical cap and left the room.

The hospital adhered to a family members only rule in the ICU, so Tucker waited outside while Marika had her short visit, after which she collapsed in Tucker's waiting arms.

"He looks terrible." Marika cried, "There are tubes everywhere. The only spot I could find to kiss was his hand. I'm so afraid he's going to die."

"Baby, he's made it this far." Tucker's eyes filled with tears. His voice choked. "He's a strong boy, and he's stubborn just like his mom." He looked directly into her eyes. "We're going to keep praying and believing. He's going to be fine."

"He's so still. I don't think he knew I was even there." Shivering, she pressed herself against Tucker's warmth.

"He knew. Honey, he has to stay quiet." Tucker's soft voice was soothing. "Remember, he's sedated. They don't want him to move. The only thing the doctors want Jamal's body to do is heal."

"He can't die," Marika sobbed.

51
KATE

Mass was packed in the morning. Mary & Martha's employees and volunteers sat between the clients and their families. Kate was surprised to see Dallas sitting in the front pew next to Nick, but the past twenty-four hours had been filled with craziness, so the two praying together just added to the list. No one looked like they had gotten much sleep. By the time Mass had ended, a local news station had set up a remote broadcast on the street corner by M&M. A reporter was relentless in trying to interview worshippers about the shooting.

Kate realized there were two types of people: a person was either camera-shy or a camera hog. There was no in between. Nick unlocked the front door for everyone, "Hey, let's have a quick meeting in the dining room," he said.

Kate with her mom and sister, Jenny, Dallas and volunteers gathered around the tables. "I spoke with Tucker before Mass." Nick's hand rested on the back of a chair. "Jamal made it through the night but is still in very critical condition. Marika has asked for us to continue to pray." He put his hand on Dallas's shoulder. "Dallas has agreed to step in to help for the next few days. I really want to thank him for his willingness to set aside past arguments to help."

Nick looked around the room. "I know we're going to be short-handed for a while, so I appreciate everyone's efforts to pull together, not only to support Marika and Jamal, but for the clients. A special thanks to Katie's family who are volunteering with us today." He put his hands in his pockets and rocked back on his heels. "Let's face it. Today is going to be hard for all of us, but I know you're all going to work to make sure people are fed and feel safe. Thank you." He smiled. "Now, let's go make it a great day."

Dallas started the clapping, and the rest of the staff joined in. Nick looked embarrassed, waving the applause away. He started walking to his office but stopped, "Oh, one last thing, the media is very interested in this story. We do not want them filming inside here, and please let me speak on behalf of M&M if there is a need."

Nick touched Kate's elbow on the way to the kitchen. "Hey, I'm sorry to blindside you with the Dallas announcement. He offered to help, and it seemed like the perfect opportunity to give him a second chance."

"I think it's a great idea." Kate smiled. "You know, I never thought Dallas should have been fired."

"I *do* know," he winked. "Let me know if you need anything."

"We're good." Kate turned away. "With Dallas, my mom, and sister helping, we should be fine."

Prepping the day's meatball casserole, green beans, and salad was accomplished in a hushed tone, until Jenny yelled, "It's time to pray." Employees, volunteers, and clients walked into the dining room.

Gathered in a circle holding hands, Nick read the day's Bible passage and offered a simple prayer, "God, thank you for this community. We ask you to please bring healing to Jamal and Jayden and give your consoling peace to the family of Benji. We ask, too, dear Lord, for your healing presence to be brought into this community, not only in the blessing of our meal, but in the spirit of the neighborhood. In your son's name, we

pray. *Our Father…*" The Lord's prayer filled the kitchen. Kate hoped
God was listening.

The conversation in the dining room during lunch was subdued yet
passionate. Everyone seemed to have seen the shooting or knew someone
who saw it. Rumors were rampant about who the shooter was and why.
Lynne wiped down tables and gathered information. "Everyone thinks
Tyrone was sending a message to Aldiez: stay away from that corner."
Lynne rinsed a towel at the sink while Kate washed dishes.

"No one's saying Jamal was involved with drugs, are they?" Kate
scrubbed a pan.

"No," Lynne said, "Everyone thinks Jamal was just trying to get here.
The news reporter is going to interview Jamal and Jayden's dads this
afternoon."

"Both of them?" Kate looked at her mom. "I didn't think Jamal's dad
lived around here. Marika never talks about him."

"I think so." Lynne pointed out the window. "It looks like they're
doing the interview now."

Curiosity got the best of her, so Kate went to watch the interviews. The
young reporter was talking with "Cool Hand Luke."

*He's Jayden's Dad? I've seen him and Sharon eating together, but I
didn't know they were a couple-couple. Where's Jamal's dad?* Kate
looked around the corner to see if there was another man waiting to be
interviewed.

The reporter started talking to Cool Hand Luke, "When I touch your
arm, that means the interview is beginning okay? You just look at me and
answer my questions. You'll do fine." The reporter smiled and began
talking to the camera. "I'm with James Cutler. He's the father of two of
the boys hurt in last night's shooting near the M&M Soup Kitchen. Mr.

Cutler, how are the boys doing?"

Kate shook her head. *What did she say? Did that reporter say James was the father of two of the boys? That can't be right.*

Cool Hand Luke stared into the camera, "My boy Jayden's paralyzed. They don't think he'll ever walk again. I talked to him and he's bein real brave." He wiped a pretend tear. "They won't let me see my boy, Jamal. He's in the ICU. They're not sure he's going to make it."

Jamal...Cool Hand Luke was Jamal's dad? Kate couldn't believe it. She'd seen the man at lunch almost every day for the past six months and not once had she seen Marika give him more than a perfunctory nod.

He was Jamal's father?

"Mr. Cutler, I'm so sorry. I know this is difficult. What would you like our viewers to know about your sons?"

"They're good boys. They love their mommas, and they didn't deserve to get hurt." He covered his face and cried.

"Anyone with information about this horrific crime should contact Crimestoppers," The reporter said.

The light from the camera turned off, and James stopped crying. "Did I do okay?" he asked.

Disgusted, Kate pulled open the door to M&M and marched inside. She bumped into Nick, who had been watching from the doorway.

"Hasn't he suddenly become a loving and concerned father?" Nick's voice dripped with sarcasm.

"I had no idea he was Jamal's father." Kate put her hands on her hips. "And he's Jayden's dad too? No wonder Marika doesn't like Sharon."

"Yep." Nick walked down the hall with her. "I found out about two years ago. Marika needed help paying for St. Katherine Drexel, and she asked James to contribute. She really struggled even going to him, but she wanted the best for Jamal. So, she confronted him. Told him he hadn't paid a dime for any of Jamal's upbringing, no child support, no clothes, no food. Could he please give her a thousand dollars so Jamal could attend the private high school?"

"What did he say?" Kate asked.

"James told her, 'No way, the public school was just fine. Jamal would be gettin' too big for his britches. Besides, he had nine kids. He had to be fair'."

"*Nine* kids?" Kate stopped, "Cool Hand Luke has *nine* kids? That's crazy, I've never seen him with *any*."

"Cool Hand Luke?" Nick laughed, "That sure fits him, and I didn't say he was a dad to any of them. I just said he had nine kids."

"So how did Marika get the money for school?"

"Jamal got a sponsor." Nick stopped at his office door.

"Is his sponsor's name Nick?" Kate gazed into his beautiful eyes.

"Nope, but you do know him. It's Dan Hamilton."

"Dan Hamilton of Hamilton Enterprises is supporting Jamal's education?"

"Yep, when he heard Jamal needed help, Dan decided to become his benefactor. It's been great for everyone. Jamal is getting an excellent education, and Dan is seeing how one person can really change a another's life."

"That's great," Kate said. "I'm taking some clothes down to the hospital for Marika and Tucker as soon as lunch is finished."

"I'll go with you, if that's okay?"

"Absolutely." Kate went back to work.

The ICU waiting room was empty except for an older man sitting with his hands clasped staring at the floor. He raised sad eyes when Kate and Nick entered.

"Dan," Nick reached out his hand. "I thought you were in New York."

"I was," Dan stood. "I decided to fly home to see if I could do anything."

Kate shook his hand. "Where are Marika and Tucker?"

"They're with the care team." Dan sat back down. "Going over the next steps. It's fucking unbelievable."

Kate sat, placing the tote bag on the floor next to her.

"Did they catch the guy?" Dan crossed his arms over his chest.

"Nope, no one knows anything." Nick sat across from Dan. He rubbed his face, "Man, I'm tired. I think this is the first time I've sat down all day." He leaned back in the chair and closed his eyes.

They all slipped into the quiet of their own thoughts. Kate looked around the room. There was a trashcan filled with crumpled tissues and tattered magazines. Styrofoam coffee cups were scattered across a small table. The decor of the space was depressing: gold upholstered chairs and light mocha walls.

Why weren't hospital waiting rooms at least pretty or interesting?

Dan opened his eyes and stared at a poster with hot air balloons floating across the New Mexico sky.

"How did I get here?" Dan slapped his legs.

"What?" A startled Kate asked.

"I mean it." Dan paced the room. "How did I get to this place?"

Nick opened his eyes and looked from Dan to Kate.

"What?" Kate mouthed to Nick, shrugging her shoulders.

"What do you mean?" Nick asked.

"How is this my life? I should be in New Mexico watching balloons float across the sky for real, not sitting in a hospital waiting room hoping to hear my fifteen-year-old friend is to going to survive getting shot."

"Tell me about it," Nick snorted, "Life never takes the direction we expect."

"Yeah, but I wouldn't be here if it wasn't for you." Dan got in Nick's face and pointed his finger. "I was enjoying my life of leisure in retirement. I was traveling, seeing the world."

"Oh, come off it." Nick pushed Dan away and stood. "How much more traveling could you do? You've visited every capital in Europe, Asia, Australia, and Africa. You've seen the seven natural wonders of the world, touched every ocean, and ridden your bike along the east and west coasts of the United States."

Nick jabbed Dan's chest. "You told me you were looking for something more. I didn't force you to volunteer at M&M. I suggested maybe there was more to life than travel and fun."

Kate listened to the two men argue without saying a word. Her eyes followed the conversation's volley like a spectator at a tennis match.

"Right," Dan shoved Nick away. "You knew I had to see the charity that caused you to commit professional suicide. I needed to see why the magnificent Nick Decker gave up his career to become a director at a non-profit." He raised his hands towards the sky. "I needed to understand why my protege, my friend, the man I expected to take the helm of my company would give it all up to work at a soup kitchen."

Shaking his head, Nick laughed. "I asked you to volunteer *one* day. It was your decision to become a regular. Why was that? Did you suddenly find meaning in your sorry-ass life?" Nick glared at Dan.

Kate's eyes were wide. *Why was Nick so angry?*

Nick took a deep breath. "Did it hurt you to help someone? I simply suggested you volunteer to give your life a purpose."

The tension in the room was palpable. The two men glared at each other. Kate attempted to calm the situation. "Dan, how long have you been volunteering at M&M?" she asked.

"I guess four years now." Dan took a deep breath and sat down next to Kate. "I'd never really seen anything like it. With all the billions of dollars spent to end poverty in America, people were still waiting in line to eat. That was shocking to me. I thought maybe it was just the day I worked, so I came a different day, but the same thing, people waiting in line to eat. I started observing the clientele. They were disproportionally black men with no direction or goals in life." He shrugged his shoulders and laughed. "They were *me* without money. I thought maybe it wouldn't hurt to serve them lunch one day a week."

"Weren't you surprised by the comradery?" Kate asked. "I was."

"Not really," Dan looked at the floor. "What surprised me was their faith. I don't get it. The clients living the way they live, still believe in God. Hell, most of the volunteers are from some church or Catholic organization and almost all the employees attend daily Mass." He looked up. "The idea of a supreme being watching over us is ludicrous to me. It's the one aspect of the kitchen I don't understand. The whole 'let's get together and pray' is an anomaly to me.

"Where's God now, huh?" Dan raised his hands towards the sky. "Jamal's a good kid. A hard worker, polite, dependable." He whispered, "Where's God now?"

52

NICK

Nick went to the hospital chapel. He shouldn't have let his old boss's comments get under his skin, but they did. Nick knew he had practically said the same thing earlier, but Dan was different. He didn't have any faith. Dan couldn't comprehend the deep spiritual calling Nick had felt to go and work for M&M, and he could never understand the step Nick was contemplating now. Hell, sometimes even Nick didn't believe the direction God was pointing him towards.

The chapel was peaceful. A stained-glass window behind a simple wooden altar. Statues of Mary and Joseph on one side of the altar and an Infant of Prague statue on the other. Tucker and Marika knelt in the first pew, each clasping a rosary. Nick slipped into the row behind them.

Their rosary finished. Tucker and Marika stood looking tired and worried.

"Nick," Marika grasped his hands.

He wrapped his arm around her shoulder and shook Tucker's hand at the same time. "How is Jamal?"

Reaching into her pocket for a tissue, Marika shrugged, "He made it through the night."

"The doctors are pleased with how he's handling things." Tucker said. "If he remains stable, they'll operate tomorrow morning to complete all of the repairs." He held Marika's hand.

"That's good, isn't it?" Nick asked.

"I guess." Marika wiped her eyes.

"Baby, it's good." Tucker put his arm around her waist.

"Everyone is praying. In fact, the Mother's Group has organized a prayer service for tonight." Nick said.

"That's wonderful, thank you, Nick." Marika touched Tucker's cheek. "Could you go for both of us?"

"You know I will." Tucker nodded.

Nick sat next to Tucker in the front pew for the prayer service. The old church looked so beautiful. Evening was Nick's favorite time to be at Holy Family, as the setting sun washed the stained-glass windows in a warm glow, making the depiction of 'Jesus's Transfiguration' even more radiant. The waning light wrapped the altar in a cocoon of yellow and orange hues, creating an aura of peace and serenity.

The church was filled. Boys and girls dressed in their school uniforms represented Jamal's entire class at St. Katherine Drexel. Sitting together, the teens held hands, some crying, but all were subdued. Members of Marika's Mother's Group took up three pews, and several other rows were filled with her GED students. Dallas, Jenny, and even Libby sat in a pew behind Katie and the cooking class, including Leon, Deacon, Ted with his grandma, and a whole host of other M&M clients and volunteers. Holy Family Parishioners welcomed the clients and worked to find seats for the crowd, eventually resorting to opening the choir loft, which had been closed for years.

Nick allowed the priests words, the Bible readings, and the age-old prayers to heal his heart and soul. He prayed for God to hear the prayers being offered for Jamal and Jayden.

Towards the end of the service, the priest invited everyone to share a sign of God's peace with each other. Nick hugged Tucker, turned to shake Jenny's hand and noticed Dan standing next to Sylvie in the last row. Catching his eye, Nick nodded. Dan made the peace sign.

Dan waited for Nick after the service.

"Well," Dan said looking at the vaulted ceiling. "I can't remember the last time I was in a church. I'm glad the roof didn't cave in."

Laughing, Nick sat next to him on the wooden bench. "I'm sure God was glad to see you here." Both men stared at the flickering votives under the Madonna and Child statue. A hum of quiet conversation buzzed throughout the church.

"Is there any update?" Dan sighed.

"He's holding his own. The surgeon said we should pray."

Dan shifted in the pew. "You know. I walked in here and saw these people chanting, and I thought 'They're all crazy—praying to a so-called supreme being. If there was a God, why did Jamal and that other kid get hurt in the first place? Why did that teenager die?'" Dan shrugged. "Bad things happen. Praying isn't going to make it better."

Nick listened.

"I don't know," Dan rubbed his hands down his jean legs. "I don't really believe in God."

Nick's eyes darted around the church. "This is probably not the best place to admit that."

"I'm an engineer, for God's sake," Dan laughed. "I believe in tangibles; ideas that can be proven. You can't *prove* the existence of God. So, is God real?" He put his arm on the back of the pew. "A doctor asking people to pray for a miracle seems preposterous to me, but here I am." He opened his arms. "And I feel better. I have this feeling Jamal is going to be alright."

"That, my friend, is faith." Nick's fist tapped Dan's knee. "This entire community has joined together to pray for one thing: the healing of those two boys. I don't think you're here by accident. I believe God called you to attend this healing service."

"God didn't call me," Dan scoffed. "I opened your email, and if God is so good, why were those boys hurt to begin with?"

"I don't know." Nick stared at the crucifix on the altar. "There's evil in the world and sometimes God gets blamed, but I know God is here. Look at all the people who came to the service. Why? They came to pray. They came because they want things to get better. They came because they need hope. God gives us hope."

"Do you really believe that?" Dan asked.

"I do," Nick nodded. "Without hope, I couldn't do my job."

"I want Jamal to be okay. I saw all those people praying and they seemed so calm, so peaceful. I want to believe there's someone up there." Dan pointed to the ceiling, "but my brain won't let me."

"Then let your heart believe. Ask God to heal Jamal, He'll hear you," Nick said.

"You want me to pray? I wouldn't know where to start." Dan shook his head.

"Don't think of it as praying, just talk to God." Nick stood. "I've got to get going. I'm really glad you came tonight, Dan. Let me know if you want to talk again."

Dan sat in the pew and watched the flames of the votive candles dance in their red vases. He stared at the statue's peaceful face and felt calm. Feeling foolish, he looked around the church. He was alone except for the old woman kneeling in the front row.

He folded his hands. "Hey, are you there?" he laughed, and looked around, feeling sillier by the minute. "Well, I want you to help Jamal. He's a good kid. He doesn't deserve to be hurt. If you're real, please heal my friend."

Dan rose and walked down the aisle, trying to decipher his feeling: peace, serenity, joy? Those words weren't quite right. He felt *hope*.

53

NICK

"Nick," Deacon stood on the church steps following the prayer service. "We've got to do something about the crime around here. It's ruining everything. We've got to get the neighbors to start carin' about each other. Maybe you could start some type of neighborhood watch or somethin?"

"You're right, something needs to be done, but I can't do it." Nick pointed at Deacon. "You live here. I don't. You should organize your neighbors."

"Oh, no, no. I can't do that, I've got the store." Deacon fiddled with his toothpick.

"C'mon Deacon," Nick waved away his protest. "You're practically the mayor here. You've lived here your whole life, you know everybody, and you're a business owner. You're the perfect guy to start a neighborhood group."

"I don't think so," Deacon looked down at the sidewalk.

"I'm not saying you should do it yourself. Get some other people to help you." Nick spied a flash of orange on the church steps. "I bet Bernice would do it."

"Of course, I will." Bernice's orange fingernails grasped the railing. "What do you need?"

"Deacon wants to start a neighborhood watch program, and he's looking for people to help." Nick smiled. "I thought maybe you could be his assistant. You can use the dining room for your meetings."

"I'd love to help." Bernice clapped her hands together. "Let's get a coffee and talk about it."

She took Deacon's arm and headed down the street.

The next morning, Deacon walked into Nick's office as soon as the kitchen doors opened. "Got a minute?" he asked.

"Sure, what's up?" Nick said.

Deacon handed Nick a piece of paper. "Bernice and I would like to have the first neighborhood watch meeting here tomorrow afternoon." He tapped his leg with a folder. "Boy, that woman's a dynamo. She thought we should have a name for the group. What do you think of *Knights of the Neighborhood*? I'm not sure, but she likes it."

Nick read the flyer.

Help keep our neighborhood safe. Become a Knight. First meeting Friday, 1:00 p.m., at M&M Soup Kitchen.

"I think this looks great. What do you need me to do?"

"Can we pass out the flyers during lunch, maybe put some up in the foyer?"

"Of course, Friday's a great day for the meeting. Kid's Cafe is off, so you won't be rushed. We'll have some snacks and drinks available too."

"Much appreciated." Deacon shook Nick's hand. "I hope people come."

"I'm sure they will." Nick handed the flyer back to Deacon. "You can plaster those all over the kitchen. We're totally behind the Knights."

Sitting back at the desk Nick couldn't concentrate on anything. The whole kitchen seemed to be moving in slow motion. Like a cog was missing in the wheel, and it was. Without Marika, the kitchen seemed off-balance. The staff was going through the motions of work, but their heads and hearts were at the hospital with Jamal.

After lunch, Katie walked into his office. "Have you heard anything?"

"No." Nick looked at his watch. "I must have checked the clock a hundred times today. I thought he'd be out of surgery by now."

"Me too." Katie sat in the empty chair. "Uh, I know it's bad timing but tomorrow is supposed to be my last day."

"Oh, Katie." Nick groaned rubbing his fingers through his hair. "I totally forgot. Marika had a whole party planned, but with the shooting... I'm sorry."

"Oh my gosh, Nick." Katie waved her hands for him to stop talking. "No! I'm not worried about a party. I wanted to let you know I'll stay until Marika's back. I'm not going to leave you in the lurch."

"You will?" Nick breathed a sigh of relief. "You're a lifesaver. I don't know what I would do without you. Thank you."

"I want to stay and help." Katie stood to leave as his phone rang.

"It's Marika," He hit the speaker button on the phone. "Hello, hi, how's it going?"

Sobs filled the room.

"Marika?" A pale Nick wrapped his arm around Katie as she began to cry. "I'll be right there." Nick said into the phone.

"No, no," Marika laughed through the sobs. "Jamal's okay, he's out of surgery. It went great. The doctor says he's going to be okay. Jamal's going to be fine. Thank you, God."

"That's fantastic, I'm so happy for all of you." Nick said. "I'm going to share the great news."

The kitchen was quiet. Nick walked through the offices, turning off lights and closing doors. He checked Padre's Pantry. Tucker had a great group of volunteers. They had kept the pantry open in his absence without missing a beat. The kitchen had kept working, feeding more people in the past two days than they had in the prior three days combined.

He was tired. He felt like the shooting had been two months ago, not two days. The shooting had refocused his attention to the real problem of the community. It wasn't poverty of things, but rather poverty of spirit. The neighborhood had lost hope. How could he fix that? Locking the kitchen's doors, he walked to Holy Family Church, the only place he could find true peace. Kneeling before the crucifix, he thanked God for Jamal's successful surgery. He prayed for the community of M&M, and he asked God for the strength to answer His call.

54

MARIKA

For the first time in days, Marika felt peace. Sitting in the ICU waiting room, she could breathe without feeling a wrench in her gut. Her son was going to live.

"Hi, there!" Kate said walking into the room. "You look like a new woman."

"I feel like one." Marika stood to give Kate a hug. "It's amazing what good news and a hot shower can do for your spirits."

"I bet. Where's Tucker?" Kate asked.

"I sent him home." Marika sat on the couch. "He's so tired, and they won't let him see Jamal, only relatives are allowed in the ICU. I tried to explain that Tucker is like a father to Jamal, but they won't budge." She played with the button on her sweater. "I know Tucker's feelings were hurt. He wants to see Jamal for himself."

Kate's voice was soft. "I saw the interview on the news. I didn't know Cool Hand Luke was Jamal's father."

"He's not," Marika paced the room. "He was just the sperm donor. I saw him on the TV, acting so concerned—what a joke. He probably couldn't pick Jamal out of a crowd. James has never been a father to him." Stopping to stare out the window, Marika's voice was derisive. "He ran the second I told him I was pregnant. Of course, I didn't know that Sharon had told him she was pregnant the week before." Her laugh was filled with scorn. "I don't think James has ever even touched Jamal. He didn't come to the hospital when he was born, even though I called him. He's never watched Jamal play football or basketball. He hasn't given Jamal one dime, yet he had the nerve to call himself his father."

She turned and looked at Kate. "That reporter should have asked *'When was the last time you talked to Jamal?'*"

"Never," Marika continued, mimicking James' voice.

"When is Jamal's birthday?" Marika's reporter voice asked.

"Not really sure, I wasn't around, and I've never been to a birthday party for him," Marika continued as James.

"What's Jamal like?" the reporter voice said.

"He's funny, he's kind, he's smart, he's honorable." Marika sat down. "Tucker could answer all those questions. He's Jamal's father in every true sense of the word. He's gone to hundreds of school events and games, helped with homework, given advice on everything from how to tie a tie to how to treat a girl. Tucker is Jamal's dad. I just haven't let him have the official title."

Marika seemed to be talking to herself. "I'm the one who didn't want to get married. I'm the one who kept saying *no* to Tucker. It's me. I've kept Jamal from having a dad, from us being a family, because I've been afraid. I let the way James treated me fifteen years ago control my life now. I let that lying showboat of a man keep me from marrying the man I love. James has been the stereotype I've judged all men by—even Tucker, who's never been anything but wonderful to me." Marika started to cry.

Kate handed her a tissue and patted her back.

"Tucker hasn't left my side since this whole thing happened." Marika sniffled. "He's been here crying with me, praying with me, supporting me, because he loves Jamal as much as I do. Tucker is Jamal's dad, and I need to make sure everyone knows that."

She stood up smiling as tears ran down her cheek. "Katie, I'm going to marry Tucker."

The Knights of the Neighborhood's first official activity was to welcome Jamal home from the hospital. Deacon and Bernice had worked non-stop over the past two weeks to organize the neighborhood watch group. They recruited neighbors to serve as street captains, established safe zones at local businesses and created a community board. Deacon had been overwhelmingly elected to serve as the group's first President, a job he seemed to relish. Bernice handled the social aspects of the group, including Jamal's welcome home celebration.

Marika's eyes filled with tears when Tucker turned onto their street. Bernice had the students of St. Katherine Drexel and Kid's Cafe create signs.

Welcome Home, Jamal.

Feel Better, Jamal.

We love you, Jamal.

Yellow ribbons were placed on each door, and the children held yellow balloons. The cooking class had baked dozens of cookies, and Leon had spent hours baking and decorating miniature cupcakes.

Stepping out of the car, a much thinner Jamal was greeted by Deacon. "Jamal, we are so happy to welcome you back home. We want you to know that the Knights of the Neighborhood are going to work tirelessly to ensure that you and everyone else in this community is safe. We love you, Jamal." The crowd erupted with applause.

Standing next to Kate and Marika on the sidewalk, Bernice, in yellow, whispered, "Don't you think Deacon is handsome? He reminds me of my dear Larry, God rest his soul."

"He is very good-looking," Kate agreed hiding a smile.

"Should I say something?" Jamal asked.

"I think you should," Marika said.

"Gosh you guys," Jamal smiled, his voice quiet and strong. "I am so happy to be home, and I appreciate all the prayers and support everyone has given me. I know they helped." He looked at the dessert table. "Now, I think I want that chocolate cupcake."

Curled up on the couch later that evening, Marika relished being home. After two weeks in the hospital, she was enjoying using her own bathroom, sitting on her own furniture and the familiar noises of home.

Tucker was helping Jamal get ready for bed. Once he'd been on the mend, Jamal had decided that Tucker was more suited to helping with his shower than his mom. "I've seen everything you've got." Marika had told him.

"But you haven't seen it this big," Jamal had answered. Laughing and shaking his head, Tucker had agreed to take over the bathroom duties.

Closing her eyes, she laid her head on the arm of the sofa. She couldn't wait to climb into her own bed knowing Jamal was safe in the room down the hall.

How was Sharon coping? Did Jayden like the rehab facility? And Briana, Benji's poor mom, how was she surviving?

Hearing her two boys laughing and talking as they completed Jamal's nightly routine, Marika drifted asleep thinking, *I am so grateful. Thank you, God.*

"Hey, why don't you climb into bed.? Jamal's asleep and I'm going to head out." Tucker's soft touch startled her awake. Rubbing her eyes, she pushed up from the couch and snuggled next to him.

"Thank you." She whispered looking into his warm, dark eyes. "Thank you, Tucker. I don't know what I would have done without you these past few weeks."

He kissed her lips. "I'm just glad he's home."

"I mean it." Marika hugged him tighter. "This whole thing has made me realize how much I count on you, how much I *need* you, and how much I *love* you." She pulled away and took both of his hands into hers. "What I'm trying to say is…" She gulped, "Tucker, will you marry me?"

Throwing back his head, Tucker roared with laughter. "I have waited my whole life to hear you say that! Yes, *yes*, I will marry you."

55

KATE

Prepping for lunch, Kate was surprised to see a frail-looking Sylvie standing on the threshold of the kitchen doorway, staring into the dining room. Jenny took her elbow. "Sylvie, I'm glad you're back. We've missed you." She walked with her into the kitchen.

"I wasn't sure I could do it, but I told myself I had to at least try." Sylvie gave a nervous smile.

"We're glad you did." Kate handed her a blue apron. "Thank you for the spinach. It looks wonderful."

"Oh, you're welcome. I'm so glad to be working in the garden again. I need to keep busy." She tied the apron around her waist. "Would you mind if I serve desserts?"

"That's perfect." Jenny wrote a note on her clipboard. "You can help Katie organize the trays before we start serving."

Rolling a grocery cart of pies to the prep table, Kate handed Sylvie a knife. "We've got to slice all of these," Kate said.

"I can do that." Sylvie took out a tin. "Oh, my. It's peach! That was Xander's favorite. He must be sending me a sign." A tear rolled down her face.

"I'm so sorry." Kate handed her a paper towel.

"No, no. I'm okay." Sylvie blew her nose. "It just comes and goes.

I'll be alright. Let's talk about something else—have you seen Rachel?"

"I have," Kate sliced into an apple pie. "She's good. She's still taking the cooking class. What about you?"

"I talked to her at the prayer service for Jamal, but not since then." Sylvie shrugged. "I want to help, but I don't want to overstep my bounds."

"Rachel is really sweet." Kate placed the pie plates onto the serving trays. "She's had to deal with a lot: the baby, Alex dying, meeting you. She'll come around, just take it slow."

"I hope you're right." She opened a second peach pie. "That baby is my last connection to Xander. I want to meet it."

"Well," Dan walked into the kitchen. "You're a sight for sore eyes. How are you?" He put his arm around Sylvie's shoulder.

"Good days and bad days." Sylvie made a so-so motion with her hand. "As hard as it was to see Xander stoned and dirty each week, I always had hope that maybe next week I'd get my miracle; he'd ask for help, get sober. But now it's real. I'll never see my son again. The hope is gone." She sniffed. "I know he's in a better place, he was tormented by his addiction, but I'd give anything for him to be here with me, completely healed."

"It's time to pray," Jenny yelled from the dining room.

"Hope," Dan squeezed her hand. "That's the one thing everybody needs." He walked into the dining room to pray.

Kate could see how happy the clients were to have Sylvie back. Sylvie remembered the regulars'; saving a blueberry muffin for the *Muffin Man* (Jerry) a cheese crown for *Crazy Maisie* (Lucy), and Boston cream pie for the *Scarecrow* (Dexter), who actually smiled when she handed him dessert. She helped even the most persnickety clients get the sweet they wanted.

"Miss Sylvie, it's so good to see you," Bernice beamed in an orange sweatsuit.

"I have a bear claw for you," Sylvie picked up the plate. "That orange is a beautiful color on you."

"Thank you, now have a blessed day." Bernice placed the pastry on her tray.

"Rachel," Sylvie's voice shook. "I don't know your favorite dessert. Is there something specific you like?

"I guess chocolate cake," Rachel wouldn't look at Sylvie's face. The young girl was rail-thin, but her baby bump was pushing out of her jeans and T-shirt.

"I've got the perfect piece for you." Sylvie moved several trays on the rolling cart before choosing a plate. "Here you go." She handed the young girl a slice of triple-layer chocolate cake. "Enjoy."

"Thank you," Rachel's eyes lit up as she took the plate.

"She talked to you." Kate gathered the empty trays from the dessert station.

"She did," Sylvie nodded. "I think somebody should donate maternity clothes to the kitchen. Don't you?"

"I do," Kate said. "That would be very nice. They should probably be dropped off on Wednesday around five, that's when the cooking class is over."

Winking, Kate carried the trays to the washroom.

56

MARIKA

Walking to M&M in the warm sunshine, Marika thought this must be how a prisoner feels when they're released from jail. It was exhilarating, just breathing fresh air. She wasn't quarantined in a hospital praying for her child to live, or stationed at her house making sure that same child didn't overdo his rehabilitation. Tucker was staying with Jamal so she could attend the cooking class. She hadn't been to the kitchen since the shooting over a month ago, and she couldn't wait to share her exciting news.

Pushing the walk button with her left hand, she smiled once again at the sparkle of her beautiful engagement ring.

I better be careful. I could blind someone with this.

Holding her hand out for a better look, she admired the diamond ring. She, Marika Johnson, was getting married.

The signal turned green, and Marika crossed the street. The memory of last night making her smile more. Tucker had called on his way home from work to say he was making his famous spaghetti and meatballs for dinner. When he'd arrived, he'd handed her a fizzy lavender-scented bath bomb and told her to go take a long relaxing bath. He wanted the kitchen to himself. Jamal would be his sous chef.

Walking into the kitchen after her soak, she saw white tapered candles flickering on the table, a vase of red roses as the centerpiece. Tucker bowed when she entered the room, an apron wrapped around his waist. "Madam," he said. May I have this dance."

"You may," she curtsied.

Jamal sat on the kitchen chair, his hand holding the side where the bullet had entered. Pushing a button on his phone, Bruno Mars started singing 'Count on Me.'

Marika and Tucker swayed around the tiny kitchen, Jamal laughing at their silly moves. At the end of the song, Tucker pulled out a chair for Marika to sit at the table. He dropped to one knee and held her hand.

"Marika," he said. "I love you, and even though you asked me to marry you, I wanted you to have a real proposal. So, after getting your son's permission, I have a question to ask you." Jamal passed him a box, and Tucker opened it. "Marika, will you please marry me?"

She was stunned. Her eyes moved from the sparkling diamond to her son's eyes twinkling with excitement, to Tucker's eyes shiny with tears.

She exhaled and shouted, "Yes, yes, yes! I'll marry you." Putting her hands on both sides of his face, Marika kissed him saying, "I love you, Tucker."

"*Finally,*" Jamal said grinning.

Arriving at the kitchen, she rubbed the diamond on her jacket.

I'm not going to say anything about the engagement. I'll let them notice my ring.

She pushed open the door. Her arms opened wide, "I'm back."

"Oh my gosh, it's so good to see you," Kate said giving her a hug as "hellos" echoed through the kitchen.

"We're just getting started." Kate pulled her over to the prep table where they were meeting.

"How is that sweet son of yours?" A red-clad, Bernice said, wrapping her in a bear hug.

"He's doing so good." Marika nodded. "Today's the first time I've left him since the whole thing happened. I think he was glad for me to leave."

Rachel pulled her T-shirt down over her swelling belly and scooted over to make room. "Oh, my goodness, you popped!" Marika said, touching the girl's stomach with her left hand.

"I know," Rachel said. "I had my sonogram last week and the doctor said everything is good."

"Did you find out what you're having?" Marika asked.

"No, I want to be surprised. I can show you the pictures later if you want?"

"I'd like that." Marika smiled.

Leon was a changed person since his medicine had been regulated—more confident, outgoing, stable. Jackie wasn't around anymore.

"Leon," Marika took his hand, "I can't tell you how much we enjoyed the cupcakes you baked. They were delicious. We shared them with the nurses, and I'll tell you, sometimes they pretended to check on Jamal just so they could take another one."

"I'm glad you liked them." Leon blushed. "I made some for the street party, too. Some people asked for my recipe."

"Tamara!" Marika opened her arms.

"I am so sorry," Tamara cried into Marika's shoulder. "I should have stopped Aldiez, but I didn't know how. Mr. Nick helped me talk to the police. Aldiez is going to jail."

"I know." Marika rubbed the girl's back. "It must have been so hard to turn him in, but you did right thing."

"I know I did." Tamara stepped back and wiped her eyes. "I can't believe he got those boys hurt. I'll never forgive him."

"How is Jayden doing?"

"He's doing okay, I guess." Tamara shrugged. "He'll be at the rehabilitation center for the next few months. Sharon's been going every day. It's just starting to sink in that he's never going to walk again."

We were so blessed, thank you God! Marika took a deep breath, offering up her silent prayer for the hundredth time.

"I'm so glad you're here," Kate handed her an apron.

"What are we making?" Marika tied the apron around her waist.

"Oh my, God," Kendra shouted, jumping up from the chair. She grabbed Marika's hand. "Is that an engagement ring?"

"It is." She fluttered her fingers in front of her. "I'm getting married!"

"How did he propose?" Rachel asked.

"Have you set a date?" Bernice said.

"Will we all get to come?" Kendra asked.

"So many questions." Marika put her hands to her face. "Oh my gosh, let's get started and I'll tell you how it happened."

Marika finished her story just in time to put the shepherd's pies in the oven. The class gathered around the table for a snack while the food baked.

"I had no idea Tucker was such a romantic." Kate took a bite of a carrot. "He even asked Jamal for his permission. Wow, that's a class act."

"What type of wedding are you going to have?" Kendra asked. "Do you have a theme?"

"No, I don't have a theme." Marika shook her head. "It's going to be small, maybe at city hall."

"You can't get married at city hall. We'll do it here." Bernice looked at the class. "We'll be your wedding planners. Tamara can help Katie with the food. Leon can bake the cake. Kendra and Rachel can work on the decorations, and I'll help with the dress. It will be wonderful."

"Oh, I can't let you do that." Marika said shaking her head. "It's too much work."

"Nonsense," Bernice waved away her protest. "We can do it, can't we?"

"Yes!" The group said in unison.

"You can count on us. We'll take care of everything." Bernice smiled.

"What do you think?" Marika asked.

"I think you're going to be a beautiful bride," Kate answered.

"Are you sure?" Marika looked at the smiling faces. "Well, okay. Thank you."

"It's settled then." Bernice stood. "You pick the date and time, and we'll do everything else. I think red is a good color, don't you?"

"Red?" Marika tilted her head. "I'm not sure about red."

"It's the color of love, it's perfect for a wedding," Bernice modeled her red ensemble.

"How about shades of pink?" Marika touched her pink shirt. "I'm not really a red person."

"Pink will work," Bernice said.

"How many people do you think will be there?" Leon asked writing in a notebook. "I need to start designing the cake."

"I think there should be lots of flowers, don't you?" Rachel pushed Marika out of the way to talk to Kendra.

"Oh my, what have I gotten myself into?" Marika laughed, shaking her head.

The buzzing of the back door stopped the conversation. Kate peaked through the peep hole. "It's Sylvie, she's donating some things. I told her she could drop them off tonight."

Rachel stood to leave, but Bernice pulled her back. "She's trying to be nice, just say hi." With a huff, Rachel sat down.

"Sylvie," Kate opened the door. "Come in. Can I help you with those bags?"

"I've got it." Sylvie walked sideways through the door carrying two huge shopping bags in each hand. "Hi, everyone, boy it smells good in here."

"Sylvie, we made the most delicious dinner." Bernice said, reaching to help with the bags. "I can't wait to see what you have in here."

"They're maternity clothes for the Mother's Group, but I thought maybe Rachel would want to go through them first." Sylvie smiled at Rachel, who sat with her arms crossed, looking down at the floor. "I wasn't sure what girls are wearing now, so I bought a variety of sizes and styles." Sylvie's voice quavered.

"Rachel, come look at this." Bernice rifled through the bag and pulled out a blouse.

Rachel didn't move.

"I can just leave this for you, I didn't mean to interrupt." Sylvie put the rest of the bags on the counter.

"You're not interrupting," Bernice's voice was firm. "We were busy helping to plan Marika's wedding."

"Show her the ring," Kendra grabbed Marika's hand. "We're going to be her wedding planners. I'm in charge of decorations."

"Well, if you need any flowers, let me know." Sylvie admired the ring. "I think my garden is going to be beautiful this summer."

Rachel ambled over to the shopping bags, watching Bernice pull out various dresses, skirts, pants, and shirts. Picking out a blue-and-white-striped fitted dress, Rachel held the bodice up to her body and admired her reflection in the stainless-steel refrigerator.

"That would look so cute on you, plenty of room for the baby to grow." Bernice handed her another dress. "This would look good too."

Rachel examined all the clothes, taking some and passing on others. Sylvie watched from across the room.

"Would you mind if I take these?" Rachel held up a stack.

"Of course not, are you sure that's all you want?" Sylvie moved closer.

"It's fine." Rachel put the clothes in a bag. "The Mother's Group is really friendly. I'm sure we'll all end up sharing anyway."

"Did you show Sylvie the sonogram?" Bernice nudged Rachel.

"No," Rachel shook her head.

"Why don't you show her?" Bernice asked.

"Oh, you don't have to—" Sylvie interrupted.

"Do you want to see it?" Rachel asked, looking at Sylvie for the first time.

"I'd love to." Sylvie smiled.

Rachel pulled the photo out of her book bag. She'd placed it between the pages of the book, *What to Expect, When You're Expecting*, a gift from Marika.

"Oh." Sylvie traced the image with her fingertip, her voice cracked. "I know this sounds crazy, but I think the baby has Xander's nose."

"I thought the same thing," Rachel laughed, pressing her shoulder into Sylvie's side to share the photo. "Isn't it cute?"

Sylvie cleared her throat. "Do you know if it's a boy or a girl?"

"I don't want to know." Rachel shook her head. "I like surprises."

"Me too," Sylvie agreed staring at the picture.

The oven timer rang, jolting everyone back to the dinner. Katie checked the pies. "I totally forgot about these. Thank goodness a shepherd's pie is so easy. They're perfect."

"And, so simple," Bernice said. "We had plenty of time to plan our wedding. Now, Marika, you just set the date, and we'll take care of everything else."

57

KATE

Kate closed the kitchen door and walked towards Nick's office. Today was the day; she was taking it into her own hands.

She'd be leaving M&M in two weeks.

There weren't any more excuses or reasons why she couldn't ask Nick out. Taking a deep breath, she smoothed down her white oxford blouse. She brushed a loose strand of hair back into her ponytail.

It was time.

Giving herself a pep talk, she walked down the hall.

I can do it. I'm a modern woman. Nick is wonderful. We won't be working together much longer, so if things don't work out it won't be awkward.

Reaching the door, she took one more deep breath. She was ready. She was going to ask Nick out on a date.

Rap, Rap, Rap. "Hi, are you busy?" Her fist rested on the door frame.

"Hey, come in." Smiling, Nick looked up from the computer.

God he's cute.

"Am I interrupting something?" She moved the box resting on the chair to the floor.

"No, I'm ready to quit." Nick tossed a spreadsheet on the desk. "I've been reviewing last month's numbers and, to be honest, it's a little depressing."

"Really, why?" Kate asked.

"We just don't seem to be making a difference. We're consistently feeding the same number of people. Don't get me wrong, I'm happy the kitchen is able to help, but I'd like to see some type of downward turn, but not this month.

Kate picked up the sheet and looked at the columns. "Have you ever thought that some people are just coming for the delicious food and camaraderie, and not just because they're hungry?"

He pointed his finger in the air as if a lightbulb went off. "I have thought of that, but if that was the case, I think we would have seen an uptick in the numbers since the food is so good."

"Right." She laughed handing him back the pages.

"Oh well, the problem will still be here tomorrow. What can I do for you?" The chair squeaked as he leaned back to place his feet on the desk. His arms crossed behind his head.

You can do this.

She gripped her hands together. "Well, uhm, I was wondering. Would you like to be my date to the wedding?"

Nick jumped up like hot water had been poured on his lap. His face turned red, he stammered "Uh, wait a minute." He hopped over boxes and papers in a rush to shut the door.

Kate jumped up too, feeling heat race from the bottom of her work clogs to the top of her head. She was going to combust with embarrassment.

"Katie. I, uh, *oh*." Nick blocked the door. He put his hands out like a defensive back trying to avert a tackle.

"It's alright, you don't have to say yes." Kate waved her hands like a referee calling a ball dead. "I just thought it might be fun to go together. I mean, I'm not dating anyone, and I didn't think you were dating anyone. I just assumed." She laughed and tried to reach the door handle, but Nick's body was still blocking the door. There was no way for her to escape.

He stared at her as he rubbed the five o'clock shadow on his face.

Move away from the door. She silently begged. *Why won't the floor open up and swallow me?*

She was mortified. He looked horrified, almost as if Medusa herself had invited him out on a date.

"Katie, I'm sorry." He took both of her hands. "Can we sit back down?"

She sunk onto the edge of her seat, while he sat on the box she'd placed on the floor.

"Really, it's alright, it was just a thought." Kate went to stand, but he pulled her down.

"Katie, please, please sit…let me explain."

What did he have to explain? He didn't want to go with her to the wedding. He didn't think of her in that way.

She could feel her face get even redder, if that were even possible.

"Katie." He looked into her eyes, keeping her gaze. His smile was sweet. "I am so flattered that you wanted me to be your date. I would be lucky to go *anywhere* with you, but I've been in the process of re-evaluating my life, and I've decided to make some changes."

He's gay. Kate shook her head. *How did I miss that? My gaydar is terrible. I would have never guessed. Why are the most attractive men always gay?*

Nick didn't hear the thoughts rushing through her brain. He kept talking. "So, after a lot of prayer and a period of discernment, I've realized I'm being called to become a priest."

"*What?*" Kate's voice croaked, and she grabbed her chest. "I'm sorry, *what* did you say?" Kate leaned closer to make certain she heard correctly.

"I'm going to be a priest." He took a deep breath. "I'm entering the seminary in the fall." He stood up. "Wow, you're the first person I've told outside of my family." He stretched his arms over his head. "Boy, it feels good to have it out in the open."

"Oh my gosh," Kate hugged him.

Wow, should I have done that...do you touch a priest?

"I don't really know what to say. Are you sure?"

"I am." He nodded. "I mean, I wasn't until you asked me out, and then I knew."

"Well, I'm not sure that's a compliment—" Kate tilted her head.

"It is." He squeezed her shoulders. "You're asking me out made my decision crystal clear. You are exactly what every man wants in a woman: you're smart, beautiful, kind, loyal. You've handled a tremendous hardship with grace and humor, but I don't want to date you. I want to be a priest." He beamed with joy.

"I had no idea you were thinking about the priesthood." Kate sat back in her chair.

"I really wasn't." Nick picked up a baseball from the desk and started tossing it in the air. "I always thought I'd get married, have a few kids. I've dated and loved some amazing women, but something always seemed off. So, I focused on my career, got my MBA, then my law degree. I worked hard and was successful. I had everything a guy could want, but I wasn't happy. That's why I started working for M&M. I thought maybe if I gave back, then... I would be content. It worked for a while, but about a year ago that feeling of restlessness came back with a vengeance."

He stopped tossing the ball. "I prayed for God to show me my next step. I promised to do whatever he told me to do." He stared at Kate. "Do you think I'm crazy?"

"No." Kate laughed. "I talk to God all the time."

"I do too." Nick smiled. "But this time, I listened, and I swear I heard God's voice." He walked to the window. "I was in the stockroom looking for some toilet paper for a client. I remember thinking, *God, what should I do with my life.* And then I heard the answer: *you should be a priest.* It was as if God was standing next to me."

"Are you sure it was God?" Kate walked to the window. "Maybe it was Dallas or Tucker playing a trick on you?"

"No kidding." Nick laughed. "I put the thought out of my mind right away, but it kept coming back, getting louder and more persistent. About two months ago, the Athenaeum was giving a retreat for men thinking about the priesthood; a kind of information weekend. By Saturday night, I knew the priesthood was for me." His face was peaceful.

"I think you'll be a great priest." Kate gave him a quick hug.

"Thanks, Katie." He squeezed her back. "I'm going to tell everyone once the wedding is over. Okay?"

She nodded.

"Hey, we can still go to the wedding together now that we both know it's not a date." Nick said.

"Sounds good." Kate started to open the door. "You know, I've had men give me all sorts of reasons why they can't go out, but you're the first to actually become a priest."

"Those men were fools, Katie." He winked. "You're a keeper."

Kate practically ran to her car. Pushing the ignition, she paused to breathe. She tried to remember every conversation she had with Nick. Did he ever say anything that would make her think he was going to be a priest? Yes, he went to Mass every day, but lots of people did. *She* had started going to Mass every day. Holy Family was so convenient to

M&M. Her Catholic guilt required her to at least attempt to hit church a few days a week. She got it when he told her Mass centered his day.

Oh God, am I supposed to join the convent? No way, a life of celibacy is not for me. Sex —oh God, did I ever say anything sexy or racy to him?

She made the sign of the cross. Putting the car in drive, she drove to the restaurant.

Sitting on the stoop, Kate closed her eyes to bask in the sun. A kaleidoscope of shapes and designs swirled across her eyelids and her breathing slowed.

Nick, a priest. It was hard enough to find a good guy to date; now she had to compete with God. Shaking her head at the irony, Kate looked at him with fresh eyes. Nick was so kind and patient with all the clients. He had been so compassionate with Leon and Sylvie. Nick was a *good* man. He would be a wonderful priest. He had a dynamic and engaging personality that people were naturally drawn to. He encouraged people to do the right thing without becoming judgmental or preachy. He was a wonderful speaker and could tell a great story, which would be a terrific asset when he gave a homily, and he was able to make the most lost person feel as if he had found a friend.

Kate smiled. Nick had found his calling. *What's mine?*

Opening her eyes, she looked at the building. The reconstruction was in full swing. Her dad had been spending every waking hour coordinating electricians, plumbers, and construction workers to ensure the project was completed on time and within budget. Her prayers had been answered. She was going to be a chef again in her own restaurant, but surprisingly the thought didn't bring her much joy.

Working at M&M, she'd truly been feeding the hungry. How would she be helping anyone but herself at the restaurant? Patrons would be spending more for one dinner at Kate's than M&M spent on feeding a client for an entire month. Owning the restaurant seemed shallow and self-absorbed now. How was she going to change that?

Kate stood. The porch was covered in shadows. Her entire business plan didn't make sense anymore. There wasn't any meaning to it other than the bottom line. She wanted the restaurant to make a difference.

58

MARIKA

Marika peaked out the door of the bride's room to look inside the church. It was beautiful. Her decorators, Rachel, Kendra, and Sylvie, had tied a white rose with baby's breath to each pew, with a ribbon of pink tulle. The altar was framed by huge arrangements of roses in various shades of pink and gold candelabras. The pews were filling up.

"Girls, the church looks amazing." Marika stepped back into the bride's room. "I can't believe all those people are here for my wedding."

"You should see M&M." Rachel stepped over Marika's train. "You aren't going to believe what we did over there."

"I can't wait." Marika swayed in the dress. "You saved your seat for the wedding, didn't you?"

"I'm going to sit with Sylvie. You look so pretty," Rachel said before slipping out the door.

"Do you need anything? It's almost time," Kate asked, fluffing Marika's train.

"No," Marika grabbed Kate's arm. "I want to say something to you, and I don't want you to interrupt me until I'm finished."

"Okay." Kate held the bride's hands in hers. "What do you need?"

Marika eyes shined with tears. She took a deep breath and squeezed Kate's hands. "I want to apologize for how mean I was to you when you started working at M&M."

"Marika, that's water under the bridge." Kate shook her head.

"No, I have to say this," Marika's voice cracked. "You have become such a wonderful friend. I've learned so much from you. You gave me the confidence to try different recipes, to plan menus, to teach the cooking class." She took a deep breath. "I know you told Nick to give me the job as head cook, and I want you to know how grateful I am. You have helped change my life."

"Marika," Kate's voice cracked. "You taught me more about feeding people than I learned in three years of cooking school. I didn't have to tell Nick to hire you, that was his plan all along. You needed the confidence to know you could do the job, and you are going to be fantastic." Kate sniffed, reaching for a Kleenex. "Now don't you dare cry. This is your day to shine."

"Mom," Jamal knocked and entered the room. "Wow, you look beautiful."

"You look so handsome, so grown-up." Marika smiled. "Come here and let me straighten that tie. How's Tucker doing?"

"It's hilarious," Jamal grinned, "He's so nervous. Nick told him he was going to walk a hole in the carpet with his pacing."

"Do you think he's having second thoughts?" Marika adjusted the pink bow tie.

"No way," Jamal shook his head. "He thinks you might. I'm supposed to text him to let him know you're here."

"Are you kidding?" Kate laughed.

"Nope, when I told him I was going to tell you he was nervous, he threatened to ground me. He said it would be his first punishment as my official stepfather." Jamal held his stomach as he laughed. "Man, he's all talk."

"Text him that I can't wait to get married." Marika nudged Jamal's arm.

"No way," Jamal took his phone out of his pocket. "I'm going to say you're a no-show."

"Don't you dare," Marika smiled.

"It's time." Bernice poked her head through the door.

Nick and Tucker stood with the priest on the altar. The music started and Kate walked down the aisle first. Still in the bride's room, Marika turned to Jamal. "Are we ready for this?"

"We've been ready for this for a long time." Jamal's voice was sincere.

"Yes, we have." Marika nodded. Taking her son's arm, she went to marry the man of her dreams.

59

KATE

The decorating crew had worked overtime transforming the dining room into a secret garden. With Dallas's help, they hung twinkling fairy lights across the ceiling. They'd borrowed plants from Dan's office, Sylvie's house, and the church, to hide the stainless-steel appliances. Bernice insisted the chairs be color-coordinated around each pink, linen tablecloth. As centerpieces, fishbowls with floating candles were surrounded by an arrangement of gardenias and roses. The scent of the sweet flowers combined with the savory aroma of dinner obscured any soup kitchen smells.

Kate watched Tucker and Marika as they greeted their guests.

"It was a beautiful wedding," Bernice, wearing a pale lilac suit, hugged the bride.

"Tucker, I didn't know a smile could get that big." Deacon slapped the groom's shoulder.

"You look so pretty," Sylvie said.

The Muffin Man asked, "Why does a man twist the wedding ring on his finger?

"I don't know, why?" Tucker said.

"Because he's trying to figure out the combination," bowing, the Muffin Man kissed Marika's hand.

The Scarecrow nodded when he walked through the door. Crazy

Maisie donned a new pair of pajama bottoms. Ted, escorting his grandma, smiled at everyone to show off his new teeth.

The cooking class students were beside themselves with excitement. Tamara brought her children, looking adorable in coordinating outfits. Kendra's mom and brothers were amazed at the transformation of the kitchen, teasing Kendra that she should become a decorator. Leon had outdone himself: the cake was magnificent. Two round tiers sat atop a square opera cream base. The buttercream white icing was decorated with swirls of pink roses, with the couple's initials integrated into the design. Real pink roses served as the cake topper.

"Leon, we saved you a seat," Kendra said admiring the cake. "The cooking class is going to sit together."

"Okay." Leon nodded, standing next to the cake. "I'm going to stay here for a bit. I want to pass out the business cards my dad got for me." He handed her a card,

Stability Sweets made by Leon the Baker.

After Marika and Tucker enjoyed their first dance as a married couple, they invited their guests to join them on the dance floor. "Miss Katie, may I have this dance?" Leon stood at Kate's chair.

"I'd love to," Kate said, taking his hand.

An hour later, she was hot, tired, and her feet hurt. Besides Leon, she had danced with Tucker, Jamal, Dallas, Dan, the entire cooking class, and even the *Muffin Man*.

"You look like you could use a drink." Nick stood next to the makeshift bar.

"I'd love a water," Kate smiled. "I was never this popular in high school."

"You look beautiful." Nick said, handing her a pink Solo cup.

"Thank you," she took a sip, "Have you decided when you're going to tell everyone?"

"I don't know." He leaned against the wall watching the dancing. "Part of me wants to shout it to the world, but another part wants to keep quiet for a little longer."

"I get it," Kate nodded. "It's hard saying goodbye to people you care about. I can't believe how much I'm going to miss this place. People keep saying, 'You can stay involved. Keep teaching the cooking class, but it's not the same." She put her cup down. "Sometimes following your heart can really cause it to break."

The DJ announced the 'Electric Slide'. Watching the partiers attempt the dance with various levels of success, Kate had an epiphany. She took Nick's hand. "A stranger walking in here wouldn't be able to tell the difference between an employee, a volunteer, a benefactor, or a client. Isn't that amazing. It's just a bunch of people celebrating."

"You're right," Nick said leading her to the dancefloor.

60

NICK

"Man, I'm tired." Dallas stretched his arms surveying the room. "I'm just going to straighten these tables before I call it a night."

"We can all help." Dan stood and moved the table next to Tucker. "When are you leaving for your honeymoon?"

"Well, tomorrow we're going to a little bed and breakfast up near Hocking Hills, and then on Wednesday we're picking up Jamal to head to the beach." Tucker slid some chairs over to Dan.

"I'm so excited," Marika said. "I've never seen the ocean."

"I'm so glad Jamal's going with you." Kate gathered the tablecloths into her arms. "It will be your first family vacation."

"I know." Marika placed the centerpieces on the counter. "Gosh, when I come back, you'll be gone."

"I know. I can't really think about it." Kate shook her head, "If you would have told me nine months ago that I would cry about leaving here, I would have said you were delusional. I was going to come in here, get the kitchen in order and leave as fast as possible. I had a real job, a real kitchen, a real profession." She grabbed Marika's and Dallas's hands. "This kitchen is an amazing place because of the two of you. You have managed to feed hundreds of people with very little, and you do it with kindness and love." Her voice cracked, "I am in awe of what you accomplish each and every day." They group-hugged.

"Hey, now," Nick interrupted. "It's not like you're saying goodbye. Tell everyone your plan."

"You don't want to wait until it's official?" Kate asked.

"No, go ahead," Dan said. "The Board is definitely going to approve it."

"Well," Kate clasped her hands together. "With Nick's help, and the support of the M&M Board of Directors, Kate's on Vine is entering into a partnership with the 'Mary and Martha Soup Kitchen'. For every meal purchased at Kate's, we'll donate a meal to M&M. We're expanding our garden so the kitchen will also share in the produce we grow. The restaurant's new business plan has the lofty goal to fund one day of meals at M&M each week."

"That's wonderful," Sylvie said, her eyes sparkling, "I'd love to help with the garden."

"I could make the desserts for the restaurant." Leon said.

"That's a deal." Kate shook his hand. "I'm also going to keep helping with the cooking class, so I'm really not leaving."

"No, but I am," Nick's voice was quiet.

"Yeah, right." Dan pushed back his chair.

"I'm serious." Nick cleared his throat. A hush filled the room. His friends looked at each other and then back at him. Their faces looked confused, except for Kate's. "After a lot of thought and prayer," Nick's voice was strong, "I've decided to leave M&M. I'm telling the Board at next week's meeting."

"But, why?" Marika walked over to his side.

He pushed in a few more chairs shuffling uncomfortably at their stares. Kate gave him an encouraging nod. "I love this place," he said, looking around the dining room at his friends. "I love all of you, and I love the clients, but I've just been feeling like I needed to do something different. I needed to change the direction of my life." He took a deep breath. "So, I'm joining the seminary. I'm going to become a priest."

"A *priest*?" Bernice gasped, "You're too handsome to be a priest."

Nick threw back his head and laughed.

"Man," Tucker put his arm around Marika. "Are you sure?"

"I think you'll be a wonderful priest, Nick." Sylvie took his hands, "You were so kind and understanding when Xander died."

"Do you know when you're leaving?" Kate asked.

"It won't be until September," Nick said, "I want to make certain the right person replaces me, and a good transition plan is in place."

"Hello? Mom?" The door opened, and a voice called from the foyer.

"Zach, how are you?" Nick went to shake the man's hand.

"What are you doing here?" Sylvie looked confused.

"It's almost midnight." Zach's blue eyes widened. "You were supposed to call me when you got home."

"Oh, honey, I'm sorry. I didn't mean to worry you. Everyone, this is my son, Zach." Sylvie took her son's hand. "This is the bride and groom, Marika and Tucker, and their son, Jamal."

"Congratulations." Zach smiled

"And this is Katie. She owns Kate's on Vine." Sylvie took Kate's elbow.

"I ate there several times; it was always delicious." Zach shook Kate's hand. His blue eyes were identical to his mother's.

"Oh, thank you," Kate's smile was warm. "You'll have to come with your mom to the grand reopening."

Dan stood next to Nick as he locked the kitchen's door. "So…a priest, that's your new calling?"

"Yep." Nick put the keys in his pocket.

"Are you sure?" Dan asked.

"Absolutely positive," Nick stated.

"So, do you have any ideas about your replacement?" Dan stopped in front of his car.

"I think so, I'm going to talk to him this week." Nick got into his truck leaving the door open. "He's been a volunteer for years, believes in the mission of M&M, and is exactly what the kitchen needs to move to the next level. He's fairly new to the Catholic teachings, but he has a really good heart and a strong desire to learn."

"Do I know him?" Dan asked.

"You sure do." Nick started the engine, "How about we go to breakfast after Mass on Monday? There are a few things I want to discuss with you."

61

KATE

Six Months Later

Kate stood on the front porch of the restaurant. The building had been repaired and renovated to its former glory; the kitchen glimmered with walls of stainless-steel refrigerators and stoves, and copper pots and pans gleamed from the hanging rack above the six-foot-long prep table. The dining room was an eclectic mix of granite tabletops and deep-seated walnut chairs, while the bar's focus remained the fireplace. Comfy sofas and chairs were interspersed with high-top tables. She'd used the extra insurance money to expand the side patio, adding a pizza oven and casual bar to serve at the café-style wrought-iron tables. Hanging baskets of purple impatiens and green ivy hung from the front porch eaves, and a light wind gently pushed the freshly painted porch swing. The lawn was filled with people holding glasses of champagne staring at her.

How could she possibly put into words what this moment meant to her?

The grand reopening was being used as a fundraiser to celebrate the restaurant's new co-operative arrangement with the M&M Soup Kitchen. The hundred-dollars-per-plate event had sold out in less than three hours, and the entire M&M staff was volunteering their time to work the party.

Dan, M&M's new executive director, greeted the clients and thanked them for their support. To date, he hadn't made many changes to the kitchen, except for cleaning up Nick's office. He had spent the last few months learning the ropes and was working to continue to improve the programs already in place.

Kate and Dan met once a week after daily Mass to discuss the partnership.

"I understand what Nick meant about Mass centering his day." Dan had told her at their first meeting. "Mass renews my focus each morning, reminding me about what's really important."

With Nick's encouragement and tutelage, Dan was becoming Catholic.

Marika and Tucker worked as host and hostess, escorting the clients to their tables. The couple had announced they were expecting a baby next year. Marika was taking the upcoming birth in stride, but Tucker was as nervous as a mother hen protecting her chicks. He had insisted Marika not carry anything, and asked Kate if there would be a place for her to sit when she got tired. Marika had rolled her eyes and made a face at this suggestion.

Kate laughed. She thought Tucker's concern was adorable.

Jamal missed the party. An honor student and class president, he was representing Drexel at a symposium in Washington DC about Charter School education. He was using the trip as an opportunity to tour several colleges. Jamal was thrilled about the baby. He had been worried about going away to college knowing his mom would miss him, but the new baby would keep her busy.

After helping at M&M while Jamal was in the hospital, Dallas had returned to his job at the Quick-Mart. He was the acting manager and was working to purchase the store from Deacon who wanted to retire. As President of Knights of the Neighborhood, Deacon's days were spent building up the community and its neighbors. Bernice continued as his assistant and companion.

Nick attended the party as Kate's special guest. It had been a shock to see him dressed in black with a Roman collar, signifying his status as a Priest in Training, but he was still the same old Nick. He enjoyed his studies and hadn't thought twice about the calling. "I'm exactly where God wants me to be," he told Kate when he accepted her invitation.

Sylvie had quit volunteering at the kitchen. It was too difficult. "I kept watching for Xander, even though I knew he would never walk through those doors again." She started to work at the M&M and Kate's Place Garden, a project perfect for her. She cultivated a team of volunteers and toiled over the plants she loved so much. It also gave her the freedom to spend time with Alex, her grandson. She and Bernice took turns babysitting Rachel's little boy. Rachel worked at the kitchen as Marika's assistant while attending college online. Rachel was a good mom.

Zach, Sylvie's son, was a frequent visitor at the garden. He had first stopped by to check on Sylvie's progress, but it soon became apparent his interest was not in the garden but in the kitchen. He and Kate had been dating for several months. Sylvie secretly hoped the wedding planners would have a new event to organize soon.

Kate raised her glass of champagne. "One year ago, almost to the day, Kate's on Vine, caught fire. I can remember standing at this very spot smelling the smoke, looking at the area that used to be the dining room and seeing only charred remains of tables and chairs swimming in wet ashes. My only thought was: *what do I do now?*"

She looked around the room, seeing all the people who had supported her on this journey. "God, in his infinite wisdom, knew I had a few things to learn. So, he sent me to the Mary and Martha Soup Kitchen. From the wonderful people working there, I learned a couple of things. One." She held up her finger. "A true chef can make the most *unbelievable* meal out of the most unlikely of ingredients." Kate toasted Marika.

"Two." She made a peace sign. "I discovered the only real difference between the clients I served at Kate's on Vine and M&M were economical.

The diners were the same in all other ways: they wanted to eat good food in a safe place with wonderful friends."

She grabbed the cloth covering the sign. "My hope is that both establishments can reach that goal together. So, without any further fanfare, I ask my friend, the soon to be Father Nick Decker, to bless our meal and our new restaurant."

She displayed the sign:

Katie's Restaurant

Acknowledgements

This book is a result of a conversation I had with God. My daughter had just left for college, and I was searching for direction. On a chilly, sunny day, I was walking the country roads near my home, and I asked, "God, what should I do with my life?"

God answered me, "You should write a book."

I ignored His request and continued to pray for the answer to what my next step should be. No matter how many ways I prayed, I kept getting the same answer…You should write a book. So… I did, The Soup Kitchen (A novel).

To say, writing a book is hard is an understatement. I had no idea where to start, but God kept sending me ideas and people to help. I am forever grateful that I attended an editing workshop at Books by The Banks taught by the amazing Victoria Ryan. She was funny, engaging, and so kind that I emailed her asking more questions. She agreed to meet with me, and a friendship was born. Her honesty and encouragement about my work kept me going. Vickie, I not only value your advice, but I treasure your friendship. I also want to thank my wonderful editor, Rebecca Roy.

Much to my chagrin, I learned that getting a novel published is hard. In all honesty, I think I was rejected or ignored by over one hundred agents. I gave up on ever getting my novel published, but God sent me someone once again…J.L. Hyde.

I read Delta County by J.L. Hyde. It was fantastic. I discovered J.L. had self- published. So, I emailed her. She shared her publishing story, and I was inspired. I re-edited The Soup Kitchen, hired the talented, Jenna Kendle to design the book cover and here we are. Thank you J.L. for being my inspiration to self-publish.

I was searching for my next step, because my amazing daughter Hayley had left for college. She had been my purpose for eighteen years, and I didn't know what I would do without her. Hayley, I love you and I'm so very proud of you. It's taken so long to get this book to print, that Hayley has graduated from college, gotten married to the fantastic Derek, and given me the most perfect grandson, Lincoln John.

To my husband, William John, you have given me an incredible life. I am able to follow my dreams because of your hard work and support. I am so grateful God gave me to you.

God has blessed me so much. I was born to amazing parents...Terry and Linda. I was gifted wonderful siblings: Tracy, Wendy, Nancy, Molly, and Jim and I had a grandma, who always believed in me, Mary Ferkenhoff.

Thank you for reading my book, I hope you enjoyed it!

All Praise and Glory to God!

A.K. Hill